Under the Family Tree

By

Gary Feinstein

Published by RiverQuest Publishing-Gary Feinstein

ISBN 979-8-9910687-0-3 (paperback)
ISBN 979-8-9910687-1-0 (ebook)
LCCN 2024915506
Cover and interior design by CoverKitchen

To my family

May 19, 2019

Chapter 1.
Notes from
a Visit to the Ohio
Reformatory for Women

Dakota had never been to a prison visiting room before. It hadn't been on her list of things to do, like seeing the Grand Canyon or riding the Millennium Force roller coaster at Cedar Point. She would have preferred not to spend her Sunday afternoon in a place surrounded by razor wire.

She took a seat in the far corner opposite the vending machine so she had a view of the entire room. It reminded her of her high school cafeteria—if you ignored the cameras and the giant armed guard styling coke-bottle glasses. There was a medicinal smell mixed with body odor. And other people doing the things you apparently did in prison visiting rooms. An older couple playing cards. A young girl holding a boy in her lap, talking to a woman with pink hair. They all seemed so casual, and for a moment Dakota imagined a day far better than the one she had originally envisioned. Then her mother stumbled into the room wearing an orange jumpsuit, and an electrified arrow shot across the room.

Dakota resisted the urge to spring out of her chair, to wave her over. She had planned this part. To put on a tough exterior. To be strong. She didn't want to be that sad little girl who turned into a pool of jelly. Except when she stood up to greet her, putting as much effort into not caring as she could, her mother penetrated her force field and gave her a big hug. Which was unexpected, and kind of nice.

They sat down, close enough that Dakota detected her mother's uneven breath.

"What's new with you?" her mother asked, like they were long-lost friends meeting for coffee.

Let's see. First off, her mother had accepted a plea deal on drug charges and was sentenced to four years in the Ohio Reformatory for Women. Then there was the panic attack she'd had in school last week, when she locked herself in a bathroom stall and hyperventilated. Oh, and last night, right before she made her big decision, she'd listened to that ambient wave audio her social worker had recommended to help her sleep. But that just made her want to go to a place with actual waves, like California, which she would have done if she had the courage, a car, and a license.

"They frisked me and checked for weapons," Dakota said instead, this being her most recent new experience. There'd been a drug-sniffing dog as well, but she saw no reason to involve an innocent canine.

"I can see why." Her mother shook her head. "You're a real threat to society."

Dakota clenched her teeth. Across the room, the young boy she'd seen earlier had stuck his arm up through the bottom of the vending machine. Perhaps larceny ran in the family.

"I moved in with Grandma Lucinda yesterday. Did you know she bought a house in Zionsville?"

Her mother let out an odd sound, somewhere between a gasp and a laugh. "They let you make phone calls after they arrest you. Did you not know that? But, what… you were aching for foster care? Should I have called Aunt Evelyn?"

They both knew that was never an option. Yet the thought of her mother placing a desperate call to Grandma Lucinda seemed just as unlikely. It would, however, connect the dots as to why the family court had placed her in the custody of her grandmother. A woman she barely knew.

"It's just kind of funny," Dakota said. "You know… how no one asked me what I wanted."

Her mother smiled then, but an evil genius kind of smile. "You're just a kid, Dakota. You don't get to make these decisions."

Her mother was beginning to annoy her. Was it possible to miss someone and hate them at the same time? And if her mom knew so much more than a kid, what was she doing in this wretched place?

"Well, actually, there is a decision I can make." Dakota paused, her insides simmering. "I've decided to look for my father."

She'd certainly surprised her mother with that one. She could tell because her mom was doing that thing she always did with her eyes when she was trying to figure out what to say, letting them wander about the room, as if she had no care in the world, before they locked onto you, like a fighter jet that just located its target.

"We both know you'd be wasting your time," her mother said. "But I don't get it. I've never heard you say a word about him. Why the sudden interest?"

This was true in some respects. Certainly, she'd wondered what it would be like to have both a mother and a father show up for parent night at school or have her father coach her on the soccer fields. But only recently had the idea of actually finding him taken hold.

Dakota forced a grin. "Is this you trying to protect me, Mom? Because I don't need that from you anymore."

"It's always been my job to protect you, Dakota. That's what a mother does. That's what I've always done."

"And you've done such a great job of it." She clapped three times. "Really. I'm giving you an A-plus for effort."

Her mother lurched forward and pounded a fist on the table. The ripples spread outward, like earthquake tremors, prompting the other inmates and their visitors to stop whatever they'd been doing and look over. The security guard pressed a walkie-talkie against his mouth.

"Listen to me, smart-ass," Mom snarled. "You're not the one in this shithole, living in a room the size of a fucking shoebox while you sit at home doing whatever you want with your grandmother—who, by the way, is a wolf in sheep's clothing. And believe me. I would have called anyone else if I'd had a choice."

"You're here because of yourself," Dakota said. "Nothing to do with me."

"Of course, Dakota. Nothing is ever your fault."

Her mother stood and held her hand up to signal there'd be no further debate. But it was when she slammed her chair against the table that a trio of corrections officers descended upon her like a band of ninja warriors and Dakota realized the conversation was truly over. Impressive, really, the way one of them pinned her right arm back while the others practically lifted her up and carried her across the floor.

"Get your hands off me," her mother pleaded, her voice echoing off the walls of the room. But it was no use. The ninjas refused to loosen their grip as they forced her out the exit and closed the door behind them.

Dakota grabbed the edges of her chair, trying to steady her hands, as the rest of the room's occupants gawked at her, not one of them minding their own business. The security guard headed in her direction. Would she be getting an escort out of the visiting room just like her mother? Her stomach started to make creepy noises. Did that vending machine have Twix bars? And what had her mother meant when she said "Nothing is ever your fault"? She likely knew the truth. That in some ways, Dakota had some responsibility for her mother ending up in the state penitentiary. That in some ways, it *had* been her fault.

May 21, 2019

Chapter 2.
Crazy Boho Skater Girl

Dakota had no desire to celebrate. With one day remaining in the school year, it all seemed premature, like lighting off firecrackers the night before the town's Fourth of July fireworks display. And besides, had she not expressed there should be no expiration date when it came to her suffering?

Rosario Peña, aka Rosie, had no interest in suffering. Which was how they'd ended up at their usual spot in Putnam Park, by a bend in the Muskingum River, perched on a flat rock outcrop underneath a large cottonwood tree.

"I heard some news about you," Rosie said, her knees drawn up to her chest, a grin leaking out from the corner of her mouth.

"Can't wait to hear it," Dakota replied, as if she could wait forever.

The sun sat above the tips of the trees behind them, shining directly on Rosie's face, highlighting her dark purple–dyed hair strands, which mixed in seamlessly with her natural black. She wore a white Petal Power tee imprinted with a red-and-pink psychedelic flower "Well, I'm gonna tell you anyway. Presumably, Will Aubrey has a crush on you."

Who the hell was Will Aubrey? She vaguely recalled

some dude named Will from remedial math last year. But as far as she knew he had no last name.

"I seriously doubt that."

Rosie did a quick shimmy with her left shoulder, and the grin she'd previously tried to cover up began to emerge. "Apparently, he thinks you're interesting."

"I've never thought of myself as interesting."

She'd once seen a documentary on leopards. Now that was interesting.

"You're not, D. You're fucking boring as hell. But you've got that crazy boho skater girl look going on. You have to admit, some guys like that."

"Mmmm," Dakota said. "I'm beginning to question your motives." Though she had to admit liking the idea of the crazy boho skater girl, even if she'd never been on a skateboard in her life. It sounded like a superhero. One that created chaos in the world, but only if it led to a greater good.

"It's my job to help you when you're being antisocial," Rosie replied, with a smug look. "And in that capacity, I recommend you come with me to the dance tommorow night."

"Sounds awesome. But that's a big noooo."

"I'm pretty sure Will will be there. You could hook up with someone for once. Otherwise, let's get real. You're just going to sit at home and masturbate."

Dakota kept a straight face. "Sounds like a plan. Maybe I'll light some candles. Make it special."

Rosie bent over in laughter, which Dakota took as a sign to remove a joint from her backpack. On the river, a family of ducks cruised by, and the sun's rays angled off the water, creating little specks of light that appeared and disappeared like glow bugs in the night. She lit the joint, took a hit, and passed it along to her friend. She flicked ashes off of her *I can see through your bullshit* tee, the one with the all-seeing eye that she'd chosen that morning to compliment her distressed jean shorts and checkerboard Vans. She scratched at something, at the back of her neck. An itch beneath her skin.

"I have something I want to ask you," Dakota then said, nervously tapping her knee. "I've decided to look for my father. And I need you to help me."

Rosie stared at her, eyes wide, mouth open as if she were catching flies. "I'm confused. Didn't your father die in a motorcycle accident when you were two?"

"Yes. That's the story."

"But now... all of a sudden... you think your mom is lying about it."

"I've had my suspicions. But when I saw her the other day at prison and I told her I was going to look for him, she practically had an aneurysm. Which made me think she's hiding something. Then I remembered. Last summer. We went swimming at the quarry and she told me that's where they threw my dad's ashes. Before that, it had always been the river."

"They both have water." Rosie cocked her head. "Could be she mixed them up. But it's funny how you never mentioned this before?"

"I'm pretty sure I have."

"Yeah... I don't think so, D. You can be very secretive."

Dakota nodded. She wasn't about to deny her secretive nature, nor the legitimacy of her friend's complaints over the past year as to how this hindered their friendship. Yet she'd lived with Rosie and her family in the month after her mother's incarceration, before her grandmother moved back into town. Rosie was the only person in the universe she trusted. And while her best friend had issues when it came to reading and mediocre grades in school, she possessed an undeniable sixth sense that could aid in her quest. Latino-Dyslexic Power, Rosie called it. You could deny it, but only at your own peril.

"You think I'm crazy to do this. Don't you?"

"I don't know about that," Rosie commented. "But you mom could be pissed because she's in jail. It doesn't mean she's lying. And it sounds like you're doing this on a hunch. Do you even have a plan?"

Dakota said she did. But truth be told, her plan consisted of a few random notes scribbled on a notebook page, starting with *can't do this alone, talk to Rosie,* and *DNA* underlined and followed by three exclamation points. Which was why she reached into her backpack, removed the old photograph, and held it out so Rosie could see it. It was the same photograph she'd shown to her friend years earlier, in the bedroom of her North Zionsville apartment. The teenage version of the person she'd been told was her father, Jimmy Ray Coleman. Looking like a cartoon character, wearing a Question Authority T-shirt and leaning against a large oak tree like he was trying to hold the damn thing up. There was the unfortunate attempt at a mustache, blond hair down to his shoulders and blue eyes set in a straight line

Rosie examined the photograph, as if seeing it for the first time. Her eyes narrowed. "I get it. You still don't look like him."

That thought had crossed her mind a zillion times. Even if she knew genetics didn't always work that way, that you could breed two purple flowers in one generation and give rise to a white flower in the next. Yet the contrast was obvious. Dakota's dark brown, almost black hair fell inches below her ears, while her brown almond shaped eyes tilted down towards her nose, making it seem like she had binocular vision. Even the complexions didn't match, Dakota's being more Mediterranean than Ohio pasty.

"And now that I think about it," Rosie continued, "it's entirely possible you were dropped off at a fire station after you were born. And a fireman took you in, and later your mom adopted you. Or your mom drove by and saw a baby wrapped up in a blanket and thought you were so pathetic looking, she had to take you home, and now she has to lie about it because it's embarrassing.

Dakota smiled. Over the years, she'd imagined many scenarios involving the story of her birth. But never one that involved total abandonment by strangers.

"Does that mean you're going to help me?" Dakota asked, hoisting herself off the rocks.

Rosie stuck her hand out, as if getting helped off the rocks would be a requirement before aiding her friend, and Dakota grabbed it and pulled her up toward the highest point of the outcrop. They paused to take in the most iconic view in town. The meandering Muskingum River, separating the two sides of town, and the Y-Bridge that connected them. North for four-dollar lattes, south for pawnshops and handguns, she'd once heard a local joke.

Rosie sighed and put an arm around Dakota. "Of course I'll help you, D. I'm your friend. I will say, though, that it's not always easy being your friend. I do hope you realize that."

She did.

9 months earlier: August 26–27, 2018

Chapter 3.
A Not-So-Funny
Eviction Story

Dakota lounged on the living room couch in plaid pajama bottoms and a black Zodiac tee. It was one o'clock in the afternoon, and she'd already read the eviction notice three times by the time her mother entered the house, trailed by her best friend, Gina Barato, carrying a case of Natty Lights, their go-to version of liquid cheer.

"We're back," Gina said, loud enough that the entire neighborhood could hear.

Dakota leaped out of her seating position, as if propelled by jet fuel. She threw her skinny arms around her mother's neck and pulled her in tight, breathing in the soapy smell of her hair. The smell had her believing there would be some sort of explanation for the notice. A misunderstanding that would soon be cleared up.

Dakota released her vise grip and straightened. "Hey, Mom," she said. "You look great. Did Aunt Evelyn pay for a makeover?"

"You need glasses," her mother replied with a grin. But to be honest there were times when Dakota was struck by her mother's beauty. On her good days, which this one appeared to be, her blue eyes, wavy blond hair, and slightly pouty lips made it so that she could have passed for a college girl even though she was thirty-two. One time, a kid in school, who had seen them at the mall, commented on how cool it was that she got to hang out with her hot older sister.

"Well, I missed you," Dakota confessed. "Gina's, like, super boring."

Gina smiled from across the room. The case of beer she'd lugged into the kitchen weighed more than she did. "I appreciate your compliment, Kota," she said, using her lazy Texas drawl. "But I must say you look tired today."

"I'm good," Dakota replied. "But you know… the end of summer. It's sort of depressing actually."

"At least you won't be a freshman anymore."

"I remember my sophomore year," her mother chimed in. "All three months of it."

Next came the sound of air being released from beer cans. Gina was responsible for that one, her face lighting up like a Christmas tree as she handed one of the opened cans to her mother, who'd joined her in their tiny kitchen. The two of them hid behind worn linoleum counters, clinking their cans together, as if making a toast. A toast to what? Adult incompetence.

Dakota reached into her pocket then. But as she wrapped her fingers around the eviction letter, she could feel sweat leaking out the pores on the back of her neck, and she wondered if she should have left the letter on the floor where she found it. She scratched at something behind her ear and let out a deep sigh. Which got her mother's attention.

"What's going on, peanut?" her mother asked. "Please tell me you didn't do anything stupid while I was gone."

Gina seemed interested as well, the two of them staring, four synchronized eyes locking onto her, making her dizzy.

Dakota pulled the letter out and waved it in the air. "Look what I found."

Her mother's eyes crinkled and she moved quickly, snatching the paper and examining it, as if it were a piece of rotting garbage.

"And you've read this," she said, halfway between a statement and a question.

"What was I supposed to do? Someone slid it underneath the door with no envelope."

"How about not reading it?"

"Sorry, Mom. It's the law of unintended consequences. Remember? You taught me that."

"What's that?" Gina asked, acting all innocent, almost childlike with her big eyes and blond pixie cut. A child with a prominent spider tattoo on her left arm. A child with a prominent spider tattoo on her left arm that drank like a fish. Still, Dakota liked Gina for some reason. Could it be that she just paid attention, dished out a hug now and then?

"It means no one intended for me to see any of this," Dakota explained. "It means someone has to tell me what's going on."

Her mother shot Gina a side-eye glance and scrunched the paper into a ball, while Gina produced a subtle nod. Suddenly, Dakota had the sneaking suspicion that the $1800 owed for back rent and next month's payment of $800, due on September 1, wasn't exactly breaking news. Not to mention the threat of eviction by the end of the year if arrangements could not be made to square things up.

"Sit down, Dakota," her mother said forcefully. "We need to talk."

Dakota took a step back and placed a hand on her hip. She knew there was plenty to talk about, but that it wouldn't be good. Perhaps if she just stood there like a statue, it would all go away.

"It's just financial crap," her mother explained. "I didn't tell you about it because I figured you wouldn't understand."

That's right. She was a dumbass fifteen-year-old girl. She'd almost forgotten that.

"Whatever," Dakota replied. "So you went to visit Evelyn to get money. What's the big deal?"

Her mother smiled then, but like one of those smiles that's been coaxed out of you by the threat of torture. "Listen. I have some decisions to make, okay? And once I make them, I'll be sure to let you know."

Yeah. And nothing says superior decision-making skills like a case of Nattys.

Dakota put her hand out to signal the end of the conversation. She felt the pressure building up between her ears. A spontaneous combustion, right around the corner. "I'm going for a walk," she announced.

Her mother narrowed her eyes into tiny, suspicious slits. "Where are you going?"

"Just in the neighborhood, Mom. I promise I won't run away."

And she was off. She had made her own decision. To experience the last vestiges of summer by spending some time outdoors. Not that she'd be alone. She would put on her headphones, check out some of the old punk music she liked listening to from her "Punkified" playlist. Especially when her anger flared up. "I Wanna Be Sedated" by The Ramones came to mind. She could follow that up with

"Search and Destroy," a classic from The Stooges. Maybe bang her head against a tree trunk.

* * *

The next morning, Dakota held a mug of coffee, dressed in the green Hilger tee she'd found at the thrift store that summer, cuffed ripped jeans, and green low-top Cons. She entered her mother's bedroom without knocking. She took a gulp of coffee, then placed the mug down on her mother's dresser between an assortment of skin creams, cosmetics, and an unlabeled bottle of pills. She removed her phone from her back pocket and pulled up the air horn app that she'd downloaded last night. Her mother was nestled in a cocoon of pillows and blankets, and she had to pull one of the blankets back to reveal her face. She put the phone inches from her mother's ear and pressed the start arrow.

Honestly, the whole air horn thing exceeded expectations, as her mother jumped out of bed with a look on her face like she'd woken in the middle of one of those Halloween horror houses. Mouth open, droopy red eyes. Sleeping Beauty she was not.

"What the fuck, Dakota."

"Good morning, Mom," Dakota said in a fake cheery voice. "Did you sleep well?"

It took a few seconds for her mother to pull herself up. "Seriously. If you don't get out of this room in a second, I'm going to kill you."

"You've said that before. Empty threat. And... you promised to drive me to school."

"When did I say that?"

"Last night. But after ten beers you probably don't remember. At least you drank light beer. You wouldn't want to ruin your hot mom bod."

"Are we starting with that again?"

"I've already decided I'm not going to concern myself with your problems. But what I am concerned about is being on a bus with a bunch of ghoulish freshmen. Do you have any idea how humiliating that will be?"

"I'm sorry, Dakota. But my head feels like it's stuck between boulders. You're gonna have to take the bus."

Dakota folded her arms. There'd been a glimmer of hope this morning. The app seemed like a good idea at the time, and she'd picked out something to wear that she thought looked decent. She'd even entertained the possibility that school wouldn't be so bad this year. But here she was, twenty minutes away from boarding the bus, prospects already dwindling.

"What is it?" her mother asked.

"Nothing," Dakota replied.

"Nothing means something." Her mother patted the mattress. "Come sit."

"No."

"It's not a question."

Dakota eased her way onto the mattress but kept her distance. Her mother's eyes were bloodshot, and she smelled of alcohol.

"What is it? You nervous about school?"

Her mother was good at this, somehow molding her daughter's anger into some other emotion, whether it be sadness or guilt. And maybe it had something to do with it being morning, and especially the mornings when she was hungover, when her semiconscious state always managed to smooth out the sharp edges of her other self.

"You know I hate school, Mom. And I just thought if I

could just get a ride I could at least get off to a good start."

"I understand. But you just have to get through it."

"And yesterday I heard Rosie has a different lunch period."

Her mother tilted her head. "Maybe this is a good opportunity for you. Sometimes I think you're too dependent on your friend. It could be time to make new ones."

"I don't want new friends."

"Okay. But you might want to try, at least."

Dakota scrunched up her mouth. She wasn't about to concede on the friend issue, especially when the specter of the eviction notice loomed in her mind.

"So, Mom. About yesterday. Do we have to move again?"

Her mother slid closer and smiled while pressing a hand against her daughter's back. "Is that what you're worried about?"

"Considering the circumstances, why wouldn't I be?"

Her mother drew her in closer. "I might as well tell you this," she started. "There's an opportunity that came up. A receptionist at Uncle Bert's car dealership will be going on maternity leave in January, and Evelyn said that I could start by filling in for a few months until she comes back. We'd have to move to Cleveland though. And live with Evelyn for a while. Which I know is not ideal. But it would give me a chance to get my shit together, maybe take GED classes at night."

The blood rushed to Dakota's head then, and she felt as if she might black out. She had expected her mother's solution to the rent problem would result in some inconvenience. But Cleveland. With Aunt Evelyn. "This is bullshit" was all she could get out, her throat beginning to tighten.

"See," her mother responded. "I knew this would upset you. That's why I didn't tell you yesterday."

Dakota pushed her mother away. She got up from the bed, backed up against the dresser, and produced a glare that she hoped would be menacing. "Right, Mom. You drop a bomb ten minutes before I have to go to school. Way better timing."

"We have to face reality." She said it matter-of-factly. Like she was talking about doing a batch of overdue laundry.

"Well, here's my reality, in case you care. I do not want to move. I have school and my friends, and I like it here."

Okay, so she might have exaggerated that last part, since she didn't like school, had only one friend, and could take or leave the town of Zionsville. And their rental house, a tiny shotgun shack with peeling white paint, was not exactly Buckingham Palace. But they'd lived there for almost three years, by far the longest they'd ever been in one place. Did her mother not realize that life as she knew it would cease to exist if she moved to Cleveland? Did they not have GED classes and jobs in Zionsville?

"I get that you're pissed, but right now this is our best option."

"What about Grandma? She's got money."

Her mother's eyes hardened. "You and I both know that's not happening."

Dakota shook her head and turned. "Well, then I have a bus to catch."

"Hold on," her mother said, moving toward the edge of the bed. "I know this is a lot to take in, Dakota. But we have some time. We've got our benefits, and Gina and I are going to try UberEats, which hopefully will cover most of the rent. I can look for something more permanent, but it's rough out there, and there's not much I can do about the $1800. But we'll make the best of it. We're survivors, you and I. Right?"

Dakota nodded. But what would their definition of survivor be? She wanted to believe that things would be okay. She wanted to believe in smiles and reassuring words. Yet she wasn't about to stand by and watch her life go down the tubes. She had to do what was right for herself, to find some way to make money and save her life as she knew it. She recalled a girl from school last year who presumably made two hundred dollars selling hideous Jesus Loves Me T-shirts on TikTok, and from what she'd heard, the girl wasn't exactly a Mensa candidate. Not that she could make T-shirts. Not that she believed Jesus loved her. As for Cleveland, she had nothing against the city itself. Only that she would not be moving there. Never. No effing way!

May 22, 2019

Chapter 4.
Hot-Sauce-of-the-Month Club

Dakota could not deny it. Grandma Lucinda made a mean taco. Double corn tortillas filled with chopped chorizo, onions, and cilantro. A bottle of hot sauce rested atop the table, calling out her name.

"This is seriously awesome," she said after her first taste, a fireworks display of flavors having detonated in her mouth.

"It's an old recipe," Lucinda replied. "And the hot sauce is from this hot-sauce-of-the-month club I belong to."

Sounded like a dare. Still, questions remained. Like what did people actually do at hot sauce club meetings? Or more specifically, what would her grandmother be doing?

Dakota engulfed her first taco in less than a minute. "Can I have another?"

"Why not."

Dakota smiled. "How about a beer?"

Lucinda nursed a Modelo, whereas Dakota drank from a glass of lukewarm water, this killing the vibe to some degree.

"Nice try," her grandmother responded with the face

of an assassin. A face Dakota had been trying to decipher ever since she moved into her grandmother's house, a white vinyl single-story prefab located in South Zionsville. She seemed a woman of contradictions. Like her dark, closely set eyes that signaled "do not mess with me," offset by cat-eye glasses that gave off crazy-cat-lady vibes. Or her lime-green Thunderbird, with hubcaps so clean you could see your reflection in them, while her salt-and-pepper hair was short and spiky. As if she'd ordered some internet contraption to save money and had an inebriated friend cut it in her kitchen.

Dakota built another taco, stuffing in some extra chorizo because it seemed like the right thing to do. "I'm gonna try the hot sauce."

The corner of Lucinda's mouth turned up ever so slightly, but she gave no warning. It was called Boneyard Hot Sauce. The label hinted at the possibility of medical attention being required if not used judiciously.

Dakota sprinkled some of the sauce on her plate and dabbed the edge of her taco in it. She stuffed it into her mouth. "That's really good," she said while chewing. However, a second later a wave of intense heat pulsed throughout her mouth, radiating toward her lungs. "Holy shit."

Lucinda laughed in a joyful manner she'd not previously demonstrated in the few days they'd lived together. "What, you don't like it?"

"You did that purposely," Dakota implied, moving her hand back and forth in a fanning action.

"How will you know if you like something unless you try it?"

"I already know I don't like extreme pain."

"Just call it a learning experience."

"That's exactly what I need in my life. Another learning experience."

After Dakota inhaled a third taco (minus the hot sauce), washing it down with multiple glasses of water, she settled back into her chair, trying to shake off her food coma. The events of the past few days made her feel as if her insides had been carved out with a hunting knife. Yet the tacos had settled her nerves, leaving a clear sense of purpose behind.

Dakota took in a deep breath, then exhaled. "Can I ask you about something?"

"Fire away," Lucinda responded.

"The social worker told me you owned an auto shop. Is that true?"

Lucinda looked down at her empty plate. She grabbed hold of the Modelo and brought the bottle to her mouth. "Not exactly. I own part of it. A friend of mine runs the branch in Florida, and I came up here to work with his brother."

"Is your shop in Zionsville?" Dakota asked. Not that she cared. The shop could have been in fucking Borneo and it would not have made a difference.

"No... outside of Dayton."

"What do you do there?"

"We restore cars."

"So you buy old crappy cars and make them not crappy?"

"Sometimes. But mostly people hire us to work on cars they bought."

"Sounds lucrative," Dakota said. Like she knew the first thing about lucrative.

Lucinda removed her glasses, rubbed at her eyes, then put them back on. "It's a living."

"Why didn't you tell me about this?"

"I'm telling you now."

Dakota let the words hang out there.

Lucinda chugged the rest of her beer. She shifted her chair closer to the table. "If there's something you want to say, you should spit it out."

Wow. Her grandmother was seriously observant. Though perhaps the obvious nature of her floundering was not so difficult to detect.

"I was thinking about something today," Dakota started. "How I don't know whether to call you Lucinda or Grandma. Unless there's something else you prefer."

"Grandma would be fine, but I don't think that's what you wanted to ask me."

Dakota felt a pit in her stomach. "It's weird, but I still remember that sweater you used to have… the one you used to wear on Christmas. If I'm not mistaken, there was a giant moose on it."

"So what you're telling me is you want to discuss a hideous sweater I used to own."

"Well, not if you don't have it anymore."

"Please get to the point."

Her grandmother's face had turned a shade of crimson, and Dakota had the strange sensation that she could explode at any second. Not that there'd been any signs of that kind of behavior in the previous days they'd been together. But if her mother had the capacity to lose her temper whenever it best suited her, would Lucinda not possess similar abilities?

"It's just strange," she said, "how you went away for all those years and no one told me why."

Not that she was totally clueless as to the reasons.

Her grandmother had moved to Florida ten years ago on account of a new job opportunity, having to do with cars. She'd raced go-karts when she was younger and once worked as a mechanic. She was a workaholic and didn't have time for them, though she never completely broke off contact. Each year, on Dakota's birthday, she sent a card with a twenty-dollar bill tucked inside. Thank god for Hallmark bullshit and Andrew Jackson.

Lucinda stared down at the table. "Listen, Dakota," she finally said. "You have to understand something. This is all new to me too. It's been a while since I lived with a teenager, and the last time, it didn't go so well. So I'd rather not burden you with the past, seeing what you've been through with your mother and everything."

Dakota gritted her teeth. "In case you didn't know it, Grandma, my life has been shitty enough as it is, so I don't think anything you tell me can make it worse. And what I really don't get is why everyone has to lie to me all the time."

Lucinda glanced up and folded her arms. "No one is lying to you."

"I don't know. I just thought... you know... since you want things to go better than the last time... maybe we should be honest with each other."

In some ways it felt wrong to be playing the self-sanctimonious card. And did honesty not have its limits? She wasn't about to tell Lucinda about her and Rosie getting high at the river yesterday. Nor was she in a hurry to reveal the sordid details of her sophomore year.

Lucinda lifted her head. She looked weary, as if she'd just gone through a tooth extraction without novocaine. "I'm sorry about not telling you about the job earlier.

And I do understand what you're saying, Dakota. But the answers to your questions are not so simple. Families are complicated."

She used the word complicated as if it were a virus you might catch if you went out into the rain without a raincoat.

"I get it. I just feel as if I'm old enough to know the truth. That we should talk about these things."

"We can do that someday."

Someday. Meaning not tonight. Maybe never.

"Okay. Then I'd like to ask you about something else."

Lucinda's brow furrowed, her eyes jumping to a state of alert. "What is it?"

Dakota felt it happening again, a rash of heat across her face that had nothing to do with hot sauce, her hands beginning to shake. She clenched her fingers into a fist, then released them slowly. "I want to find out more about my father. And I've been looking into a DNA test. But you have to be eighteen to open an account. So I would need your help with that."

"I don't understand."

"If you're worried about the money, it's only fifty-nine dollars. I can give that to you."

"I don't care about the money. I'm just wondering what you're up to."

"I'm looking for information. Like… what if he were alive?"

Lucinda leaned forward. "What makes you think a DNA test will help?"

Dakota had been well aware of the test's limitations. On *Dateline*, a show she and Rosie liked to watch, DNA unlocked the secrets of murder investigations, but when applied to a family tree, things were not so simple. The customer support representative at AncestryDNA had explained it all to her last night. How the test results would provide an ethnicity pie chart, so if she were descended from Scandinavians (Vikings would be cool) or had ancestors from the Scottish Highlands (Do girls get to wear kilts?), then that information would show up on the final report. But the chances of confirming whether or not Jimmy Ray Coleman or anyone else was her father depended on there being a DNA profile of them in their database. When it came to Jimmy Ray, Dakota knew next to nothing about him apart from the photograph and what, in her mind, that insinuated. Either way, she couldn't picture him sticking a swab in his mouth just to find out where he came from.

Dakota needed to go on the offensive. Her grandmother's question had been nebulous at best, and at this point, she had no ability to provide answers other than spewing out a bunch of genetic jargon, which, frankly, she didn't always comprehend herself.

"Did Mom ever tell you Jimmy Ray Coleman was my father?" she asked.

"Of course," Lucinda answered.

"And he had a motorcycle accident and died when I was two."

Her grandmother appeared confused. "I'm not sure this is the best time to discuss this."

Dakota felt the air being slowly sucked out of her lungs. "Did you go to his funeral?"

Lucinda shook her head. "I ain't never been to a funeral for Jimmy Ray Coleman. And I never heard anything about an accident. That don't mean he's not dead."

"What do you mean?"

"Right after you were born, he joined the army. Did a few tours in Iraq. From what I heard, he was pretty messed up when he came back. Then he just disappeared, and we never saw him again. So I don't know what happened after that. And your mom… she was good at keeping secrets."

"What about friends that might know something? Did she have anyone she hung out with around that time?"

Lucinda paused. She appeared to be searching for something in her memory, her eyes flitting about, down toward the ground, up at the ceiling, her right hand contorting to massage the back of her neck. Dakota feared she was conjuring up polite ways to end their conversation, when her eyes finally steadied. "Well, there was Anika, of course," she said. "Anika Powers. But that friendship kind of fizzled out, so I'm not sure how much she would know."

Anika Powers. She'd never heard that name before.

Lucinda sprang up from her chair then, muttering something about cleaning up. An obvious shut-down move if there ever was one.

Dakota stood up as well, an empty plate in her hand. "I can help you with that, Grandma."

It had ended up being a decent evening, with good food and what she considered to be the first real conversation with her grandmother in ten years. Yet afterward, a single, stubborn fact gnawed at her, like an itch she wanted to scratch but couldn't quite locate. Her grandmother had never actually agreed to help her with the DNA test.

August 27, 2018

Chapter 5.
A Little Help
from a New Friend

Back to school. Honestly, it could not have been more gruesome. At least Dakota used her morning classes to fill her daydreaming quota for the day, which mostly consisted of her conjuring up scenarios where she made enough money to help her mother pay off what she owed. A scratch ticket came to mind, though she was too young to buy one legally. Dog walking could work, and she recalled seeing a woman at Putnam Park last summer walking five dogs at once. Would anyone dish out cash for her to generate supercool playlists for them? Probably not.

Afterward, she navigated through a maze of tables in the cafeteria before ending up in the food line. The noise in the room was deafening, as if all the pent-up energy of the summer had been released at that precise moment. Banners advertising school activities. A big football game on Friday night. Exhortations to join the drama club. Her stomach rumbled with a combination of hunger and nervous energy, and she picked up a bag of Cajun fries, hoping to deal with the hunger part. Then the nutrition police got into her head and she grabbed one of the apples, strategically placed in a wicker basket at the checkout counter. She took out her public-assistance-free-lunch-or-whatever-the-hell-they-called-it card and handed it over to a woman with wiry black hair and crooked teeth. The town's education department had made a decision last year to make all the lunch cards look the same, such that the lunch ladies, or anyone else for that matter, would not be able to distinguish between the deadbeats (like herself) and those with money. Except when the crooked-toothed woman jammed her card into the reader, she raised her eyebrows slightly and Dakota could have sworn she passed judgment. *Fuck off* is what she wanted to say, but didn't. Instead she tucked the apple into a side pocket in her backpack. She bit into a fry, reveling in its spicy goodness.

Dakota made her way to the courtyard, by far her favorite spot at Zionsville High School. An outdoor oasis, with red brick pillars and a series of circular concrete benches surrounding raised wooden planters with a bunch of green spindly plants. She claimed an empty spot on one of the benches, then, in what she considered to be a brilliant strategic move, folded up three Cajun fries and jammed them all at once into her mouth. The sun shined brightly, and as she chewed she slanted her head back and soaked in the rays.

Suddenly, she heard a voice that sounded familiar, and she brought her head back down. About twenty feet away, just over her shoulder. A dealer from her neighborhood. Abraham, or was it Abe? She couldn't be sure, since she'd only met him once. Nevertheless, she couldn't help but stare as he conversed with a group of kids, moving his hands around in animated fashion. Everyone seemed to like Abe, and Dakota deduced he was one of those rare creatures that seamlessly drifted between the various social groups at Zionsville High. Perhaps it didn't hurt that he wasn't bad looking. Not exactly tall, but with long, gangly arms and short wavy black hair. Like that kid in *The Outsiders*, from the old movie she and Rosie had watched a few times. Pony Boy. Definitely Pony Boy. Before he dyed his hair blond.

Dakota twisted her body to get a better look. Abe had finished talking and was moving in her direction. It could have been a coincidence, but what if it wasn't?

"Abe," she shouted out.

Oh shit. What had she done?

Abe came closer, and it soon became obvious he hadn't a clue as to who she was. "Hi," he said.

At least he had good manners.

"I'm Dakota. Dakota Lodi. We met this summer. At the circ."

The circ. A round clearing in their South Zionsville Kings neighborhood where kids gathered to party. That much Abe would know.

Dakota continued. "I smoked weed with you. You had this crazy-assed bong. It was, like, made of glass. Pink and blue, I seem to remember."

Abe pursed his lips. "That would be Bertha."

"Oh… you name your bongs. How very personal."

"Bertha's dead though. Some dickwad dropped it."

"How sad is that. Well, I'll be sure to say a prayer for Bertha tonight."

Abe smiled, then pointed at his nose. "I remember you now. Dakota. You're the girl with the nose ring."

Not exactly a nose ring. More like a stud. A zirconia stud that her mother bought for her on her fourteenth birthday and Gina put in using a sewing needle sterilized with a flame from a lighter. But why quibble with distinctions.

"So, Abe. I was wondering if you knew where I could score some weed?"

Abe lifted his eyebrows. There wasn't much there, as if they'd been trimmed. Or else he suffered from some genetic malady that made it difficult to grow eyebrow hair.

"How much are we looking at?" he inquired.

"Not really sure."

She could see no reason to reveal details about her dire financial situation. If nothing else, it might ruin the good karma she was beginning to feel.

Abe let out a noise, something akin to humming. "How's your schedule look?"

"Well… right now I'm eating fries. Then I have math."

"What about after school," he suggested, motioning with his hands for some reason, as if that could make the time go faster.

Dakota paused. She didn't want to seem too chill, as if she might have something to do after school. Nor did she want to appear eager. Except, being a dealer meant Abe was basically an entrepreneur. If nothing else, he could have some decent ideas on how to make money.

"Yeah," she finally said, "I should have some time after school."

* * *

As it turned out, Abe lived right down the road from her home in South Zionsville, and so after school she hopped onto one of the dirt paths that crisscrossed through the homes in their tightly packed neighborhood. She had texted

Abe that she was on her way, to which he immediately replied with a thumbs-up emoji. But you never knew with guys, and so when she reached his trailer, she was surprised to see that he was already outside, sitting on his front step, and shirtless no less.

"Hey, Dakota," Abe said.

"Nice shirt, Abe," Dakota said, flashing a smile.

Was this some kind of seduction ploy? Remove your shirt when the neighborhood girl comes over to buy pot? Not that she minded. Abe wasn't exactly built, but his arms had outlines of muscle and there were clearly defined ripples in his abs. If there happened to be any hair on his chest, it was not visible to the naked eye.

Abe ran his fingers through his hair as he surveyed the neighborhood. It consisted of the Band-Aid-brown trailer he lived in and a dirt cul-de-sac with just two other trailers on it, beyond which existed a gravel-lined path that led to the circ and the Kings trailer park.

"How was your day?" Abe asked.

Dakota shrugged. "I pretty much nailed the first-day-at-school thing. I did, however, almost fall asleep in geometry. But it's not like we're ever going to use that shit."

"Well, the good news is: I have some weed for you. It's a sativa strain they call Train Wreck."

They. A bunch of potheads sitting around, coming up with wacky marijuana names related to public transportation, probably smoking pot while they did it.

"Sounds like a train I'd like to board," Dakota responded. "If I could afford the ticket."

Abe let out a laugh, and she used that moment to make what she considered to be a bold move, sitting down beside him on the front step. She put her legs close together and placed a hand on each knee. They were close, and she felt heat coming off his body.

"You're talking premium stuff here. I hear it even increases brain activity."

Was this guy serious? Increased brain activity. If there existed a person on earth that smoked pot to increase brain activity she'd like to meet them.

"I'm interested," Dakota said with enthusiasm.

"Good. I can hook you up," Abe replied. "What are we looking at?"

"I have five bucks."

So much for the mic drop.

Abe pitched his shoulders, let out a sigh. He was likely disappointed, but what did he expect from a fifteen-year-old girl living in a neighborhood where people weren't exactly rolling in dough? Perhaps Abe wasn't all that swift.

"I'll tell you what. I can sell you a joint, but in the future, you may want to buy in bulk."

Dakota handed Abe the money.

Abe went back into the house and came out wearing a Mastodon T-shirt, one of those metal bands she'd heard some of the stoners liked. He sat back down on the step and inched closer to Dakota, their legs a fraction of an inch from touching. Dakota detected the odor of aftershave. Had Abe gone inside to clean up? It was something to consider at least. And the question became more significant when he handed over a tightly rolled joint while looking into her eyes. It made her nervous and tingly at the same time, and for the first time she noticed the actual color of his eyes. Grayish blue with some brown around the edges. Something a wolf might have.

"So, Abe," Dakota started, trying to break the spell.

"You live here with your parents?"

Abe shook his head. "Just my dad. My parents divorced last year."

"Sorry to hear that. I live with my mom on Bramble Street."

"How's that going?"

"Let's just say my mom knows her way around the liquor store. And she gets Christmas cards from all the bartenders in town."

"That's kind of nice, actually. I mean the part about the cards."

Dakota nodded, as if her mother having a circle of friends bound by the common denominator of alcohol was a good thing.

"Hey," she said, conjuring up a subject change. "I heard there was a fight in the stairwell today and they had to call an ambulance. Someone said it was Katie Larsen again."

Abe shrugged. "Don't really know her."

Except everyone in their neighborhood would have at least known of Katie. She lived in one of the Kings trailers and could be seen down by the circ on most nights. She had a stocky build and straight blond hair. She appeared older, like one of those actors in a teen movie that looked like they'd graduated five years ago.

"She beat up Brianna Dyson in the stairwell. Apparently she said something nasty about Katie's boyfriend."

Abe wrinkled his nose. "Who's the boyfriend?"

"Joey Vinson." Joey had been in her math class last year. A bit of a clown, to be honest.

"Don't know about that."

Dakota agreed, not wanting to debate a subject she didn't give a shit about. Though she'd heard through the grapevine that Katie was skilled at oral sex, and perhaps that had something to do with it.

At some point the conversation began to fizzle out. Dakota had no desire to overstay her welcome and was about to remove herself from the front step, and make some bogus excuse about having way too much homework, when something in the yard of the adjacent trailer caught her attention. A bicycle. Not a nice one, by any means. But old-school. Could be decent transportation if it weren't covered in rust. Could lead to something if it actually worked.

"Hey, Abe," Dakota said. "Whose bike is that?"

Abe put his hand above his eyes as if to shield himself from the sun. "That piece of shit... that's Ray Kelly's."

"Do you think he'd give it away?"

Abe produced a sarcastic grin. "Ray Kelly's not giving away anything."

"What if I offered him something for it?"

As far as she knew, Ray Kelly wasn't exactly the master of commerce. Just some random dude in his twenties, rumored to have an aptitude for delinquency.

"Why would you want to do that, Dakota... and besides, aren't you broke?"

"Let me figure that out. Could you talk to him for me? Tell him I'm interested."

"Sure... why not," Abe said, although he didn't seem too pumped about it.

"Good," Dakota said. "I've got an idea that could benefit both of us."

Abe scratched at his chin. "What is it?"

"I kind of have to work it out first. You know... in my mind."

But she already had visions of helping her mother pay the rent. Of finishing up her sophomore year in Zionsville instead of moving to Cleveland. Perhaps that was how entrepreneurial geniuses worked. Sitting around like Isaac Newton, in your front yard one day, and an apple falls down and hits you on the head.

May 23, 2019

Chapter 6.
Knickknacks in the Attic

Rosie fiddled with the music app while driving aimlessly around the back roads of South Zionsville, a recipe for disaster if there ever was one.

"Let me do that," Dakota suggested. In her mind, the danger of her best friend attempting to multitask had reached its apex. "What are we looking for?"

Rosie turned her head and shot out an are-you-fucking-with-me look.

"Got it," Dakota said. She navigated the Spotify app until she came upon their killer mixtape playlist, titled "Killer Mixtape." She selected a Bad Bunny track and cranked up the volume.

"That's what I'm talking about," Rosie proclaimed, suddenly tapping her fingers on the steering wheel. Ever since she'd obtained her license, the contents of the playlist had become their traveling jam. And once the weather turned warmer in May, they routinely cruised down Main Street with the windows down. Two dweebs in a Subaru, pretending like they were pop stars, bellowing out whatever tune happened to be on. Even the ones in Spanish, which Dakota memorized, with far more gusto than she'd ever used in her actual Spanish class.

When the playlist transitioned into Doja Cat's "Bottom Bitch," they had no choice but to sing, Rosie starting it off, followed by Dakota syncing up in less-than-perfect harmony. And if ever there was a time to sing, would it not be after the last day of school? Except in the midst of the chorus, Rosie eased the car over onto a dirt pullout and shifted into park.

"What are you doing?" Dakota asked.

"Honestly, D," Rosie replied. "I'm not sure I can listen to you anymore. You sound like an out-of-tune hyena."

"So you're saying there could be in-tune hyenas?"

Rosie smirked and pushed aside a stubborn strand of hair. "I'm just saying you're a bad singer."

"You're not exactly Beyoncé."

"Fair enough. But still."

"So," Dakota then said, trying to conjure up a way to say what she wanted to say in a sensitive manner. "You are aware that the house we're going to is in North Zionsville?"

Rosie tilted her head. "So what?"

"It's just that we're presently located in South Zionsville."

"You think I don't know that?"

"I don't know what you don't know. Only you would know that. Then again, maybe you don't."

"Are you calling me an idiot?"

"I would never use that word. You might be a bit soft in the brain though. It could be all those paint thinners you use."

Rosie let loose a right jab to Dakota's shoulder.

As it turned out, their ultimate destination happened

to be 46 Brunson Avenue, located on the Northside, across the bridge, just a few miles east of downtown. Rosie ending up on the Southside was not as bad as you might think due to a quirk in town geography, where parts of North Zionsville bled into South Zionsville on the other side of the Y-Bridge. Between that and her sore arm, Dakota felt no need to continue needling her friend about her navigational disabilities, and she punched the address of Stanley and Helen Powers into the Subaru's navigation app. She'd found it last night using a Google search. It took her a whole thirty seconds. But no Anika Powers. Likely, she'd gotten married and taken on her husband's name, and so the purpose of their unannounced visit would be simple. Find out Anika's last name. Procure her address and/or phone number. Limit the meaningless conversation. No tea or scones. Get the information. Get out.

Minutes later they found themselves outside the home of Stanley and Helen Powers, a modest ranch in a neighborhood filled with modest ranches and a smattering of cool-looking Craftsman homes.

They exited the Subaru and met up by its front hood. Dakota wore a white tank over green cargos, whereas Rosie had on a white vintage Care Bears tee over wide-leg yellow floral sunflower pants.

"Do we have an actual plan?" Rosie asked.

Dakota wiped sweat off her forehead. She could already sense her nerves beginning to jangle.

"We don't need a plan," she replied. "I'm just going to tell the truth. Anika was an old friend of my mom's. I'm looking to get information about my father. I'd like to ask Anika a few questions to see what she remembers."

"So telling the truth. That's your plan."

"At this point in our investigation, I don't think we need to lie."

Dakota took off, briskly making her way toward the house. At the front door, she kept moving her feet, nervously tapping them on the ground.

Rosie came up from behind, placing a hand on her friend's back. "Breathe," she instructed as she rang the doorbell.

They heard a stirring from behind the door. Footsteps. Muffled voices. The door creaked open, revealing two people behind the screen.

They presented as an odd couple and not only because of their disparity in height. Helen, they presumed, a tall wisp of a woman, looked sharp in a button-up floral-patterned blouse over white pants, with alert dark eyes and a helmet of expertly styled white hair that could double as a bird's nest. Then Stanley, lurking behind. He must have to buy his clothes at a big-and-tall store. Stocky, with wide shoulders that slumped slightly forward, allowing an expansive view of his bald, egg-shaped head. He appeared festive in his Hawaiian shirt over blue Bermudas. Dakota feared they might have interrupted piña colada hour.

"Can I help you?" the woman asked in a tone that signified she might consider helping.

Dakota swallowed. "Mr. and Mrs. Powers... uhh... my name is Dakota Lodi... and this is my friend Rosie. My mom... Victoria Lodi... she was a friend of your daughter's."

Stanley nudged his wife out of the way. "Which daughter?"

They hadn't counted on more than one. But no biggie.

"Anika," Dakota said, trying to project confidence.

"Is this some sort of scam?" Stanley inquired.

They could see him more clearly then. Dakota's first impression: a used car dealer. A guy that would sell you a shitty car, then later contend he hadn't a clue as to it being shitty. A guy with a set of intensely brilliant blue eyes that appeared ready to pop out of their sockets. At waist level, she noticed him gripping a large cigar in his hand. He twirled it around for a few revolutions before jamming it into his mouth.

Rosie offered a half smile so that the Powers could catch a glimpse of a dimple. "We can assure you we're here for legitimate reasons."

Stanley chomped at the cigar for a few seconds before removing it from his mouth. He waved it in the air as if chasing away a swarm of insects. "Us seniors have to be careful, you know."

Helen glared at her husband. "Knock it off, Stanley." Then to the girls: "He thinks he's being funny."

Stanley just stood there. If he felt emasculated, he didn't let on.

"We just wanted to ask you a few questions," Dakota chimed in. "I'm trying to learn more about my father, and I know Anika was a good friend of my mom's around that time."

Helen gave Stanley a subtle nod, then opened the screen door. "You girls might as well come in, but we don't have much time. We have a reservation at Bixby's. At five."

Bixby's. Overpriced burgers and steaks, although there could be discounts for the early bird special.

Dakota attempted a genuine smile. "Thank you so much."

"I've heard Bixby's is good," Rosie said.

Typical Rosie. She despised Bixby's but loved chatting up strangers. Irritating sometimes.

"Oh, we just love it there," Helen replied.

They were in the vestibule. A narrow nothing of a room, where people removed their shoes and likely passed through without noticing. The house smelled of baked goods with a hint of cinnamon. Dakota pushed her desire for snacking aside and observed that Helen and Stanley had formed a blockade of sorts, pinning them into the corner of the room up against a wooden console table.

Stanley parted his lips slightly, revealing an unruly set of yellow teeth. He inserted the cigar back into the corner of his mouth. It appeared as if he had no intention of smoking it. "So, what kind of questions are we talking about here?"

"We don't want to take up much of your time," Dakota replied. "If you could just give us your daughter's address, or maybe her phone number, we'd be on our way."

Helen folded her arms in a way that signaled grave concern. "I'm not sure we feel comfortable giving out our daughter's information. It's not that we don't trust you, but like my husband said, we're seniors. We have to be careful."

"I totally understand," Dakota explained. "But you must remember something about my mom."

Helen exchanged looks with Stanley, and you could tell something passed between them. "Our Anika was quite popular back then," Helen contended. "It's hard to remember all the girls who came through here."

"And honestly, I have a hard time remembering yesterday," Stanley claimed, trying his hand at stand-up.

"What if I gave you my cell number?" Dakota proposed. "You can pass it along to Anika. Then she could make the decision to call me or not."

Helen appeared to be deep in thought, as if she were running the proposal over in her mind. She turned toward her husband. "Stanley, there's a pad and pen in one of the kitchen drawers by the phone. Why don't you get that for her?"

Strange. Why wouldn't they just give her the number to put in her phone?

Stanley smiled. "I've been reduced to an errand boy," he quipped before disappearing somewhere into the house.

"Sorry about that," Helen said once her husband had vanished. "He's just protective of his daughter. Even if she is in her thirties."

"Some things never change," Rosie offered.

Helen turned toward Dakota then, and her eyes drifted up, then down, as if performing an examination, the air in the vestibule turning thicker by the second. In the background, they heard the sound of opening and closing drawers. "You don't look like her," Helen observed.

Dakota felt a rush of adrenaline. "You remember her?"

Helen nodded. "You'd have to be brain dead to forget Victoria Lodi. And the two of them together. Let's just say the word wild doesn't do them justice."

"Wow. So, like… you would know things about her. Like who she was dating. Who got her pregnant when she was sixteen."

Perhaps she'd gone too far with the who-impregnated-my-mom thing, because Helen just shook her head, a hint of annoyance sneaking into her posture. "I never concerned myself with the personal lives of Anika's friends. We had enough to worry about back then."

"It's not easy being a mother of teenage girls," Rosie said, smiling, as if she'd contributed to that universal problem.

"And honestly, it never ends. I would have no problem giving you my daughter's information, but Stanley wouldn't like it. And Anika would definitely flip out. She's a very private person. And she's quite busy with her business lately, so I don't think she'd appreciate the disturbance."

"I can certainly understand that," Rosie said. "My mom has her own business. And god help you if you happen to interrupt her while she's even thinking about it."

"Can I ask you something, Mrs. Powers?" Dakota then said, an idea suddenly churning about in her head. "Where did you get these?" She pointed at some items she'd been examining on the console table. A couple of glass candle holders and a glazed wine bottle, each of them with etched monograms in fancy script lettering.

"Oh… I'd guess you'd say they were gifts."

Originally, Dakota hadn't pegged the candle holders as gifts. *God is love* was inscribed on one of them, *The best is yet to come* on the other. They could have been purchased at any secondhand knickknack store, but the wine bottle appeared to be more personal. "Do you mind?" she asked, her fingers already wrapping themselves around the bottle's mouth.

Helen's mouth formed a perfect oval. "No… of course not."

Dakota picked up the wine bottle and turned her body slightly so that Rosie could see it as well.

"That's beautiful," Rosie said.

The bottle was made of greenish-colored glass and glazed such that you couldn't see directly through it, but transparent enough that you could discern a set of fairy lights winding their way from the top to the bottom of the bottle, like a vine on a trellis. "It's a lamp," Dakota declared.

"They call them upcycled bottles," Helen said. "I never heard about such a thing until my daughter told me about it."

"So your daughter made these?" Rosie asked.

Helen said that she had.

"Happy fortieth anniversary. Stanley and Helen Powers," Dakota read out loud.

"Forty years," Rosie said. "That's some accomplishment."

Helen's face flushed. "Thank you."

"And Anika gave this to you?" Dakota asked.

"Not really. She made it. But I heard it was our grandkids' idea. Actually, Maggie and Katelyn's. They're older, you see. Matthew and Lauren's names were on the card, but they're too young to come up with something like that on their own."

"Do you get to see them often? Your grandkids."

"Well… Matthew and Lauren live in Columbus. Maggie and Katelyn are close by though."

Close by. Could be evidence they lived in town, which could be good, unless Anika was the one responsible for the grandkids in Columbus. Not that they couldn't get to Columbus. Rosie on the highway though. Could be dicey.

"You know," Rosie said, wrapping a locket of hair around one of her fingers. "My parents' anniversary is coming up in a few weeks, and I was wondering what to get them."

"Your mother would love something like this," Dakota

added, although they both knew Mrs. Peña hated kitschy stuff and that if Rosie did bring home a monogrammed wine bottle lamp, it would likely end up in their attic.

"Is there any way I can order one of these?" Rosie asked.

A smile enveloped Helen's face, lifting her cheeks up toward the sockets of her eyes. "I don't see why not. It's Anika's Creations. Except you have to order them on the internet, and I can't remember where."

"Etsy?" Dakota said.

"Yes… Etsy… that's it. How did you know?"

"Lucky guess."

Just then, Stanley returned. "Sorry about that," he said. "I found the pad by the phone, but there were no pens."

Helen shook her head. "There are pens, Stanley. They're in the third drawer."

"Don't think so. I had to go to my office to find one. I swear, gremlins are stealing all of our pens."

"It's a well-known fact," Dakota said. "They come in at night. While you're sleeping."

"Happens all the time," Rosie added.

Stanley smiled and held up the pad and pen as if finding them had been one of life's great accomplishments.

Helen, however, was not so impressed. She snatched the pen and pad from her husband and gave them to Dakota. "Men" is all she said.

August 31, 2018

Chapter 7.
Liar's Poker

Dakota initiated Project Freedom the very next day. It signified freedom from the shackles of impending eviction and from moving to Cleveland, with freedom from the humiliation of riding the bus to school each morning as a decent side benefit. All she needed to execute her plan was to buy the bicycle. And it all seemed possible when Abe, whom she'd met out by the courtyard that day, implied that Ray Kelly would be willing to part with it for twenty-five bucks.

So when Dakota arrived home that afternoon, there was a sense of impending change. Especially when she found her mother and Gina at the dining room table playing Texas Hold'em while nursing whatever alcoholic concoction they'd drummed up for the evening. It presented an opportunity of sorts, as sometimes the inebriated version of her mother agreed to things she'd normally not agree to when sober.

"What are you guys drinking?" Dakota asked, pulling up a chair.

"Mojitos," Gina replied in a gleeful manner. She took a sip, then dealt the three face-up cards for the flop.

Her mother examined the cards, then shifted her cement-filled eyes without moving her head. "Where you been?"

Dakota sat down, leaned back, and crossed one leg over the other. Ace of clubs, ten of hearts, and five of spades, along with the two hole cards. Nothing special.

"At the library," Dakota replied.

"You're not gonna make friends at the library," her mother insisted.

"You'd be surprised," Dakota responded, recalling the article she'd read in *National Geographic* about polar bears but not feeling the need to explain.

Her mother pushed a few chips into the pot. Gina matched the bet.

"You guys playing for money? Dakota asked.

"IOUs," her mother said.

Gina dealt the turn card. "Tell that to my bank account." A seven of clubs. She had as much chance of winning the hand as being elected president of the local PTA chapter. A fact that became obvious when, without hesitation, her mother moved a large cluster of chips into the pot, causing Gina to fold. Which she surely regretted once the hole cards were revealed and it became apparent she would have won the hand with a pair of tens. Her mother had shit for cards.

"So, Mom," Dakota started, having intentionally waited until the hand was over. "I was wondering if you could lend me twenty-five bucks. There's a bike I want to buy."

"What kind of bike costs twenty-five bucks?"

"An old one," Dakota said. "It's a friend's."

An incredulous look appeared on her mother's face, and Dakota couldn't tell if it had to do with the old bike costing twenty-five bucks or her mentioning a friend. Maybe both.

"You know things are tight, Dakota."

She already knew that. Her mother had made it perfectly clear last night as they discussed the specifics of their grim financial situation. Their benefits would not be enough to cover both rent and food, not to mention utilities. She'd even floated the idea of Gina temporarily moving in so they could pool resources, which would not have been much of a lifestyle change, since Gina had lived there the past two weeks. Not that Gina didn't have her own issues to deal with. Car payments, insurance, credit card debt, three months left on her own apartment lease, and the stubborn fact that she drank as much, or more, than her mother.

"Think of it as a loan," Dakota suggested. "I'll pay you back."

"Oh," her mother said, shaking her head, "and how might you do that?"

"I'm going to ask Mrs. Peña for a job. Rosie told me they need help at the diner."

"Seriously, Dakota," her mother scoffed. "What makes you think she's giving you a job?"

"I don't know. She likes me."

"Here's some info for you, peanut. That woman doesn't like you. And if she gives you anything, it's only to make herself feel better."

A brutal analysis for sure, but if that were so, how did it account for Mrs. Peña inviting her to all those Friday night dinners, the zillion sleepovers with Rosie, and Mr. Peña allowing her to use his Spotify account, which Mrs. Peña certainly would have put a stop to if she had any problems with her?

"I don't know, Mom. I think you're underestimating her generosity. And besides, if I were to work there on weekends, I could take home some serious bank. I could pay you back and contribute some of it for stuff. Like food, maybe."

"Some of it."

"Yeah… it would be my job." She had emphasized the word *my*, intending to be snarky about it, knowing that if she somehow managed to get a job at the diner, she'd have to figure out a way to prevent her mother from suctioning off all of her take-home pay while keeping enough to help her mother with rent. A delicate balance, for sure.

"We'll see about that. But as far as me giving you money for the bike, I don't think so. You get the job. You pay for your own bike."

"Kind of like you getting a job and paying for your own booze."

Her mother fixed her with mega laser-beam eyes, and Dakota smiled back at her, knowing how it would piss her off, but also knowing that she could have gone further. Hit her mother with some simple math zingers. That adding up her recent alcoholic beverage purchases, combined with sure-to-be-future jaunts to the Handlebar Tavern, would more than pay for the bicycle. And she could have brought up the unlabeled bottle of pills she'd seen yesterday on her mother's dresser. Instead, she let out a sigh of mock resignation as her mother dealt the next hand. Instead of sulking, which would have done no good, Dakota procured a bag of tortilla chips from the kitchen pantry and a bottle of spicy salsa from the fridge. Chips and salsa. Typical Lodi dinner fare.

After the flop, both of them checked. Gina raised an eyebrow, a sure tell if there ever was one.

"You should play, Kota," Gina said to her, rubbing her fingers together. "I'm tired of getting my ass kicked."

"No thanks. My mom gets bitchy when she loses."

Gina chuckled. "She's bitchy when she wins."

Her mother gave Gina a killer look, then peered over her shoulder as Dakota spooned some salsa into a bowl. "The only way you're beating me, peanut, is if you blind-fold me. Even then I'd probably take you."

Her mother didn't kid around when it came to poker. She'd even taught the game to Dakota when she was in third grade, beating her like a drum continuously, having no problem making her daughter cry. But at times she overestimated her ability. She had no problem fleecing a bunch of inebriated local yokels at the Handlebar Tavern and had gone as far as placing, and winning, money at some of the Lions club tournaments in town. But eventually she would run into someone better. There was always someone better.

Dakota smiled but for the most part ignored her mother as she gathered her dinner and brought it over to the coffee table in the living room, far enough that she didn't have to smell the alcohol on their breath, close enough to hear the clacking sound of chips being tossed into the pot. She scooped a chip into the salsa bowl and stuffed it into her mouth. By then she'd resigned herself to certain undeniable facts. Not that Gina folded again, but that her mother wasn't going to give her a freaking dime. Though in the Project Freedom flow chart she'd developed in her head, an entire branch had been created for such a scenario. Ask Mom for money. Mom says yes. Buy the bike. Mom says no. Go to plan B, the details of which she hadn't yet ironed out but would need to do pronto.

Dakota pulled out her phone and earbuds. She laid them on the coffee table and grabbed hold of another chip. Outside, the wind had picked up, and for a moment she considered detangling her earbuds, perhaps working on her R&B playlist, when she felt movement on the couch and her mother plopping down beside her.

Dakota turned. "What's wrong, Mom? Gina run out of money?"

Her mother smiled and moved closer. "I know you think I'm being hard on you, Dakota, but you know how I feel about these things."

"I get it, Mom. I was just trying to help."

"I know you were. But the world isn't about to do you any favors, and you need to take care of yourself. We've talked about this before, so I'll assume you remember."

Dakota nodded. "Yes. I have to be independent... and strong."

"And smart. Don't forget smart."

Yeah. Independent. Strong and smart. And now she was supposed to make new friends, dream up some way to buy the bike, and make enough money to stave off eviction and the move to Cleveland. Honestly, it was a lot to remember.

May 24, 2019

Chapter 8.
If Life Hands
You Melons

The sticker on Rosie's laptop read *If life hands you melons you might be dylexic.* A statement that Dakota always found inspiring, the way her friend could be self-deprecating about something that had caused her problems over the years. But as she positioned the laptop on the bright yellow island in Mrs. Peña's kitchen, and hopped about the Etsy store for Anika's Creations, she wished for her own source of inspiration.

"This feels weird," Dakota said. "You know… intruding on people's lives like this."

"Are you serious?" Rosie replied. "People put shit on social media because they expect you to look at it. And a girl has a right to know who her father is. I say fuck 'em."

Words of inspiration, for sure. And she certainly felt a burst of positive energy when she found a snapshot of said owner of the store, Anika Renfors. After that, a collection of mediocre photographs. Wine bottles, candle holders, along with gratuitous comments like *beautiful, perfect birthday gift, and made our holiday* that made them think they were wasting their time, until Dakota scrolled down and came upon a silver globe-shaped Christmas ornament with *joy to the world* etched in black. It wasn't necessarily the ornament itself that caught her attention, but a comment by someone named Jenna Beal. "Fabulous," Dakota read out loud. "Always knew you were creative."

"It's more personal," Rosie observed.

"'Always knew,'" Dakota added with a wry smile.

They followed the link to Anika's Facebook account. It didn't take long to find a friend.

"Bingo," Dakota exclaimed enthusiastically.

"They could be sisters," Rosie said.

She had a point. Anika with short blond hair. Jenna's hair, longer and slightly darker. Both of them, with cherub faces and bright eyes, produced half smiles for the camera.

The next steps consisted of going through their Facebook and Instagram pages. Anika with a photo of her and husband Al on vacation in the Bahamas. Jenna with an Insta shot that appeared to be from the same vacation, Anika and Al along with Jenna and her husband, Jeremy, all sitting at an outdoor restaurant table. A whole set of Insta photos, again from Jenna, dated last August, from what appeared to be a retirement party for the Public Works department of Zionsville. In fact, a retirement party for Stanley Powers. Stanley cutting a cake. *A Happy Retirement, Stanley* banner. Stanley, Al, and Jeremy, with a caption: *Public Works. One down, two to go,* implying that the three of them were coworkers.

"I think we've learned something," Dakota commented, trying to digest what she'd actually learned.

"Well, Stanley is retired," Rosie said. "That explains the Hawaiian shirt he wore the other day."

"It's nice that the Beals and Renfors seem close."

Rosie's eyes widened. "You know, we should check out Twitter. Business owners use it all the time. My mom posts menus and specials for the diner."

Seconds later, they were on the @SunriseDiner Twitter account, where they struck out on anything for Anika's Creations but did find a personal @AnikaRenfors account, although you wouldn't exactly call Anika a big-time tweeter. The occasional random comment about events in town, but nothing that appeared pertinent until they came upon a tweet from last year, linked to a photograph from something called the Ohio Women's Conference.

Just came back from the Ohio Women's Conference in Dayton. What a wonderful weekend. So many great events. Kudos to the keynote speaker, Marjorie Jennings. Marjorie, you are always an inspiration to me.

They weren't exactly sure if the tweet had any value, but they did manage to confirm that Anika and Marjorie were in fact friends. Well, at least on Facebook. Not to mention the photograph of the two women posted a few months earlier that they'd discovered on Marjorie's Instagram, which made them go back to the original tweet and a tag that led to Marjorie's blog, a publication-style newsletter with entries about women's issues. Women juggling work and raising kids, postpartum depression, relationship advice, job interview tips when dealing with male asshole authority figures, as well as a blurb about changing the false narratives on sexual violence.

"Interesting," Rosie observed. "But what does it really mean?"

"Marjorie looks older. More sophisticated," Dakota replied. "Can't see her being my mom's friend."

In the end they both agreed that while it was fascinating

that Anika Renfors had a business engraving knickknacks, went on vacations to Caribbean islands with her friend, had a retired father, and was curious enough about women's issues to attend a conference, that it all deflected from the main problem. At some point they'd have to find a way to talk to her. Unless they struck gold with their Jimmy Ray Coleman search. In which case, however Anika Renfors lived her knickknack-engraving, Facebook-Instagram-posting, Caribbean-vacationing life would make no difference.

Their search began on Google, where they discovered a Jimmy Ray Coleman in Elgin, South Carolina, buried in the Spears Creek Baptist Church Cemetery. Or in Carson, Texas, where James R. Coleman, who presumably loved working with wood, had died doing what he loved. And a deceased hog farmer in Eldon, Ohio, that had gone by James Coleman. They switched things up then, adding keywords like obituary, funeral, and accident. They included the town of Zionsville, after which they took out the Ray, substituted James for Jimmy, and later replaced Zionsville with neighboring towns such as Somerset and Philo and cities like Dayton and Columbus, all of it leading down a road to nowhere until Dakota typed in "Coleman Grave Zionsville" and a portal to an unseen universe opened: George Coleman on findagrave.com.

Rosie leaned closer. Dakota felt her friend's breath brushing the side of her neck as she fixed upon the grainy photo: a headstone in St. Joseph's Cemetery in Zionsville with *George Coleman 1958–2018* carved onto the stone. The other side of the page contained an obituary, which Dakota read out loud.

George R. Coleman entered into eternal rest on Friday, November 9, 2018, at his home in South Zionsville.

He was the husband of Marion Coleman. He was born in Dayton, Ohio, son of the late Raymond and Estelle (Stinson) Coleman. George was an employee at Daniels Propane and a graduate of Zionsville High School. He loved hunting, working on his Ford truck, and keeping his yard and vegetable garden green. He was an avid fan of Ohio State Football and the Cincinnati Reds. Survivors were brothers Michael Coleman and Richard Coleman, sister Beatrice Flanagan, daughters Christine Boland and Maureen Bonardi, son James Coleman, and grandchildren Ashley Boland, Adam Boland, Samuel Bonardi, and Elaine Bonardi. He was predeceased by son Greg Coleman.

The passage was a Venus flytrap, revealing itself slowly before ensnaring its prey. Sadly, George Coleman was dead at the age of sixty. Dakota didn't care that he liked working on his truck, harvested his own tomatoes, or watched football. But George's father's name was Raymond, and so there was a chance his friends called him Ray. There was a surviving son named James or Jimmy. Parents liked naming their kids after their own parents, and so Jimmy Ray seemed logical. Yet according to the obituary, Greg was dead and Jimmy was not.

Could it be?

Jimmy Ray Coleman.

Alive!

Which meant her mother had lied. No surprise there. Even Lucinda had expressed reservations as to his death. Though it was strange how she never mentioned a brother that passed. Especially when Dakota looked up Greg Coleman on findagrave.com and discovered he died in 2005, the same year that Jimmy Ray presumably had his accident. Could that be why she'd abruptly ended the conversation about her father the other night and brushed off the DNA test? Could it be her grandmother was a liar as well?

September 1–2, 2018

Chapter 9.
Plan B

Outside with bike, Dakota texted Abe, before placing her bony ass on the Schwinn Sidewinder, booking it around the cul-de-sac with a degree of verve she had clearly not expected. Starting with circles and moving on to crazy eights, she pumped her legs to get the kinks out of the clunky gears while dreaming up ways to pitch her idea to Abe. The sun over the tops of the trees beat down on her. The warm feeling in her stomach was getting warmer.

Abe came out of the trailer and perched himself on his front step.

Dakota shot him a quick glance, pretending her heart hadn't just fluttered. "Look," she shouted out, "no hands." She had raised them into a victory formation before bringing them back down and slamming on the brakes, spraying out dirt. She disembarked from the bike with some difficulty. The seat would need to be adjusted, and she'd have to do something about the rust so the bike didn't look like something a junkyard might reject. Yet she could not deny there'd been a sense of exhilaration. As if she'd discovered something she never knew she'd been missing. And when was the last time she'd even ridden a bike? Nine, maybe ten. Her mother had bought her one of those cheap BMX look-alikes, and she did jumps with the neighborhood kids in the parking lot of their subsidized apartment complex in North Zionsville. She'd been decent at it too, but it likely wasn't something she'd try as a fifteen-year-old. Still, it was true what they said about bicycles. About never forgetting.

Abe pulled at the shoulder of his tie-dyed shirt and smiled. "Are you trying to impress me?"

Dakota returned the smile, hoping there might be a hint of seduction in it. "Was it that obvious?"

"So what's it gonna be, Dakota?" Abe said, suddenly all business. "Ray Kelly let you test the bike out, but he's getting impatient."

Yeah. She'd noticed that when she'd taken the bike from him that morning. You would have thought she was asking for one of his kidneys.

"Well, I'm interested," Dakota said, walking the bike over to where Abe was sitting and leaning it against her side. She'd already observed the kickstand needed tightening and didn't want to just drop it on the ground, thinking that might prove Abe's original theory about it being a piece of shit. Nevertheless, she had the urge to sit down next to him just as she'd done the other day. Maybe closer this time.

Abe scratched at something behind his ear. A few hairs on the back of his head stood up, like vagabond feathers. "So why don't you tell me what you're trying to do here."

"Okay... hear me out. You lend me the twenty-five bucks to buy the bike and I fix it up. Then I have transportation to school and you get to expand your pot business. It's a win-win."

Abe looked as if he'd been hit in the face with a frying

pan. "Huh," he replied. "You want me to buy the bike for you?"

"Think of it as an investment. Right now, you're only selling in the neighborhood. It limits your upside."

"Upside," he mimicked.

"The rich kids on the Northside won't come over to the South, and it's too risky selling at school. Instead, I act as your courier and deliver anywhere in town. I would expect some compensation, of course. And you can deduct the twenty-five bucks from our first sale."

"I don't know about this."

Dakota rolled her eyes. She'd hoped Abe would have demonstrated some vision. Sure, the bike was not aesthetically pleasing in its current condition, and her small-girl-delivering-pot-on-a-bicycle business model represented out-of-the-box thinking. But sometimes, did you not have to see the forest through the trees?

"Sure you do." Dakota smiled and brushed aside a strand of hair that had wandered across her eyes, thinking that might do the trick.

"I get it, Dakota. But it's not like we're the only ones selling pot in this fucking town."

"But we'd be the only ones delivering pot," Dakota said, a bit miffed by Abe's reluctance. "And from what I hear, you have lots of contacts."

She'd heard zippo about Abe's contacts, only deducing that he might have them from the way he interacted in the courtyard that day.

Abe shook his head. "I'm just saying there's competition out there. It's like you've got McDonald's, Wendy's, and Burger King on the same block. And they all sell fucking burgers for the same price."

"But McDonald's has the Egg McMuffin and Burger King chargrills their burgers."

"What's your point?"

"They differentiate. Like I said, we push the delivery angle. The convenience of getting high without leaving your couch. Except then I'd actually have to go into their house. Not sure I'm down with that. Depends on the house and the person, I guess. Do you deal with lots of creepers, Abe?"

Abe hesitated before displaying a half grin. "I guess it's not the worst idea in the world. But you have to fix the bike up. And pay me back."

Dakota felt the edges of her mouth stretch out. She wanted to dump the Sidewinder onto the ground and rush over to him, drape her arms around him to show her appreciation. Perhaps slip in a comment about the two of them together not being the worst idea in the world either. Instead, she just stood there with her bicycle, squinting at the sun. She'd never had a boyfriend before. Didn't quite know how to go about it. Though if Abe were impressed with her undeniable business acumen, could things not work out between them?

"Awesome," she proclaimed, jumping back into a reality bereft of hot juvenile delinquent boyfriends. "Now all we need is customers."

* * *

Next came the culmination of the beginning stages of Plan B, when on Sunday afternoon, Dakota rode her bicycle to Rosie's house in North Zionsville, a bold turquoise-colored ranch with light blue vinyl siding. She'd been cruising all day, crossing the bridge into Philo, then back up on the other side toward downtown, and by the time she reached her friend's driveway, her legs had transformed into a pair of lead sticks. She dismounted and had to steady herself to keep from stumbling, before heading toward the refurbished shed in the corner of the backyard, which doubled as Rosie's art studio. To Dakota, it seemed as if she'd spent half her life in that shed, playing DJ on Mr. Peña's stereo, compiling her playlists as she lounged on the cushy leather chair while Rosie painted, the two of them not always feeling the need to say anything.

She eased her bike onto a blue tarp laid out on the grass and then made her way into the shed, where her best friend stood, staring at one of her paintings. *The Octopus.*

"Come here," Rosie said, having sensed her friend coming up from behind. She had on her painting outfit. Denim overalls, with a variety of stains encompassing most of the color wheel, over a green-and-white-striped tee, a paisley bandana tied around her head. "What do you think?"

What could you say about *The Octopus?* A humongous kaleidoscopic sea creature, with eight appendages and what must have been one hundred suction cups, suspended in a brilliant cobalt-blue background. Beautiful, actually.

"I love this one," Dakota said.

Rosie turned. "So I've been talking to this woman at one of the galleries in town. They have a young artists show every summer that I'd like to be a part of. So she came over yesterday, and she's looking at Señor Octopus, and she says..." Rosie lowers her voice an octave. "Well... Miss Peña, you obviously have talent, but there is a small piece missing, something from your heart that doesn't translate onto canvas. You're good... but you could be better. Remember… art is alive. It should stimulate all of your senses."

"Like all five of them?"

"Yep… go ahead." Rosie flicked her hand forward. "Try it."

Dakota hesitated. Did her friend want her to feel the canvas, to smell it? It sounded ridiculous. Still, she moved forward, put her face right up to the canvas and sniffed.

"Do you smell the sea?" Rosie continued. "Do you feel the cold water rushing over you?"

"I don't think she meant that literally."

"Of course not. It just means I have to work harder. Spend more time on this. Which I will do because I want this."

Dakota took a step back. There was no questioning Rosie's effort when it came to her art. Scattered throughout the room were half a dozen canvases, some on easels, others leaning against the walls, all in various stages of completion. If nothing else, her friend was productive, though she often worked on multiple paintings at once, going from one to another, depending on the day, the light, or even the phase of the moon. A process that Dakota never totally understood.

"What does your mom think about this?"

"She says painting is a nice hobby."

"But if you get a piece into the exhibit next summer… which you will… she might see things differently."

Rosie shrugged. "Don't think we're gonna solve that problem today." She rapped Dakota on the shoulder. "But let's see that shitty bike of yours."

They went outside then, and Dakota stood like a statue as Rosie walked around the bike, looking it over, shaking her head a few times. "So let me get this straight," she started. "I'm about to paint a bike that you got from a sketchy neighbor of some guy you're crushing on, and you're too embarrassed to ride the bike to school because… well, look at it… and you somehow talked this guy into buying the bike for you, and you have to pay him back with money you earn from a job you don't have yet."

Dakota smiled without revealing any teeth. "Sounds about right. Except for the crush part."

"Please, Dakota. You're, like, so obvious. So tell me about this guy. Do I know him? Is he cute?"

Dakota let out a breath. "Not sure I'm into an interrogation today. Don't we have work to do?"

Rosie furled her lips. "I'm the one doing you a favor here. And I seem to remember you asking about a job at the diner. So that's two things you owe me for. Big-time."

Jeez. What ever happened to giving for giving's sake?

"Honestly," Dakota replied, "there's not much to say. His name is Abe. He's a junior. I hung out with him after school the other day. Then I went home."

Rosie cracked a smile. "Please tell me he hasn't sent you any disgusting sex emojis?"

"Huh?"

"Last year, this guy texted me a peach. And when I sent him back a question mark, he fired off an eggplant. You know what I'm saying?"

Dakota shook her head. No one had ever texted her a fruit. Or a vegetable, for that matter.

"Well, I'll assume this guy is your only option," Rosie said.

"I could have other options," Dakota responded. "It's been a whole week. I could have lots of male suitors by now."

"Sure… maybe that happens… in Dakotaworld."

"Hey. Don't be dissing Dakotaworld. I have to live there, you know."

Rosie laughed, then reached out and pressed a finger into Dakota's ribs. "So, by the way, I talked to my mom last night about you getting a job at the diner. She said you're in if you don't mind washing dishes."

"Are you serious?" Dakota replied with a burst of excitement. "I love washing dishes."

"If everything works out, you'd be working weekends with me. You have to start tomorrow though. We open at six-thirty, but she wants you in at six. She wants to talk to you first."

Dakota couldn't deny a tinge of fear about talking to Mrs. Peña, but as Rosie stood before the Sidewinder, applying neon yellow paint from a spray can, a smile emerged, covering the entire surface of her face. At that precise moment, her dreams of helping her mother avoid eviction seemed within reach. And if she had to reciprocate at some point, then so be it. Wasn't that what friendship was all about? Doing things for each other. Respect. Trust and honesty. Oh yeah. Honesty. She took in a shallow breath and faced the facts of what she'd just done: lied to her best friend. A lie of omission, but still. Not that she wouldn't use the bike for riding around town, commuting to school, and now to a job that her friend had gotten for her. More to do with the bike's other purpose. That there'd be a different kind of job: a pot courier, if you were to put a delicate spin on it. A drug dealer, if you didn't.

May 25, 2019

Chapter 10.
I'm Not Afraid
of No Hornets

They made it to the car just as the rain started coming down, sheets pelting the windshield like machine gun fire. Rosie wiped drops of water from her forehead with the back of her hand, then adjusted the rearview mirror so she could see herself. She combed her fingers through her hair, as if she were getting ready for a date. Meanwhile, Dakota, perfectly oblivious to her appearance, pulled up Adam Boland's Facebook page on her phone. There'd be some time, as she knew Rosie would want to wait out the storm before getting back on the road.

"I have something to show you," Dakota said. She leaned over, and the two of them huddled around the phone. "This is Adam Boland. I got his name from the obituary. He's the son of Christine Boland, who's the daughter of George Coleman, which would make him George's grandson, Greg and Jimmy Ray's nephew, and my cousin."

Rosie drew her knees up. "That's confusing."

Dakota enlarged the profile photo. "Check it out."

"Such a handsome devil," Rosie offered with dripping sarcasm.

Dakota ignored her friend's commentary and swiped down to the other photograph on the page. Three guys posing in front of a bright red truck with three dirt bikes held down in the truck bed with ratchet straps. Behind them was a large blue sign with the words *Columbia Machine* in white script. The photo's caption read *All play, no work.*

"There he is again," Rosie said.

In the snapshot, Adam Boland stood in the middle between a large muscle-bound guy with a shaved head and a shorter hippieish-looking dude with long brown hair. Compared to the profile pic, you had a better view of his thick dark beard, and he wore a red baseball cap whose brim partially covered his eyes. He folded his arms, no smile, striking a tough-guy pose. His intentions seemed clear. Surely he wouldn't post a picture of some random truck with random people in front of a company he did not work at. He'd be the kind of guy that wanted you to know something about himself. That he was a machine-working, truck-driving, dirt-biking son of a gun with no less than two friends.

"So I'm thinking we should visit him at work," Dakota proposed.

"What makes you think he's there?"

Dakota had been prepared for Rosie's skepticism. And so she hopped aboard the Columbia Machine website just as she'd done last night. It contained all sorts of valuable information. For instance, their place of business happened to be in the town of Duncan, located on the east side of the river, which meant it was close. And they had a mission statement that ended with the phrase *Keep Junk Alive*, with signs depicting those exact words plastered throughout the workplace.

"I didn't know there was too much junk dying in the world," Rosie commented.

"Me neither," Dakota replied, "but I guess sometimes you can learn shit on the internet."

According to the site, Columbia Machine specialized in small-quantity machine repairs, requiring the expert use of lathes, mills, and surface grinders, as well as welding and fabrication services, using skills such as bending, shearing, and torching.

Rosie didn't seem impressed, which caused Dakota to follow the next branch of her decision tree, navigating to the HR portal. "You can apply for a job here."

"Is that something you wanted?"

Dakota produced a fake incredulous look. "What... are you saying a girl can't bend, shear, and torch?"

"No, I'm saying if you did, I'd feel sorry for the machines."

"Fair enough. But look at this." She clicked on the FAQ section and scrolled down to a blurb about the company's hours. Two shifts, seven days a week, one from eight to four thirty and the other three thirty to midnight. "The Facebook photo was taken in daylight. I'm betting he gets out of work at four thirty. I say we go there and see if the red truck is there. And if it is... we wait."

"Then what?"

But by then, the corners of Dakota's mouth had spread out into a devious-looking grin, and Rosie stared back at her with parted lips and raised eyebrows, as if she already knew the answer to her own question.

Later, they found themselves in the parking lot of Columbia Machine, where they discovered Adam Boland's red Ford F-150. It hadn't been all that difficult to find, as

Columbia Machine wasn't exactly Amazon, just a modest building with white cinder block and blue-and-gray trim that almost looked like an auto repair shop, with a couple of bays. They'd snaked through the back lot for not more than a minute before they located the truck, its shiny redness sticking out like a swollen thumb. Rosie eased the car right up to it, the two of them noticing the proliferation of bumper stickers, which Dakota recited out loud.

On the tailgate:

Gone Fishing. Back by Hunting Season.

I Heart Your Hunting Spot.

Born to Hunt, Forced to Work, with two bucks on either side with intertwined antlers.

Yes, This Is My Truck. No, I Won't Help You Move.

NICE TRUCK... Sorry About Your Small Penis.

And on the rear windshield:

Bigfoot Doesn't Believe In You.

"Wow," Rosie observed. "I don't even know what to say."

Dakota kept a straight face. "I'm not gonna lie. I'm a little disappointed in Bigfoot."

Afterward, they waited on a residential side street with a prime view of the lot until four thirty, when Adam and his partners in crime from the Facebook photo emerged out the back door of Columbia Machine and slid into the red truck. Before you knew it, they were peeling out onto the adjacent road. Rosie fired up the Subaru and they followed behind, keeping their distance to remain inconspicuous. But they only had to travel a mile down the road before the Ford F-150 pulled into the parking lot of Golden Bud's Bar and Grille. They parked one row down from where the truck had settled. But even from that distance, Dakota detected heavy metal music blasting from its speakers, and she could have sworn they were passing a spliff back and forth.

The Golden Bud's Bar and Grille wasn't the fanciest shindig in the world, which was good, since they were dressed casually. Dakota wore her black Pink Floyd *Dark Side of the Moon* tee over cuffed jeans and her Sk8-Hi Vans. Rosie was adorned with a gray-and-pink tie-dye mushroom tee, frayed denim cutoffs, and gray Cons.

They found two seats at the oval-shaped bar. They'd already located Adam and his friends sitting at a corner table, and it was the perfect spot to keep an eye on him without being noticed.

The bar looked as if it had been carved out of wood, with an island in the middle with tiered shelves of liquor lined up in neat rows. The bartender, a young woman in her early twenties with spiky blond hair streaked with purple, came up to them. She had an arm sleeve tattoo, something to do with two-headed snakes, dragons, or some other creepy members of a pretend animal kingdom.

"Can I help you girls?" she asked, a tinge of danger hidden in the simple question.

"Can we get something to eat here?" Dakota asked.

"For sure," the bartender replied. "You are aware this is a bar though."

"You know… my mother once told me I was conceived in a bar."

"How would I know that?"

"Oh… I do that all the time. Begin sentences with *you know*."

"The story has potential," the bartender contended. "But you need to work on your presentation."

Dakota put her hand on the wooden rim of the bar and slid it along the lacquered surface as the bartender plucked out a couple of menus from underneath the bar.

"What's good here?" Rosie inquired.

"Just about everything," the bartender responded. She flipped the menus onto the bar like she was dealing from a deck of cards. "Where you girls from?"

Rosie told her.

The bartender looked at Rosie, then back at Dakota. "For a second, I thought you two could be sisters. But now I don't see it."

"Sisters from another mother," Rosie countered, with one of her million-dollar smiles.

"Great. Two wiseasses. Must be my lucky night."

"So how's the nachos?" Perhaps Rosie sensed the bartender could go off at any second and that inquiring about a specific menu item could be the right kind of diversion.

"They're killer."

Rosie glanced over at Dakota, who gave a thumbs-up sign. "We'll go with the chili nachos, no sour cream, and can we get jalapeños on that?"

"Most definitely," replied the bartender. "What about drinks?"

"Two screaming orgasms, please," Dakota declared.

She and Rosie had once looked up crazy drink names on the internet and decided the screaming orgasm would be their drink of choice if they were to have one.

The beginnings of a smile began to form on the bartender's mouth. "You girls are a riot. Think you might be able to handle some soft drinks?"

They settled on water with lemon and ice so that they could save money for dessert. Dakota had spotted the words key lime pie on that particular section of the menu, and so to some degree, their fate had been sealed. Meanwhile, and thankfully, the bartender had moved over to the other side of the bar to deal with some thirsty customers.

"Are you intentionally being an asshole?" Rosie said.

"I'm just trying to establish some ground rules," Dakota replied.

"And what might those be?"

"We need an ally here. Someone to help us gather information. And bartenders know everyone."

"I don't think she likes us."

Dakota shrugged. "We don't want her to think we're intimidated by her."

"But we are intimidated."

"Of course. But we can't let her know that."

"So you guys have names?" The bartender was back. This time with a plate of nachos the size of Wisconsin. She had two small plates and far too many napkins that she said they'd most likely be using. Had she pegged them as messy eaters? This being part of some evaluation bartenders were required to do as part of their job description.

"I'm Rosie, by the way," Rosie said, her mitts already excavating a clump of nachos. "And this is Dakota."

"Angela," said the bartender. She looked happier now. Maybe one of the other customers had said something nice to her. Complimented her appearance, or hair, or the snakes and dragons on her arm or whatever the hell those were.

"Well, it's nice to meet you, Angela," Dakota said, attempting her take on charm. "Have you been working here for long?"

"About a year. Ever since Marty bought the place and hired his brother, Ed, as the cook. That's why the food's good. Before that it was a salmonella factory."

"We work in the food industry ourselves," Dakota said. "Rosie's mom owns a restaurant."

"Oh yeah, what restaurant?"

"Sunrise Diner," Rosie told her. "In Zionsville."

Angela eyed them suspiciously. "I've been to that place. It's good. But I've never seen either of you there."

"We work behind the scenes," Rosie explained.

"I must say though," Dakota said, "these nachos are extraordinary."

"You might want to try eating some of them," Angela suggested, putting a finger on her chin.

"Oops. Sorry about that." Some chili had found a resting place around her mouth, and half a jalapeño rested atop the *Dark Side of the Moon* pyramid. She raided the napkin inventory and dealt with it accordingly.

"So, you girls checking out the competition?"

"We're looking for jobs, actually. Rosie's mom pays us shit."

Rosie shot Dakota a dirty look.

Angela continued. "Well, this place ain't so great, although some nights the tips are good. I'm saving up to go back to school."

"What are you going to school for?" Dakota inquired.

Angela produced a sly grin. "Actually, I want to be a pilot."

"For some reason that doesn't surprise me, Angela. Although I'll reserve judgment on whether or not I'd ever fly with you."

"Do you want to work for an airline?" Rosie asked.

"No. I prefer small planes."

"Like rich-people planes?"

"More like charters going into remote areas. Like a bush pilot."

"Sounds like a bad sex metaphor," Dakota said.

Angela grinned. She tilted her head, like a dog does when it's not sure of your intentions. "So," she said. "I need something from you girls."

"What would that be?"

"You can tell me what the two of you are really doing here."

Dakota eyed Rosie, as if exhorting her to speak first, but Rosie gave a quick shake of her head to indicate she wouldn't. Which was about when her hand began to tremble. She made a fist, tapped her toes against the leg of the barstool. "Umm... well... we were just passing by... and..."

"Cut the bullshit," Angela said, following it up with one those smiles you see on people before they're about to hurt you. "You've been looking over there all evening. What is it? You stalking some guy?"

"That's a little harsh, Angela."

Angela hardened her eyes, then picked up a dish towel and started wiping away at a vacant spot on the surface of the bar. Dakota considered her next move. They certainly hadn't come to Golden Bud's Bar and Grille to seek help from a cool bartender previously unbeknownst to them, but sometimes in life opportunities presented themselves and you had to take advantage of them. Besides, Angela looked as if she might jump over the bar at any second.

"Okay," Dakota said. "There's this guy over there at that table in the corner. He's wearing a baseball cap."

"What about him?"

"His name is Adam Boland."

"Tell me something I don't know."

Dakota's eyes popped. "You know him?"

"I'm a bartender. I know everyone, except for you two clowns."

"What's he like?"

"He's kind of a player. Not my cup of tea. But his sister Ashley is nice. Actually, she's getting married in a few weeks. Shotgun wedding, from what I hear."

"Well, good for her. But here's the thing about Adam… and Ashley, I guess. I think they could be my cousins."

"How do you not know that?"

"It's kind of a long story, Angela. You know, long-lost family stuff."

Angela bit at her bottom lip. She raised the dish towel. "Why don't you just go over and talk to him instead of wasting my time? You guys are being a bunch of chickenshits."

Dakota was a bit taken aback by Angela's observation, yet she could not deny her perceptiveness. She was being a chickenshit. It could be she actually was a chickenshit. Not that she hadn't thought about going over to speak with Adam, the dozen or so times she'd looked over at him. Watching him carefully. Trying to drum up a clever opening line, if she were to go up to him. He seemed like the jovial type. Drinking. Laughing. One time standing up and waving his arms around, perhaps telling a story about how his truck got stuck in the mud and some yahoos in a tow truck had to pull it out.

She felt a hand on her shoulder. Rosie. "Do you want me to go with you?"

"No," Dakota replied. "I have to do this myself."

And so they waited, ordering the key lime pie because

it seemed like the right thing to do, Dakota keeping an eye fixed on Adam in case he made a move toward the men's room. By her count, the group at their table had almost finished off their second pitcher of beer, so unless Adam had a supersized bladder, she figured it might happen soon.

Angela brought the pie over and gave them a quick shimmy of her head along with two clean forks and a set of fresh napkins. Dakota stabbed at the pie, hoping it was half as good as Mrs. Peña's version. She had an ongoing love affair with the world's greatest dessert, and seconds after inserting the combination of graham cracker bottom and tangy key lime mixture topped with whipped cream into her mouth, she almost forgot about Adam Boland. Until, from across the room, she observed him getting up from his chair and stretching his arms. He then stepped away from the table. Dakota took one last bite of pie and swiveled in her chair, wondering how she could possibly wait outside a men's room without dialing up the creep factor. Except, by the time she'd removed half her ass from the barstool, she noticed that Adam had taken a detour. Instead of turning right toward the corridor that led to the restrooms, he was zigzagging around tables and moving in the direction of the bar. No need to panic. He'd likely been sent on a mission to procure another pitcher. But if that were the case, why was he looking in their direction as he walked? Closer and closer—until he stopped. Adam Boland, the object of their surveillance, stood right before them.

"Is there some reason you girls keep staring at us?" he asked.

Dakota's heart began to pound. She inserted another piece of pie into her mouth, whereas Rosie produced a sly smile. Adam remained stationary, likely awaiting some kind of explanation. He appeared more imposing than he did in the photograph. Tall, with broad shoulders and a slight beer gut. His beard was a dark tangled forest, practically obscuring his mouth.

"You're just so handsome," Rosie said.

Adam adjusted the bill on his Bass Pro Shops cap, revealing his bloodshot eyes, the perfect stoner giveaway. "Just to set things straight, you girls are on the young side for me."

"Major disappointment," Rosie responded. She winked at Dakota, then turned back at Adam while attempting a hair flip.

Without warning, Adam inserted himself between the two of them, his back up against the bar, but angled so that he faced Rosie. "Well," he proclaimed, looking right at Rosie, "I would say... that if I were younger, I would definitely be interested."

"Aren't you a charmer?"

"We could always revisit this moment. Let's say a few years from now."

"A girl can dream."

"You understand what I'm saying, chica."

Rosie's expression suddenly changed. "Did you really just call me chica?"

Adam pulled at his beard. "What's wrong with that?"

"Tell me you didn't just learn that in Spanish class and thought you might try it out tonight."

"I don't go to school," Adam explained. "I'm a working man." He had emphasized the man part of his statement, then glanced over his shoulder at Dakota, as if seeking assistance.

"She's a chica, for sure," Dakota chimed in, swallowing down the last chunk of pie, "but you probably shouldn't call her that."

"I don't see a problem here," he said defensively. "You are a girl, are you not?"

Rosie kept her lips sealed, and Adam made the error of continuing. "By calling you chica, I feel as if I'm honoring your heritage in some way."

"Really." Rosie smiled. Not a happy smile. She balled up her fist, and Dakota feared she might slug him.

Adam returned the smile. "I have a good eye for these things, you know. What are you, Puerto Rican? Mexican?"

"Adam... Adam," Dakota interrupted, not recognizing her mistake. "I would suggest you stay away from the multiple-choice format on the racial insensitivity test."

Adam grimaced. "What did you just say?"

"I'm just saying you might want to think before you talk. You know... use that oversized brain of yours."

"You called me Adam."

"That's your name, isn't it?"

"But I never told you that."

Dakota shot a quick glance at Rosie, who shook her head in a manner that indicated she wasn't about to help her stranded friend. "You sure about that, Adam? You look pretty stoned tonight. Maybe you just forgot."

Adam's cheeks turned a shade of magenta. "Okay," he said, "the way this is going to go now is you're gonna tell me what the fuck is going on here."

Dakota took a deep breath. "Would you like to sit down?" A chair had opened up next to her, the theory being if she could get him off his feet, then maybe he'd relax.

Adam shook his head. He looked like a deer staring

into headlights, except the vehicle containing those headlights was about to run him over, leaving his dead body in the road for the buzzards to claim. "Is this one of those hidden-camera deals? Tell me I'm not going to be on TikTok."

"Honestly, Adam. Do we look like TikTok girls?"

"I can see that you're stalling now."

It didn't look like Adam was going anywhere. Dakota decided to come right out with it. "I'm here because I think you could be my cousin."

Adam's eyes rolled up toward the ceiling. "This is bullshit."

"It could be," Dakota admitted, "but my mom told me years ago that Jimmy Ray Coleman was my father. Which would make you my cousin."

Adam shook his head. "How'd you find me?"

"You're on Facebook. In front of a truck next to where you work. It wasn't that hard."

"So you're a stalker."

"We're not stalkers, Adam. And it's not like we told you to post on Facebook."

"What do you want from me?"

"I'd like to ask you some questions."

Adam paused and furled his lips into his beard. "What's your name?"

"Dakota. Dakota Lodi."

"Listen, Dakota. Maybe you're a stalker. Maybe you're not. You might even think this bullshit story is true. But this... whatever this is... it's not going to happen."

Dakota let out a deep sigh. Something other than key lime pie had lodged in her throat. "I understand, Adam. And I apologize. I should have come over earlier and introduced myself. It's just that I was really nervous."

Rosie put a hand on Dakota's shoulder. "You really should be more sympathetic, Adam."

"Okay… I get it. I'm the bad guy here. But you don't know anything about my family. Believe me, if you keep this up, you'll be heading into a hornet's nest. In some ways I'd actually be doing you a favor."

"The thing is," Dakota said, trying to act tough while rubbing at her watery eyes. "I'm not afraid of no hornets."

"Well… I guess you'll be doing what you have to do. But don't say I didn't warn you."

"Give me your phone, then."

"No."

"Don't be a prick, Adam," Rosie said. "Give her the phone."

"I'm gonna give you my number," Dakota contended. "The second I walk out of here, you can delete it. Or maybe you could talk to your mom about this. Tell her I'd like to talk to her. Tell her I'm not trying to stir up trouble. That I just want to know the truth."

Adam clasped his hands and started rubbing them together. His eyes drifted to Rosie and then Dakota, as if he wanted their faces imprinted in his mind for future reference. He cleared his throat, then reached into his back pocket. He took out his phone and handed it to Dakota.

September 8, 2018

Chapter 11.
Complications
at the Sunrise Diner

On Saturday morning, the first day of her legal employment, Dakota boarded the Sidewinder and made her way down Bramble Street, the stillness of the early morning enveloping her, only the sound of the wind whistling through her ears. Across the Y-Bridge, a boxcar whizzed by, and down below a dense fog hovered above the water, barely visible in the dull, early morning light. She rambled onto Main Street, passing a bank and a shop that sold greeting cards, before entering the Sunrise Diner. The smell of brewing coffee and baked goods tickled her nose, and her eyes fell upon the giant mural Rosie had painted on a yellow wall. It consisted mostly of family scenes related to food. A large gathering around a dinner table. A smiling mother and daughter dicing herbs and vegetables around a kitchen island. An old man picking tomatoes in a garden. Quite stunning.

Rosie rushed over to greet her. "Hey, D," she said. "What's happening?"

"Well, I've pretty much discovered I'm not a morning person," Dakota replied, still staring at the mural.

Up from behind came Mrs. Peña to join the welcome committee. To say she looked exactly like an older version of her daughter would be an understatement. Same wavy hair, skin tone, and facial features minus the dimples, and both of them four inches taller than Dakota. Mrs. Peña carried a few extra pounds than her daughter, though you wouldn't mention that to her if you valued living.

"Hi, Dakota," she said. "Are you ready for this?"

"I am," Dakota lied, her fingers tapping rhythmically against her thigh. "I'm nervous… but excited too."

"You'll be fine," Mrs. Peña then stated, in a manner that might have been intended to calm her down, but for some reason had the opposite effect. She couldn't pinpoint the feeling exactly, the effect her best friend's mother had on her at times. It could have had something to do with her being a person you didn't want to disappoint, or perhaps because the Peñas represented such a coming-to-America success story. Mr. Peña was a second-generation Guatemalan immigrant who taught economics at the community college. Mrs. Peña, whose parents originated from the Sinaloa region of Mexico, owned and operated a diner.

"You're probably right," Dakota replied, as if she could be fine. As if pigs might fly. As if her entire life as she knew it didn't depend on her not screwing up.

Mrs. Peña turned toward her daughter, fixing her with a hard expression. It was an almost subliminal message, which Rosie obviously received, because she rapped Dakota on the shoulder, whispered, "Good luck," then skittered off toward the coffee station.

Mrs. Peña took in a breath. Her eyelashes were lined with a thick layer of black mascara. "So, Dakota," she said, "I've been meaning to ask you. How are things at home?"

Quite the thorny question, since it basically meant *What kind of crazy shit is your mother up to lately?* And with Mrs. Peña, it was hard to tell how much she might already know, since most of it would have come from Rosie. Either way, Dakota wasn't about to get into her mother's troubles at a diner on a Saturday morning with her best friend's mother. And no way would she tell her about the eviction notice or her own desperation when it came to making money and not moving to Cleveland. She hadn't even told Rosie about that part.

"Well… you know," Dakota said, "things are a bit tight for us. So I really appreciate this opportunity."

Mrs. Peña offered a look of mock sympathy. "You're welcome. But just to make things clear. This is a trial run for you. To see if this is something you want to do… if you fit in."

"I get it," Dakota said, her stomach fluttering at the word trial, its hidden meaning quite obvious. Fuck up and you're gone.

Dakota secured her bike to the dumpster in the back alley and was led into the kitchen, where the head chef, Mario, barely acknowledged her, and the prep chefs, Bennie and Eduardo, just nodded.

"And this is Manuel," Mrs. Peña said, walking over to the far corner of the room and stopping beside a guy in a blue sleeveless muscle shirt. A workout shirt. Not a wifebeater. "He's our toastmaster."

Toastmaster. Somehow she pictured an after-work scenario, all of them sitting around, drinking beers, while Manuel dealt out a series of clever one-liners. Or did he actually make toast? If that were the case, it would be a pretty cushy job, for sure. She had no experience in the real work world, but maybe that was how things transpired. You started with shit jobs like washing dishes, then one day you woke up and you were on top of the world, making freaking toast all day.

"Manuel. This is Dakota."

Manuel said, "Hey," but didn't appear all that psyched.

"I'm gonna leave you two together," Mrs. Peña added, her eyes then shifting to the other end of the kitchen, more specifically at Mario, who appeared to be scolding Benny.

Manuel glanced in that direction as well. "So, you're Rosie's friend."

"Yes," Dakota replied, but her attention had diverted from an examination of Manuel's muscular arms and his black-pattern neck tattoo to the curious scene before her, Mrs. Peña and Mario arguing in Spanish while Benny and Eduardo looked on with apparent delight. "What's going on over there?"

Manuel crossed his arms and smiled. "It's nothing. They're just warming up."

He dropped his arms, then ran his fingers over the stubble on his face, and Dakota considered whether or not the stubble was a permanent style choice or if he'd just forgotten to shave that morning. Nevertheless, you had to admit he was a good-looking guy. Late twenties, blackish-brown hair with a fade cut. A long, angular face with a sharp chin.

"How old are you?" Manuel asked, maintaining solid eye contact.

"Fifteen," Dakota replied. "I'll be sixteen in March."

"I'm just deciding whether or not to go easy on you today."

"I don't think that's necessary, Manuel. I'm a big girl."

Manuel smiled again, but in a creepy way. "So you don't mind if I kick your ass now and then?"

Dakota batted her eyes. "Only if I deserve it."

Manuel beckoned her to follow him, and they ended up by the large double sink at the far end of the kitchen. In the distance she could see Mario feigning punches at Benny's stomach, as Eduardo cracked eggs into a large metallic bowl. Just then, traditional Mexican music bubbled up from some undetectable sound system. It was the same music that Mrs. Peña often played during their Friday night dinners, and immediately it signaled a change in the action. Eduardo twirled a whisk in his hand while shaking his hips. Benny juggled onions before placing them on a cutting board, while Mario sprayed something on the griddle and sang along with the chorus.

Manuel exchanged looks with her. "I know. It's like the fucking circus came to town."

Dakota tried to suppress a giggle.

"So, this is the Hobart," Manuel then said, as if introducing a degenerate cousin.

Dakota inspected the humongous metallic dishwasher. "Why do you call it the Hobart?"

"It's the manufacturer's name. But I see it as human. Like a temperamental woman."

The sexist observation jolted Dakota briefly, but she wasn't about to debate feminism at six in the morning with a guy in a muscle shirt sporting a neck tattoo. "Honestly," she replied instead, "if I were a girl named Hobart, I'd consider changing my name."

Just then an alarm went off, an obnoxious pinging sound, causing Manuel to check his phone. "Excuse me for a second," he said, taking off toward the far end of the kitchen. When he returned, he held out a giant metal rack with a half dozen steaming loaves of bread on it.

Dakota's eyes turned into giant saucers. "Ohhhh... my god."

"So you thought I just popped bread into the toaster all day." Manuel lowered the rack onto a steel table beside the toasting station.

"That's why they call you the toastmaster."

"It's okay. I don't expect you to bow."

"Funny. But seriously, Manuel. I'm not gonna be able to work under these conditions. You know... like I'll be hungry all day."

"Don't fret. I'll make you slices of the honey wheat later. And we make our own butter."

"So it's cool to eat here?"

"As long as Mario doesn't catch you."

"What happens if Mario catches you?"

"Then we all go to your funeral."

It didn't take long for things to pick up. Especially during the peak breakfast hours, which started at seven thirty and according to Manuel would drift into noon, after which the diner would switch over to lunch service. Super Mario the magician cooked eggs and pancakes while tending to batches of sausage, bacon, and home fries. Benny the octopus used all of his appendages to grate cheese and chop onions, tomatoes, and mushrooms. Eduardo had two bowls of batter going at all times, one for pancakes and the other for waffles, which he was responsible for making, using a series of three waffle irons.

Meanwhile, Manuel kept the toaster rolling, cranking up the bread slicer and the eight-position toaster to dish out honey wheat or marble rye toast onto plates of food waiting for him on a large butcher block table next to the toasting station.

Dakota could only play the role of chief observer until the dirty dishware started coming through, after which she dumped any leftover food scraps into the swill bucket, washed off the plates with a spray washer, and then loaded it all into the dishwasher according to Manuel's prior instructions. Then it was just a matter of pouring the liquid detergent into the appropriate chamber, closing the Hobart's door, and pressing start. Easy peasy.

The first signs of something amiss came around eight thirty, when Dakota noticed a worried look on Manuel's face, before he bolted from the toasting station and vanished beyond the confines of the kitchen.

From her angle, Dakota could only see the backs of a few customers' heads and the coffee station, where Rosie appeared to be pouring freshly brewed coffee into one of the urns. But soon Mrs. Peña entered the kitchen with an expression of grave concern and began discussing something with Mario as he flipped an omelet.

When Manuel returned, his face was flushed and he appeared out of breath. "Don't panic," he instructed.

Great advice. Except when people told you not to panic, it generally meant you should at least consider panicking.

"What is it?" Dakota asked.

"The place is packed. There's a line out the door."

"Is that unusual?"

"Not since the paper wrote a feature about us," Manuel stated in a tone that signified annoyance. "And that was two weeks ago."

"Mas platos," Mario cried out from across the room.

"More plates," Manuel translated.

"I know what mas platos means," Dakota replied, using a tone far too snippy for a person whose knowledge of the language came from middle school Spanish class and Friday night dinners at the Peñas' house.

Mario pounded his fist on the prep table. "Rapido, rapido."

She knew that one as well.

Manuel abandoned the toasters and joined Dakota by the Hobart, where Mrs. Peña had already situated herself, putting a hand on her hip. "We're out of dishes," she said.

"I know," Manuel answered.

"You're gonna have to show her how to do a manual wash and dry."

"How fucking hard is it to wash and dry dishes?"

"Manuel," Mrs. Peña said, as if chastising a teenager.

"Fine." He turned to Dakota as Mrs. Peña slid away to fight the next fire over by the griddle, where Mario had a scowl that could turn someone into stone.

In an attempt to be proactive, Dakota opened the Hobart, and immediately a blast of steam smacked her in the face. "Fuck," she yelled out.

"Big surprise," Manuel said. "Steam is hot."

Sure, Dakota had messed up that part of the dishwashing continuum, but there was still time to force some positive momentum. She bent down and simultaneously removed a stack of five dishes from the bottom rack, but as she gathered them in her hands and straightened, two of the dishes slipped out of her hands and shattered around her feet. In the background, everyone turned to look at her. Mario raised a hand and made a slashing motion across his neck.

"Are you intentionally trying to find ways to fuck up?" Manuel asked.

Dakota took in a deep breath. A lump had formed in her throat, but the last thing she wanted was to cry in a hot kitchen with a bunch of crazy people watching and waiting for her to cry. "Is there a dustpan somewhere?" she said.

"Back there." Manuel pointed to the other end of the kitchen, past the prep benches. "Just don't run anyone over. And in the future, I'd suggest not filling up the Hobart all the way the first time you use it each morning. It's all about timing. Check the crowd. Adapt."

"Thanks," she said, coming to the realization that the future would do little to help her in the present.

The rest of the morning unfolded like a fire drill where no one could find the exits. Dakota followed Manuel's instructions as best she could, but always had the sense of being a step behind. And as Manuel lost himself in toastworld, the rest of the crew appeared flustered for reasons that apparently had nothing to do with her shoddy dishwashing. There was no juggling, shaking of the hips, or singing when Mrs. Peña and Mario faced off over an incorrect order that had just been sent back to the kitchen.

Mario deflected blame by holding up the order sheet. "I can't read this shit," he explained, apparently referring to its less-than-stellar handwriting.

Mrs. Peña snatched the order sheet away from Mario and waved it before his eyes. "That specifically says scrambled," she scolded. "Either you can't read or you need glasses, Mario."

Just then, Benny escaped the scene and playfully punched Manuel in the shoulder as he walked on by, stopping at the sink and wiping at a river of sweat trickling down his nose with the back of his arm.

"It sure is hot in here," Dakota said to him, attempting

to break the ice.

Benny shook his head and spit in the sink, then went back to the prep station.

"Hey, chica," Mario shouted out seconds later, beckoning Dakota to join him by the griddle, then shoving a plate in her face. "You see that?"

Dakota took a step back to get a better view at, yes, a clearly visible microscopic dot of dried egg yolk. "I see," she said, snatching back the plate.

Mario rapped her on the arm. "Next time you do better."

Dakota had the plate in question and a piece of steel wool over by the sprayer when Mrs. Peña came storming in. "We need more coffee cups."

"Coming right up," Dakota replied, noting the two minutes left on the Hobart's dry cycle.

"You need to fill this to capacity, Dakota," she said, arms folded as she inspected Dakota opening the Hobart, standing off to the side this time, allowing the steam to release into the air rather than her face.

"Okay," Dakota replied, but after Mrs. Peña left, she gave Manuel the evil eye.

"Remember," Manuel said. "Adapt."

"I have an idea," Dakota replied. "How 'bout we get more dishes. Since, you know… we have more customers. More customers. More dishes. More cups."

She had hoped Manuel might sense a trend in her rant, but it appeared as if he didn't.

"You can always make that suggestion to Mrs. Peña," he said with a smug shake of his head. "Or else you can put it in the suggestion box."

"We have a suggestion box?"

"What do you think?"

When it was over, and after the cleanup to prepare the diner for the next day, Dakota expected there'd be some kind of update as to the status of her future employment. Instead, Mrs. Peña just passed her in the kitchen without acknowledging her, while Manuel rushed by like a hot rod on the freeway. Resigning herself to reality, that she was undeserving of positive reinforcement, that she might have messed up an opportunity to make enough money to help her mother pay rent and would perhaps need to come up with a Plan C, she went out back and unlocked her bike from the dumpster. She wheeled it through the kitchen, into the dining room, and said goodbye to Rosie, who sat splayed out on a chair, wiping sweat from her forehead with a towel, barely able to produce a wave. Outside, Dakota boarded the Sidewinder, head down, all bleary-eyed and exhausted. She put one foot on the pedal and pressed down, slowly guiding the Sidewinder into traffic.

May 27, 2019

Chapter 12.
Rumble at
Muncy's Tavern

They faced off around the kitchen table, the smell of per-colating coffee saturating the air. Dakota slapped three crisp twenties on the table and leaned back in her chair. Up above, a single ceiling light filtered through opaque glass, making the atmosphere cloudy and mysterious. As if they were in a dingy bar somewhere, making decisions about some future criminal enterprise.

Lucinda eyed the bills. "You want to tell me what that's for?"

"DNA test," Dakota replied. "You know. The one you haven't opened an account for yet."

Lucinda examined her with a steely expression. "Listen, Dakota, I thought we already talked about this."

Her grandmother hadn't exactly lied, but shouldn't a conversation involve two people? Not one person telling the other what she wasn't going to do.

Dakota braced herself. "I guess I don't see it that way. You told me you'd think about it. Then you told me you weren't sure about it. And now it's a week later."

The coffee maker stopped its sputtering, and Lucinda

placed a finger in the air to signal a pause in their discussion. She made two stops at the kitchen counter, first to fill up two cups with coffee, which she brought over to the table, sliding one of the cups over to Dakota, and a second where she removed two raspberry scones from a paper bag and gently positioned them on plates. Dakota had wrangled the scones from the Sunrise Diner, and they were relatively fresh, Manuel having made them that afternoon.

Dakota took a bite out of her scone and washed it down with a gulp of coffee.

Lucinda rubbed at the rim of her cup as wisps of steam rose into the surrounding air. "It's my job to take care of you," she said. "So if I think something has the potential to hurt you, I'm going to protect you from it."

Dakota said, "But I don't need to be protected. You are aware I'm not six anymore."

Lucinda crinkled up her forehead, rows of straight lines appearing out of nowhere. "That was a low blow."

"Truth squad."

Last night, her grandmother had lectured her about rules, the main gist of it being she didn't have lots of them. First she addressed the pyramid of dirty clothes on the floor of Dakota's room that resembled Mount Vesuvius and mentioned the laundry room down the hall. She wasn't too crazy about profanity and had no intentions of chasing after a teenage drunk or drug addict. Most of all she valued honesty, even when things weren't going well. Even when the truth meant hearing something you didn't want to hear.

Perhaps Lucinda didn't recall this, as she split her scone in half and turned one of the pieces over in her hand. "Lots of raspberries" came out, before she stuffed the scone fragment into her mouth, taking her sweet time chewing before gulping down more coffee. By then it had become obvious that her grandmother's use of superior baked goods was just a method of deflection. Funny, how those who espoused truth were the most sensitive when confronted by it. Not that Dakota had intended to be cruel. She was just tired of being trampled on. Did she not have some basic human rights? To get what she wanted once in a great while? It was only a test. A stupid fucking DNA test.

Dakota took in a deep breath. "I asked you for this out of respect," she started. "Because it's important to me and I didn't want to do it behind your back. But I've already started my investigation, and I will find a way to get the test, one way or another. I have the money. I have no problem with saying I'm eighteen on the application. I know it's a crime, but I'm willing to take that chance."

"What kind of crime?" Lucinda said, grinning.

"Like, impersonating an older person on an internet application. In the first degree. Pretty sure it's a felony. CPS might want to take a look at that."

Her grandmother ran a hand through her hair. She fixed her eyes on Dakota, but the grin was still there. "You remind me of your mother sometimes."

"How so?"

"You've got her moxie."

"What's that?"

"It can be a superpower," Lucinda said, her eyes hardening. "But only if you use it well."

Dakota smiled. "Like the Force."

Lucinda shook her head, and her eyes shifted up toward the ceiling as if she might be praying.

"So, you just told me you started your investigation.

If I agree to this test thing, I want to know what you're doing out there."

Another game of Truth Squad. This time with the tables turned.

"Okay… umm… first we talked to Helen and Stanley Powers. Anika's parents. Then we looked up Anika and some of her friends on social media."

"Who's we?" Lucinda asked.

"Oh. My friend Rosie and I. She has her license, and her parents bought her a Subaru. It's like the safest car, in case you didn't know. Anyway, we found George Coleman's obituary the night before. Did you know George died last year?"

"I didn't."

"And guess what? Jimmy Ray had a brother, Greg, who predeceased George. Not Jimmy. Then I found Adam Boland on Facebook. He'd be my cousin, and so we went to his work, and later we followed him to Golden Bud's Bar and Grille."

Lucinda said, "You went to a bar?"

"Well… it's a bar and a restaurant. We had nachos. And key lime pie. Which was excellent, I might add."

"I appreciate the food review, but I'm assuming you did something else there."

"Of course. We actually talked to Adam for a few minutes. Can you believe it? Honestly, I wasn't all that impressed, but if he's my cousin, I guess I'll have to be more understanding."

Her grandmother paused to consider what she'd just heard. Then she stood up and said, "I need a drink." Out came a small bottle of whiskey. Lucinda poured some into a small glass and swirled it before taking a swig.

"So, what do you know about this, Grandma?" Dakota asked, sensing an opportunity. "You said you don't remember anything about Jimmy Ray dying, but he and Mom must have been dating back then."

Lucinda shook her head. "Definitely not. But they were best friends since grade school. The guy spent more time at our house than his own."

"What about other boyfriends?"

Lucinda smirked. "Well, that's where it gets complicated. Your mother was, how do you say... quite active around that time. Now, when she had you and she lived with me, I sort of knew what was going on. But after she turned eighteen, she moved in with Jimmy's brother. He'd rented half of a two-family on the west side."

Funny how her mother had never mentioned Greg before. But her living with him, shortly after giving birth, put a whole new spin on the story.

"Do you think she ever... you know..." Dakota made a circle with her fingers on her left hand and thrust the index finger of her right hand in and out of the circle. "Hooked up with Greg?"

"Jesus," Lucinda said, blushing, then covering her eyes. "What does Greg have to do with this? She moved in with him after you were born."

"Hey... I'm just saying."

"Yeah... well, I don't know about that. Though there was definitely some friction between her and Jimmy about her living there."

"Where was I during all of this?"

"You went back and forth, but mostly you lived with me."

Dakota shot an incredulous look at her grandmother,

but in some ways her mother's maternal negligence did not surprise her. "So my mom moved in with Greg and left me with you?"

"More or less."

"What about when I was born? Were either Jimmy or Greg at the hospital?"

"Nope. Only me. Jimmy joined the army right before you were born, and they shipped him over to Iraq. And Greg would have been the kind of guy not to show up."

"What happened after that?"

"About six months later, she moved back. After I told her I wasn't about to raise you on my own. No offense."

"None taken. But why would my mom tell me some bogus story about Jimmy?"

"I can't answer that. All I can tell you is, Jimmy was alive when he came back from Iraq. You would have been two around that time. Maybe that's not a coincidence."

"And you don't think it's strange that Greg died around the same time?"

"It's certainly strange. Especially the circumstances. Him being murdered and all."

Dakota's mouth dropped. A sudden surge of blood pulsed through her veins, throbbing against the inner surface of her skin. "You're shitting me."

Lucinda shook her head and drained the last of her whiskey. Then the story trickled out like a slow drip. How Greg Coleman was shot execution style in his truck while parked in the vacant lot next to Lucky's Dry Cleaners in South Zionsville, as revenge for a bar fight a few nights earlier, during which Greg beat up one of the leaders of a biker gang. The particular gang had been heavily involved in dealing drugs in the area, and so the theory went that had something to do with it. But fourteen years had passed and no one had ever been arrested for the crime. Although, according to recent news articles in the local paper that cited the possibility of overlooked evidence, the case was being reopened.

Afterward, Dakota leaned back in her chair while processing what she'd just heard. "That's kind of crazy" was all she could say, to which Lucinda just shrugged. As to the murder, and what, if anything, it had to do with her father, she could not tell. And while it seemed far-fetched that her mother was involved, there was something about the details of the case that made her think she needed to dig deeper. But how? Her grandmother had likely revealed most of what she knew. She couldn't picture her mother coming clean on the topic. Nor would the cold-case detectives hand her a dossier of all their evidence. But Lucinda had mentioned a local news article that had to be written by an actual person. A person she could talk to. A person that out of the goodness of their heart might be willing to help a distressed sixteen-year-old girl, desperately searching for her long-lost father.

October 20, 2018

Chapter 13.
Train Wreck

On Saturday afternoon, Dakota rode her bike to John Moran's house, located in the northernmost part of Zionsville, about two miles past the town center. She pumped her legs furiously, guiding the Sidewinder up the driveway for what seemed like forever as it twisted through a canopy of trees, blotting out the sky from above.

When she reached the apex, she parked her bike and plopped herself down on the ground. Her legs breathed fire, and she traced the breath coming out of her mouth. From the Moran's front yard you could see half of Zionsville, part of the downtown area, and a church steeple piercing through some trees in the distance. And behind her was the house itself, a two-story brick monstrosity about a hundred times the size of anything she had ever lived in. Which kind of explained how a high school kid could afford the three hundred dollars' worth of prepackaged pot in her backpack.

She had her earbuds on, "London Calling" from her "Punkified" playlist pumping away. An array of Halloween lawn decorations closed in on her: a family of zombies with patches of white hair and red lights for eyes, a witch on a broomstick, and a mini graveyard with *RIP* etched into black gravestones. Next, she selected "I Don't Wanna Go Down to the Basement" by the Ramones. She liked matching music to her current mood or environment, and the track seemed appropriate, soothing her nerves for the moment.

Two minutes and thirty-seven seconds later, the Ramones had finished, and she made her way up a set of brick steps with black cast iron railings and rang the bell. Off to the side, six cars were parked in the driveway by a basketball hoop, which meant either the Morans were rich enough to own six cars or other people were getting a jump on the party. She guessed the latter when she heard a pounding bass noise coming from the house. Should she have worn a costume? Her orange sweatshirt over black skinny jeans and black Cons were not cutting it, nor was the black wool cap she'd taken to wearing lately during her morning bike rides to school. She could always tell John that she was dressed as an undercover narc. But perhaps he wouldn't think that was funny.

Dakota rang the bell at least a dozen times before John Moran answered, wearing a red Ohio State T-shirt that exposed his modest biceps. He had short blond hair with a bit of a fade cut, except for a curly patch that looked as if it had been grafted atop his head. Initially, she hadn't pegged him as a player, but during study hall, when she'd overheard him talking about his father bringing him back a hookah from Istanbul last summer and that his rents would be gone for the weekend, thus necessitating a Halloween rager, his fellow students seemed drawn to him. Then again, it could be that rich kids having parties in big houses vacated by their parents might exist in their own universe, attracting fake friends like flies.

"Hey, Dakota," John said, shooting off a goofy smile that revealed a set of perfect white choppers. "Any trouble finding the place?"

"Not at all," Dakota replied. "But you have quite the hill, I must say."

"Come on in," he said, forcing a chuckle.

"You have a beautiful house."

"Thanks." But he had a weary look on his face, like he'd been told that a million times before.

Moran beckoned her to follow, past the front entrance with its twenty-foot ceiling, through a myriad of rooms whose purpose Dakota could not discern. She'd heard about rich people whose houses were so big, they had rooms in them they never actually went in. Mud rooms, sitting rooms, playrooms, dining rooms. This was different from her mother's rental, where you could sit, play, dine, and scrape mud off your shoes in the same location. Not that she had time to think about it, since she basically had to run to keep pace with Moran, who was quite the strider. By then the bass noise she had heard earlier had increased in volume, and its vibrations shot up through the floor, making her bones vibrate. There were voices and music, which likely accounted for the bass. Suddenly, Moran slammed on the brakes and said, "This is it," as if they'd discovered the Emerald City.

Moran called it the game room, but calling it a room was like describing the planet Earth as a small rock. First of all, you could drive a tractor through it, plenty of room for the dozen or so people already there. For some reason she made a fist when she saw them, digging her nails into her palms as she surveyed the scene, her eyes darting about to take in all of the room's occupants. A girl with dark hair lounged on one end of a green leather sectional while a couple canoodled on the other end. A tall muscular dude stood in front of a brick fireplace, tending to a fire. Beyond that, a bunch of guys wearing blue-and-black Zionsville High football jerseys played a game of pool and drank beers. Some appeared interested in a football game playing on the big-screen TV with the sound turned down, as Kendrick Lamar blared from some unseen stereo. Dakota had a sense she'd stumbled into the dreamworld. One of those nightmares where you end up in a place you're not supposed to be.

Moran tapped her on the shoulder. "Just hang here for a while," he said. "I've got some calls to make." Then he was off. Striding again.

Calls. What the fuck. Had she not clearly stated the transaction price when she closed the deal with Moran by the bike rack three days ago? Then again, Johnny boy could be dealing with shit she wasn't aware of, perhaps clouding his memory. It would certainly be a bitch, your father buying you a hookah but not leaving you three hundred buckaroos to purchase the pot for it. Like leaving your kid a Beamer with no gas. Still, there was something off about the situation that made her eyes twitch. Could it have to do with Project Freedom being on life support and she having no other options but to see things through? That she'd somehow managed not to lose her job at the diner, but that working only Saturdays and the occasional Sunday meant she didn't earn nearly enough to help her mother pay rent?

Dakota trudged onward. The crowd, likely juniors and seniors, appeared somewhat intimidating. Yet she didn't want to loiter in the game room's doorway either. What would be the harm in taking a few steps forward? She could avoid the scene around the pool table and head over by the fire to warm her hands. Sure, some guy was already there, stoking the fire, but the inhabitants of the couch didn't seem to know she was even there. The dark-haired girl was studying something on her phone while the canoodling couple had upped their game to a full make-out session.

Once she actually took the steps though, the guy by the fire must have had supersensitive hearing, because he turned around and Dakota instantly recognized him. Joey Vinson, of boyfriend-to-Katie-Larsen fame. The same Katie Larsen that beat Brianna Dyson to a pulp in the stairwell last month.

"Who the fuck are you?" Joey said, pointing a hot poker at her.

Not exactly politeness-man. And clear evidence of steroid overload. Seriously, the guy could carry an elephant on his back without much problem. And his physical appearance didn't help much either. Gnarly hair, black as charcoal, eyes like tiny slits, squinting at some imaginary indoor sun. And the pained expression painted across his face, like he'd just bitten into a lemon.

"I'm Dakota," she told him.

Joey smirked. "Like South Dakota."

She'd never heard that one before.

"Or North."

"What are you doing here?" Joey pushed the poker down into the carpet.

"I have something for John. He told me to wait here. Said he'd be right back."

Joey's brow furrowed, wavy lines traversing his giant

forehead. "Well, you're not the pizza delivery girl or else you'd have pizzas."

Dakota tried on a fake smile. "You have a sharp eye for the obvious."

Laughter from the sectional. The couple on the couch released their grasp on each other and the girl who'd been previously obsessed with her phone looked up. In the distance, some of the football players erupted in cheers.

Joey grinned as if he'd thought of something clever. "You must be selling Girl Scout cookies, then."

"But then I'd be a Girl Scout."

"How old are you anyway?"

"You were a sophomore in my freshman math class last year. That should be a clue."

The girls both laughed. Phone girl said, "Hey, Joey, I have a math problem for you. What's the circumference of that tiny fucking brain of yours?"

Joey growled. "Shut the fuck up, Adele."

Adele smiled, and Dakota thought she might have winked at her. "You'll have to excuse him," she said. "He's in a pissy mood 'cause he misses his girlfriend."

Joey lifted the poker and pointed it at the sectional. "I already told you. She's not my girlfriend."

"Oh, I forgot," Adele said. "The slut just lets you fuck her."

Joey gave Adele a death stare but offered no verbal response as he returned to the now substantial fire. He admired it for a few seconds, placed the poker in a rack alongside the other fireplace tools, then turned back to face Dakota.

"So, what's your name again?"

"I'm kind of hurt you don't remember, Joey. South Dakota."

"What kind of name is that?"

"My mom gave it to me. You'd have to ask her."

Joey appeared puzzled, as if the logistics of questioning Dakota's mother provided an obstacle he could not overcome. "You should sit down. You're making me nervous." He motioned toward the couch where Adele and her cohorts rested.

"I'm good. John said he'd be back soon."

"But I'm guessing he's jerking off somewhere. It could be a while."

"You wouldn't think that would take long."

Joey tilted his head. "You're kind of a wiseass. I'm not sure if I like that."

Dakota clenched her teeth. She had the urge to tap her feet together, chant "There's no place like home," and be done with it.

Joey continued. "So, are you, like, one of John's neighbors?"

"That's a big no."

"And what's with the fucking backpack? What are you, like five?"

Dakota put a hand on her hip.

"And that stupid hat."

"Enough with the inquisition, Joey." Adele again. "You're being an asshole."

Joey bowed for some reason. "Can't help it," he said, as if addressing an audience. "The assholiness flows from within me."

Dakota glanced over at Adele. "It's fine."

"Well, you might as well come to the party tonight," Joey proposed out of nowhere. "There's gonna be like a hundred people here. We're gonna trash the place."

Great. One hundred more people she had no desire to meet.

It was at that moment that the messiah in the form of John Moran returned, but he looked flustered, as if a situation he'd wanted to control had somehow gone off the rails. "Did you meet everyone, Dakota?"

"Hey, Johnny," Joey shouted out before she could answer. "What's with the new girl?"

"Nothing you need to worry about."

"What kind of loser buys drugs from a sophomore?"

Dakota's heart skipped a beat. The fact that Joey Vinson possessed any perceptual powers whatsoever had startled her.

"Unless it's your new girlfriend. You're in luck, South Dakota," Joey continued. "Johnny boy likes 'em young."

Moran glared at him. "Knock it off, Vinson."

Joey smiled. "The pinker the meat, the sweeter the treat, I always say."

Moran shook his head, but the edges of his mouth widened and it almost looked like he was trying to repress a smile. Dakota repressed her own urge: to kick Joey Vinson in the balls. But if these guys were friends, then maybe this kind of banter was normal for them. Which became somewhat obvious when Moran feigned a punch to Vinson's stomach and said, "Honestly, if you weren't such a dick for brains, I'd let you test out my hookah tonight. This weed will kick your ass. Believe me. They don't call it Train Wreck for nothing."

At the time, Dakota didn't think much about Moran revealing the name of the pot strain, nor did she consider Vinson's reaction to it, his mouth open, his eyes widening as if he'd just been given an impossible calculus problem to solve. Especially once she followed Moran into the dining room and the transaction went off without a hitch. She handed over the plastic bag of pot, wrapped in a paper bag and for some reason secured by Abe with multiple revolutions of duct tape.

"I really do appreciate this, Dakota," he said, handing over three hundred bucks like he was purchasing a Big Mac at the McDonald's drive-thru.

"I'm the one that should be thanking you," she replied.

Moran grinned. "And if you're not doing anything tonight, you're welcome to come to the party."

Dakota smiled. She liked that Moran was inviting her. He seemed like a half-decent guy. "Maybe I will," she said. But she didn't tell him how she really felt: that she'd rather be torn apart by wolves than attend his Halloween party.

Afterward, she tucked the money into her pocket and made her way to the front door. And she'd almost made it there when the faint sound of footsteps filled the air behind her and she turned. Joey Vinson. Again.

The space between them closed, and he grabbed ahold of her wrist, spun her around, and pushed her against the wall. He squeezed, but his palms were sweaty and Dakota somehow managed to free her hand. He came back at her, but she slapped his hand away.

"I'll scream if you do that again," she told him.

Joey said, "No one will hear you."

"I have pepper spray," she lied.

He smiled and pushed his body against her, backing her into the wall, his face right in front of her. He exhaled, and she smelled beer mixed with onions.

"You want to tell me about Train Wreck."

Dakota shook her head.

"Where'd you get it?"

"None of your business."

"I'm making it my business. You know who my girl-friend is?"

"No," she lied again.

"Either you got it from her, which I highly doubt, or you're selling it for someone else. So I'll ask you again. Where'd you get it?"

Somehow she'd stumbled onto an episode of *Narcos*. But one whose plot she couldn't decipher. She would ask Abe about this, but if he and Katie Larsen were selling the same variety of weed, what was the big deal? When it came to Zionsville and drugs, she'd never once heard about a turf war. The general mantra in town, when it came to these things, had always been "the more, the better." But maybe Katie Larsen was a different beast. There'd been plenty of school history behind that theory.

She kept her eyes on Joey, not saying anything, but her legs were shaking and she wondered if he noticed that. He seemed to be pondering something, mapping out his next move, when suddenly he took a step back. Dakota side-eyed the front door, making her own calculations.

"So, here's how it's gonna happen," he started. "I'll give you until Monday to think it over. If you come to your senses, you'll tell me what's going on here. If not, I can't be held responsible for what happens next. And don't think I won't find you. I remember you from math class last year, and I know your locker is right around the corner."

The fact that Vinson remembered her and knew the location of her locker creeped her out to some degree, but she acted all stoic, as if it didn't bother her, bobbing her head up and down to signify she'd consider his proposal, then slipping out the front door, afraid that a sudden move would disturb him. That he might change his mind and come after her again.

Once outside, she quickly straddled the Sidewinder. She pulled the black cap down over her ears and gripped the handlebars, her hands trembling. She downshifted and made her way back down the long winding driveway.

May 28, 2019

Chapter 14.
Go Ask Alice

The next day after work, Rosie dropped Dakota off at the Zionsville Record, the town's only newspaper, located in a weathered brick building about a half mile down a side road off of Main Street. She passed the Zionsville Record's white portico and pushed through the front door, which had the name of the paper stenciled on the front of it, with the "d" in Record partially peeled off. The office had a reception area with white-painted walls, beyond which were two rows of desks, each with computers on them. Framed photographs covered the walls, mostly scenes of Zionsville: a church, the Y-Bridge, and assorted nature shots from the river. A middle-aged woman with glasses and short blond hair sat at one of the desks, a half-eaten sandwich nestled before her in a cocoon of waxed paper. The room smelled like cigarette smoke and cold cuts. Dakota went up to the counter and cleared her throat.

The woman glanced up with a placid expression. "Can I help you?" she asked, her voice like gravel on a blacktop.

"I hope so," Dakota replied. "I'm looking to get information on an article."

"Which one?"

"The Greg Coleman murder."

The woman's eyes suddenly widened. She sprang up from her chair and strode over to the counter. Her thin build and running shoes made Dakota think of a person obsessed with exercise.

"And who are you?" the woman asked. Not exactly friendly.

"Dakota Lodi."

"You can read articles online, you know."

"Right. But then I'd have to get a subscription."

She'd found that out last night when she attempted to read one of the articles Lucinda had referred to. But no way would she pay for it. If there was anything she cared less about than the goings-on in Zionsville, she couldn't think of it.

"Got it," the woman snapped. "So what's your angle?"

Dakota heard the hum of an air conditioner in the background, yet she could have sworn the temperature in the room had been dialed up. "It's possible Greg Coleman was my father."

That shut her up for a second. The woman folded her arms and cocked her head, as if she were inspecting a slab of meat. "Possible?"

Very investigative reporter–like. Picking out the key word. Sorting for facts.

"It's complicated," Dakota replied, intentionally being vague, not wanting to hand over details. Not yet, at least.

"Try me."

Dakota put her brain on hold. The woman was like a gargoyle guarding a moat that contained a family of crocodiles impatiently waiting for their dinner. Not someone you wanted to relate your life story to. Then it came to her. Her angle. But first she'd have to make sure she was speaking with the right person. Not a gargoyle in a windbreaker eating a sandwich.

"Do you think I could talk to the person that wrote the most recent articles?" Dakota asked.

At first the woman didn't seem to appreciate the can-I-speak-to-the-manager moment, but then a faint smile creaked across her face. "You're looking at her," she claimed. "I'm Alice Benning."

"Oh. I'm sorry. Well, it sure is nice to meet you, Alice."

Alice didn't return the compliment. Either she was rude or she had far more important things to do than entertain a snotty sixteen-year-old girl with a shady family tree.

"So you're a reporter," Dakota continued, filling in the silence. "How exciting."

Alice perked up. Perhaps she coveted flattery. "I'm actually the editor now, but I wrote the piece you're interested in. In fact, I was a rookie reporter fourteen years ago, and I covered the initial story."

"So you would know everything about the case, then."

"I know a lot," Alice boasted. "But you still haven't told me why you're here."

"I have a question first," Dakota replied. "What's your motivation for writing these articles? Is it just to get information out to the community, or are you interested in solving the case?"

"Both," Alice answered without hesitation. "My job as a reporter is to keep the community informed, but if I were to discover information that led to the solving of the case, then of course my career might benefit."

She had counted on Alice being ambitious. Not that there was anything wrong with that.

"Good," Dakota replied. "I think we might be able to help each other, Alice. You see, I just started my own investigation. Greg's brother was Jimmy Ray Coleman. My mom told me he was my father and that he died in a motorcycle accident when I was two. But recently I discovered that Jimmy Ray might be alive and Greg's the one that died when I was two."

"Interesting story. But I don't see what it has to do with a murder. And with all due respect, you're awfully young."

"That's exactly why I can help you. The kinds of people involved in this case, I've lived around them my whole life. They won't talk to cops. Or a reporter."

"Not sure they'll talk to you either."

"Let me read the article at least. It's public knowledge, and it's not like you have anything to lose."

Alice slumped her shoulders and let out a sigh. "You are quite persistent," she said, motioning Dakota to follow her into the office area.

Alice fired up the computer. According to the most recent piece in the *Zionsville Record*, a newly formed cold-case unit at the Zionsville Police Department had reopened the case in February. Its intentions were to reexamine the evidence and conduct additional witness interviews. The basics in that particular article, as they pertained to the murder, pretty much followed the version she'd heard from Lucinda but with far more details. The bar fight occurred two days prior to the murder at Muncy's Tavern, just outside of South Zionsville. The president of the Runaways motorcycle club, based in Columbus, Ohio, Shamus Westwood, had been beaten up by Greg during the fight. He spent one night in a local hospital. One day after his release, Greg was found murdered, a single bullet to his forehead, in the front seat of his Chevy truck. The police investigated Shamus, who had an ironclad alibi, having been back in Columbus at the time of the murder. Instead, it was postulated that an enforcer for the Runaways likely pulled the trigger. The fight, so the story went, had something to do with a dispute over a drug deal. But in the end, no confirmation as to that theory's veracity could be made. The police had their suspicions, but arrests were never made. They cited the lack of physical evidence, the reluctance of locals to offer information, and an oath of silence taken by the club members as being the main obstacles to their investigation.

"You're a very good writer," Dakota observed after finishing the article.

Alice smiled. "Thanks. Did you get what you wanted from this?"

Dakota shrugged. "So other than the cold-case unit, there really wasn't anything new to report?"

"That's one way of looking at it."

Dakota had seen enough *Dateline* to know that detectives sometimes had tunnel vision. That a set of new eyes, looking at the same evidence, often led to breaks in cases that previously were unsolved. But she also knew that detectives were not about to release all their theories about an ongoing case to a reporter at the *Zionsville Record*. Not that Alice wouldn't have sources. Not that Alice wouldn't have her own theories about the case she wasn't about to share.

"Can I ask you for a favor, Alice? I'd like to see some of the original reporting, if that were possible? You know… the stuff you wrote fourteen years ago."

Surprisingly, Alice acquiesced. Nothing in their previous conversations had indicated her desire for any kind of partnership, but perhaps Dakota's story about a girl without a father tugged at her heartstrings. Or else she was just being a clever reporter, leaving all doors open.

Alice went back to her desk. She lit up a cigarette, holding it between two fingers and blowing out tiny smoke rings as Dakota traveled back in time, pulling up the original articles. The stories ran over a period of weeks, in just about every issue of the *Zionsville Record,* until they trickled away to nothing. It all began with the initial report on the murder, written the day after it occurred, and followed up with assorted articles focusing on the police investigation. There were also features on Greg Coleman, the Runaways motorcycle club, and even Muncy's Tavern. Much of this was interesting but not entirely relevant from Dakota's perspective, except for the photograph of Greg Coleman, who had a square-shaped face, small angry eyes, and dark hair just like hers. She was about to give up when she came across an unrelated police blotter report, detailing the previous week's exploits of the town's local petty criminals: disorderly conduct and vandalism, two neighbors coming to blows over a barking dog.

"Hey, Alice," she said, raising her voice but still at a volume below shouting. "Was there anything in the paper about the actual fight after it happened?"

"We're a biweekly," Alice responded quickly. "We had something written, but after the murder we combined the stories."

"Would there be a police blotter in that edition?"

"I would think so."

It didn't take long to find it, going back to a story about the tavern fight that Dakota had already read, but on the back page: a list of those arrested after the brawl at Muncy's.

Greg Coleman-Zionsville, Ohio
James Coleman-Zionsville, Ohio
Albert Renfors-Zionsville, Ohio
Orville James-Zionsville, Ohio
Shamus Westwood-Columbus, Ohio
Randall Cronin-Columbus, Ohio
Lenny Braverock-Manderson, South Dakota
Jake Weston-Rapid City, South Dakota

As Dakota digested the report, Alice stationed herself behind her shoulder, leaning into her back while providing context to the names on the screen. The story went something like this: Shamus and Randall had come up to Zionsville to meet up with Orville, a longtime member of the local Runaways chapter. Whereas James and Albert were at the bar with Greg, presumably in case there was trouble with the bikers. The South Dakota guys happened to be innocent bystanders, drinking at the bar, that got caught up in the fight. They worked for a company that set up conventions all around the country and had been staying in Columbus over the weekend. They'd been unlucky in some respects, making the one-hour drive to Muncy's just to end up in the wrong place at the wrong time.

Afterward, Dakota bit down on her lower lip. She had no desire to insert herself into a murder investigation. Yet there was something about the police blotter report that tugged at her. The fact that Jimmy Ray, Greg, and the husband of her mother's ex-best friend were at the bar that night. What if it were all related? The murder. Her father. The reasons for her mother's lies.

Dakota turned to face Alice. "You don't believe any

of this. Do you?"

"I've told you enough," Alice replied, a weary look spreading across her face.

"Honestly, Alice, I don't give a shit who killed Greg Coleman. I'm trying to find my father. But some of these people might talk to me, in which case I can feed you information. Which I'm guessing might be to your benefit."

Alice let out a sigh. "It's not a matter of what I believe. It's the cold-case guys. They think the original detectives were too focused on the bikers."

"How so?"

"Common sense told them it was the most likely outcome. Greg beat up one of the bikers. The bikers were not opposed to violence."

"But there's more to the story."

"Perhaps. From what I've heard, Greg Coleman rubbed a lot of people the wrong way. So they could be looking at other suspects."

They exchanged numbers, for whatever that was worth, and Alice escorted her back into the waiting area, mentioning something about trust and not revealing any of the information she'd disclosed.

"Sure thing," Dakota replied, but once outside she felt a smidgen of guilt about lying to Alice Benning.

Seriously though. Who tells a secret to a sixteen-year-old girl and thinks she won't phone her best friend immediately upon leaving the confines of the Zionsville Record and tell her all about it?

October 22–26, 2018

Chapter 15.
Seemed like
a Good Idea
at the Time

On Monday, things took a turn for the worse when, after school, Dakota came out and could not locate her bike. Her first inclination was not to panic, yet it should have been easy to find, since she had chained it to the bike rack after a lunch-period joyride in the exact spot she stood. Her brain cells fired up as her eyes took in the entirety of the rack and the grassy hill behind it, until something in her peripheral vision caught her attention. Out by the parking lot, the sun was reflecting off something metallic. She ambled over and picked up her bike chain. She dangled it in front of her eyes. One of the links had been severed, and its edges were bent but smooth, as if someone had sliced through it with a bolt cutter.

Her heart sank like an iron chest in the ocean. Her rational mind told her that the theft of a bicycle was not uncommon, but for some reason that explanation seemed too coincidental to the moment. And bolt cutters? Was that not overkill for a twenty-five-dollar bicycle? A twenty-five-dollar bicycle she loved, but still. She didn't want to believe that it had anything to do with her running into Joey Vinson that day, because in her mind a response to his threats had not been necessary. When she met up with Abe Saturday night to give him the money and take her own cut, she'd told him all about the night's escapades. But Abe had brushed the whole thing off, saying it was just a misunderstanding and that he'd take care of it by the end of the weekend. But now her beloved Sidewinder was missing, and she needed to do something about it. She fired off a text to Abe.

Someone stole my bike! Need to talk. NOW.

Abe replied immediately. *K. Im home.*

She took the bus home. How embarrassing. Not to mention, she'd hyperventilated through most of the ride, her mind venturing into dark places, conjuring up worst-case scenarios by the dozen. If Abe had taken care of business like he said he would, then he hadn't exactly done a good job of it.

When she reached Abe's trailer, he was already outside waiting for her, sitting out on his front step and looking all casual.

Dakota ran up to him, panting. Sweat oozed out the pores on her forehead, and she wiped at it with the damp back of her hand. "Someone stole my bike," she blurted out between breaths.

"Yeah… I read your text," Abe replied.

"You said you'd deal with this."

"I did. I talked to my supplier, who said it wasn't a problem."

"How is it not a problem? Joey Vinson threatened me, and now my bike is gone."

Abe bit down on his lower lip. You could tell he didn't like being challenged. "Not sure you're thinking clearly, Dakota. And besides, you don't know for sure who stole your bike."

"Let me lay it out for you," she said. "Katie is Joey's girlfriend. Joey assaulted me and said his girlfriend wouldn't like me selling pot at the party. And Katie is a psycho bitch. Are you gonna tell me she wouldn't steal my bicycle out of revenge?"

"I have no idea what Katie Larsen would or would not do."

Dakota folded her arms. Abe hadn't exactly answered her question, but he hadn't contested her revenge theory either. "Here's the deal, Abe. I'm going to get my bike back one way or another. Now, I have no clue where Joey Vinson lives. But we both know Katie lives somewhere in the Kings trailer park."

"I don't like where this is going."

"Then just tell me where her house is and I'll go myself."

"What makes you think I know that?"

Dakota rolled her eyes.

Abe shook his head. "This is fucked."

The King Street Trailer Park consisted of equally spaced rows of mobile homes in a grid pattern surrounded by King Street, curving around most of the park, and Royal Avenue out past the east side.

They started on King Street, a pockmarked, dirt-encrusted road that you had to be careful just walking on to keep from breaking an ankle. They passed a gang of middle school kids, all wearing orange kneepads, jumping their bikes over a makeshift wooden ramp, just a sheet of plywood propped up by an old tire, after which Abe suggested they head down Prince Street. Apparently he'd been to a summer block party there, which Katie Larsen had attended, giving him the idea that she might live in the vicinity. Except by the time they turned down Prince Street, the sun had dipped below the horizon, shading the entire neighborhood in a hazy purplish light, and all the trailers looked to be the same shade of white.

Dakota kept her head on a swivel, moving slowly, searching for something that stood out. There were men huddled around a car propped up on cinder blocks. Two old people rested on Adirondack chairs, staring up at the sky, a carved-out pumpkin visible on the ground behind them. Suddenly she stopped, her eyes fixing on a spot four trailers down. "I see it," she said softly, almost a whisper.

Abe turned and she pointed to it, an upright bicycle parked behind a truck with its tailgate down. Even in the dim light she could make out the bike's silhouette. The way it leaned slightly to one side when parked. Its handlebars sitting up high, stretched out in a straight line.

"What about the light?" Abe asked.

A light was on in the trailer. Three girls around a table on the side nearest the truck.

"I bet the front door is on the other side of the trailer," Dakota replied. "We need a diversion. You go to the front door and ring the bell. Then I'll take the bike."

"I'm not ringing the fucking bell, Dakota."

"You're not there for a social visit, Abe. Knock. Ring the bell and run."

"I hate to break it to you, but there are three people there. They won't all get up to answer the door."

"You have a better plan?"

"Yeah… let's get outta here now."

"If you weren't going to help me, then why are you here?"

Abe moved his foot around in the dirt. "Fine," he said, but he seemed anything but fine.

They crept up on the trailer, trying to act inconspicuous, except when they got closer, a woman came out from the house across the street and started sweeping her front steps with a broom. Dakota waved at her, trying to be friendly about it, but the woman ignored her and kept on sweeping.

They were one house away. Dakota crouched down, about ten feet away from the truck. She nodded to Abe, who then slipped between trailers, crossing over onto Queen Street. Less than a minute later, she could only assume Abe had rung the bell when a girl with blond hair stood up and the other girls at the table turned their heads. Adrenaline shot through her veins, and she dug her nails into the dirt. She counted to ten, then sprang up from the ground and sprinted toward the bike. She turned it around and hopped aboard, her legs heavy as she began to pedal, slowly picking up speed as she headed down Prince Street in the direction they'd just come from. She turned right, passing the same group of kids and the bike ramp she'd seen earlier. She stood up in her seat to get more leverage, to go faster, until she approached the Royal Street entrance, where she eased up to avoid crashing into the woods. She veered out of the park and down a straightaway until she was on the part of King Street outside the park. She settled onto the right side of the road, racing down the hill, a rush of wind blowing her hair back. A sense of exhilaration invaded every cell in her body. She could see no reason to pump the brakes or look back. She was flying.

Dakota kept a low profile for the next few days, keeping the Sidewinder inside her room and taking the bus to school. She encountered Joey Vinson outside his locker on Tuesday and told him she wasn't a snitch and that she'd be retiring from the pot delivery business, and she was sorry for the misunderstanding. "All right," Vinson had replied, but his eyes had hardened a bit, and she wondered if her explanation had fallen short.

At lunch period, out by the courtyard, she'd thanked Abe profusely for his help in getting her bike back. And when she clued him in on her pot delivery decision, he hadn't exactly acted surprised. "It's cool," he had commented, with that snarky little half grin of his that always seemed to make her heart beat faster. Dakota suggested they still hang out now and then, and Abe smiled at that and said, "Most definitely."

On Friday, she told herself enough was enough. She'd originally intended to wait until the following week to bring her bike out of hibernation but couldn't stand it any longer. Those four days of taking the bus to school, having to come up with bogus explanations to her mother as to why she wasn't riding it, were beyond tortuous. If there was a silver lining to her ordeal, it was that she'd gained a new appreciation for her bike. How she almost couldn't imagine living without it. Sure, she'd fucked up that part of her Plan B. Yet there was more to consider: that her bike signified a different kind of freedom. On Thursday night she could hardly contain her excitement. She texted Abe.

Taking the bike out tomorrow!
Thx so much for helping again
I so appreciate it :)

Abe replied:

Dont ride 2 fast. I hear cops r givn tickets

Dakota:

LOL

Smiley face emoji

When Friday lunchtime came around, Dakota decided to take the Sidewinder out again. Her morning ride had jazzed her up, such that all she thought about during her early classes was getting out on the road again. And it didn't hurt that the weather had warmed up considerably throughout the day.

She went out the west exit of the school, underneath the rotunda by the gymnasium. She had parked the bike in the rack by the school's side entrance, reasoning that a change in location from where her bike had been stolen might bring her good luck. As she moved closer, butterflies pinged in her stomach. A sense of anticipation filled the air. Her plan was to ride into town, get a snack, then make it back before English class. Except for some reason she had trouble locating the bike. No biggie. There were other bikes parked there, and perhaps hers had been sandwiched. She circled the rack, her eyes darting about, when suddenly the sensation in her stomach turned. Up ahead, a few feet away off the back road, among a set of tire tracks, she spotted her mangled bicycle lying on the ground. An invisible force tightened around her throat. Tears collected in the back of her eyes. Both the tires and the chain were gone. The bike's body was almost folded in half, unrecognizable except for the scuffed-up orange paint. She closed her eyes and let out a howling noise that rose from deep within her core. She kneeled and gripped the handlebar. She stood up, clenched her teeth, and lifted what remained of the bike, then flung it back to the ground.

Boiling water coursed through Dakota's veins as she started back toward the school. Under the rotunda and into the gymnasium locker room, she rushed past kids in their gym wear going in the other direction, pushing some of them aside to reach the stairwell. She sprinted up the stairs, and picked up her pace as she made her way down the hallway. Once in the cafeteria, she stopped for a second to look around. Something ominous bubbled up inside of her, coming up to the surface. She could see tables filled with students eating their lunch and a banner out by the courtyard exit hyping the homecoming dance. Other students carried their trays as they left the lunch line and filtered out to their tables. Dakota gazed past them at the far end of the cafeteria. She'd seen Katie Larsen eating lunch in that vicinity before. She headed in that direction.

She took in a deep breath before slowly approaching Katie's table, until she stood right in front of it. There were other girls at the table who did not see her, along with Katie, who did.

"Cat got your tongue, Lodi?" Katie said. She didn't look so intimidating sitting in her chair, but there was something about her eyes. They seemed to move in multiple directions at once, as if someone were positioning them with a remote-control device.

"You know why I'm here," Dakota told her. She slapped her hand against her thigh a few times to stop it from shaking.

"Educate me." Katie flashed an evil smile, and her lazy eye drifted off to the side. She looked around at the other girls, who were now interested.

"It's about the bicycle."

"I don't know anything about a bicycle."

"You stole mine last week. I know that because I found it outside your trailer and took it back."

"So now you're admitting to stealing my bike."

"What kind of fucked-up logic is that?"

Katie tilted her head. "A mouth like that will get you in trouble, girl."

"The way I see it, at a minimum I deserve some compensation."

"How 'bout I give you nothing and you go back to middle school." The girls at the table laughed in unison, and Katie shifted in her chair.

"I'm willing to negotiate on this."

"How's this for a negotiation? You go away and I let you live."

It occurred to Dakota that living would be good, but she resisted the urge to run.

"You're dumb as rocks," Katie said, smiling again. Not a happy smile.

Dakota felt a switch go off in her brain. "At least I'm not dumb and ugly," she said, emphasizing the *and* part.

*Oh*s and *aah*s from the peanut gallery.

"What'd you say?"

"Oh… so now you're deaf, dumb, and ugly."

Katie Larsen stood. She might have been attractive in a sporty kind of way if it weren't for her broad shoulders and cement-filled eyes. She tied her medium-length blond hair back with a band she plucked out of her pocket. Voices came out from the table, saying "knock her out" and "fuck her up." Out of her peripheral vision she could see people standing, and some were moving closer.

Dakota moved fast, landing a foot to Katie's groin. She

balled up her fist and hit her as hard as she could in the nose. "Fuck," Katie yelled out, but she was charging now. The first punch came out of nowhere and smashed Dakota in the mouth, then a roundhouse that landed above her eye, followed by a barrage of rapid-fire strikes. Mouth. Eye. Eye again. Another above the nose. She lost her balance, tilting sideways when Katie slashed a forearm across her head. Dakota hit the ground. She tasted blood in her mouth and heard loud voices in the background. "How do you like this, you little cunt," Katie declared, straddling her, grabbing a clump of Dakota's hair, and slamming her face against the tile floor. Dakota could barely make a sound before another whack in the back of her head, but somehow she'd freed her right arm. She jerked her elbow up, hitting something hard, giving her a split second to roll into a ball with her hands over her head. Katie punched again, but her blows glanced off Dakota's arms. She growled, got up, then stood over Dakota. She took a step back, wound up her leg, and moved forward. Dakota felt the foot in her ribs and screamed. A sharp pain pulsed throughout her body, and it was as if someone had vacuumed the air out of her lungs. She coughed, trying to regain her breath. She opened her eyes and coughed again. She could see blood pooling on the floor. She touched her mouth and saw blood on her hand. Then a thought. What had happened to Katie? Her voice projected out from a distance, but was that even possible? She rolled on her side and opened her eyes, but everything was all blurry. She blinked. Two people had Katie in a vise grip, and one of them looked a lot like that guy Carlos, who'd come into the diner last weekend after hours to help bring in the new freezer. There were other people around her now, and some guy with dreadlocks handed her a towel and said, "You're bleeding." She placed the towel over her mouth. Her head hurt, and the pain in her side throbbed like a continuous drumbeat. She glanced up again to see Katie being escorted out of the cafeteria. She lay back down on the floor and closed her eyes.

"You okay?" someone asked her.

She forced one of her eyes to open. Carlos, crouched right beside her. From her vantage point he looked like the most beautiful human on Earth.

"Should we call an ambulance?" he proposed.

Dakota tried to shake her head but could not be certain it actually moved.

"Why don't you try sitting up," he then suggested. "I'll help you."

Carlos slid his arm underneath hers and lifted her slowly into a sitting position on the floor. Dakota groaned and grabbed at her side.

"Fuck, that hurts."

"No problem. We can sit here for a while."

Dakota did just that. She had the sense people were staring at her. Her vision drifted in and out of focus. The guy with the dreadlocks again. Some girl she didn't know, handing over a water bottle. She tried drinking from it, but most of the water dribbled down her chin. The bloody towel lay by her side, but it was too much effort to pick it up and dry her face.

"You got some good shots in, actually," the dreadlocks guy then observed.

"Yeah," she replied. "I'm a natural-born killer."

Then another voice. Deeper than the others. "What's going on here?"

"She could have broken ribs," Carlos explained.

Dakota giggled, making the pain worse. "Dr. Carlos, paging Dr. Carlos."

The man with the deep voice said his name was Dawkins. An industrial arts teacher who sometimes patrolled the cafeteria. Wood shop, if she was not mistaken.

Carlos and Dawkins exchanged glances as if they were deciding what to do next.

"We should get her to stand up," said Dawkins in a manner that projected confidence.

"I don't think so," Dakota protested, but it was almost as if the two of them had not heard her, because they positioned themselves on either side of her, each one picking an arm.

"I'll count to three," Dawkins said, "and then we're going to lift."

They counted to three and lifted her up.

"Aaaahhhh!" Dakota blurted out.

Dawkins continued. "We're going to walk now. One foot in front of the other."

"I know how to walk," Dakota told them.

Then, as if to prove it, she put one foot in front of the other. She did it again, then fell to the ground.

May 29, 2019

Chapter 16.
Pendejos

At the Sunrise Diner, Dakota received her first assignment of the summer: train the new guy on how to use the Hobart. The success or failure of this mission had a domino effect, as promotions for both Dakota and Rosie were at stake. If it all worked according to plan, Dakota would be clearing off tables and refilling the customers' coffee cups in her new position, while Rosie would graduate to waitress, both of them receiving modest increases in pay and working six days a week for the entire summer.

There existed a complication, however. The new guy happened to be Carlos. Yes. The same Carlos that had saved her life seven months ago in the Zionsville High School cafeteria. Not to mention he was Mario's nephew.

"You let me know if there's trouble with him," Mrs. Peña said to her the second Dakota entered the diner on Wednesday morning, nipping the whole nepotism factor in the bud. "I'll deal with Mario if I have to."

Dakota had no expectations of trouble. In her mind, a halfway-intelligent farm animal could be trained to wash dishes as long as you were willing to accept some trial and error in the beginning. Except not knowing much about

Carlos, other than his bravery, she said, "Don't worry about it, Mrs. Peña. If he can't handle the heat, you'll be the first one to know."

Mrs. Peña seemed satisfied by this approach, whereas Rosie had an entirely different angle when it came to Carlos, this having more to do with his off-the-charts hotness. She'd been arranging mugs in neat rows by the coffee station in a manner that suggested a serious case of OCD when Dakota came up from behind her and tapped her on the shoulder. Rosie turned and smiled. In the background, the sounds of dicing vegetables and something sizzling on the griddle filled the air as Bennie sang along to a mariachi song he liked to start off each morning with.

"Hey, D," Rosie said. "Are you ready for training today?" She winked, not once but twice.

Dakota narrowed her eyes. "Is there some reason you just winked at me?"

"Carlos."

"What about him?"

"You don't remember? You had that sex dream about him."

Why had she told Rosie about that? Big mistake. Yet truth be told, Rosie knew Carlos as well, since their families had known each other for years and he'd helped install the diner's new freezer in October. Though on that particular day, Carlos said hello to Rosie and only nodded at Dakota, as if he were acknowledging a less-than-attractive potted plant stationed in the wrong location. Which for some reason had led to the sex dream. And her pleasing herself afterward. Although she hadn't told Rosie that part.

"I do remember Carlos," Dakota admitted, "but it's not like he'd be into me." The words sounded pitiful, almost to the point of nausea when they came out.

"At least he hasn't seen you for a while," Rosie countered. "He might think you're someone else."

"So you're saying I can use that to my advantage. Especially since the last time he saw me, I was bleeding out on the cafeteria floor."

"Can't hurt. And when you work with someone, they get to know the real you." This was code for *otherwise you'd have no shot.*

"What I don't get is, if he's so hot, then why aren't you making a play for him? Is there something wrong with him? Let me guess. He has herpes."

"It's not that. He's Mario's nephew. It would be wrong. You know what I'm saying?"

"Not really," Dakota said, her eyes darting about, catching a glimpse of Carlos engaged in conversation with Manuel through the opening in the kitchen. Then back to Rosie, biting down on a fingernail, chipping away at her peach-colored nail polish. "Why are you so nervous?" Dakota asked, quenching an obvious need for a subject change.

"I had this nightmare last night," Rosie answered. "Someone ordered pancakes, but I spelled it wrong and they got eggs instead."

"Not sure how you get from pancakes to eggs. But you practiced last night, and I'm sure you'll be great." Dakota put a hand on her friend's shoulder. "And Mario gets shorthand orders all the time. He'll just have to get used to yours."

"Yeah... right."

"I'll talk to him about it... tell him I'll kick him in the cojones if he gives you a hard time."

Rosie laughed hard at that one. Months ago, the thought of Dakota talking to Mario in that manner would have been beyond absurd. Except over time, their relationship had morphed into something else. Not exactly buddies, but for some reason Mario trusted her palate when it came to testing out lunch recipes, all of this starting when Dakota tried out some of his pork chili verde one day and made the suggestion that he add more hatch chiles to the recipe. Later, she gave two thumbs-up to his green tomatillo enchilada sauce and helped pick among competing pork marinades for the tacos al pastor. Once she even suggested adding more jalapeños to the pico de gallo.

"But gringos don't like spice," Mario protested at the time.

"Fuck the gringos," Dakota told him, as if she weren't a gringo herself. "Make what you like, and people will respect that. If not, they can go to fucking Burger King."

Back in the kitchen, Dakota found Carlos chatting with Manuel by the toaster. He wore a Zionsville High soccer tee that looked as if it had been painted on, but she already knew that he played on the varsity. Rosie had once mentioned something about it, that he was a striker. Whatever that was.

"Hey," she said to him. "Remember me?"

"How could I forget," Carlos replied, the corners of his mouth turning up slightly.

Dakota felt an immediate buzz. A shot of adrenaline mixed with dizziness, topped off with a dose of horniness. Oh no. What the hell was wrong with her? She really could use professional help. And with the search for her father just beginning and all the crap she had to deal with in her life, did she really need to obsess over some guy? Some guy that obviously didn't give a hoot about her. Even if he had saved her life. But let's face it, Carlos was pretty damn good-looking. Though more in a cute than conventionally handsome way, with his closely cropped brown hair that appeared disheveled and almost sculpted at the same time. His nose flared out slightly at the edges as if it had come out of a panini maker.

"Earth to Dakota," she then heard from Carlos.

She snapped to attention. "Oh… yes. Sorry. I was just thinking… about what we had to do today. And… okay. Let's see. Have you met Manuel?"

Carlos fixed her with his brown eyes, another item on her why-I-should-crush-on-Carlos checklist. "I did."

"Well, don't pay attention to him. He's a jackass."

Manuel had been laboring by his toasting station but had likely been listening to their conversation the whole time. "And good morning to you, Miss Dakota," he said, flashing one of his ambiguous smiles, somewhere between a friendly waiter and a pervert.

"Are you giving Carlos work advice?"

"I told him you're trouble. To watch his back."

Dakota punched him in the arm. "What's on the menu for today?"

"White chocolate macadamia scones."

"Ohhh. Seriously, Manuel. If you weren't such an a-hole, I'd ask you to marry me."

"A sixteen-year-old bride," Manuel said, handing her one of the scones. "I'll be sure to tell my parole officer about that."

Dakota smiled, then turned to Carlos, who was shaking his head.

"What?" Dakota asked.

"Nothing," Carlos replied, making it sound like something.

She took a step forward. Perhaps too close. "It's weird for you, seeing me here. Isn't it?"

"A bit. But, like, obviously I knew you worked here."

"Except you have to work with me and I have to train you, which you think could be a problem. I will say, though, that I'm pretty easy to work with. And I promise I won't hit you. Unless you try stealing my scone."

She got another grin out of Carlos with that one. "Well, I'm glad you won't hit me. And I won't touch your scone. And of course there's no problem. Really. The whole thing. It wasn't a big deal."

But it was.

"Great," Dakota said, a lump beginning to form in her throat. "So, are you ready to wash dishes?"

She started with the basics. Dishwashing 101. Things like proper placement of plates, bowls, and utensils, and when to use the spray washer, as well as where to load the dish soap and setting up the control functions. Dakota went back and forth from clearing dishware off of tables to supervising Carlos, who at first had no problems with the basics, adeptly filling up the dishwasher and getting it ready to run, when something became apparent. Dream-world Carlos might have possessed mad sack skills, but the real-life version hadn't a clue how to start the Hobart.

"Is there a problem?" she asked him, while knowing there was a problem.

"I think the dishwasher's not working," he claimed.

Dakota immediately knew what to do with the dishwasher but didn't want to let on, as seeing a new flustered side of Carlos made her giddy in some respects. And wasn't fucking up at the diner part of your initiation?

"You think we need a new one?" Dakota asked, pretending to want his input.

"I'd say so."

"In your free time, you can suggest that to Mrs. Peña." She kicked at the door of the Hobart, and instantly it revved up.

"How'd you do that?"

Dakota shrugged, as if her getting the dishwasher to work was just an example of dumb luck. Then she ambled over to Manuel, who'd been observing the whole scene from afar.

"Pendejo," she muttered under her breath.

October 26–28, 2018

Chapter 17.
Damaged Goods

Dakota woke up in her hospital bed and opened one eye. Up above, a fluorescent light shined its artificial rays, making her squint. She detected a faint chemical smell, like disinfectant mixed with urine. Over the intercom, someone paged Dr. Brantley. She turned her body, and a sharp pain, unlike any she'd felt before, pulsed down her side. *Fuck*, she yelled out to the universe.

She then experienced a strange sensation other than pain. Could there be something wrong with her brain? It was as if snippets of time had actually vanished. She remembered the fight, Carlos and the industrial arts teacher (what was his name again?) helping her to stand, and a doctor mentioning stitches and X-rays, but everything else existed in a void. And now, here she was in a hospital bed, hours, maybe days later for all she knew, a drab gray curtain drawn across the room, behind which she could hear groaning noises and people talking. Two strangers then passed by, both staring at her, as if she were part of some freak show they might consider paying for if the price was right. *Fuck off,* she wanted to say. Instead, she closed her eyes and tried shifting her body. More pain. Oxygen drained from her lungs. She tried to compensate by taking in a deep breath, but it felt like she'd been stabbed in the abdomen. She tried opening her eyes, but only one complied. Rosie sat in the chair beside the bed, legs crossed, wearing pink pants and a brown sweater with white, pink, and sky-blue geometric patterns on it. Her hair was pinned back with a pink beret.

"Hey, D," she said, all casual about it, as if she were welcoming her to the diner on a Sunday morning.

"Oh," Dakota replied. "I didn't see you there."

"No big deal. I've just been sitting here for two hours watching you sleep."

Dakota opened her mouth to respond, but nothing came out except a gurgling sound. She cleared her throat. She touched her left eye, which by then she'd determined was not working properly. But the second her finger grazed against a bulbous mass where her eye should have been, she recoiled as if stung by a bee and then had the nightmarish thought that perhaps the eye had been gouged out.

Rosie shook her head. "I'm not gonna lie, D. You look like an extra in a zombie movie."

"Huh."

"You have this purple welt above your eye, which for your information is closed. And those zigzag stitches around your mouth. Let's just say you won't be kissing anyone anytime soon."

She felt a modest wave of relief after hearing Rosie's eye diagnosis. But there were other matters to resolve. "Why does it hurt when I breathe?"

"You have broken ribs."

"Oh," Dakota replied, but she had no memory of anyone telling her about broken ribs. Had a doctor talked to her about it? Or had she been sleeping the entire time? And what was the deal with pain meds in this place? You'd have thought they'd have something decent in a hospital.

Just then the nurse came in. A short blond woman in blue scrubs. She had a nameplate on, but Dakota couldn't read it. "You're alive," she chirped.

Nurse humor. Not funny.

"I can't see out of one eye," Dakota told her.

The nurse rotated a thermometer in her hand. "It's just swelling. We iced it earlier, but it will take a few days to go down. But the good news is you didn't break your orbital bone. Wish I could say the same about your ribs though. You nailed two of those bad boys."

"You think I could get some meds for that?"

"Sure thing. But I need to check your vitals first."

The nurse took her temperature and checked her blood pressure, then typed something into a laptop. "You should drink something. I'll bring you some water."

Dakota nodded, which honestly took more effort than you might have thought.

"And if you're hungry," the nurse continued, "I can score some applesauce. How does that sound?"

Sounds awesome. Since after you get the crap beaten out of you and end up unconscious in a hospital, naturally you're jonesing for some applesauce once you come to.

Dakota tried nodding again but couldn't be certain she pulled it off.

"So. Are you gonna tell me what happened, or do I have to beat it out of you?" Rosie asked as soon as the nurse was gone. She had moved her chair up to the bed and pressed her index finger into Dakota's shoulder.

"Please don't do that," Dakota said, referring to the

finger, but at the same time wondering if a communal hospital room was the best place for a confession.

Rosie withdrew her finger but not her gaze. "Take your time. But I'm not going anywhere."

"I need water first," Dakota said, which wasn't exactly a lie, since she required something to soothe her parched throat before she could talk for the length of time it would take to tell the whole story. And so they waited, listening to the sounds of the hospital, the constant beeping noises, pages, conversations around the bed behind the curtain, until the nurse returned, bringing along a cup of water, a sealable container of applesauce, a plastic spoon, and two white tablets. She placed all of this atop a portable table on wheels, which she then slid over the bed. She adjusted the mechanical bed into a more upright position and stuffed an extra pillow behind Dakota's head for support. "Just remember, you had fourteen stitches in your mouth," the nurse reminded her.

"Does this mean my modeling career is over?" Dakota asked.

"Nahhh," the nurse replied with a smile. "We'll get you back on the runway in no time."

Once the nurse left, Dakota reached for the water and brought the lip of the cup to the top of her bottom lip. She hardly opened her mouth to take in a few sips of water, letting the liquid trickle down her throat. But when she tried the same technique with the spoonful of applesauce, she had to open her mouth wider, which made her wince.

"You're just stalling now," Rosie told her then, her brow all furrowed, lips pinched into a thin line.

"Can you just hold it for a second?" Dakota snapped. "I'm going to tell you everything." And she did, after giving the applesauce another try, then washing the pills down with more water. Starting with the eviction letter and her mother's threats about moving to Cleveland. Abe. Ray Kelly. The bicycle and her plan for the pot delivery business. Meeting up with John Moran by the bike rack. The trip to Moran's house with three hundred dollars of Train Wreck. The entire Joey Vinson experience. The stealing, re-stealing, and crushing sequence of events when it came to a bicycle. Her, flying into a rage, confronting Katie Larsen in the cafeteria and kicking her in the groin. A detailed play-by-play of as much as she could remember about the fight and its aftermath, including Carlos and the industrial arts teacher being Good Samaritans.

To say Rosie had a stunned look on her face afterward was not an exaggeration. But she didn't say anything for what seemed to be an eternity, her eyes wandering around the room, glancing up, as if there were answers inscribed on the ceiling tiles. Until finally she brought her head down and locked eyes with her best friend. "I'm not sure how to process all of this, Dakota. It's like you had this secret life that I knew nothing about."

"I know. I know. I feel really bad about that."

"Do you really? And why would you sell drugs? My mom gave you the job at the diner. I painted your bike for free."

"I don't think it comes down to one reason."

"What, then? Did you do it for Abe? Please tell me you're not having sex with him."

"No. Definitely not."

"Then what the fuck, D. None of this makes sense. We can go to school on Monday and find half a dozen people that sell pot. Why would Katie Larsen only be pissed off at you? Did you make a play for her boyfriend?"

Dakota grimaced. "Are you serious?"

"Then there must be something else you're not telling me."

"I don't know what to say to you, Rosie. I've literally told you everything."

Rosie smirked, then took out her phone.

"What are you doing?" Dakota asked.

"I'm texting my mom to pick me up."

"Oh... okay."

Rosie sat up straight in her chair and brought her legs together, placing a hand on each knee, one of them still holding on to the phone. "Listen. My mom's been asking all kinds of questions about this, so I'm gonna have to tell her something."

"You don't have to lie for me."

But what if her friend didn't lie? Would Mrs. Peña forbid her daughter from being her friend? Would Dakota lose her job at the diner, all but obliterating her already wounded Project Freedom?

"Rosie," she then pleaded, searching for some meaningful words to follow.

Rosie rubbed her eyes, then stood up. "I'm gonna wait in the lobby," she said, her voice all shaky. "Maybe I'll see you later."

Then she was out the door.

* * *

Dakota began her convalescence at home two days later. Her mother set her up in her bedroom with a protective shield of pillows and blankets, and she listened to the Gang of Four's "Damaged Goods" on her headphones.

There were glasses of water, continuously refreshed, and a half dozen Ritz crackers for lunch, which went down like shards of glass. After a three-hour nap, they settled on a lukewarm bowl of chicken soup for dinner, which her mother brought over on a cutting board. She stood in front of her bed, waiting not so patiently.

"Are you gonna sit up, or do I have to stand here all night?" she asked, her mouth all scrunched up on one side.

"No prob," Dakota replied. But as it turned out, sitting up with broken ribs was like planning a military operation. You had to strategize how to wriggle your body from a prone to partial upright position, avoiding the minefields along the way. Best to use your arms or lower body, which in theory sounded simple. Except that every kind of body movement known to humankind required some usage of ribs or their surrounding muscles. All it took was one wrong move and POW!

"Ahhhh," Dakota cried out. She had tried shifting her body in a deliberate manner to avoid the usual pain cycle but ended up with the ripping-off-the-Band-Aid method, having reached the conclusion that it made no difference either way.

Her mother shook her head. "Will you be making that noise each time you sit up?"

Dakota delivered a faint smile. "Only if it annoys you."

"You look better, at least."

"Really."

Her mother shrugged. "Do you feel better?"

Tough question. The aftereffects of the concussion still made her foggy, but a tiny slit in her left eye had opened up and her mouth only presented a problem when she talked, ate, or brushed her teeth. Of course, there were her ribs, which the doctor told her would be the most stubborn of her injuries. As well as her mental well-being. She was to be cooped up in a bed for who knew how long, with only her mother and Gina as company. Rosie hadn't returned her FaceTime request last night.

"Not sure," Dakota replied. "But this soup sure tastes good."

She couldn't deny the warm, salty liquid, slimy noodles, and small pieces of chicken comforted her as it all slid down her throat and coated her stomach without much required in the way of chewing. And she didn't even mind eating in bed, although her mother had originally protested that move by trying to coax her into the dining room. But in the end, drinking soup from a bowl precariously balanced on a cutting board turned out to be the right thing to do.

Afterward, Dakota let out a yawn and her good eye turned cloudy. It was crazy how much she'd been craving sleep lately, although the doctor had implied that might happen on account of the concussion. Which, at the time, made her recall an article she'd once read about koalas, and how they slept up to twenty-two hours a day. A blissful existence, if you could pull it off.

Except her mother had other ideas.

"I'm worried about you, peanut," she said, somewhat out of the blue.

"It's okay, Mom. I'll be fine."

"I think we should talk about your fight. I was quite surprised when I heard about it. I never thought of you as a fighter before."

Dakota forced a smile and pointed at her eye. "Well, obviously I'm not."

"What on earth happened?"

"This girl, Katie Larsen, destroyed my bike. I think she ran it over with a truck."

It happened slowly then. A slight change in her mother's constitution, and no sound whatsoever as the blood drained from her face. "Shit" was all she said, before placing both hands over her head, rocking gently back and forth. She took in a series of rapid-fire shallow breaths.

"Are you okay, Mom?"

Her mother went silent.

"Mom. What's wrong?"

More silence.

"Are you taking those pills again?"

That got her attention. Her mother dropped her hands and turned. Beads of sweat pooled on her forehead. "It's not that," she said firmly.

"Should I call an ambulance?"

"No. Please, no. I'm fine… really."

Her mother had stamped out the ambulance suggestion, which perhaps was a bad idea in the first place. No need to overreact and get the authorities involved. And it wasn't as if she'd never witnessed her mother having a panic attack before. Although this one seemed to come out of nowhere. Not a trigger in sight.

"You should lie down." This was her next brilliant solution, which her mother promptly ignored.

"Why would she do that?" her mother suddenly asked in a soft voice. "That girl… Katie."

Dakota was surprised by the question. It didn't seem like something a person on the verge of passing out might ask. "She didn't exactly tell me."

"You're gonna have to do better than that."

What could she do? Lying about the fight didn't seem right. But she'd already told the truth to Rosie, and that hadn't worked out so well. Under the circumstances, getting her mother more riled up didn't appear to be the right move.

"Okay," Dakota said, her heart beginning to pound. "Well, first she stole it from me, then I stole it back. So maybe that had something to do with it. Or it could be that she saw me talking to her boyfriend in the cafeteria. She's a bit loco that way. She has a reputation, you know."

Her mother rubbed at her suspicious eyes. "So, you're telling me she ran over your bike, then started a fight in the cafeteria?"

"Uhh… no. I'm the one that sort of started it. But honestly, Mom, I was super angry. Because of the bike, you know. And so I went to her in the cafeteria and told her she needed to pay me for the bike. Which I thought was reasonable. But she didn't like that. Then she stood up, and I knew she was coming for me, so I kicked her and punched her in the nose, which I guess made things worse."

Her mother's eyes popped. "What the fuck, Dakota. Haven't we talked about this before? About you using your head. There are people out in the world that play by different rules. And let me tell you, girls like Katie are bad news. Believe me… I know. A girl like that gets all fired up about shit in her own life she can't control. Next thing you know, she's taking it out on innocent people like you."

Innocent. Ha ha. But her mother sure knew a lot about Katie Larsen. Or the kind of person she was, at least. Then again, there were likely bullies just like her back in the day her mother attended high school.

It was then that her mother gingerly placed a hand on

her shoulder. Not moving it, just keeping it there as if to hold her daughter in place. "Just promise me this is over."

"It is, Mom. I've definitely learned a lesson."

"Good," she said, leaning in closer, their heads almost touching. A solitary tear dribbled down her mother's cheek as she rubbed at the space between her daughter's shoulder and neck. It was all a bit unnerving. Apparently it took a beating from Katie Larsen for your mother to know that you were alive. And it was good that she didn't know the whole truth, that she had tried to stave off their eviction but failed. That her entire world had gone up in smoke.

May 30, 2019

Chapter 18.
Hard to Explain

After work, the girls piled into the Subaru and headed across the bridge to South Zionsville. The events of the past few days, as well as the information obtained from Lucinda and Alice, had been swirling around Dakota's brain like a swarm of angry bees. The murder of Greg Coleman. Her mother possibly shacking up with him shortly after her birth. Jimmy Ray and the husband of Anika Renfors showing up on the arrest report for the brawl at Muncy's Tavern. And yesterday, when she and Rosie had discussed their next steps, they couldn't agree on a direction. Rosie had suggested they concentrate on the Colemans, perhaps find a way to speak with the aunts, Christine and Maureen, whereas Dakota sent a friend request to Adam Boland on Facebook (which Rosie staunchly opposed) and expressed the desire to meet up with her mother's friends, Anika and Jenna. In the end, they'd settled upon Anika. Being her mother's best friend around the time of her conception and Greg Coleman's murder, she'd likely be able to shine light upon all the confusion. Of course, there was something else to consider. Dakota had given her contact information to Helen Powers to pass along, but Anika had never responded. Which meant they were showing up uninvited.

Dakota directed Rosie toward the Royal Avenue entrance of the King Street Trailer Park, but once they veered onto Queen Street, her stomach began to flutter, the same feeling she'd gotten when she first looked up Anika Renfors on Google and found out that her address was 21 Queen Street.

Dakota draped her hand over the side of the Subaru's passenger window and tapped against the car door. The smell of charcoal smoke filled the air, and they passed a trailer beside a patch of green grass, and another with pots of purple petunias. Rosie pulled the car up to a drab off-white trailer and cut the engine. They exited the Subaru and crossed the dirt driveway, after which Dakota froze in front of a lilac bush. Immediately, the flutter in her stomach turned hard.

"What is it?" Rosie asked.

"I've been here before," Dakota replied. "The night I stole back my bike from Katie Larsen."

Rosie seemed skeptical. "Are you sure about that, D? I mean, these houses all look the same. Maybe you're just mixing them up."

Perhaps Rosie had a point, yet there was something about the branches on that damn lilac bush and the way the edge of the driveway tapered off that made her think otherwise. Then again, checking wouldn't hurt, and she took out her phone and googled Anika Renfors once more. But 21 Queen Street came up again, which coincidentally matched the *21* in gold metallic letters nailed to one of the trailer's shingles. A fact that she shared with Rosie, sticking the phone in her face, just for emphasis.

Rosie ran her fingers through her hair. "It doesn't mean

she lives here. The chances are slim. It would be like being struck by lightning."

Dakota chewed on her lower lip. There were no vehicles in the driveway. No black truck. Could it be her mind had been playing tricks on her? Still, she hesitated. Rosie's analogy didn't exactly scream out comfort. Didn't lightning kill hundreds of people each year? "I'm thinking we should wait in the car," she said. "Observe for a while."

Rosie shook her head. "No fucking way am I waiting. We either go or we don't."

They approached the trailer slowly. When they reached its front entrance, Dakota stepped onto a set of wooden stairs and rang the doorbell. They heard noises. Someone fumbling with the door. Then a girl who, from a distance, didn't look anything like Katie. Tall, but with short blond hair. She examined them through the screen, perhaps making a decision on whether to engage them. Or not.

"Hello," Dakota said in a friendly manner, thinking that might help her decide.

The girl came out through the screen door and onto the front step, turning slowly to face them. She had brilliant blue eyes and a sharp, pointy nose. A grin slowly spread across her face, like liquid diffusing through a blank piece of paper.

"Oh," Dakota said, her voice parched. She grabbed ahold of Rosie's arm and took a step back, pulling her friend along with her.

"You here for a rematch?" asked the one and only Katie Larsen.

"Uhhh," she managed to force out, her jaw unhinged, the edges of her peripheral vision all blurry. Questions arose. Did her life exist in someone else's dream, where all control had been relinquished? If there was a god, had he (or she) created the universe for the sole purpose of tormenting her? Or was Katie considering whether or not to slug her in the mouth again?

"At least you've brought reinforcements this time," Katie observed, sounding amused, like either way she would have been up for the challenge.

"Oh... yes... this is my friend Rosie. Rosie... Katie."

For some reason she felt bad for Rosie after the introductions, which played out more like an ambush, even though she'd prefaced it with her déjà vu moment. She had this catatonic expression on her face. But truthfully, Dakota had had no sense of recognition the instant she'd seen Katie Larsen. The shorter hair had framed her face differently, softening the edges of her jaw, highlighting her blue eyes, dared she say, making her more attractive. Faced with such circumstances, and the fact that she hadn't seen Katie since the fight, on account of her being expelled from Zionsville High for being a habitual offender, how was she supposed to know?

"Sorry. I didn't recognize you," Dakota told her, pointing to her own head. "Your hair is shorter. Actually... it looks good. You look good... with short hair, that is."

"You broke my fucking nose."

Had she really? She'd heard rumors to that effect, but thought it to be a Zionsville High urban legend. Something someone made up to offset the fact that she'd been pulverized in its cafeteria. Score one for the underdog.

Dakota swallowed. "Well... okay. But you broke my ribs. And I needed stitches in my mouth. And I had a concussion."

Katie smiled again. Perhaps she had totaled up all their

injuries and had come to the conclusion that they were even. "What are you doing here?"

"I must be in the wrong place," Dakota explained. "I'm looking for Anika Renfors. Does she live around here?"

"I would say so. She's my mom."

"But... I..."

"Larsen's my father's name."

Dakota glanced over at Rosie, who offered up a what-do-you-want-me-to-do-about-it look, then back at Katie. That she was Anika Renfors's daughter seemed like a product of some nonsensical fever dream. "So maybe you didn't know this," she said, "but your mom was a friend of my mom's back in high school."

"And I'm supposed to care why?"

"I should explain. I'm trying to get information about who my father is. And I thought she might know something about that. Which is why I'm here. Not to see you. Not that I mind seeing you. It's just that I'm not here to start trouble."

Katie put both hands on her hips. Somewhere in the distance a dog barked. "She's not here right now. You can wait if you want."

"Sounds good," Dakota replied.

It was then that something passed between them, Katie eyeing her as she sidestepped up the stairs, opened the screen door, then inserted herself aside it. Half in. Half out. "What," she said, "you want me to invite you in? Should I make tea?"

Katie didn't wait for an answer, though she smiled once again before going back inside the trailer and slamming the door behind her.

The two of them looked as if they'd witnessed the

beginnings of the zombie apocalypse as they inched their way over to the side of the trailer's yard and lowered themselves upon a bench of an old wooden picnic table. At that moment, the return of Anika Renfors seemed immaterial. Dakota had her knees drawn back into her stomach. Her eyes closed as she concentrated on the rhythm of air going in and out of her lungs. A gentle breeze floated by. There was the sound of water coming through a faucet in the trailer. Minutes passed without them speaking, until Rosie said, "Well, that was certainly weird."

Dakota opened her eyes. "I know."

"Are you okay?"

"Not really."

Rosie nudged her shoulder. "I was just thinking. Remember in the hospital? All that stuff about her that didn't make sense?"

"Vaguely. It was a long time ago."

"I don't know, D. I mean, there's only so much coincidence in the world."

Coincidence. She was having a hard time processing that part of it. Reliving the fight, its aftermath, and all the things that didn't add up around that time, including her mother's panic attack, which instantly appeared shaded in a completely different light than it had in her bedroom that day. Instead, and perhaps out of an act of avoidance, she focused more on the last time she'd been at this exact location. Abe helping her take back her bicycle. The exhilaration she'd felt, flying down King Street at the time, when suddenly the hum of an engine came up from behind them, bringing her back to reality. A black truck pulled into the gravel driveway across the yard. The same truck she'd seen months ago with its tailgate down, her Sidewinder set down right beside it.

A woman with curly blond hair down to her shoulders exited the truck and walked around to the passenger side, where she removed a grocery bag. "Excuse me," Dakota cried out, and instantly they were moving toward her.

The woman turned. She held on to the grocery bag with her left hand, causing her shoulder to droop. Dakota tried imagining her, years ago, galivanting around town with her mother. And she could almost see it. Anika looked just like the photos of her on Instagram and Etsy, but she was one of those women, like her mother, who had aged while still possessing traces of her youthful beauty despite the few extra pounds and the lines winding across their foreheads.

"Mrs. Renfors," Dakota started. "I'm Dakota Lodi, and this is my friend Rosie. We were wondering if we could have a minute of your time."

Anika put down the grocery bag. "Did you say Lodi?"

"Yes. I'm Victoria Lodi's daughter. You were friends with my mom in high school."

"You don't look like her."

Dakota stepped forward. Anika had the same blue eyes as her daughter and a smattering of freckles on her cheeks. "Yeah… I hear that a lot."

"Do you need help with those bags?" Rosie offered.

Anika flashed a look of annoyance. "That won't be necessary."

"I just wanted to ask you a few questions," Dakota said. "About my father. I figured you might know something about him."

"How'd you find me?"

"We visited Stanley and Helen the other day. I gave them my number to pass on to you. I assume you got it."

"I didn't. Now answer me or else I'm calling my husband."

Sounded like a threat. Get ole Albert involved. Albert, the family enforcer. One phone call and Albert shows up in a Cadillac with a baseball bat.

Dakota exchanged glances with Rosie before fixing her eyes on Anika, trying to appear tough. "It wasn't that hard to find you. Between Etsy and Google."

"And you're on Instagram and Facebook," Rosie added with a perky smile.

Anika let out a laugh, but the kind of laugh that says you're not amused. "Are you guys stalking me?"

"Your stuff is not private," Dakota explained. "Did you not know anyone can see it?"

"Okay. I've had about enough of this."

"Please, Mrs. Renfors. I promise it won't take long."

Anika blinked. Once. Twice. Three times. "Listen. I knew your mother once, but I wouldn't say we were ever friends."

"So you know nothing about Jimmy Ray Coleman? Or his brother's murder?"

"I don't."

"But if I'm not mistaken, your husband showed up on the arrest report for the fight at Muncy's Tavern."

It had been a Hail Mary shot. An attempt to change the momentum of events that appeared to be headed downhill. Except at that very moment, Anika's eyes hardened, and you could almost feel the heat oozing out the pores of her body. She lifted up the grocery bag and shifted her body in the direction of the trailer. "I don't have time for this shit," she said. "I wasn't married to Al back then, so I don't know anything about a fight. And like I said, your mother and I were never friends."

"But maybe you heard something about her and Jimmy Ray."

"Anything you could remember would help," Rosie said.

But by then, Anika had forged her way up the front steps of the trailer and had made her way inside.

Back in the Subaru, they tried making sense of what had happened.

"I'm not gonna lie, D," Rosie started. "That was beyond surreal."

Dakota secured her seat belt as they exited the trailer park. "Well, Anika had no problem lying."

"Are you sure about them being friends?"

"That's what my grandmother said."

Down by the river, they crossed over the Y-Bridge, veering left onto the west side of the river, which led to the northernmost section of North Zionsville. Last night they'd traced a single post on Jenna Beal's Instagram about the Coffee Break Cafe in North Zionsville to the café's Facebook page, which had a photo of its manager, Jenna Beal.

The café itself was wedged in the middle of a tiny strip mall. Table and chair sets had been placed out on the pavement, and an older couple lounged there, nursing their coffees. Indoors, customers positioned themselves around a counter set up against a large window. At the far end of the café, a giant chalkboard listed a dizzying array of choices: lattes, espressos, cappuccinos, americanos, along with caffè macchiatos. And the ultimate in coffee drinks: *JAVA EXTREME!!!* A combination of dark-roast coffee and cream supercharged with Java Monster energy drink. Like caffeinated speed.

The girls stepped up to the counter, and a young guy with long dark hair wearing a black Coffee Break tee greeted them. "Can I help you?" he said in a nasally voice.

"Sure," Dakota replied. "Is Jenna Beal here by any chance?"

Of course, she had already recognized Jenna from the photos. She was only a few feet away from the counter, tugging at a strap on her purple apron while listening to a girl with green hair who, from the looks of her, seemed to be in the midst of a crisis. Beside them, a skinny dude with sandy hair and blue glasses, who obviously didn't give a shit, forced a series of far too many baked goods inside a glass dome tray.

Nasal-voice guy interrupted Jenna's counseling session to explain the situation, and instantly she turned and moved toward them. "Hey, girls," she said, flashing a smile. "What can I do for you?"

Seeing Jenna Beal in a photo, then in person, were two different things. The snapshots failed to capture the aura surrounding her, and how that likely made her prettier than she appeared on film. She had medium-length brown hair and sparkly blue eyes that latched onto you when she spoke. She wore silver hoop earrings and a dream catcher necklace. There was a strong undercurrent of contentment, drawing you in like a magnet, making you feel as if you'd be missing out by not getting to know her.

"Hello, Mrs. Beal," Dakota said, offering up her own smile, trying to return the positive energy. "I'm Dakota Lodi, and this is my friend Rosie. We were wondering if you had a minute to talk to us about something important." She had added the word important, thinking it might stimulate Jenna's interest.

Jenna fiddled with her necklace. "Mmmm. Dakota Lodi," she observed, taking in a deep breath. "Aren't you a blast from the past. You were like, what… one, the last time I saw you."

The revelation startled her. Yet, it made sense that her mother's friends would have seen her around that time. And unlike Anika, it appeared as if Jenna favored the truth.

"Honestly," Dakota replied, "I have trouble remembering last weekend. So don't hold it against me if I draw blanks on that one."

Jenna smiled again, but this one seemed forced. "So, tell me, then. What's so important?"

"I'm trying to find my father, and I thought talking to my mom's friends might help."

Jenna tilted her head. "Not sure I understand. You don't know who your father is? Or you do and just can't find him?"

Dakota sighed. Anika had never asked her that question, which only added to the oddities of that particular conversation, as if maybe she already knew the answer. "I could say yes to both. Which I guess is the problem."

"We just want to see if you remember anything," Rosie chimed in. "It won't take long. We'll even buy coffee."

You could tell Jenna liked the coffee part, because she took a step forward and leaned against the counter. "How old are you guys?"

"Sixteen," Rosie answered. "We just finished our sophomore year at Zionsville High."

"Go Blue Devils," Jenna said sarcastically.

"So, what do you think?" Rosie again. "Can you help us?"

Jenna shook her head, but not in a way that said no. "The two of you are cute. A couple of heartbreakers, I bet."

"Yeah," Dakota said. "We swat them away like flies."

Rosie nudged her in the ribs as Jenna removed her apron and went back to the row of industrial-sized coffee makers lined up against the back wall. She came back carrying three cups of coffee on a round serving tray. "On the house," she said, directing them to a table in the corner with a prime view of the parking lot.

They settled into their chairs. On the street beyond, a police cruiser sped on by, its red lights flashing. An uncomfortable silence filled the air, which in some ways had been part of their recently formulated plan. Don't let Jenna know about their meeting with Anika. Wait for her to talk. Look for discrepancies.

Jenna took a sip of her coffee, then leaned back. "Should I assume you've already talked to your mother about this?"

Dakota nodded. "I have. But sometimes she lies."

Jenna's cheeks flushed, and her eyes began to shift back and forth between the two girls, finally settling on Dakota. "I'm not sure that I can help you much, Dakota," she started. "I met your mom through a mutual friend, Anika. I grew up on the same street as Anika, and we've been best friends since second grade. But that's where it gets tricky. Around ninth grade we started to drift apart. Anika met your mom, and the two of them started hanging out. They were definitely alike. Both of them into drugs, alcohol… lots of guys. That just wasn't my scene at the time. I was a good student. I played clarinet in the band. I didn't have a boyfriend until my senior year. But Anika and I had a childhood bond, and that wasn't so easy to break. So there were times when she'd invite me to go out with them and I'd go."

"Like the third wheel," Dakota commented.

"Exactly. Except here's the thing. I really liked your mom. She could be brutally honest, and there was no such thing as boundaries. But for some reason that never bothered me. Maybe because she was always really nice to me. Like it was no big deal for me to tag along with them. It meant a lot to me at the time. And for some reason I found her easy to talk to. She was super witty, which I liked, and we talked about stuff you wouldn't expect to talk about when you were getting wasted. Though I always felt as if she were trying to tell me something."

It was then that a tear began to trickle down Jenna's cheek, and she took out a napkin and dabbed at it. "Sorry about that," she said. "I get overly emotional about these things. When I think about how young we all were. And the two of them. Such troubled lives."

"What kind of troubles did Anika have?" Dakota asked.

Jenna's eyes narrowed. "I can't get into that. She's still my friend, and I'm not about to betray her confidence."

"I totally understand," Dakota said. "Maybe you can tell me about Jimmy Ray Coleman."

Jenna looked as if she'd just walked into a surprise party. "Jimmy? I mean, he was a friend of theirs. But he never said two words to me. I barely knew him."

"What if I told you he was my father?"

"I'm not sure what you want me to say about that. I never knew them to be a couple. But after your mom left school, I never saw much of her. It was kind of sad, actually."

"What about Greg Coleman?" Rosie asked.

You would have thought Rosie had tossed a dart right

between Jenna's eyes, because she pursed her lips and shook her head vigorously. "That guy was bad news," she claimed. "With a capital B."

Rosie continued. "What can you tell us about him?"

Jenna turned to Dakota. "I don't mean to be rude. I just don't feel comfortable talking about any of that."

"That's fine," Dakota replied. "But you said earlier that you met me when I was one. Were you with Anika?"

"Yes. We'd been at our neighborhood block party. And after, we went to see your mom at your grandmother's house."

"And the subject of who the father of this cute one-year-old is never came up?"

Jenna laughed. "No. It didn't."

Dakota had intentionally kept Anika's lie about not being friends with her mother to herself to see if Jenna would confirm it. Which she had. If Anika went with Jenna to Lucinda's house when she was one, then obviously they'd still been friends at that time. Could something have happened later to cause their relationship to end? Or to fizzle out, as Lucinda had implied? Did it have anything to do with the murder of Greg Coleman? In that case, in Anika's mind, it might have canceled out everything that came before it, such that Anika would not consider her we-were-never-friends statement to be a lie. Either way, Dakota felt as if she'd wrung as much as she could out of her mother's friends. And she could tell Jenna was getting fidgety, as she probably needed to get back to work.

"You've been very helpful, Mrs. Beal," Dakota said, trying to wrap things up. "We really appreciate it."

"Not a problem," Jenna replied. "But I wanted to tell you one more thing, Dakota. I felt awful when I read about what happened to your mother. It must be difficult for you. How are you doing with it?"

"I live with my grandmother now," Dakota revealed, appreciating Jenna's concern since, for the most part, people she came in contact with avoided the subject. "So it's cool."

"Well, hopefully she can recover from this and turn her life around. She's certainly smart enough."

Dakota agreed with Jenna's assessment, mostly because she had no desire to challenge it. She knew all about her mother's so-called intelligence. Her superior poker skills. The documentaries she liked watching on television where animals tried to eat each other. Even the game shows, where she sometimes answered questions before the contestants did. No doubt, her mother was smart. But dumb at the same time. Smart and dumb. It was hard to explain.

November 12, 2018

Chapter 19.
You Kind of Get
What You Deserve

With only six weeks remaining in the year, Dakota faced her stark reality. The looming eviction, questions about her job at the diner, not to mention her best friend freezing her out during her time of need. And to make things worse, she was back at Zionsville High School for the first time since her battle royale with Katie Larsen. A bit later than expected though, on account of Dr. Donaghue, the reviled vice principal of Zionsville High, suspending her for ten days. The good doctor claimed that witness testimony pointed to her starting the fight with Katie Larsen. That breaking rules came with consequences, in which case you kind of got what you deserved.

Whatever. She did the best she could, cruising through the hallway, adorned with a patterned olive-green hoodie over her black Ramones tee, ripped blue jeans, and black Cons. She even stuck to the periphery, hoping no one would notice her, dialing up "Cannonball," a killer 90s tune by the Breeders from her "Punkified" playlist. Kim Deal, the band's leader, had once been an Ohio high school girl—just like her—in Dayton, where as a young girl she played country music covers at a truck stop. But as the last notes of the song faded, she was struck by a sudden burst of nausea. Someone had obviously dismantled the school's ventilation system in her absence. The smell of teenaged boys and girls rushing by her overwhelmed her nasal passages. Sweat, deodorant, perfume, hair spray. Some combination of motor oil and cigarettes. Yuck!

At least she made it through the morning. A surefire miracle, considering all the stares and whispers. During homeroom, she fired off a text to Rosie, thinking that might be a remedy. *Back to school today!* With a melting face emoji. Which just made her check her phone after each period just to see that her friend hadn't responded. And then there was the matter of her schoolwork, pressing down on her chest like a giant anvil. An overdue paper in English on a book she hadn't yet started. A history project on the Civil War. So when lunch period came around, there was a sense of relief. Not that she had any intention of going within a mile of the cafeteria, the scene of her recent humiliation, though at some point she'd have to go back there. Not just to eat, but to thank Carlos and Mr. Dawkins and perhaps even dreadlocks guy for helping her. Instead, she would head to the second floor and venture toward the art classroom where Rosie would be. Her goal: to smooth things over with her best friend and find out if she still had her job.

It didn't take long to find Rosie, stationed by a large wooden table in the center of the room. She wore a white sweatshirt covered with yellow lemons over lime-green pants with darker green squiggly stripes, and a matching green headband. It was one of the things she always loved about her best friend. The fact that you could always pick her out in a crowd within seconds.

Dakota came up from behind and tapped her friend on the shoulder. Rosie turned immediately, a pair of black scissors in her hand. It looked as if she'd been cutting construction paper. Likely for one of those mixed-media projects she always complained about.

"What are you doing here, D?" she asked. "Can't you see I'm in art class?"

They both knew that didn't matter. Mr. Kramer's art classroom was well-known for its absence of structure, with stragglers coming and going at all times of the day to visit with their friends or to hang out with Mr. Kramer himself.

"Can I talk to you about something?" Dakota asked.

"Talk," Rosie replied, her face a block of stone. At least she put the scissors down.

Dakota locked eyes with her friend, her insides churning. "Is there some particular reason you're ghosting me? You've barely spoken to me lately. You don't return my calls or texts. Honestly, you've been kind of a dick. Like, what did I do that was so wrong?"

Rosie widened her mouth. She appeared on the verge of laughter. "Well, the fact that you have to ask me that and call me a dick tells me everything I need to know."

Okay, so her dick statement was regrettable. Except her friend had pissed her off by not responding to her text that morning. Could she not have taken a second to respond with a thumbs-up or a heart emoji? Even a middle finger would have indicated she was worthy of a response. That being said, she should have learned how to better navigate confrontations. To avoid saying the wrong things. Perhaps there was a YouTube video for that. Confrontation 101.

The one without violence.

"I didn't mean that, Rosie," Dakota said, attempting a backtrack. "I'm sorry… and I admit that my behavior has been highly questionable. It's just that I've been through a bad time lately, and I thought you could be more understanding."

Rosie shook her head. "I've always been understanding, Dakota. But it's different this time." She paused. "I need a break. From you. From your drama."

"So… what? You don't want to be my friend anymore?"

"Friendship is supposed to be a two-way street. You might want to think about that for a while."

What did her friend mean by that? Was she canceling their relationship or laying out conditions for a reconciliation?

Dakota cleared her throat. "I'm pretty sure we can work this out."

"What difference would it make? You'll be moving to Cleveland soon."

"Actually… I have no idea if I'm moving. My mom has been wacky lately, and she won't talk about it."

"Well, you'll need to tell my mom. If you move, that is. She'll have to get a replacement."

"Oh… Does that mean I still have my job for now?"

Rosie lifted her eyebrows. "Of course."

Dakota felt a flash of optimism. Keeping her job constituted a victory of sorts, except all would be negated if she lost her friend.

"I appreciate that," Dakota said. "I really do, Rosie."

Rosie picked up the scissors and rapped them against the table. She pursed her lips and her face appeared all droopy, as if she were on the verge of tears. "I need to tell you something," she started. "Before you ended up in the hospital, I'd been fighting with my mom. She thinks I should be killing it in school, and obviously I'm not. She says I have tools to deal with my dyslexia and that I'm just lazy. That I need to work harder and spend less time painting. She even threatened to put a padlock on the shed. So I was already in a bad place before your fight. I'm not gonna lie, D. I'm still pissed at what you did. But the worst part was when you told me you would be moving. It felt like you were deserting me."

Rosie's statement startled her. Dakota had been so wrapped up in her own efforts to avoid the move, she never once thought of how her friend might feel about it. "I never intended to desert you, Rosie. Everything I did was because I didn't want to move. And sure... I made mistakes. I should have told you everything. Even the thing with Abe... I actually thought he liked me. But after I left the hospital, he never once asked how I was doing and then he ignored all of my texts. It's kind of pitiful, to be honest."

"Fine, D. I get it. You fucked up. Everyone fucks up. It just feels like sometimes you don't take me seriously. That you think you're only my charity-case friend."

"I never once thought that."

"Good. Because I'm far from perfect, and I need you sometimes. I like hanging with you, but you're my friend because you've always supported me."

"I guess I never thought I could support anyone."

"Well, you can." Rosie held her hand up then, probably to signal Mr. Kramer, who was glaring at them from across the room. "Okay, then," she continued. "I have to get back to work before Kramer has an orgasm. But here's the deal. My mom's making tamales tonight. You might as well come over."

"What kind of tamales?"

"The pork ones. Your favorite."

Dakota smiled. The corners of her mouth stretched out so wide they almost hurt. "Okay," she replied. "I can definitely support you with that."

Rosie punched her in the shoulder. "Great... now get out of here before I change my mind."

June 13-14, 2019

Chapter 20.
Wedding Rehearsal
Party Crashers

Ashley Boland had documented the upcoming events for her entire wedding weekend on Knot, an app that Rosie had clued Dakota in on, claiming her cousin Maria had used it for her big day last year.

"Did I not tell you this would be a gold mine?" Rosie boasted.

Dakota just nodded. She hated to admit her friend had hit upon something. But what could she say? They'd been racking their brains, trying to figure out ways to talk with members of the Boland and Bonardi families, when Rosie recalled Angela telling them about Ashley's upcoming shotgun wedding. Operating under the assumption that even scary bartenders with whacked-out serpent tattoos could be purveyors of accurate information, Dakota had hopped aboard the Knot site. And voilà!

On the home page was a photograph of her potential cousin Ashley with Brett Simmons, holding hands and staring into each other's eyes beside a pond with lily pads. Dakota's initial observation: Brett Simmons had won the marriage lottery. Ashley Boland was seriously hot, in an earthy, crunchy way. Wavy blond hair down past her shoulders with lighter highlights on the tips. A wide mouth, her lips highlighted by a trace of pink lipstick. Whereas Brett was a tall, somewhat athletic-looking guy, but with a mop of unruly dark hair and a long rectangular face that looked as if it been squished in some kind of medieval torture device.

"I don't see it," Rosie commented, upon closer inspection.

As it turned out, there was plenty to see on the site. Mostly logistic details, such as there being a wedding rehearsal party at the Boland house on Friday, June 13, at 6:00 p.m., to be catered by McKinnons, and the wedding itself Saturday, June 14, at St. Mark's Church in Zionsville at 4:00 p.m., followed by a reception at Tillman's. In addition, there were snapshots of the bachelorette party: girls drinking champagne at a fancy spa, all dressed in denim-colored robes except for Ashley, who wore a pink robe with *Bride* stenciled on it. As well as a registry list from which guests could purchase wedding gifts and a section called *Our Story*.

"Is it normal to register at BestBuy?" Dakota inquired.

"It is if you like your electronics," Rosie replied.

"And what's *Our Story?*"

"My cousin did that. It's like a blog that tells you how they met." Rosie smiled. "Like a love story."

Dakota winced. "Should I assume it includes Ashley's unwanted pregnancy?"

"For sure," Rosie replied, taking the bait. "And let's not forget the moment he impregnated her in the bed of his truck."

"Brett drank too much that night. He had a spot of trouble performing."

"But Ashley came to the rescue and lent him a hand."

"Now that's a love story."

The two of them bent over in fits of laughter over their manufactured version of *Our Story*, but unfortunately the actual blog included none of that. Just a bunch of boring shit. Ashley and Brett, playing in a coed soccer game. Brett inadvertently running over her. Him tending to her on the sidelines, the two of them pleased that no blood had been spilled and that there were no broken bones. Afterward they went to a bar to play darts and sing karaoke, Brett having the far superior voice. And the rest was what you might call history, ending up with Ashley and Brett being soulmates.

"So, what are you thinking, D?" Rosie said after they'd digested far too much of Ashley's Knot epic. "Wedding crashers?"

Dakota tilted her head. "Not sure about that. We'd have to get dressed up for a wedding."

"And the food sucks at Tillman's."

"I'm thinking wedding rehearsal party. Everyone we'd want to see would be there. We could knock 'em off with one visit."

And so the next day, after work, Dakota and Rosie drove to the northeasternmost section of North Zionsville, where the Bolands lived in a tan split-level on Roast Meat Hill Road. An impromptu parking lot had been set up at the northern edge of the property, with about a dozen cars already parked there in two asymmetrical rows. Rosie eased the Subaru by the far end of the second row beside a Lincoln Navigator and shut off the ignition. They exited the car. Dakota pulled at the collar of her striped baby doll tee, which she wore over khaki cargo shorts.

Rosie, on the other hand, looked super sharp in her Sampic orange floral-print beach mini with Y2K straps. Both of them had their hair brushed and nails painted: Dakota's a subtle shade of peach, Rosie's orange to match her dress. If nothing else, they would look good.

They walked around the side of the Bolands' house, commando style, instead of ringing the front doorbell and announcing their presence, where they came upon a large grassy backyard surrounded on all sides by tall trees. Country music played in the background, and there were already a dozen or so people mingling about. Some sat around one of the four circular wooden tables laid out on the lawn; others stood beside a large cooler, as if they were guarding it. A set of rectangular tables with white tablecloths had been set up. An older woman deposited a bowl of fruit salad on one of the tables, then turned to face them.

"Oh," the woman said, stepping forward, an enormous smile covering her face, her eyes fixed upon Dakota for some reason. "You must be Charlotte."

Who the fuck was Charlotte?

Dakota smiled. It appeared to be her best option.

"I'm Aunt Bea."

Bea. Beatrice. George Coleman's sister from the obituary. She'd read it again last night just to get the names straight. "Nice to meet you, Aunt Bea," she replied, the muscles around her chest tightening.

"And I'm Rosie," Rosie said with a bit too much verve. "Charlotte's friend from school."

Bea's smile seemed to be painted on, and she accentuated it by stretching the sides of her mouth out further. She had dressed to kill: a sleeveless yellow-and-blue floral dress, gold costume jewelry, and black flats. Her hair poofed up like a gray beehive. Not to mention the stratified layers of makeup. No doubt someone would need a chisel to get that shit off.

"You girls are so adorable. But young. Brett said you were going to college next year, Charlotte. For engineering."

"Charlotte's graduating early," Rosie said. "She's like a math prodigy."

"Yeah," Dakota said. "I don't like bragging about that stuff."

"There's nothing wrong with being modest," Bea implied. "But very impressive."

Was this the wrong time to bring up her history with remedial math freshman year, for which there'd been no remedy? Her recent D in algebra?

"And how was your flight?" Bea continued. "We'd heard it was delayed."

Flight. Okay. She could do this.

"About what you'd expect."

No reason to give out details. Didn't most flights suck? Turbulence. No leg room. Obnoxious passengers. Not that she'd ever been on a plane before.

"And you're all from Arizona."

"Ahhh... yeaaah," Dakota let out, sounding like air being released from a tire.

"I hear the heat there is insufferable this time of year."

"You have no idea."

"Well, it sure is nice to meet you, Charlotte. We've heard so much about you. And you too, Rosie. Unfortunately, they've put me to work here, so I can't stay to chat. But you should mingle." Bea's eyes then surveyed the lawn, perhaps scouting out the best minglers. "Hey,

Adam," she shouted out, while waving to a group of guys hanging out by the cooler.

Oh shit!

They all turned, but it was obviously Adam Boland that Aunt Bea had called out to, then waved at, beckoning him to come on over. Which he obliged, lifting a can of beer in the air to acknowledge them, but moving slowly, as if he were avoiding landmines. And you could tell he hadn't recognized her immediately. Not necessarily by the look on his face when he first saw her, which was a shade of neutral, but the way it changed as he came right up to her and their eyes locked. Perhaps it had something to do with her wearing nicer clothes than she had at Golden Bud's or having applied a dab of gel to her hair so that it didn't automatically fall across her eyes. But at that precise moment, you could almost detect the trigger going off in Adam's brain. Like someone who'd just opened a Christmas present they'd most surely return.

Bea, totally oblivious to the current state of events, fired off the introductions. "Adam, this is Charlotte... Charlotte, Adam."

For some reason Dakota repressed the urge to laugh. The whole scenario bordered on the absurd. Bea beamed as if she'd just orchestrated an overdue family reunion, while Adam wiped at his brow, looking like he might spontaneously combust.

"Charlotte just flew in from Arizona," Bea said.

"Her arms must be tired," Adam replied, all deadpan.

"Why don't you be a gracious host? I'd bet these girls could use a refreshment."

"I'd like that," Dakota answered, winking at Adam.

"Me too," Rosie added.

By then the caterers had arrived, which to be honest was excellent timing. Two guys wearing identical red polos set up aluminum chafing dishes on wire racks by the fruit salad, stuffing Sterno cans underneath. Bea abruptly apologized, then split, as if her pants were on fire. And the two of them were alone. Once more. Adam vs. Dakota. Part deux.

Dakota smiled. "You look sharp today, Adam."

He really did. Spiffy tan shorts, a Hawaiian shirt with, like, fifty colors on it, tan Docksiders. From the looks of it, he'd even trimmed his beard.

Adam shook his head. "What are you doing here?"

"Never mind that," Dakota replied. "You want to tell me who Charlotte is?"

"Brett's cousin," he said, producing a Cheshire cat grin. "I guess she's some kind of teen internet star. An influencer. Whatever that is."

"I thought she was going to school for engineering," Rosie remarked.

"Don't know. Maybe she has a lot going on. But you still haven't answered my question."

Dakota put a hand on her hip, trying to act defiant. "I don't know, Adam. What did you expect to happen when you don't accept a girl's friend request?"

"Not this."

She hit the pause button. The party had picked up. Guys in red shirts lighting Sternos, a woman with long dark hair, wearing a blue dress, barking instructions behind them. Partiers streaming through cracks in the foundation. The mood was jovial. Hugs, smiles, and laughter. She almost waved at Ashley, who looked beautiful in a multicolored peasant dress, but she seemed preoccupied with her wedding party friends. The cooler appeared to be gaining in popularity, and someone had turned up the volume of the music. One of Ashley's friends started singing. Kacey Musgraves. "Golden Hour."

Dakota swayed her hips. "I like this song."

Adam said, "You have no idea what to do right now, do you?"

Dakota shrugged. "Well… why don't we start with you introducing me to your mom?"

Adam brought the can of Bud Light up to his mouth and took a series of swigs, a lump in his throat bulging and contracting, like a beating heart, as the liquid made its way down his throat. "Ahhh," he proclaimed when he was done.

"Okay, then who's that?" Dakota asked, pointing to a woman with brown curly hair wearing a red dress. The woman held a martini glass in the air, but she was one of those people who moved their hands when they talked, and the glass kept tipping, its contents occasionally going overboard.

"Aunt Maureen."

"She looks wasted."

"Come back in an hour if you want to see wasted."

"Sounds like an invitation."

Adam shot a quick glance at Rosie. "You here for protection?"

"Hey, amigo," Rosie said, wagging a finger. "Don't you start with me."

Adam shrugged and took another sip of his beer. Perhaps he'd learned his lesson: not to mess with Rosario Peña. "Listen," he then proclaimed. "You should know something. They had a meeting about you."

"Oh yeah?" Dakota replied, not knowing if a meeting would be a good or bad thing. Leaning toward bad. "What kind of meeting?"

"Maureen came over. My mom and dad were there. Then they kicked me out. Said they had to talk about something."

"Even though you were the one that told them about me."

Adam narrowed his eyes. "What... you show up at a bar, tell me a bullshit story about my family, and you think I'm gonna keep that to myself?"

Dakota's face flushed, bad adrenaline backing up inside of her. "It's not bullshit, for your information. It's my life, okay. I'm just trying to find my father, which shouldn't be such a big deal. But apparently everyone feels the need to lie and be assholes about it."

"Seriously," Rosie said. "You'd think we killed someone."

Adam's eyes rolled upward. A surefire tell of his building exasperation. In the background, someone called out that dinner was ready, but no one seemed to be in a hurry to eat, as only a handful of partiers approached the the food tables.

"I'm sorry, Adam," Dakota admitted. "I didn't mean to imply you were an asshole, because you're not. I'm just feeling a little frustrated here. And I'm betting you're frustrated as well. They kicked you out of a meeting you should have been in on. I can't imagine you weren't curious about it."

"You must have heard something," Rosie added.

Adam appeared to appreciate the apology, and perhaps Rosie's interest. He took a deep breath, then let it out slowly. "All I know is Maureen did most of the talking.

She called you a stalker. Said we should avoid you. Then they started talking about your mom for some reason."

"What about my mom?"

"Not sure, to be honest. But I got the feeling Maureen didn't like her."

Dakota just nodded, as if she had expected this revelation, yet she couldn't deny the grievances against her mother were starting to pile up. Jenna had implied some of their classmates weren't quite buying her act, Anika lied about them being friends, while Lucinda claimed their friendship fizzled out. And now Maureen. She couldn't tell what this had to do with her father, but her mother seemed to be quite the divisive figure.

"What about your cousins?" Dakota asked. "Are they here?"

Adam's eyes wandered about. "I don't see Elaine. But Sammy is over there… by the big tree. The kid with the long hair."

Big tree. Well, that narrowed it down. Which meant it took her a while to spot Samuel Bonardi. Much younger than Adam and Ashley, either in or just out of middle school, with that middle-school awkward-boy look, somewhere between short and tall, brown hair grazing his shoulders. He wore grungy gray cargos and a black tee with some kind of logo on it. If there'd been a family memo to dress up for the party, Sammy either ignored or hadn't received it.

"Mmmm," Dakota said, "I sense a skateboarder vibe."

"The kid's a legend in his own mind."

"Good to know. And where's your mom?"

"Over by the food tables. Blue dress."

Ahhh. The woman she'd seen earlier talking to the

caterers. Definitely a person who liked being in charge. But smiling while she did it.

"Call her over," Dakota said.

Adam stuck out his chest. "No."

"Just do it, Adam. Then you can be done with me. Forever, if you want."

"Promise?"

Dakota punched him in the shoulder. More of a tap. Which he didn't seem to mind.

Christine Boland didn't appear all that stoked when her son interrupted whatever she was doing with the caterer guys, tapping her on the shoulder and saying something into her ear. Still, she turned and began walking in their direction, her dark eyes landing on Dakota upon her arrival, moving up and down, examining her. Christine was attractive in a middle-aged-mom-driving-a-minivan-in-a-TV-commercial type of way. Tall and thin. Long dark hair. A few gray streaks, which she hadn't bothered to dye out for the wedding.

"I like your necklace, Mrs. Boland," Dakota said, wanting to put the kibosh on the visual examination. "Is that a dragonfly?"

A halfway-blind person could tell it was a dragonfly. Wings, turquoise with dark blue tips. Silver rhinestones on its edges. Its tail was made up of a series of individual purplish-blue gemstones. Very cool.

"Yes, it is. My husband got it for me on our anniversary."

"Well, it looks great on you, I must say."

"Very sharp," Rosie added.

Christine smiled. "Thanks. And you must be Charlotte."

Dakota shot a quick glance at Adam, who grinned back at her. He'd definitely pulled a fast one on her. But enough with Charlotte already. She was really starting to dislike the girl.

"Nope. I'm Dakota. Dakota Lodi. And this is my friend Rosie."

Chistine's eyes suddenly widened. Her face flushed, like one of those horrified characters in a graphic novel, with bulging eyes and a contorted face accompanied by a blank speech bubble. She locked eyes with her son, flashing a look of disapproval. "Why don't you leave us alone?" she snapped.

Adam didn't seem all that disappointed in his sudden dismissal. The corners of his mouth peeked out from the confines of his beard, and he offered an over-and-out wave before saying, "See ya later."

"What do you want from us?" Christine then asked, getting right down to it, her face having morphed into a block of granite.

"My mom told me—"

"I know what your mom told you. What does that have to do with me? With us. And what made you think you could show up to our party with a guest, uninvited?"

"I'm sorry about showing up at your party, Mrs. Boland. It was rude of me. And if you want me to leave now, I will. I just thought if you had a minute or two, you might be able to help me."

"I don't see how."

"One of your brothers got my mom pregnant. Is it so crazy to think you might know something about that?"

"Not sure where you got that information."

"I have my sources."

Christine firmed her mouth. "Do you have siblings, Dakota?"

"No."

"Well, I'm the oldest. Seven years older than Jimmy Ray. I graduated from college when he was a high school freshman. I barely knew your mother. And I certainly wouldn't know who she slept with."

Christine had a point about the seven years. But if Jimmy Ray and her mother were besties for as long as Lucinda claimed, then Christine should have been more aware of them. And what about her mother living in Greg's house around that time? Would she have been totally oblivious to their relationship? Not likely. Christine was hiding something. They all were.

"What about Maureen, then? Was she closer in age to Jimmy and Greg?"

Christine cracked a smile. "I'd say they were very close. In fact, she and Greg were twins." She intertwined two of her fingers.

"Then what you're saying is, Maureen would know more about this. I should talk to her."

Christine shook her head. "I wouldn't recommend that. Maureen wasn't a fan of your mother. Didn't trust her for some reason. Now... me, I don't know anything about that. And I don't want to judge you, Dakota. For all I know, you might be a nice girl. And you have some guts coming here, I'll admit that. But I can't help you."

"Fine," Dakota said, her eyes drifting downward, focusing on her shoes. A wave of dense air came up through her chest, pressing against her throat.

"You need to leave," Christine then added, putting a ribbon on it. "Your mother is the person you should be talking to. Not us. But if you're thirsty, you can help yourself to some water over there before you go. Okay?"

Dakota forced a smile, as if it could be okay, as if the consolation prize of a lousy cup of water had been what she'd wanted all along.

After Christine's departure, she surveyed the scene. Never having been unceremoniously tossed from a wedding rehearsal party before, she didn't exactly know what to do next. She was pretty damn sure you weren't supposed to cry about it. Perhaps you'd be expected to exit immediately with your head down and tail tucked between your legs. But Christine had mentioned she could get a drink of water.

"We should get some water," Dakota said, an idea suddenly taking flight in her brain. In the distance, Sammy Boland strutted toward the water station, like a middle school mafia chieftain, if there were such a thing. Hands gently swinging, head held up high.

Rosie tapped her on the shoulder. "This place is trouble, D. We should leave."

"I have one more thing I need to do on my own. You should go back to the car and wait. If there's a problem, I'll call."

"You're making me nervous. Are you sure you know what you're doing?"

Dakota lied. Said that she did.

Once her friend had left, Dakota sauntered over to the food table, where she discovered a tray of corn bread. As the rehearsal party revelers made their way through the food line, she snuck in through the back side and grabbed one. She took a bite out of it, ignoring the dirty looks from the patrons, then ambled over to a large glass urn filled up with water and a zillion slices of cucumber. It seemed like a waste of perfectly good cucumbers, but she needed the water to wash down the mediocre corn bread, which she imagined to be like biting into a dried-up sandcastle. Nothing like Manuel's orgasmic version, moist, sweet, inflected with bits of jalapeño. And wouldn't you know it, Sammy was there as well, staring in her direction as she approached.

"How's it going, Sammy?" she said, trying to get the jump on him.

"It's all good," he replied.

"I'm Dakota."

"Do I know you?"

Dakota had used his first name right off the bat, figuring it might faze him, but she could tell it hadn't. Perhaps Sammy was used to not recognizing people who knew his name. And he grinned as if this particular dynamic pleased him, assuming a buffalo stance, hands stuffed in his pockets, revealing the logo on his shirt: a crude version of a spaceship above some random geometric patterns that looked like trees. The spaceship was either taking off or landing. You couldn't actually tell.

"Don't think so," Dakota replied. "But I will say you do look familiar. Maybe you saw me at the Sunrise Diner, where I work."

Sammy bounced on his toes. "Never been."

"Then I'm guessing you go to Zionsville High?"

"I'll be a freshman this year."

"Wow... so you're, like, fourteen. You definitely look older."

"Thanks."

"I'll be a junior, so I'll probably run into you."

"Cool. Are you, like, one of Brett's relatives?"

"Honestly, Sammy, I pretty much crashed this gig. But tell me this. What's it like being with a bunch of relatives and your cousin's friends, and they're all getting wasted and you can't join them?"

Sammy didn't hesitate. "It sucks, actually."

"So if I told you I had some pot that would knock you on your ass… that might be something you'd be interested in?"

Sammy played it cool. Not responding immediately. And you could tell he wasn't about to be the kid acting all eager about some older chick coming on to him at his cousin's wedding reception party.

Dakota winked at him, then followed that up with what she hoped to be a seductive smile. She could be quite the temptress where fourteen-year-old guys were concerned.

Eventually, Sammy relented, and Dakota followed him off to the side of the yard, where a dirt path between the Boland and Bonardi houses led into the woods and down a hill lined with boulders, which you had to navigate carefully until you came upon a small pond. By the water, an old wooden bench stood next to a crude firepit outlined with rocks. Inside the pit were burnt logs, charred glass bottles, and on the perimeter, a presumed-to-be-empty box of Cheez-Its.

"This place is seriously lit, Sammy," Dakota said. Ordinarily she would not have used the word *lit* in a sentence, but it felt like something a delinquent fourteen-year-old boy might appreciate.

"Party central," Sammy replied, pumping a fist.

Dakota smiled, and they both sat down on the bench, gazing out at the still water. At the far end of the pond, two ducks floated aimlessly between lily pads, and a red-winged blackbird landed on a cattail.

She pulled out the joint from the pocket of her tan pants, lit it, then cupped her hands to shelter it from the wind. She took a single puff herself before passing it on to Sammy, who engaged in a succession of multiple hits, inhaling, then holding it in each time for what seemed like minutes before letting out a wisp of smoke.

"I gather you like this," Dakota said.

Sammy laughed, more like a cackle. Which made the blackbird take off. "I'm getting seriously torched."

Dakota smiled while quickly organizing her thoughts. Christine had told her to leave after drinking some water, and she'd been fairly certain some of the wedding party revelers had seen her leave with Sammy. For all she knew, they could come rumbling down the path and bust them at any second.

So, Sammy," she started. "I have a proposition I'd like to run by you."

"Oh yeah?" he replied. "What's that?"

"First of all, and this is going to sound crazy, there's a possibility that your uncle Jimmy Ray is my father. Which would make you my cousin."

Sammy's eyes narrowed. "That's not a proposition. That's just some stuff you made up."

"It's what my mom told me. She said he died when I was two."

"Well, right there I know you're fucking with me. Because then I would have talked to a dead person."

Dakota felt a jolt of electricity. Her toes curled, and she drummed her fingers against her knee. "What are you saying, Sammy? You talked to him? You talked to Jimmy Ray?"

"I wouldn't say we talked. He sat across from me. At

Applebee's."

"When was this?"

"Labor Day weekend. Last year. In Illinois."

Dakota bounced on the wooden bench, knees knocking, hands shaking. This was it. Wasn't it? What she'd been looking for. What she'd always wanted. And sure, she'd always had her suspicions, except hearing it in person made it real.

Finally, something true.

Labor Day.

Applebee's.

Illinois.

Her mother's lies.

"Holy fuck, Sammy," she shouted out. "Hoooly fuck! You have no idea what this means. You talked to Jimmy. Jimmy Ray's alive."

"No shit," Sammy said, appearing alarmed by her sudden display of emotion. "But I think you should calm down. You're, like, freaking me out here."

Dakota stood up. "I can't calm down." She kicked at a rock. "I can't. Illinois, you said. Right? He lives in Illinois."

"Don't know about that. I heard he's got a cabin in the woods somewhere. Could be anywhere. Like, he's a hermit or something. That's why they picked a place halfway between us to meet."

"Who's they?"

"Huh?"

"You said they. They picked a place."

"Everyone. The whole family. Except for my mom."

"Why didn't your mom go?"

At that precise moment, Dakota could see the mistrust starting to fester in Samuel Boland, his nose wrinkling up, eyes turning into tiny slits. Her question had struck a nerve.

"I'm not doing this," Sammy protested.

Dakota ignored him. "Was your mom angry with Jimmy about something?"

He shrugged.

"Are you afraid your mom will find out about this?" she asked. "Because she won't. Okay? I can keep a secret."

Sammy sighed. "Mom and Christine had a fight. It was after the cops came."

The cops? Could this have something to do with the reopened case that Alice had mentioned? If that were true, then it would be reasonable to assume that certain members of the Coleman family would have been interrogated. But why would Maureen not go with the rest of the Colemans, who traveled hundreds of miles to share a meal with her hermit brother?

"What were they fighting about?" Dakota asked.

Sammy picked up a rock and tossed it in the pond. "You should stop asking me questions."

Dakota put the brakes on. She'd come up against a brick wall and needed to keep her eye on the ultimate prize. She could push aside potential reasons for the Coleman family feud in exchange for finding a way to contact Jimmy Ray. If she were successful in that endeavor, if she could find some way to meet up with him, would anything else really matter?

"Fine," she said. "Give me your phone."

"I'm not giving you my phone."

"Listen to me, Sammy. I'm the one that grew up without a father here, okay? All I'm asking for here is a little help. Just get me Jimmy Ray's phone number. Or his address. Then I'll do the rest."

"How am I supposed to do that?"

Dakota pressed her toes into the dirt and rolled her eyes. Were all conversations with fourteen-year-old boys this frustrating? "I don't know. Talk to Adam or Ashley. Maybe your father or grandmother. Figure it out. Now, take out your phone. I'm gonna give you my number."

"This is fucked up," Sammy claimed, his head slowly moving from side to side as he removed a phone from his back pocket. He held on to it for what seemed like forever. Making her sweat. Wrapping his fingers around it. Flipping it over a few times... before handing it over.

November 29, 2018

Chapter 21.
Turkey Day

Four weeks until D-Day, and her mother still hadn't announced her moving decision, which was wrong on so many levels. How was she supposed to move on with her life with so much such uncertainty? Would she have to give her notice at work? Was there enough time to make things better with her best friend? Though what she really wanted was to stay in Zionsville for the unseeable future. Had she not made that clear?

And so it had come to this. Turkey day. Dakota, sitting at the kitchen table, pondering her next move, while looking on with a sense of bewilderment at the scene before her. Prior to that moment, she would have stated with a high degree of confidence that there was as much chance as spotting a Galapagos land iguana on their living room couch as there was Victoria Lodi and Gina Barato cooking in the same kitchen together. Yet there they were. A previously frozen turkey procured from the fire department giveaway was cooling on a cutting board, all crispy and brown. A steaming pot of Stove Top stuffing. A recently opened can of cranberry sauce.

"I'm not quite the Iron Chef," her mother declared

as she produced a knife the size of her right arm. Dakota closed her eyes as her mother began to carve.

Meanwhile, Gina had finished stirring the gravy, which she then poured into a porcelain bowl. "Outta my fucking way," she said as she bumped Victoria aside and opened the oven to take out the sweet potatoes. Presumably they'd been coated with some kind of miracle bourbon sauce, which might have explained why the kitchen appeared as if it had been ransacked by a marauding band of raiders: a half stick of butter beside a bag of brown sugar next to a bottle of apple cider, a whisk dripping viscous brown liquid all over the counter, not to mention a pint of bourbon and a few beer cans randomly dispersed.

Eventually, they all made their way to the kitchen table, where the feast had been set out. But before they could dig in, Gina held her hand up. "I'd like to say a prayer first."

She'd never pegged Gina as the religious type, except Thanksgiving was a special occasion, and maybe that was how they rolled in Texas.

Gina bowed her head. "Oh, Lord. We thank you for this bounty you've given us on this day of Thanksgiving. May you look over and protect all of us. Especially little Dakota here, who has to put up with her mother and her crazy friend. Amen."

Then came laughter, though not from her, and the sound of clinking glasses. Dakota, holding out her water, Gina and her mother with glasses of bourbon. Only a small amount had been used for the actual sauce. and there was no point in wasting the rest of God's bounty. Because if he (or she) had created turkey, gravy, and stuffing, then he (or she) had likely created bourbon as well. Perhaps on the eighth day, when no one was looking.

Dakota got down to business. She wasn't about to let uncertainty cancel out her hunger. She scooped up some stuffing with her fork and stabbed at a piece of turkey drenched with gravy, making a combo of sorts and cramming it into her mouth. "This is great," she said while chewing. Next, she tried the sweet potatoes, which honestly were quite amazing. "Wow, Mom. Where'd you get this sauce?"

"Your grandmother used to make this," her mother answered.

"So you got it from her?"

"Yep. We exchange recipes all the time."

Her mother wore her poker face, but Dakota sensed a trace of sarcasm. Neither of them had seen Grandma Lucinda for almost ten years, and it seemed unlikely that their feud had been put to rest by sharing a bourbon sauce recipe.

"Well, at least we didn't have to go to Aunt Evelyn's this year."

Her mother paused, her glass of bourbon suspended in midair, her eyes narrowing. "What are you up to, peanut?"

Dakota flinched. Her mother should start a mind-reading business. "I was stating a fact. You know... since we've gone there for, like, what... the last five years. And sure, I don't like it there because Cousin Benny's basically a pedophile, and Evelyn doesn't like me, but it seems strange... you know... one month before we're supposed to live there."

"First of all, Benny's not a pedophile. You saw him coming out of the shower once."

"Well, okay. That's your story. It's just that I've been wondering what was going on, because you haven't said anything about if we're moving or not, and I'd like to know because I would have to give notice at the diner."

Dakota had said what she wanted to say, but her mother didn't respond immediately. Instead, she exchanged looks with Gina, some kind of secret communication thing they had going on, which was like nails on a blackboard. "I wouldn't worry about giving notice," she finally said. "I'm pretty sure the fate of the Sunrise Diner doesn't depend on you."

"Right, Mom. But there's such a thing as common courtesy."

"If I were you, I'd make the assumption we're going. But I've got a few things I'm working on. So there's that."

"Things? What things? Let me guess. You're robbing a bank. No, that's not it. You're selling a kidney? No biggie. You've got two of them, Mom."

"How much can you get for a kidney?" Gina asked, as if it was a viable consideration.

Her mother leaned forward, shortening the space between them. "Listen to me, Dakota, and listen hard. I'm the adult, and you're the kid. You don't get to make the decisions in this family."

Dakota stood up then. "Yeah," she said, pushing her half-finished plate into the center of the table. "Well, that's pretty fucking obvious."

She was off then, into her room, where she launched herself like a projectile onto her bed. Her mother was like a CIA operative when it came to keeping secrets, and so there was no sense going back to that well. Nevertheless, if they were, in fact, moving to Cleveland, wouldn't Evelyn have known by now? She'd have to organize her house and get rooms ready for them. Inform Cousin Benny that his crazy cousin Dakota would be moving in, and her husband, who'd have to get the paperwork ready for her mother's job at the car dealership. Which meant something else was going on. Something she'd have to get to the bottom of.

She got off the bed. She slipped her phone into her back pocket and put on her Baja hoodie. Out in the hallway, the two women were on the couch. Gina was watching football while her mother thumbed through an old *People* magazine.

"I'm going for a walk," Dakota said to no one in particular. "I'll be back for pie."

Then she was out the door, strolling down one of the neighborhood dirt paths before veering onto an unmarked trail in the surrounding woods. She tried her best to relax, listening to Beach House and Weyes Blood from her "Psychodrome" playlist, a supercool collection of trippy pop music she deemed to be in sync with the natural world. But at that moment, the trees appeared ominous and creepy, as if they could fall down and crush her at any second. She sat down against a large pine. She ripped off her headphones. She zipped up her coat and steadied herself. She took out her phone and dialed up Aunt Evelyn.

June 18–21, 2019

Chapter 22.
Did Not See
That One Coming

The text message came over on Tuesday morning, from an unknown number. It was not the one she expected or wanted.

Those who keep digging make their own grave.

What the hell did that mean? Her initial thought: perhaps someone had played a practical joke on her. Rosie came to mind, but the perfectly spelled message nixed that theory. She could have used the voice control feature, except from what she'd observed of Rosie over the years, her best friend could barely function that time of the day, let alone speak in a complete sentence. Maybe she'd underestimated Adam's devious nature and he'd purchased a burner phone for the sole purpose of torturing her. Or else Sammy the Shark had something to do with it. Anika would be the only other person that possessed her phone number, but she'd spoken to her mother's old friend weeks ago. Under what circumstances would Anika wake up after all that time and decide to threaten her?

At the diner, she found Rosie talking to Manuel and Carlos by the coffee station. They all turned their respective heads when she came in. Manuel shot off a finger gun in her direction, whereas Carlos gave her a I-don't-give-a-damn nod. In the background she could hear voices in the kitchen and the music starting up. Dakota made a subtle motion with her head, and Rosie rushed on over. She opened the message app on her phone and showed the text to her friend.

"What the fuck," Rosie said, a look of astonishment sweeping across her face. "This is not good."

"You're telling me," Dakota replied.

"Who sent this?"

"I didn't recognize the number. But Adam, Sammy, and Anika are the only ones I gave my number to."

Rosie scrunched up her face. "Mmmm. You might want to expand that list. Who's to say Anika didn't give your number to Albert—or Katie, for that matter? Sammy could have given it to his mother. And let's not forget about Helen and Stanley. You gave your contact info to them, not Anika."

Dakota let out a fake laugh. "Somehow I can't picture Helen Powers drinking her morning coffee and deciding to threaten me. But yeah. You make a pretty good point."

"I'm just saying. We should avoid tunnel vision."

Dakota tapped at her thigh with a nervous energy. She felt like a juggler with too many balls in the air. "I just wanted to find my father. I honestly don't give a crap about solving a murder."

"I get it, D. But what if it's all related? Like, you have to open one door just to get to the other door. And that's where you find him."

Everything related. Doors opening. Doors closing. Answers leading to more questions. It was enough to turn her insides all jiggly. Not that it stopped her from checking her phone a half dozen times throughout the day, hoping for more messages that never came, as if there might be one that said *never mind* or *just kidding*. Which led her to the assumption that the *keep digging* part of the message had to do with the murder. She concluded that Adam and Sammy were likely too young to know much about it and that Christine didn't seem like the kind of person to threaten a sixteen-year-old girl. She knew nothing about Ashley or any of the other Colemans, except for Maureen, who perhaps sent the message in a drunken stupor and wouldn't remember sending it. It had been interesting that Rosie mentioned Albert and Katie. She still had questions concerning her fight with Katie and what her motivations had been, yet she couldn't fathom what that had to do with the murder, since she would have been three years old at the time. Whereas Albert had shown up on the arrest report for the Muncy's Tavern fight. Then again, why would they threaten her? Could the act of just bringing up her mother and asking about her father have triggered the threats? Perhaps her mother knew something about the murders. What if she or her father had actually been involved, or possessed information that might implicate someone else who had no problems threatening a sixteen-year-old girl? Not to mention it would be a decent excuse for a lying mother to protect her daughter.

At least Dakota got through the early morning without a panic attack, which in some ways constituted a moral victory. But all of that changed when she heard a disturbance in the rear of the diner. She went back to the kitchen, carrying a stack of plates, and observed an unusual scene. Mario had Carlos in a headlock.

She tiptoed through broken pieces of porcelain, then gingerly laid the plates beside the sink. Carlos, in an attempt to wrangle himself free from his uncle, went down on one knee and produced a strange groaning sound.

Dakota rapped Mario on the shoulder. "What are you doing?"

"Mind your own business," he replied, not loosening the grip on his nephew.

Dakota hit him again. This time harder. "Get up."

Mario released his hold and sneered. "You looking for a fight, chiquita?"

"I was just thinking you wouldn't want Mrs. Peña to find out about this."

Mario straightened and flexed his arms. No doubt he ruled over the kitchen domain, but at the same time, everyone knew who the boss of the diner was. "What are you looking at?" he said to Manuel, who'd just come over from across the room.

Manuel put two hands up in a show of surrender, then grabbed the dust broom and pan. "I'll take care of this," he said to Dakota, and the two of them exchanged glances.

Out in the dining room, Mrs. Peña chatted up some customers. It would be best if she didn't know about this, and so quickly disposing of the evidence seemed like the best path forward. In the meantime, Carlos had taken advantage of the opportunity to run for his life and was nowhere to be seen. Whereas Mario just let out a growling noise and lumbered back to the grill.

"I'm gonna talk to him," Dakota said to Manuel.

He dumped the shards of porcelain into the waste barrel and shook his head. "I wouldn't do that if I were you."

But by then she was gone.

At the grill, Mario hacked away at a mound of hash browns with his giant spatula, as if he were clearing brush with a machete.

Dakota came up from behind him, keeping her distance. "What's happening, Mario?"

"Leave me alone," he snarled.

Dakota moved closer. "I'm not afraid of you." Yet she couldn't deny a drop of fear. Mario acting like a dick at the diner before wasn't exactly news, but never once had he resorted to physical violence.

Mario turned. The hard line of his mouth opened slightly. "Go back to work, Dakota."

"Not until you tell me what's going on."

"Nothing's going on."

"You just attacked your nephew. I'd say that's something."

He glared. "It's not your business."

"Well, I'm making it my business. As an employee of the Sunrise Diner, I should be allowed to exist in a violence-free workplace. It's a rule. Which you just violated."

"Are you serious?" Mario laughed mockingly.

Dakota nodded. "I don't get it, Mario. When I started working here, I sucked big-time just like Carlos. I broke plates, but you just yelled at me and gave me dirty looks."

"You're a girl. I don't fight girls."

"Now you're just making excuses."

He scratched at his head, perhaps hoping Dakota would go away. Which she didn't. "Don't get me wrong," he said. "I love my nephew. But he's a spoiled brat. You fucked up when you started working here, but I could tell that you cared. That's the difference. Carlos only cares about Carlos."

Mario's personality analysis startled her in some respects. She couldn't deny Carlos had a slice of I'm-too-good-for-this-place attitude, and most likely he'd said something snarky to his uncle that triggered his anger. Yet at the same time, Carlos had once saved her life, not something a person who only cared about himself would do. Though when she'd thanked him in the cafeteria, weeks after her fight with Katie, he'd just shrugged and said, "No problem," as if rescuing a fifteen-year-old girl was equivalent to cleaning his room.

Dakota sauntered back to the dishwashing station. She hadn't exactly resolved the problem between Carlos and his uncle, nevertheless, the situation had been defused for the time being. Except, Carlos was still AWOL.

"Where is he?" she asked Manuel.

He dropped a few slices of bread into the toaster. "The boy wonder?" he said. "Probably out the back alley."

A sudden thought struck her then. That if Carlos quit, it would jeopardize her new promotion, since there'd be no guarantee Mrs. Peña would hire a replacement dishwasher. And she liked her new job. Not just the increase in pay, but the fact that she got to interact with customers and that by the end of the day her T-shirt wasn't saturated with sweat from working in a hot kitchen all day. Carlos's undeniable hotness aside, she wasn't about to let him ruin that for her.

Dakota found Carlos hanging out by the dumpster in the back alley. The place reeked of rotting garbage. "You gonna sulk all day?" she said to him, swatting away a swarm of flies.

"He tried to kill me," Carlos replied.

"You're exaggerating. I've been here almost a year now, and Mario has yet to kill anyone."

He pointed a finger. "Even a serial killer starts someday."

"He's your uncle, Carlos. He's not going to hurt you."

"But he's a different person here."

"Point taken. But if you go back, then you send a message that you're not afraid."

Carlos let out a chuckle. He was obviously terrified of his uncle.

Dakota continued. "Do you think you're the only one to break a plate in this place? When I started working here, I broke more plates than there were plates."

"That's not possible."

"You need to open your mind, Carlos. I honestly think your uncle just wants you to try harder. He wants you to care."

He huffed. "You don't know shit about my uncle or what he wants."

The comment stung. Though, what did she really know about Mario other than he was a talented chef and a tyrant in the kitchen? Rosie had once mentioned him having a wife and two kids. Perhaps Carlos was right and Mario existed as a completely different person away from the diner. Maybe he took his kids to swimming lessons and read them bedtime stories at night.

"Let me ask you this," Dakota started. "You play soccer. And from what I hear, you're good at it."

Carlos stuck his chest out. "I'm very good."

At being obnoxious too.

"So hear me out. I'm guessing that to be good at soccer you have to work hard. Like, you probably work out and have to do a shitload of running. Right? And you try hard at practice because if you don't, your coach yells at you. And sure... maybe he doesn't assault you. That wouldn't be cool and he'd probably get fired. But you know what I'm saying."

"I don't, actually."

"That we can't pick and choose when we try at something. Because you never know when you might miss an opportunity because you blew something off."

Carlos tilted his head slightly, and she wondered if he could tell that she was full of shit. Not to mention a hypocrite. She certainly worked her ass off at the diner, and compiling all of her Spotify playlists required some diligence, but when it came to school, she hadn't exactly reached the top of the effort meter. Or the middle, for that matter. Still, she smiled at Carlos, sending him a telepathic message. Like what if *she* were the opportunity he could be missing?

He sighed and leaned against the dumpster.

Dakota stared at the small indentation on his upper lip, and despite her current opinion of him, of being a lazy, conceited dickhead, she had the sudden urge to kiss him on the mouth. Push him right up against the dumpster. Flies be damned.

"Let's go," she said to him instead, beckoning with a wave of her hand.

"I'm not sure about this," Carlos said, but then he followed Dakota back into the kitchen.

Afterward, something between them flipped. She couldn't delineate the precise moment it happened, or how it happened. Only that her intuition told her it had. Perhaps it had something to do with the words of inspiration she'd delivered out by the dumpster. Though it wasn't as if they spoke the rest of the day. And even once the workday ended, as she and Rosie slumped down on chairs, exhausted, sipping their iced coffees, chomping at lemon squares, Carlos had briskly walked past them, with barely any acknowledgment. "Later" was all he said. But then she felt it. A tap on her shoulder as he walked on by.

She turned, which Rosie noticed.

"What are you looking at?" Rosie asked, likely already knowing.

"Nothing," Dakota replied, except she'd caught a glimpse of Carlos's ass and noticed the way his hips and shoulders moved in unison, almost like a cheetah. It was then that she felt the primal urge rise up within her. After identifying what she thought it might be, she tried tamping it down. But it just wouldn't stick.

The next day, Dakota carried a stack of plates that weighed more than she did back to the kitchen.

"Hey, Carlos," she said in a somewhat flirtatious manner. "I brought you a present."

Carlos wiped sweat off his forehead, but a few stubborn hairs remained, plastered to his head. "How very thoughtful of you, Dakota," he replied, the corners of his mouth turning up ever so slightly.

On Wednesday afternoon, a crack in the conversation dam appeared. Dakota in the kitchen again. She'd procured a couple of dry towels from the storage room out back and tossed one of them to Carlos, who by then looked as if he'd come out of the rain.

"I won't say anything about the heat if you don't," Dakota remarked, using one of the towels to wipe at her brow.

"Sounds like a deal," he replied, using the towel to dry off his head, then in sequence his arms, neck, and the back of his shoulders.

"You need another towel, Carlos?"

"Nah, I'm good… but I do have a question I've been wanting to ask you."

Dakota raised an eyebrow.

"It's kind of personal though."

"Oh…personal. Okay. Why not?"

"Is it true your mother's in prison?"

The question startled her. "Where'd you hear that?"

"Manuel told me. He said you were going through some bad stuff and that if I wasn't nice to you, he'd fuck me up. Those were his exact words. The fuck-me-up part."

Didn't sound like Manuel. But why would Carlos make that up?

"Yeah. It's true. She's in the Ohio State Reformatory for four years."

"Wow. Sorry about that, Dakota. That's, like, really tough."

She just shrugged. What more could she say?

"And I heard you don't know your father," he continued. "I mean, I overheard. You and Rosie, that is."

"So you were eavesdropping," Dakota said, pressing her lips together, trying to act as if it pissed her off.

"Well… yes… I admit it. I'm an eavesdropper. Do it all the time, actually."

Dakota recognized her advantage. "Here's the deal, Carlos," she started. "One, you're correct about my father. And two, I'm willing to forgive you for your transgression. But only if you tell me something about yourself. Something that surprises me though. Not like… ohhh… 'I really like Taylor Swift.'"

"I do like Taylor Swift."

"Everyone likes Taylor Swift. It's too common."

"So this is like a game?"

Dakota smiled. "Not for me, it isn't."

"I like math," Carlos blurted out. "And I'm taking AP Calculus next year."

"Not bad," she replied. She certainly hadn't pegged him as a math geek.

"And you have interesting eyes. That's not surprising, other than I just said it."

Interesting eyes. Not pretty ones.

"Honestly, Carlos," she said, "I'm not all that interesting."

On Thursday, they reversed roles and Carlos started up with the game, asking her to reveal something surprising about herself. "And don't give me any bullshit," he instructed her. "Like you love glitter or you played with Barbies as a kid."

Dakota touched his arm and laughed. "I'm gonna say no to the glitter, but what if I undressed the Barbies, then separated all the body parts and stored them in plastic bags?"

"Are we talking separate bags or just one?"

"Multiple bags."

"That's a little disturbing, then. Why don't you tell me something else?"

"Okay. How 'bout this one. Theoretically speaking, if you were in a poker game with me, I would take all of your money. There's no doubt. I mean, you'd be destitute. Maybe even homeless. I might even feel sorry for you then."

"Mmmm. We might have to test that out sometime."

"I wouldn't recommend that. Your turn."

Carlos didn't hesitate. "My dad wants me to go for a college scholarship, and he thinks I'm going to get one because of soccer. But the thing is, I don't like soccer that much, and I don't want to play in college. I'd rather go for engineering. I even thought about joining the robotics team at school."

"You should do what you want, Carlos. Otherwise you won't be happy."

"It's not that simple. I've got good grades, but what if that isn't enough to get a scholarship? My dad's always telling me how expensive college is. And he's been invested in my soccer life since I was a little kid."

Dakota smiled, wanting to be sympathetic, but she had a hard time relating to his plight. She knew less than nothing about disappointing fathers, college, and what it took to pay for it or get there. And she sure wasn't ready to tell him about her own shitty grades and the fact that even the act of applying to colleges, for her, would be equivalent to booking a trip to Neptune.

"You'll figure it out," she said to him instead. "But what you told me is super geeky, Carlos. Not sure if I can be seen with you anymore."

On Friday, they intentionally bumped into each other a few times. Grazing hips, bumping shoulders. Acting as if it were accidental. Dakota, coming up from behind him and playing that juvenile elementary-school trick where you tap someone on the shoulder and make them look in the opposite direction from where you're standing.

"Real mature," Carlos said to her.

Dakota's smile widened so much that it hurt, and a flash of heat radiated up and down her arms.

"Just so you know it, Carlos," she said, "I have a library card and I use it."

"I played Dungeons and Dragons last year," he admitted. "And I actually liked it."

"I'm really into music. I've got a dozen playlists with, like, a thousand songs. And I'm pretty sure you've never heard of most of them."

"Sometimes… when I'm alone at night… I listen to K-pop."

"What are you doing?" Manuel said to her later that afternoon, after she'd hip-checked Carlos against the sink.

"I'm working," Dakota responded. "What are you doing?"

"You don't think everyone sees it? You and the boy wonder."

"Don't know what you're talking about."

Manuel wagged a finger at her. "The guy's a player. You need to be careful."

"Maybe I'm a player too," Dakota said, feigning defiance. "Maybe he's the one that should be careful."

"You may be lots of things, Dakota," Manuel said with a smirk. "A player ain't one of them."

It was around closing time on Friday when the woman strolled into the diner. Dakota had been minding her own business, wiping down a table next to the only remaining customers, an older couple nursing cups of coffee by the window. The smell of Mario's pork tamales rested in the kitchen, creating an additional distraction, making her stomach rumble. Not to mention all of her interactions with Carlos during the week still buzzing around her head. Though at some point, she heard the footsteps. Even raised her head slightly to catch a glimpse of her. Short and stocky. Black skirt and a white blouse. Very businesslike.

"I'm sorry," Dakota said to her, "but we're closing."

"You're Dakota Lodi." The woman scowled.

It wasn't a question.

Dakota clenched. "Well, yes. That would be me."

"I'm Maureen Bonardi. You were at our wedding party reception the other night."

It hit her then. Bonardi. Sammy's mom. Greg Coleman's twin sister. At the party, she'd only seen Maureen from a distance. She seemed to recall a red dress and a mop of curly black hair. But this woman's hair had been straightened out, making her wonder if the curls had been manufactured just for the party.

"Can I help you?" Dakota asked, although Maureen Bonardi didn't look like she'd come to the Sunrise Diner for assistance. Her buzzard eyes fixed upon her as she wrinkled her pointy nose.

"You did drugs with my son."

Dakota felt her skin prickle, a weight suddenly pressed up against her chest. "I don't know what you're talking about."

Maureen smirked. "We both know that you do. But maybe you think it's funny, preying on a fourteen-year-old like that."

Dakota forced a laugh. "I hardly preyed on him."

Maureen pursed her lips. It appeared as if she might bite off the bottom one. "I can see now. The apple doesn't fall far from the tree."

"What do you mean by that?"

"I knew your mother. Sad to say, you might be a useless piece of shit just like she was."

Dakota took a step forward. She smelled alcohol on Maureen's breath. "You don't get to talk about my mother that way."

"My son left the party with you and came back smelling like pot. Are you telling me you had nothing to do with that?"

"I didn't tell you anything."

So, Sammy the Shark had morphed into Sammy the Rat. She should have known. In the future, she'd think twice before trusting a fourteen-year-old.

Maureen continued. "I guess I should believe the daughter of a lowlife whore instead of my son."

"You should probably leave now. I have work to do. And like I said, we're closing."

"I'm not going anywhere. And I didn't come here to be disrespected."

"Well, since I'm a useless piece of shit, maybe you should worry more about your son than me. Your son is quite the pothead, in case you didn't know it. Sad to say, that has nothing to do with me."

Maureen's hand came up from her hip and slapped Dakota across her cheek.

"What the fuck," Dakota cried out.

The rest of the diner sprang to life in choreographed movement. The old couple stood up from their seats. Mario and Manuel stared out through the opening in the kitchen, and Rosie, who had been cleaning up by the coffeepots, lifted her head. Suddenly, Mrs. Peña emerged, and as Maureen cocked her hand, perhaps to give it one more go, she moved quickly to step in front of Dakota.

Maureen appeared startled by Mrs. Peña's sudden presence but stood her ground. "This is none of your business."

Mrs. Peña smiled. "You make it my business when you assault a worker in my diner."

"This is between me and little miss slut face over there."

"I can call the police, if you'd like. I bet they could resolve this."

Maureen glared at Dakota. "I'm not done with you."

Dakota returned the glare. "There's something seriously wrong with all of you," she started, "but if you all went to therapy together, I bet you could get the fucked-up-family group rate."

Mrs. Peña looked at Dakota and shook her head.

Maureen said, "If I find out you talked to my son again, I'll come after you."

"And what," Dakota replied, "you gonna sucker punch me again?"

Mrs. Peña put her hand up. "Dakota."

Dakota let out a snarl under her breath and stamped her foot. Maureen stood there, perhaps pondering her options.

Mrs. Peña took another step forward. "You just hit a sixteen-year-old girl. And then you felt the need to insult her as well. So I'll let you know this, so that you can make a wise decision. Dakota is part of our family here, and there's more of us than you."

Maureen examined Mrs. Peña with a bewildered expression, and for a second it seemed as if the two of them might duke it out in the dining room. And when Maureen clenched her fist and tapped it gently against her thigh a few times, Dakota could have sworn it was about to happen. When suddenly, you could tell something changed in Maureen's calculation. Something that perhaps told her that a fight between two middle-aged women in a diner might not end well for her. Especially once you considered the scene: Mario standing next to Benny by the grill, while making an obvious demonstration of sharpening his largest knife; Manuel, coming up next to Mrs. Peña, folding his arms; and Rosie and Carlos right behind in formation. All Maureen could do was shake her head and make one last *hmph* noise. Then she turned around and stomped out, but not before shooting one last glance at Dakota, parting her mouth slightly, moving her lips, as if to let Dakota know she'd be thinking about her.

November 29, 2018

Chapter 23.
Ghosts and Memories

There was always something about Aunt Evelyn's voice that surprised Dakota. Two years older and two inches taller than her mother, she had a mop of curly brown hair and big dark eyes that made her appear young and attractive. Until she opened her mouth and you thought you could be talking to a grizzled sailor that swigged grain alcohol and smoked two packs a day. Not that Evelyn did either. Still, when her aunt answered the phone and offered a simple "Hello," there was a sense that she'd dialed the wrong number.

Dakota swallowed, then spoke: *Hi, Evelyn. This is Dakota.*

There was a pause, and Dakota's initial fear was that her aunt had hung up the phone. Getting a call from her niece was highly unusual.

Evelyn: *Oh… Dakota. This is a surprise. You do know it's Thanksgiving.*

She considered making a joke about eating half a turkey but decided against it. If there was a person in the world that had less of a sense of humor than Aunt Evelyn, she hadn't met them.

Dakota: *Well, yes. I do know. It's just that I wanted to ask you about something. About us moving in with you next month.*

Evelyn: *I'm not sure I understand.*

Dakota: *Mom came to visit you in September. Right? You lent her money and told her that we could move in with you guys in January. That Uncle Bert had a job for her at the car dealership. So I wanted to know if that was still on.*

Evelyn: *Is this some kind of game, Dakota? Did your mother put you up to this?*

Dakota: *No. It's not a game.*

There was another pause, and she could hear Evelyn's breathing through the phone. Her aunt was obviously pondering her next words, but Dakota wasn't about to wait.

Dakota: *Is my mom lying about this? Is any of it true?*

Evelyn: *Yes. Most of it is, actually. The part about the money and the job and you moving in with us. But your mom never came to visit me in September. I lent her five hundred dollars, but a few weeks later she called to tell me she lost it all in a poker tournament. After that we had a big fight and I rescinded my offer.*

Dakota: *So you're saying my mom knew in September that we wouldn't be moving?*

Evelyn: *Not sure what your mother thought. She kept trying to get more money... to keep our arrangement. But I had to stay strong. Your mother thinks she can push me around. I just got sick of it.*

Dakota: *This is messed up.*

Evelyn: *It is. And believe me, Dakota, I've done all I can to help your mother over the years. I just thought... this time... if I could get her out of that town, away from all those ghosts and memories, that it would be good for her. But this was the last straw. I have my own life to worry about. My own family to take care of.*

Ghosts. Memories. What the hell was Evelyn talking about? And why would her mother lie about visiting in September and them moving to Cleveland? Even an hour ago, in the middle of their Thanksgiving meal, she'd propped up that possibility as if it still might happen.

Dakota: *I understand. But do you think she went to play poker the weekend she was supposed to be with you? I mean, she wasn't here. She went somewhere.*

Evelyn: *I don't know where your mother went. I'm just telling you what she told me.*

Dakota: *It doesn't sound right, Aunt Evelyn. I don't think my mom would lose five hundred bucks playing poker.*

Evelyn: *I think you overestimate her ability.*

Dakota: *Well, yeah. It's possible. But the entry fees for tournaments are only a few hundred. And if she played open tables, she wouldn't lose that much. It's weird, but she's actually very disciplined when it comes to poker.*

She heard a sound then, the sucking in of air. Almost a gasp.

Evelyn: *Jesus… Dakota… Is your mother doing drugs again?*

Dakota felt her heartbeat then.

Dakota: *No. I don't think so. I mean, she takes pills for her back.*

Evelyn: *You know that's not what I'm talking about.*

Evelyn's suggestion pierced her like an arrow. Yeah. She did know. And Evelyn knew as well, since three summers ago Dakota had come to live in Cleveland with them, on account of her mother going to rehab. A rehab that Evelyn likely helped pay for. But the big H? Heroin? No. It couldn't be.

Dakota: *Honestly, Aunt Evelyn, I don't know what to say about this. Could you talk to her, maybe? See what's going on?*

Evelyn: *No, Dakota. No. Please... leave me out of it. I can't deal with that again. Your mom has sucked all the oxygen out of my life for years, and I need to breathe.*

When it was done, Dakota rearranged her butt against the ground and stiffened against the pine tree. In a fifteen-minute phone call, her life had changed, but she couldn't tell exactly how. In some ways, she was pleased that they were not going to move, but what Aunt Evelyn had inferred had the potential to be far worse.

And of course she'd have to deal with it on her own. As usual.

June 21–28, 2019

Chapter 24.
Who's Down for
an Info Exchange?

After her confrontation with Maureen Bonardi at the Sunrise Diner, Dakota felt as if she would have no choice but to clue her grandmother in on some of the recent events in her life. For one, the slap heard round the world had left a red mark on her face and would require some explanation. In fact, in a certain light, you could almost make out the imprint of a hand.

"I definitely see a finger," Lucinda observed, handing over a bag of frozen peas. They were out by the patio. A perfect summer evening with hardly any breeze.

Dakota pressed the bag against her cheekbone. "Manuel told me it looked like a peace sign."

Perhaps Lucinda didn't appreciate the irony, because she just shook her head and pressed her lips into a thin line. "You want to tell me about this?"

In the end, what else could Dakota do but confess. To most of it, at least. Meeting up with Anika and Jenna. A basic primer on Coleman family history, along with a sob story about how she'd tried talking to them about her father at the wedding party reception. Though she left out some minor details, such as getting stoned with Sammy the fourteen-year-old snitch and anything to do with Katie Larsen. She also omitted the part where Maureen called her a useless slut. Funny, actually. A virgin slut. A pretty decent oxymoron, if you thought about it.

"Some people don't like it when you get into their business" was how she wrapped it up. "And that woman is a serious alcoholic. The whole family knows it. Like, I have no idea what she was so pissed about."

Lucinda sighed, and you could tell frustration had begun to set in. "It comes down to this," she said. "We had an agreement and you broke it."

Dakota's throat tightened, and she could feel tears welling up behind her eyes. "I just thought you could trust me, Grandma. That I didn't have to tell you everything I do."

"I would love to be able to trust you, Dakota. But you're not making it easy for me. And who the hell thought it was a good idea to crash a wedding party?"

She already knew it had been a bad idea. Yet trust was a two-way street, and she'd only been living with her grandmother for a month. But she could work on that. They could work on that. Which could have been why she slid her phone over the table so that her grandmother could read the threatening text message.

Lucinda picked up the phone and examined the message before placing it back down on the table. She crossed her arms and leaned forward. "Why would someone threaten you by text, then show up in person to assault you?"

"Don't know," Dakota replied.

Her grandmother had obviously made the assumption that Maureen was responsible for the text. But on the ride home from the diner that day, she and Rosie came up with the alternate theory that Maureen had nothing to do with it, that the two seemingly related occurrences were unrelated.

"Something must have happened between the threat and today," Lucinda proposed.

"Nothing happened, Grandma. I swear."

"And you got this message on Tuesday. Why didn't you tell me about it?"

"But that's what I'm doing?"

Lucinda bit down on her lower lip, the tips of her teeth visible. "Not sure you should be a smart-ass right now."

"I'm sorry. But I honestly did not know what the text was for. At first I thought it was a practical joke. Kids do stuff like that."

She felt bad about her lie. Or half lie, since she had been confused by the threat when she'd first seen it and kids actually did mean shit like that on social media all the time. It then occurred to her that the concept of brutal honesty might be challenging for her.

"Okay," Dakota continued, trying to change the momentum. "So now I'm wondering if Anika had something to do with this. When we talked to her the other day, she lied about being friends with Mom. Why would she do that?"

"Not sure," Lucinda replied. "From what I recall, those two were attached at the hip. Believe me, I could tell you stories."

"I'd sure like to hear one."

"All right," Lucinda started. "This one time, the two of them went to a Kenny Chesney concert in Columbus. It was on Friday night, and I let them use my car. Except they didn't come back until Tuesday. I had to miss two days of work for that one."

"Where were they?" Dakota asked.

"Supposedly, they met some guys at the concert and took off to some country music festival in Iowa."

"When did this happen?"

"That would have been the summer before you were born. We had quite the tiff after that."

"But you said they drifted apart later. Did that have something to do with the murder?"

Lucinda paused briefly to consider the question. "Not sure about that. It wasn't as if they were friends one day and not friends the next. It could be that their lives just changed. Anika had her own baby to take care of."

Later that night, pleased that her conversation with Lucinda had ended on a less hostile note, Dakota fired off a couple of messages. In some ways, she saw it as an act of defiance, not directed at her grandmother, whom she would clue in from then on, but to the person who had threatened her.

First, she sent a second Facebook friend request to Adam Boland, along with a message.

Please help me Adam!

I just want contact info for JR

Nothing more

Promise :)

Then a text to Alice Benning at the Zionsville Record:

You down for an info exchange

She enabled her send read receipts, then stared at her phone all night, awaiting a response from either of them, but by 11:00 p.m., nothing had come over. She went to bed then, lay on her back with the lights on, eyes focused on a fly cruising across the ceiling. She was about to insert her earbuds, thinking some tracks from "Psychodrome" might help, when suddenly her phone buzzed.

A text from Alice. One word.

Depends

Dakota acted quickly, taking a screenshot of the threatening text message she'd received and sending it along with her own response.

Just got this

Blinking ellipsis. Blinking ellipsis.

Who sent this

Dakota smiled. She'd learned a few poker moves from her mother over the years and knew what to do next.

Don't know. I talked to lots of people. Any evidence you could pass along might help

I'll have to talk to Detective Waller

What do you know? A familiar name.

Oh. I know Waller. Tell him Dakota Lodi says hi. Smiley face emoji. Huh. Confounded face emoji

My mother has lots of friends

Afterward, things didn't quite turn out the way she'd hoped they would, as the rest of the week, then the weekend, drifted by with no word from Alice or Adam Boland. Once Tuesday came around, she resigned herself to a set of simple facts: Alice would not be willing to trust her career to a sixteen-year-old girl with questionable street cred, and Adam hadn't warmed to her as much as she'd thought. It all led to her weeklong sulk fest, her coworkers at the diner giving her a wide berth. Manuel didn't engage in his usual verbal tit for tats. Mario didn't ask her to test taste any recipes. Even Mrs. Peña seemed to be avoiding her, whereas Carlos waited until Tuesday afternoon to address the situation.

"Are you okay?" he asked.

Dakota gritted her teeth. "Couldn't be better."

"I can see why you're bummed, Dakota. Though I don't think you should give up. When something bad happens, there's usually something good around the corner."

Dakota raised her eyes. It sounded like pie-in-the-sky bullshit. "You get that from a fortune cookie, Carlos?"

"I did. It went great with my lo mein."

Dakota couldn't help but smile, which Carlos might have taken as a signal to put a hand on her shoulder. "I have a feeling," he proclaimed, very preacher-like, "things are gonna work out for you."

She didn't quite buy into his optimism. Still, the way he'd expressed his sympathy made her wonder. If she were to put the whole father thing on the back burner and not think of it every second of her life, then perhaps his fortune-cookie analysis could come to fruition. She could use the rest of the week to chill, perhaps work on a new playlist. Except, around closing time, it became obvious that Rosie had her own ideas about how she should be spending her time when she informed her that the two of them, and Carlos, would be going out to Mack's Treats for ice cream after work.

"Why would you invite Carlos?" Dakota asked incredulously, although she had to admit liking his hand on her shoulder.

"You're being a Debbie Downer," Rosie replied. "I just figured you needed to get out. And it's not like you're not crushing on Carlos."

"Whatever."

"Are you saying you don't like him?"

Dakota shrugged. "Why don't you go out with him?"

"You're deflecting."

"I'm, like, really suspicious of your motives right now."

"My motives are clear. I'm helping you."

"I don't need your help."

"Apparently you do."

"I'm not going."

"We're not going to a fucking orgy, Dakota. It's just ice cream."

Some of the stragglers in the diner turned to look at them. Perhaps talk of an orgy had piqued their interest.

"Fine," Dakota finally said, "but I don't like setups."

Though she had to admit liking Carlos. And ice cream. Especially the coconut almond chip at Mack's.

They waited for Carlos to join them on the two-block journey toward Mack's, and he came up from behind and forced his way between them, simultaneously tapping on both of their shoulders, a humongous grin plastered across his face. Rosie broke apart and moved off to the side, while Carlos slid his hand down the blade of Dakota's shoulder and onto her back, holding it in place for a few seconds before removing it.

Outside, the after-work bustle of downtown Zionsville had picked up. Cars moving to and away from the Y-Bridge. A six-car traffic jam at the Cross Street stoplight. A decent crowd at Starbucks, drinking iced coffees. Up ahead, something caught her attention. A truck had slid into one of Main Street's many parallel parking spots. No big deal, really. Happened every day. And didn't half the people in town drive trucks? And weren't some of them red trucks? Then again, a *Sorry About Your Small Penis* bumper sticker wasn't all that common. Dakota suddenly stopped, her face flushed.

"What is it?" Rosie asked.

Dakota pointed, eyes fixed straight ahead, as Adam Boland came around the front of his truck and stood before them, no more than six feet away. Black T-shirt and jeans. A Bass Pro Shops hat covering his eyes until he lifted up its brim. "Whaz up, cuz?" he said.

They all stopped. Carlos offered a look of confusion. Rosie grabbed Dakota's hand and squeezed. She leaned over and whispered into Dakota's ear, "Do you want me to stay?"

"No," Dakota replied. Wasn't this what she wanted when she'd sent the friend request and the message? "You guys go. I'll meet you there."

As Rosie and Carlos made their way down the street, Dakota took a few steps forward, narrowing the gap between herself and her potential cousin. Meanwhile, Adam fidgeted, digging his nails into the palm of his hand as her eyes landed on his other hand. The one gripping what looked to be a folded-up piece of paper.

"What's going on, Adam?" Dakota asked, acting as if her insides were not bubbling.

"Not much," he replied. "Thought I'd stop by. See how you're doing."

"You're concerned about my welfare, are you?"

Adam lifted his shoulders. "I feel bad about what happened."

"Yeah. Me too."

"And if it's any consolation, Sammy felt guilty about it."

"I guess it probably wasn't a good idea to get high with your cousin."

"Probably is not the word I'd use."

"Fair enough. So, you came here to pay your respects,

or is there something else you wanted to tell me?"

"Got something for you," Adam said, waving the paper in the air. "Think you might be interested."

Dakota snatched the paper from him and unfolded it. Atop the page in black ink was an address: 4 Little Fork Lane, Three Lakes, Wisconsin. Her neurons began to fire up. Was this some kind of joke? A Coleman-family scavenger hunt posing as one last humiliation?

"What am I looking at here?"

"Your father's address," Adam replied. "The infamous Jimmy Ray Coleman."

At just the sound of the name, Dakota's heartbeat quickened. She glanced up at Adam and then back to the paper again. "Where'd you get this?"

"My mom gave it to me."

"Really… Wow. Like, I don't even know what to say."

"You don't have to say anything. But I should mention Jimmy doesn't have a phone."

No phone. Interesting. Then again, you wouldn't expect a hermit to have a phone. Except that would mean she'd have to find some way of getting to Wisconsin.

"I don't know how to repay you for this, Adam. You've done a really good thing, and I super appreciate it. And your mom. You have to thank her for me. Can you do that?"

"No problem."

"I am curious though. How did this even happen?"

Adam furled his lips and glanced up at the sky, as if looking for counsel in the stratosphere. "I was in the kitchen, you see, pounding a brewski, when the two of them came in. Fighting, as usual. So I say to them… you guys are being paranoid dipshits. The girl just wants to meet her father. She's not gonna hurt anyone. Then I may have called you a little shrimp. You know, since a shrimp wouldn't hurt anyone. Then I say, give me the address. I'll go down to the diner and give it to her."

"That's redundant, Adam," Dakota said, producing a grin that stretched from ear to ear. "You could have just said shrimp. It's already little."

He smiled, slapped at his knee. "I'm not exactly a wordsmith."

She laughed at that one. Adam the wordsmith.

Afterward, they said their goodbyes, and Adam wished her good luck before heading back to his truck. Dakota heard the engine start up, and as the truck merged into traffic, she wiped away a few tears.

They were not sad tears.

For once.

November 30, 2018

Chapter 25.
Sneaky Little Bitch

It was strange seeing her mother home on a Friday evening, slumped down on their living room couch. Especially the Friday after Thanksgiving, when all the old homies returned from wherever they'd been hibernating and gathered at the Handlebar Tavern for an evening of *remember when*. Which of course presented Dakota with an opportunity of sorts.

In the meantime, she'd been arranging thoughts in her head on how to best approach a conversation with her mother about what she'd learned on her call with Evelyn. And the fact that she'd actually spoken to Evelyn, which she figured might not be well received. But as she approached her mother, there was a sense that the timing could be right.

Dakota dropped herself onto the couch and swung her legs onto the cushions to face her mother, to look her in the eye. "How come you're not out tonight, Mom?"

Her mother returned the gaze. "Didn't feel like it?"

"So, I talked to Evelyn last night," Dakota said, getting right down to it, her nerves firing up. "I know we're not moving."

Her mother perked up then, her eyebrows slowly lifting. "Aren't you a sneaky little bitch."

Yes. She was a sneaky little bitch, but she wanted to keep the mood on the light side, if possible. No way would she be conducting an intervention. Best to acknowledge her clandestine bitchiness, then slip in a probing question.

"I appreciate the compliment, Mom," she replied with a smile. "Except she told me that you never visited her in September and that you lost the five hundred dollars she lent to you playing poker. So I'd kind of like to know what's going on here."

"And you believed her?"

"Well… I'm kind of questioning the poker part. But she thinks the money's gone and you had to go somewhere that weekend. So, like, what gives?"

"Hollywood Casino. That's what gives. I entered a tournament for a buck fifty. And unfortunately, Lady Luck wasn't smiling on me that day."

This always happened with her mother. Address one question and three more popped up as a result of the answer. Such as, why would her mother hide the fact she went to the casino? It was no secret that she'd been there before. And if she only lost one hundred and fifty dollars, which Dakota tended to believe, then why would she lie to Evelyn about that? Unless she thought she could get more from her sister, perhaps squeeze more juice from the lemon. Or, as her mother had alluded to during their Thanksgiving dinner, a more lucrative opportunity had presented itself. *I've got a few things I'm working on.*

Dakota put her hands against both temples to prevent her head from exploding. "Why would you tell your sister that you lost all the money?"

"Not sure you need to know all the details, peanut. Didn't we talk about this yesterday?"

"I guess we did. But now it looks like you blew that job opportunity. Evelyn told me we're not moving to Cleveland. She said she doesn't want us there."

"Evelyn likes talking shit."

"She also said you might be using again."

There. She'd popped the zinger. And now she waited for the blowback. Which, surprisingly, didn't come. Her mother looked almost serene as her eyes wandered about the room before turning toward her daughter.

"Is this what you wanted to talk about?" her mother asked, but still calm, as if they were about to discuss takeout options.

"Please, Mom," Dakota pleaded. "Don't be angry with me. I just want to know the truth, and I promise I won't judge you."

"That's nice for a change."

Dakota ignored the dig. "You've been taking the oxies? For your back, right? But your bottle has no label on it, which means it's black market... and expensive."

"Jesus. Where the hell did you learn all this stuff?"

"The internet, Mom. And in case you didn't know, I'm almost sixteen. I'm not a little kid anymore."

"Well, that's pretty fucking obvious."

"So when did you start with the heroin? Are you shooting it?"

Her mother hesitated for a few seconds before letting it out. "A few months ago. A friend of Gina's gave it to me at a party. It's cheap. And no... I smoke it. You know I don't like needles."

Dakota brushed aside the details. She needed to stay

grounded. "So, this is good. I can handle this, Mom. Maybe even help you this time."

Her mother bowed her head. "Not sure about that."

"But we could talk about it. I want to understand."

"It's complicated. Adults have adult problems."

She recalled Evelyn's comments about memories and ghosts and decided to take a chance. "Does it have to do with your father dying?"

She could see her mother clench immediately, her muscles tightening. They both knew the story of Jameson Lodi's heart attack. Her mother had been eleven at the time. Evelyn, thirteen. But it was her mother that discovered him slumped over a chair in the kitchen and made the 911 call.

"Maybe," her mother replied, rubbing her eyes. "That was rough. And I've lost a lot over the years. But I'm not making excuses."

It struck her then. An explanation for most of her mother's losses. And not a good one.

"It was because you had me. Wasn't it? And you had to drop out of school. And you and Grandma started fighting and she moved to Florida." She left out the part about her own father dying. That would have been a loss as well, yet she knew next to nothing about his relationship with her mother and saw no point in piling on. Then again, was she not the common denominator in those situations?

Her mother slid over. She put an arm around her daughter's shoulders and pulled her in close. "Listen to me, Dakota. You are by far the best thing that has happened to me in my life. Not even close. So don't for a second think otherwise."

Dakota buried her head in the crook of her mother's neck. She could feel tears pooling behind her eyes.

"And my god," her mother continued, "you're becoming such a cool young woman now. It kind of freaks me out sometimes, to be honest. How fast you're growing up. But I just love you so much, Dakota. So much it hurts sometimes."

"I love you too, Mom. I just worry about you."

"You don't need to worry. I'm going through a phase… and once that's done… once I get everything settled, I can do what I need to do. We can do what we need to do. The two of us."

Dakota nodded into her mother's shoulder, but by then she was sniffling, tears streaming down her face. She'd lost control of the intervention, or whatever that had been. And it didn't help that her mother had said many of the same things three years ago. That everything was under control. That she was a functional human who just liked to experiment. She would never be the person having their stomach pumped in the emergency room or living underneath a highway underpass, shooting up with dirty needles. And sure, her employment history had been spotty, and they'd crisscrossed the river just about every year to live in new, crappy apartments. Dakota had attended every elementary school in town except St. Catherine's, because you had to pay for that one. Her mother explained it away as if it were part of her education.

It was then that Dakota came to a realization: That her life was just a circle that she traveled around, like a rat stuck in a maze. Repeating itself every few years so that she could pass by all those familiar places once again.

July 2-3, 2019

Chapter 26.
Three Lakes
in One Day

After Lucinda guided the Audi past the Wisconsin border, she began her geography lesson.

"Did you know there's fifteen thousand lakes in Wisconsin?" she asked.

"I did not," Dakota replied.

She hadn't known about the Audi either, since apparently it had been in storage the past month.

"And what's interesting is, Minnesota's license plate says it's the land of ten thousand lakes, even though Wisconsin has more."

"So if there were a lake contest, you're saying Wisconsin would win."

"Not only that, but you've got your Wisconsin cheddar."

"Lakes and cheese," Dakota said. "Sounds like paradise."

And it almost seemed like paradise once they reached the north woods of Wisconsin, the landscape changing to dense forests of pine trees with the occasional glimpse of some of those fifteen thousand lakes. They were heading toward a region with twenty-eight of those lakes, part of the Eagle River Chain, about an hour south of the Canadian border. Lucinda had discovered a travel blog that professed it to be the world's largest chain of freshwater lakes. Which of course made it a tourism hot spot, especially the town of Eagle River itself, which presumably had all kinds of shops, bars, and restaurants to go along with all the bait-and-tackle outfits. Not that Dakota cared one iota about any of this. Because if things went according to plan, she would be meeting her father, Jimmy Ray Coleman, for the first time in her life.

Around midday, they arrived at the town of Three Lakes, which signified the Three Lakes portion of the Eagle River Chain, the quieter, less touristy side according to the blog. At the general store, they turned onto a side road, and Lucinda opened the windows to let in some of the mild northern Wisconsin air. Outside, the road twisted among a series of lakes, sparkly blue water visible through gaps in the trees and the occasional cabin. By then, Dakota's adrenaline began to surge, and she rubbed her sweaty palms against her shorts and clenched her teeth. She was fairly certain that a stream of vomit would soon be completing its voyage from her stomach to her throat.

"I'm kind of freaking out here," she proclaimed.

"You're gonna be fine," Lucinda replied, her eyes fixed straight ahead as the Audi veered off the main road onto a strip of gravel.

Her grandmother had obviously tossed out the first words that came into her mind, but not knowing what else to do, Dakota entertained the possibility of them being true. What if she could be fine? It wasn't as if she hadn't planned for this moment, coming up with opening lines she might use upon meeting her father for the first time.

Hello, Dad.

Whaz up, Jimmy Ray?

Surprise!

Hello... I'm your daughter... descended from a distant galaxy, delivered in a robotic voice.

She'd even assembled decision trees, with multiple choices of responses, each depending on Jimmy Ray's reaction to seeing her. But each response she considered led to more questions that made her then doubt her responses, until the entire mental exercise developed its own weather pattern and she had to shut it down. In some ways, had it not been easier to think of Jimmy Ray as some kind of apparition? She'd take out the picture of him and imagine him to be alive, but in a dicey predicament that prevented him from contacting her. Possible explanations included the witness protection program in some remote corner of the US, a double agent in a foreign country whose identity could not be revealed, or trapped in a Turkish prison for a crime he did not commit. But Three Lakes did not exist in a foreign country, nor would it house a Turkish prison. And so she had to deal with the reality that some other reason existed for Jimmy Ray not wanting to be a part of her life.

The Audi bounced up and down as the road turned to dirt interspersed with small rocks. They climbed a small embankment with deep ruts on both sides, likely carved out by rainwater or melted snow. On the other side, they went down into a gully, and the outlines of a small A-frame cabin with grayish clapboards and a silver metallic roof slowly came into view. Lucinda eased the Audi onto a large patch of dirt and parked beside a beat-up Chevy truck that might have been blue at one point in its existence but had faded over the years and was now spotted with rust. Stands of large pine encircled them, and through the branches, you could see portions of what she assumed to be Little Fork Lake and the outlines of a dock down below. She had expected something dingier, something barely habitable. However, this exceeding of expectations did nothing to make her feel better, which she tried communicating to Lucinda.

"I can't do this," she said.

"I'm pretty sure you can," Lucinda replied.

"What if he's not there?"

"Then we come back later."

Dakota cradled her head in both her hands. "What if he takes one look at me and slams the door in my face?"

"That's not exactly the power of positive thinking."

"I don't need sarcasm right now, Grandma."

Lucinda shrugged. "Fine. But think of how bad you'll feel if you come all this way and do nothing."

"Think of how bad I'll feel when he slams the door in my face."

"Listen. I'll wait for you here. If it doesn't go well, we split and check into the hotel. Then we go for a nice dinner where there's a view of the lake and watch the sunset. How does that sound?"

Dakota nodded as if she were convinced. As if a sunset would make everything better.

She had pictured a hermit. A lost child of Charles Manson or someone resembling the Unabomber, but the man that finally answered the door after multiple rings looked more like a dirty-blond Jesus, except that Jesus never wore a black Allman Brothers T-shirt or faded blue jeans.

"And who are you?" the man said, in a tone more curious than anything else.

Dakota eyed the man she now assumed to be Jimmy Ray Coleman, analyzing the age progression from the old photograph she'd seen millions of times. A few lines had surfaced around his tanned face where his darker-colored, somewhat unruly beard ended, and the long blond hair falling a few inches below his neckline contained more streaks of brown than they used to, but the vivid blue eyes and shit-eating grin had aged well.

"Hi. I'm Dakota Lodi," she said, thinking it a solid beginning.

The man didn't shut the door in her face, but his eyes narrowed and the grin suddenly vanished. "Well, then, Dakota Lodi. Do you like chili?"

"What?"

"I made some venison chili. In the crockpot. No way I can eat all of it."

She hadn't prepared for the food-based branch of her decision tree, but in the spirit of adaptability she said, "Sure… I can help you with that."

Dakota followed him into the house. Inside, the walls were covered with lacquered wood panels, and the flooring consisted of darker wood planks that looked as if they'd been transported from a previous century. The living room had a couch, a coffee table possibly erected in a high school woodshop, and a standing lamp with a shade covered by bird prints. On the wall hung a series of three framed snapshots: Jimmy Ray standing on the shore holding a fish, Jimmy Ray in a boat holding a fish, and a group of about four people standing outside a log cabin around Jimmy Ray holding a fish. Dakota examined the photographs. She highly suspected the same fish was in each scene, but her father looked pleased with himself in these particular environments, his go-to pose being a flash of white teeth, barely visible in a sea of facial hair.

Jimmy Ray divvied up the bowls of chili, while Dakota pressed her nose up against a sliding glass door just outside the kitchen. There was a deck and a white-painted picnic table. Down below was a dock with a small blue fishing boat tied up, and beyond that the lake itself. In the distance, a troop of paddlers in brightly colored kayaks, suspended between ripples in the silvery blue water.

"This is beautiful," Dakota said.

Jimmy Ray said, "Yes," like it was all too obvious.

"Have you been here long? In this house, I mean."

Jimmy looked up from the crockpot. "It's sure been awhile," he said, but at that moment she could tell that something outside had diverted his attention, because he turned his head sideways, peering out the dirt-encrusted window at the parking area and, likely, her grandmother's Audi.

"Who's that? In the car out there."

"Oh. That's my grandmother. She drove me here."

"Think she might be hungry?"

Dakota shook her head. "She's just waiting for me. I'm supposed to call her."

"About what?"

"I guess… if everything was cool here, she'd go and pick me up later."

"Is everything cool?"

"I think so. But it's possible I'm being presumptuous."

"I wouldn't go that far, but somehow you stumbled upon my property."

Dakota felt pinpricks in her fingers. "I'm really sorry about that. I should just go."

Jimmy Ray let out a nervous chuckle. "I'm joking."

"Oh. Okay."

"You didn't think it was funny."

"No, it was. I'm laughing. Inside, I am."

"Mm. So that's Lucinda in the car."

"Yes. It is."

"Okay, then. Make the call. We'll do lunch out on the deck. And later I'm taking the boat out if you want to come along."

"Are you sure?"

Jimmy said that he was. Dakota smiled and took out her phone. Perhaps this was one of those fatherly moments she never knew she was missing.

They ate lunch out on the deck. Dakota lopped down spoonfuls of chili, the hot peppers that had obviously been added to the concoction scorching her mouth but not tasting all that bad once you acclimated to the heat. She washed it all down with gulps of iced water and gazed out at the water, which almost looked like a painting, with the boat bobbing gently against the dock, beside a swath of tall grass with brown feathery tips. Meanwhile, Jimmy Ray worked on a Corona, seeming satisfied to not say much of anything.

"When did you move in here?" Dakota then asked, breaking the silence. She'd almost added Jimmy to the end of her question but stopped herself, on account of her not exactly knowing what to call him. In retrospect, Jimmy probably would have been fine, whereas Jimmy Ray seemed awkward. She could have called him Dad, but that seemed out of the question.

"Let's see," Jimmy Ray replied while scratching at his chin. "I bought this place about twelve years ago."

Dakota did the math in her head. By her calculation, her father had left Zionsville fourteen years ago, which left a gap of two years between then and the time he purchased the cabin. "What did you do before that?"

Jimmy guzzled the rest of his beer, then rotated the empty bottle in his hand. "I bounced around a bit. Rented a room in town while I saved some dough. Used that with some of my veterans benefits to buy the cabin."

"Did it need lots of work?"

"Let's put it this way: the place was hardly fit for vermin."

Dakota forced a grin. "Well, it turned out great. Honestly, if I lived here, I'd spend my whole life on this deck."

Jimmy smiled, and it appeared he might talk about life on a deck, what it was like to fix up the house, or something else important, but then he just pursed his lips and said nothing.

After lunch, Dakota followed Jimmy Ray, carrying a cooler with more beers and bottles of water down a small grassy hill to the dock, where the boat had been tied up to a post.

"Be careful when you get in," he told her, putting on a pair of sunglasses that had been dangling on a string around his neck. "The boat can get tipsy."

Dakota carefully placed one foot in the boat while the other remained on the dock, and the boat gently rocked, making her think she could be doing a faceplant at any second, until she quickly lifted her previously dock-bound foot and settled it into the boat. "Oh yeah," she said, wavering a bit but maintaining her balance, moving her arms out like a surfer might do.

"Now take this," he told her, handing over the cooler, "and put that in the stern."

Dakota took the cooler. But where the hell was the stern? She didn't want to appear as if she knew nothing about boats, while knowing all along that she knew nothing about boats. Yet Jimmy Ray hardly noticed when she dropped the cooler behind her, then nudged it toward the back of the boat with her foot. He'd been busy untying a rope from one of the dock posts, after which he motioned Dakota to sit down by the center console. As the front end drifted away from the dock, he gracefully came aboard and sat down beside her. He started the boat up and the engine revved, sending waves back into the shore.

By then they were moving, puttering through their tiny inlet and out to the open water. Around them the lakeshore spread out, spotted with mostly small cabins but some expensive homes as well. All of them with docks and boats tied up. The kayaks she'd seen earlier were out in the distance, along with a few boats buzzing around. Up ahead, a family of loons drifted.

"Check it out," Dakota then said, pointing to the loons. At first, they didn't react to their presence, but at some point the mother veered away from their boat, her two babies following close behind, while what she assumed to be the father dove underneath the water. He stayed there for what seemed like an eternity before showing up about twenty feet in front of them, as if to escort them away. Dakota giggled. "Did you see that?"

"They are beautiful," Jimmy Ray commented. "And they say the same ones come back every year."

"How can you tell?"

"You can't. They kind of all look the same."

Minutes later, Jimmy Ray asked her to get another beer, and as he commandeered the boat underneath a bridge, Dakota went back to the cooler. Inside, there were two Coronas and she pulled out one of them, twisted off the cap, and brought it over to the center console, placing it in one of the cupholders.

"Thanks," he said, bringing the bottle of beer to his mouth, guzzling down about half of it, then gripping it in one hand while steering with the other. "So, we're on Island Lake now," he added, as if it were vital information. "In fact, Three Lakes has three separate lakes, which I guess makes sense."

"Of course," Dakota replied. "If it had four lakes, that would be messed up."

Jimmy Ray let out a laugh, then broadcast the names of the lakes. "You've got Island, Round Lake, and Planting Ground Lake. And the thing is, they're all connected. You can see all of them in one day."

"Sounds great," Dakota replied. And it really did. Three lakes in a single day. Not that they were in a hurry to see them all, as it appeared Jimmy Ray preferred cruising to speed boating. And there was something about the water that relaxed her. The sound of the engine drone as the boat cut a path in the water, the wind blowing back her hair. You could get used to a life like this, which perhaps Jimmy Ray had been considering as he downed the rest of his beer, let out a belch, then announced, "Round Lake," as if he were a train conductor alerting passengers of their next stop.

Dakota smiled but didn't say anything. Keeping her head on a swivel, she checked out some kids on jet skis, two guys fishing, and a pontoon boat, which was basically a living room on the water with couches and tables. In the distance, a few boats anchored around a sandbar, country music blaring while an American flag wavered in the breeze.

"It sure is busy here," Dakota remarked.

"This is nothing," he replied. "You should see it on

weekends. Drunk boater city. Marine Patrol has a field day."

"So I'm guessing you don't come out on weekends." It seemed a reasonable assumption. If Jimmy Ray happened to be a hermit, wouldn't his hermit-like behaviors transfer to life on the water?

"Have no choice. I do fishing and sightseeing tours during the tourist season. It's how I make my living."

"Sounds interesting."

But Jimmy Ray just turned up the corner of one side of his mouth and added a smirk. As if interesting did nothing to define his reality.

Eventually they made their way through Planting Ground Lake, and Jimmy Ray veered the boat into a narrow labyrinth-like channel and cut the engine. He dropped an anchor and they drifted, the only sounds coming from the buzzing of insects and a few frogs croaking now and then. The shoreline around them had low-growth vegetation by the water and beyond that stands of pine trees. "We can sit up by the bow," he then said. "You can put your feet in the water if you want."

And so they did. Jimmy Ray grabbed another beer and a bottle of water from the cooler. The two of them sat up by the bow. Dakota removed her shoes and lowered her feet into the cool water, swirling them around in circles as a school of minnows swam on by.

"This is my favorite spot," he said. "I don't like being around people all the time, and it's always quiet here."

"Nothing wrong with that," she replied. "But it must be tough in the winter here."

"You get by any way you can. I do some odd jobs. A few snowmobile tours now and then."

"Do you hunt?" Dakota asked, wondering about the venison in the chili and where that might have come from.

"I don't," Jimmy Ray replied. "Lots of fishing though. Even in the winter."

"Like ice fishing?"

"Yep."

"How does that actually work?"

"Once the lake freezes over, you put out your ice fishing hut. Bring in some chairs. A cooler with beer. Maybe some whiskey. Then you cut a hole in the ice and drop a line down."

"Do you catch anything?"

"Sometimes."

"I see. So it's basically an excuse for drinking."

"I like to think of drinking as an excuse for fishing."

The two of them exchanged smiles, then Jimmy swigged some of his beer.

Dakota sensed an opportunity. At some point, she would have to bring up what she'd come to Wisconsin to talk about in the first place, and so she removed a small wallet from the back pocket of her shorts and unzipped it. "I have something I wanted to show you," she said to him, taking out the old photograph, the one with him leaning up against the oak tree. She handed it over to him while taking in a deep breath.

Jimmy Ray's expression suddenly changed into something Dakota couldn't quite decipher. "Where did you get this?" he asked.

"My mom gave it to me."

He studied the photograph and picked at his teeth. Dakota could see it had elicited something inside of him, and that whatever that something was had rearranged the space between them. He glanced down at his feet, then up again, his eyes hardening. "You wanna tell me what you're doing here and how you found me?"

Suddenly, Dakota felt a tightness in her chest. She took in some of the lake air, letting it out slowly while she considered what to say next, not coming up with anything that made sense other than the truth.

"Your nephew Adam gave me your address because I asked him for it. My mom always told me you were my father but that you died in a motorcycle accident when I was two, which was obviously bullshit."

Jimmy Ray tilted his head, and Dakota could see that his hands were shaking. She had put him on the spot but wanted him to know she wasn't angry with him in any way, that she could be understanding of a person that split town after coming back from war, having his brother murdered, and fathering a baby with a woman that didn't want to be with him. If she could somehow communicate this to him, then perhaps he'd find a way to feel better about it.

"I know this is a shock to you," she started, "but I don't want you to think I expect anything. I just wanted to meet you. And if it's just this time and you don't want anything to do with me after this, I can try to understand that."

"I'm not your father, Dakota."

"What?"

"I'm not your father."

The words were like pinpricks piercing her skin, the pain channeling slowly, seeping into her internal organs. Any positive energy she previously possessed now escaped the confines of her body and drifted away like helium balloons disappearing into the sky. "You don't have to lie about this. I told you. I'm not angry."

"Listen, Dakota. You seem like a really nice person, and I'm glad you turned out that way. But if you were my daughter, I never would have left Zionsville. Except you're not. And the reason I know that is because I never had sex with your mother."

"What if you got drunk one night, and the two of you got together? Maybe you don't remember."

"I had a crush on your mom from the first time we met in third grade. If I slept with her, I would have remembered that."

Dakota put her face in her hands. A knot formed in her stomach. She thought back to her decision tree and how foolish she'd been not to include a scenario such as this.

"This is totally fucked. Like, why would she lie about this?"

"I have no idea. Your mother's always been a mystery to me."

"But you joined the army right after my mom got pregnant. Did you do that because Greg was the father?"

"I joined the army because I wanted to join the army."

He hadn't answered the question. And did boys really enlist in the army because they wanted to? Not to mention there'd been a war going on at the time. She believed Jimmy Ray when he said he wasn't her father. Nevertheless, when it came to his brother, he was obviously hiding something.

"Okay, then," Dakota said, her heartbeat beginning to accelerate. "What about the bar fight? At Muncy's Tavern. You were there."

Jimmy Ray's face contorted into a grimace. "What does that have to do with anything?"

Dakota remembered Rosie's comment. The two doors. One opening into the other.

"I think it does. She was trying to protect me from something."

"I know nothing about that."

"Was my mom at the bar that night?"

"No."

"Just so you know, in case you think I don't know anything about this, I've read the articles about the fight. I've seen the arrest report. I know you were there."

"Never said I wasn't."

"And you do know that the police reopened the case."

"Of course. They came up here a few weeks ago to question me."

A few weeks ago? Jimmy Ray's admission shocked her. Then again, it made sense that cops would want to speak with him.

"What did they want from you?"

"They're trying to solve the case. But I told them the same thing I told the detectives fourteen years ago. That I don't know who killed my brother. That the fight may have ended with the bikers, but that's not where it started."

"What do you mean that's not where it started?"

"Greg got into a beef with one of the Mexican dudes, not the biker. They came into the bar with Anika."

Mexican dudes? Anika! New information, for sure. She'd not read about it in any of the articles. And Anika sure as hell hadn't mentioned it. Did the cops know about this? Could Jimmy Ray be conjuring up a ridiculous story just to stop her from prying?

"What was the fight about?" Dakota then asked, trying to act as if the new revelation hadn't rattled her.

"Don't know," Jimmy Ray answered. "I'd been talking to Albert at the time, but you could tell Anika was pissed with Greg about something. Next thing you know, all hell broke loose."

"Did you know the Mexican guys?"

"Never seen them before."

"When you told the cops this, did they believe you?"

At that precise moment, Jimmy Ray dropped his chin down and shook his head. He looked tired, beaten down, and you could tell he had likely answered his last question. In some respects, she felt sorry for him. Like her, he'd been caught up in a cyclone of events beyond his control. And did anyone really want to go digging around in the past? Especially when it was dark and messy.

Jimmy Ray lifted his head then, a look resembling sympathy in his now watery eyes. "I'm sorry, Dakota," he said to her, his voice all shaky. "I know you expected something else when you came up here. But I just can't get into this anymore." He paused, took in a breath. "I hope you can understand."

Dakota said she did, but nothing she could see existed in the realm of understanding. And so she just sat there, kicking at the water as Jimmy Ray lifted up the anchor. Suddenly, an acute awareness of her environment enveloped her. How it had been one thing on the ride up and now it would be something different. How in the blink of an eye everything had changed. The sun, an angry red ball scorching the earth. The water, a dark blue hole with no bottom. She had the urge to dive in. Do the breaststroke until her arms and legs stopped working. Float on her back and stare up at the sky. Drift aimlessly. Live there forever.

February 21, 2019

Chapter 27.
Missing

Her mother always turned the heat down in February, which meant you had to dress like you were attending Winter Carnival in their house. Outside, the snow piled up in drifts, and arctic air seeped in through seams in their walls. Dakota did the best she could, dressed in her flannel shirt jacket over a black hoodie and a tan wool cap as she rifled through the kitchen cabinet above their refrigerator, scavenging for something to eat. On Monday, Gina had driven her to the local food pantry, where they'd loaded up on ramen, spaghetti, tomato sauce, cereal, coffee, bread, peanut butter, and jelly, and so for once there was plenty to choose from.

She ended up going with the ramen, thinking it might be the best antidote for frostbite. But as she slurped the combination of hot broth and slimy noodles, a feeling of dread began to spread throughout her body. She tried stamping it out, taking her phone out and calling her mother, then Gina, for the twentieth time that day, but both calls went directly to voicemail for the twentieth time. She took a deep breath and sorted the facts. Her mother had mentioned a party in town she was going to on Tuesday evening, and here it was, Thursday evening, and she hadn't seen her mother since.

Under such circumstances, Victoria Lodi going AWOL for a day or two usually wouldn't be out of the ordinary. She'd certainly slept off benders before, coming home the next morning. The time she and Gina stayed overnight at the casino and forgot to tell her about it. And of course, her mother's DUI a few summers ago, when she totaled her car and hurt her back, ending up in the hospital, which Dakota didn't know about until the next day. But it felt different this time, as if it could be time to panic. And she'd seen enough *Dateline* to know what happened to the missing. The police holding useless news conferences as community members put up posters and formed search parties. A body found weeks later, half-buried in the woods. Yet in this situation, calling the police didn't seem like the right thing to do. Then again, neither did waiting around. Which was about when a better option presented itself. Was there not a place where she might get information as to where her mother might be? A place where her mother had spent a substantial portion of her life and money?

Dakota put on her quilted green bomber jacket and black boots and trudged outside. The town of Zionsville had done a decent job of plowing, except a thin layer of slush still coated the roadside, and she had to concentrate to keep from falling on her ass and sliding down Bramble Street. Down by the river, the wind smacked her in the face as she made her way past the Y-Bridge and veered onto Crown Street. The locals called this part of town the Tire District because of its two competing tire shops, though it also included a bail bonds office and the Handlebar Tavern, which had nothing to do with tires. Though it had a decent relationship with Mr. Crowley, the bail bondsman.

As Dakota crossed the threshold of the Handlebar Tavern, she unzipped her coat and had a look around. It had been a few years since she'd last seen the place, but it was like entering a time capsule where nothing ever changed. The smell of cigarettes and dingy lighting. Beer posters and schedules for the Bengals and Zionsville High football on the walls. A dartboard in the corner. Merle Haggard on the jukebox, lamenting about Kern River. She had an inkling to give the pinball machine a try, but instead made her way to the bar and sat down on one of the stools. The bartender had his head down, and at first he didn't notice her.

"I'll have a whiskey," Dakota said to him, trying hard to suppress a smile.

The man glanced up, and instantly his eyes widened. "I'll be damned," he said. "Dakota?"

"How's it going, Wilson?"

What could you say about Wilson Vanderbilt III? Not quite royalty, as his name might suggest, but owner and part-time bartender of the Handlebar Tavern. Dakota once heard someone joke that he resembled a Denzel Washington that had come through the wrong end of a time machine, with graying hair that matched a neatly trimmed beard of the same color. He also happened to be a decent friend of her mother's.

Wilson moved closer and leaned up to the bar. "Haven't seen you in a while. You find a better place to do your homework?"

Dakota smiled. During her middle school years, her mother often picked her up from school, then stopped at the tavern to have a few pops before dinner, while Dakota settled at one of the corner tables doing her schoolwork. Although if you totaled it up, she'd probably spent more time playing pinball.

"I'm not interested in homework anymore," Dakota replied with a smirk.

"Well, you've definitely grown up, I'll give you that. And it is good to see you. Though I'm guessing you're not here for the ambience."

"Have you seen my mom recently?"

Wilson narrowed his eyes. "Depends. How far back we talking?"

"Today?"

"Nope."

"Yesterday?"

"What's this about, Dakota?"

On the walk over, she had anticipated this moment. That Wilson Vanderbilt III would pop the big question and that she'd have to come up with an honest answer. He wouldn't be the kind of guy to help you if he thought you were tossing him bullshit.

"My mom is using again, Wilson. And she didn't come home the last two nights, and I haven't seen her today, and I'm kind of freaking out about it."

Wilson straightened and scratched his chin, but it wasn't as if he looked surprised by her revelation. "You sure about this?"

Dakota nodded. "She told me about it… after Thanksgiving."

"Okay. Well, at least she's honest about it. Is she shooting?"

"Not sure. She's good at hiding stuff."

Wilson kept scratching. "This is a serious situation,

Dakota. But you should definitely get some Narcan. Some of the heroin in town has been laced with fentanyl, and that shit can kill you."

For an old bartender, Wilson sure knew a lot about heroin. Then again, a kid from her high school had died last year of a fentanyl overdose, so perhaps this was common knowledge.

"Where would I get Narcan?"

"The community center distributes it. I can look into it and get back to you."

"Thanks. But I feel as if I need to do something now."

"Have you called the hospitals in town?"

The suggestion startled her, but if her mother overdosed or had been involved in an accident, then it made perfect sense.

"No, I haven't."

Dakota sighed and tapped her fingers against the bar's surface, but Wilson ignored her, shifting his attention down the bar a bit, where a couple of guys were nursing beers and minding their own business. He cleared his throat, but only the guy with the long brown hair turned. He looked like he could have fronted a grunge band twenty years ago, and he lifted his glass as if a refill were required. Whereas the taller one, sporting an old-school 'fro, was either content with what he had or lost in his own universe.

Wilson did a quick head jerk in Dakota's direction. "This is Dakota Lodi. Tori's kid." Then back to Dakota. "This here is Roscoe. The one not paying attention is Leonard."

Roscoe lifted his glass again, perhaps his sign for hello.

Leonard turned and shot off a finger gun. "I'm paying attention, Willie. I was just thinking."

"First time for everything," Roscoe offered.

"Dakota says her mom went missing two days ago," Wilson asked. "You hear anything?"

The two guys consulted each other without actually saying anything, then, apparently satisfied with what passed between them, shook their heads in unison.

"Any place she could have gone?" Dakota interjected. From her experience, drunks occasionally responded to prodding by a teenager, so it was worth a shot. "Like a party or something." Which of course she already knew, thinking she'd throw it out there anyway.

"Something went down at Rainey's Tuesday night," Roscoe said immediately. "Might be worth checking on."

Leonard turned to his sidekick. "Rainey's is a crack house. You gonna send this girl to a crack house?"

"I ain't never said go there. I said check on it."

"Sounds like the same thing."

Dakota paused, taking stock of her situation. Her mother had talked about going to a party in town, but would she have gone to a crack house? Then again, she knew enough about those kinds of places to know they weren't just for crack addicts. That they could be especially inclusive when it came to drug users. And besides, how many parties would there be in town on a Tuesday night? Zionsville might not be Deadsville, but neither was it the city that never slept.

"Did you guys go to the party?" Dakota then asked, all casual, as if she were inquiring about the weather.

"No way," Roscoe responded. Leonard followed that up with a vigorous head shake.

"Where is Rainey's? You know, just for my information."

"On Caldwell," Leonard replied. "From what I remember."

"Yeah," Roscoe agreed. "It's like this big ole house on a dead end."

Wilson furrowed his brow, and you could tell that his patience had eroded. "Listen, Dakota. Not sure what you're getting at here, but if you're thinking of going to Rainey's, I have to recommend against it."

"I need to find my mom. She could be in trouble."

"You're better off contacting the hospitals. Like I told you."

"I will definitely do that. But what if she's not there?"

Wilson took a moment, glancing over at Roscoe and Leonard, who were studying their beers, showing no inclination of increasing their involvement. Then back at Dakota. "You do what you have to do, I guess. But don't be coming back here telling me I was right."

Dakota smiled. "I can handle this, Wilson. I'm not thirteen anymore."

"I can see that," Wilson replied. "And I can see you're stubborn too... just like your mom."

July 8–9, 2019

Chapter 28.
The Girl with
the Blue Hair

At first glance, the text from Alice Benning did nothing to lift Dakota out of her catatonic state of depression. The revelation concerning Jimmy Ray Coleman not being her father had twisted her insides into a series of gnarly knots, raising the possibility of Greg the dead asshole Coleman being her actual father, which would be even more depressing. Unless Lucinda had been correct in her assessment that her mother got around, in which case her father could be anyone. The bouncer at Muncy's Tavern. A Starbucks barista. Some random UPS driver dude.

Alice: *Talked to Waller. He says hi. Smiley face emoji*
Dakota: *Awesome. Any news*
Alice: *Yes. I hear they're concentrating on the murder weapon. There's something unique about it but that info's not being released to the public. Still no motive unless you believe original story which Waller doesn't. Also there was a partial boot print outside the truck. It rained that night so the print is useless but they found tar residue. Not sure if it means anything. Waller was mum on that.*

Well, hell yeah, it meant something, the neurons in her

brain firing up, a sudden surge of adrenaline mixed with recent memory. More specifically, the Instagram photo of Stanley Powers's retirement party. A party held to commemorate Stanley's years of service at the Zionsville Public Works department. A department that also employed Albert Renfors, the husband of Stanley's daughter. And wouldn't working in that department require the occasional paving of roads? And wouldn't paving those roads involve the use of tar?

Dakota: *Interesting. Thinking face emoji*

Alice: *You have anything for me?*

Loaded question, for sure. And one she'd have to respond to if she wanted to maintain her relationship with Alice, and perhaps open one of those doors Rosie had referred to. And while she figured the tar could implicate Albert or Stanley, and Jimmy Ray had mentioned Anika was pissed with Greg about something, she still couldn't see a motive for any of them to commit a murder.

Dakota: *Jimmy Ray is not my father. But he said the fight at the tavern started with some guy that came with Anika Powers. Anika Powers is now Anika Renfors. She married Albert a year after the murder. Anika was best friends with my mom but they had a falling out. Something may have happened to Anika that caused all of this but not sure what that is or how it relates to murder.*

Alice: *Confounded face emoji*

Spot on, Alice.

* * *

"I'm getting sick of this place," Dakota said the following afternoon, her head halfway out the window as Rosie guided the Subaru down Queen Street.

255

"No one's making you do this," Rosie observed, a look of exasperation creeping in.

Ignoring her friend for the moment, Dakota waved at a woman carrying supplies out to a camper, as a truck rambled past them in the opposite direction. "Over there," she instructed, pointing to the yellow double-wide off to their right where she wanted her friend to park.

"I'm not sure about this, D. Someone will definitely call the cops on us."

Dakota offered a snarky smile. "That's not the way it works here. They'll just come out and shoot us. No warning shots fired, if you know what I mean."

Rosie cut the engine and turned. "It might help if you told me what we're actually doing here."

Dakota said, "Did you not get my tar theory?"

"Totally. But are you telling me the cops didn't look into this already? That a sixteen-year-old space cadet thought of something they didn't?"

Dakota produced a look of indignance. "Not sure you want a battle of the space cadets right now."

"Fine," Rosie replied with a shrug. "It just seems to me you're taking an unnecessary risk. Let's say that Albert or Anika sent the text message and that they're involved in this. Why talk to Katie? She had nothing to do with this. And… I would propose the risk factor is no different than talking to her parents. Or have you forgotten that Katie Larsen tried to kill you last year?"

No. She hadn't forgotten. In fact, she still had nightmares about it. One just a few nights ago, in which she came up for air in a swimming pool filled with blood and found herself staring into the face of Katie, who laughed and said, "Take this, you little cunt," before pushing her back down into the pool. Yet the feeling that something was off about their encounter had always nagged at her. And at a minimum, questioning it could constitute a decent segue into what she really wanted to ask Katie about. Such as why Anika lied to her when they first met. Would Anika confide in her daughter when it came to that lie? Perhaps not. But it appeared to be their best option.

"I'm good," Dakota insisted, trying to placate her friend. "I promise to be careful. And if we think Anika or Albert might be there, then we turn around."

"Well, I'm coming with you," Rosie announced.

"Awesome," Dakota said, thinking that she could use the support, hoping two space cadets were better than one.

As it turned out, there were no other vehicles outside of Katie's trailer that might signal the presence of her parents, and so they proceeded, Dakota knocking on its front door, then taking a few steps back to stand by Rosie, under the theory her nemesis might come out swinging. That being a few feet away from the trailer would give them a head start in case that happened. But when Katie answered the door, she eyed them in a casual manner that did not suggest violence, then sauntered out to join them.

"Hey, Katie," Dakota said with a grin. "How's it going?"

"Pretty much living the dream," Katie replied, a bored expression plastered across her face.

"I like your shirt, by the way."

Not that Katie would be debuting at fashion week anytime soon. Her ensemble consisted of a black Nirvana tee, brown cargo pants, and black high-tops. Her short hair was tied back in a poor excuse for a ponytail.

"Thanks," she replied

"Nirvana's cool," Dakota said. "Although I must admit I've never been a huge fan of grunge."

Katie kept a straight face. Dakota recalled she'd been sent to a special school for social-deviant types after her expulsion from Zionsville High. Perhaps she'd been medicated as well. "Is this the musical discussion part of the program?"

Dakota laughed awkwardly. "Uh… no. Actually, I wanted to talk to you about something."

Dakota sensed the tension building behind Katie's eyes. It reminded her of one of those nature shows where the snake coils up, acting all disinterested until it strikes and swallows the mongoose. "I wanted to tell you that I'm sorry about everything that happened and that I take responsibility for my part in it. You took away something that was important to me, but I lost my cool and I shouldn't have."

"I honestly don't care what's important to you."

"Well, yes. You made that clear. I guess the thing I don't get… what I wanted to talk to you about… is why. Like, if you didn't want me delivering pot anymore, you could have just said something to me and I would have stopped."

"What made you think I gave a shit about that?"

Dakota's right eye began to twitch, and something pulsed beneath her skin. In the distance, she heard sounds of people laughing. The smell of woodsmoke. "Joey Vinson implied it could be a problem. And I just assumed he mentioned my bike."

Katie smiled, creases forming on either side of her mouth. "I already knew about the bike."

"Huh."

"You were working for me. Abe told me about it. Of course, I didn't know it was you at first. All he said was there's this girl that wants to deliver pot using her bike, and I thought well, that's a pretty rad idea. Let's try it. It wasn't until Monday, when I saw the two of you flirting in the courtyard, that I put it all together. That's when I knew it was you."

"So this was about a guy," Rosie chimed in.

"You were with Abe. And Joey," Dakota added incredulously.

"What?" Katie replied. "A girl's not allowed to have some fun?"

Dakota felt the blood draining from her head. The words coming out of Katie's mouth sounded like an endless jumble. Yet one thing was clear: she'd been an undeniable, certifiable fool of megawatt proportions. The fact that she'd been working for Katie without knowing it, that Abe could be way more of a rat than she'd initially thought.

"Well, just for your information, I never did anything with Abe. And to be honest, he ended up being kind of a dick. So all of this was for nothing."

"You really don't have a clue, do you?"

"Yeah, well, I've had enough of this bullshit."

"Ms. Klinger's class. Third grade. Northside."

Yes. She had in fact been in Ms. Klinger's third grade class at Northside Elementary for a total of three months on account of her mother being evicted from the Willowbrook Garden Apartments in North Zionsville, which honestly wasn't as nice of a place as it sounded, there being no gardens. But what did that have to do with Katie Larsen?

"I went by Katelyn back then," Katie continued. "I had blue hair."

A flash of memory. Katelyn. The girl with the blue hair. "Okay," Dakota said, still not sure where any of this was going but feeling fairly confident it had nothing to do with some sketchy third grade class reunion.

"We were in this bogus Thanksgiving play together. We both played pilgrims, and after the play, we were talking. You made some joke about the Indians bringing canned cranberry sauce. I thought it was funny. I may have laughed."

"That is funny," Rosie offered. "And insensitive."

"But when we drove home that night, my mom said to me, 'I don't want you talking with that girl again.' That girl being you. Then she says something about your mother ruining her life."

"How'd she do that?" Rosie asked.

It seemed to be a logical question, but Katie hardened her mouth, then shook her head, as if she had no intentions of answering it.

Dakota felt it then. The fire building in the pit of her stomach, just like it had last November before she made the fateful decision to kick Katie Larsen in the groin. The devastation of a crushed bicycle replaced by a catalog of her now apparent idiotic blunders mixed with her mother reaching across the years to fuck with her life once again.

"Our moms were best friends in high school," Dakota started. "Your mom lied about that to me the other day, but I live with my grandmother now that my mom's in the slammer, and she told me all about it. I guess they were kind of wild back then. And of course they both had babies. We're proof of that. I'm guessing we even knew each other back then."

"Why are you telling me this?" Katie asked.

"Because I want you to know where I'm coming from."

"And talking about it could help," Rosie added.

Katie turned to face Rosie. "What are you, my fucking therapist?"

"Whatever," Rosie replied, putting her hands up in a sign of surrender. "You wanna act all hard-ass, that's your choice, Katie. But I think there's a pretty cool person locked up inside of you, if you ever wanted to let her out."

Katie appeared riled up by something. Maybe no one had ever called her a cool person before. She rolled her eyes up to the sky, and Dakota got the feeling she was holding back tears. She wiped at her eyes with her forearm. She took in a deep breath, then let it all out, as if trying to calm herself down. Maybe she'd been taught that at her new school. Breathing exercises for social deviants about to lose their minds.

Katie opened her mouth, but the words came out seconds later, as if on tape delay. "Your mom introduced someone to my mom that raped her. She tried reporting it, but no one believed her. Including your mom. Which kind of fucked up her life. Which kind of fucked up my life."

The revelation hit Dakota like a hurricane, the ramifications almost too much to take in at once. Anika's rape and its trickle-down effect through the ages. Her mother's involvement. Could it be related to the murder of Greg Coleman? Or her mother lying about her father? It was honestly too much to process. Though Jenna had hinted at Anika having a troubled life, and Marjorie Jennings wrote a blog on sexual violence and spoke at a women's conference that Anika had attended, so perhaps the tea leaves had been right in front of them all along.

"Do you know who raped her?" Dakota asked, a solid theory already taking shape in her mind.

Katie shook her head. "I'm not talking about this."

"But I think we should. It will be good for both of us."

"Like you want to be my friend now?" Katie replied, all snarky.

"I don't know about that," Dakota answered. "But we don't have to be enemies. We were little kids when this stuff happened. It's not like any of it was our fault."

Katie shook her head, and you could tell she wasn't buying it. "Why don't you tell me what you're actually doing here, because I'm pretty sure you didn't come here to reminisce about the old days, and I don't have all fucking day."

"Fine," Dakota said. "So after I left the other day… did your mom talk to you about me or my mother?"

"No."

"What about Albert?"

"Why would he care about you?"

"You get along with your stepdad?"

"Albert's a prick. But he's consistent."

"Does Albert own a gun?"

Katie's mouth dropped. "What kind of question is that?"

"What about Stanley?"

At that precise moment, they both saw it. The blood draining from Katie's face, the slight tremble in her lower lip. How she balled her right hand into a fist. "I'm gonna have to ask you to leave now," she said in a quiet voice, almost a whisper.

"Is there something we should know about Stanley?" Rosie asked.

Katie narrowed her eyes, focusing them on Rosie. Dakota had seen that look before. "I'm like two seconds away from smashing you in the mouth."

Dakota grabbed Rosie's wrist and took a few steps back, pulling her friend along with her. It had become obvious she wasn't getting anything else out of Katie Larsen.

"Thanks for talking to us, Katie," Dakota said, thinking of nothing more substantial to say. "And I hope your new school isn't too bad. If it's any consolation, your old school still sucks."

Out of nowhere, Katie offered a smile. It almost seemed genuine. "You girls have a nice summer," she said. Then she turned and slithered back into the trailer.

February 21, 2019

Chapter 29.
Crack House

After calling both Genesis and Parkland Hospitals, neither of which had a patient named Victoria Lodi, Dakota followed the river further south, to a part of town she usually avoided. Thankfully, it had turned dark outside. In the light of day, she would have seen a series of dilapidated two-family homes, the remnants of the old ink factory and its parking lot, weeds growing through cracks in the cement. So it wasn't until she reached Caldwell that it all hit her. Each step she took set off a series of chain reactions in her body—her hands shaking, a tingling sensation in her feet, tiny hammers pounding away in her chest—until she reached the house at the dead end, just where Roscoe said it would be.

Dakota paused, took in a few meditative breaths. The house was much larger than she'd envisioned. Extra wide, with two stories. More like a crack hotel. Cars were parked off to one side in no discernible pattern. There was a trailer on the other side. She passed by a firepit made of rocks, filled with ash and glass bottles. Then up the front steps. They had a doorbell, so she rang it. Once. Twice. No answer. For all she knew, uninvited people walked into crack houses all the time, though she rang one more time, just in case, waiting a minute before turning the doorknob and making her way inside.

She found herself in a dark hallway. She smelled dirty laundry mixed with something sickly sweet, like burnt caramel. In the distance was a light and the muffled sounds of automatic weapons. She moved forward, placing her hand against the wall to steady herself, when she came upon a room with by far the largest television she'd ever seen in her life. It practically covered the entire wall opposite a couch, where two kids sat, playing a video game. Something violent, obviously. Not that the carnage disturbed the third kid, apparently asleep on a recliner in the room's corner.

"Excuse me," Dakota said.

On the screen, some dude killed a dozen people in ten seconds.

"Excuse me," she said again, louder this time.

Someone paused the game. The big kid most likely, because the other one turned and said, "What the fuck."

"Who are you?" the big kid asked. He had made a 180, shifting onto his knees and peering over the edge of the couch. Definitely older than a high school boy, though not by much.

"Oh, hi," she replied. "I'm Dakota."

"Well, nice to meet you, Dakota. But did you think it was a good decision to break into someone's home?"

"Oh, no… of course not. I rang the bell. Three times, actually."

"That bell hasn't worked for years. Which doesn't mean you're not trespassing. Did you know I have the legal right to shoot you now?"

The smaller kid let out a snicker, and in the corner, the

sleeper stirred. The big kid had threatened her, although his tone didn't seem all that menacing. Then again, she knew nothing about him. Perhaps uninvited strangers got shot in crack houses all the time.

Dakota forced a laugh. "I'm hardly a threat."

"How would I know that? You could be here to rob us. Or worse."

"I'm here to look for my mom. I think she went to a party here… a few nights ago. She's a little taller than me with wavy blond hair. Oh… and her name is Victoria."

The big kid smiled for some reason. "Don't know any Victorias." He turned to his friend, who just shrugged.

"Can I have a look around, at least?" Dakota replied. "I'm pretty sure my mom is here. And I promise I won't take anything."

"A look around. Well, sure. But we should ask Grant first. See what he thinks. Hey, Grant," he yelled out to the boy who had been sleeping.

By then, Grant had entered the valley of the living. He stood up, stretched his arms out, then ran his fingers through his shoulder-length dirt-colored hair. "No offense," he said to her, "but you should probably leave."

"I don't think so," Dakota replied, goosebumps forming on the back of her neck.

"If my mom finds out you're here, you'll wish you had."

"What about Rainey? Could I talk to him?"

"Rainey is our mom," Grant replied, emphasizing the *is* part of his declaration. "And she's in the kitchen with our brother Kent, who's like two hundred and fifty pounds and likes to hurt people. So I'd say you best consider leaving."

"Can't we just avoid the kitchen?"

Grant opened his mouth, but nothing came out, while

the big kid lost interest and resumed the video game, filling the silent void with pretend gunfire. Dakota considered her options. Common sense told her that if Rainey was a mother, she'd be more than willing to help a young girl find her own mother. Though perhaps common sense wouldn't apply to a messed-up family living in a crack house. Instead, she went for the direct approach.

"My mom's here," Dakota said, looking him in the eye. "Isn't she?"

Grant shook his head, but he didn't say no.

Soon thereafter, they were in the beginnings of a hallway, a pair of voices audible in the distance. "Follow me and keep quiet," Grant whispered. He pressed a finger to his lips, then motioned with his hand to follow, and she trailed behind as they climbed a series of steps. From behind, the clear sounds of a woman yelling at someone echoed, and she quickened her pace, as if the sound were chasing her.

By then they had reached the second floor and she kept close to him, passing by a series of rooms, each of them with groups of raggedy-looking people in them, some draped over couches, others on floors, who appeared to be unconscious or sleeping. The smell of pot smoke mixed with that caramel odor again. The sounds of jam band music emanated from an unseen stereo.

"All right," Grant said, suddenly coming to a stop by another room, this one with its door closed. "So, I don't know if it's your mom, but the woman in here has blond hair. I should warn you, though. She fell down the stairs the other night and hurt herself. She's a bit out of it."

"Seriously, Grant," she said incredulously. "You decided to save that part for now?"

"We didn't have time for a fucking debriefing. Do you want to see your mom or not?"

What was she supposed to say? That she'd come all this way just to turn around because her mom was hurt and out of it, even if the thought of seeing her mother that way made her want to turn around? "Of course," she replied.

After that, Grant decided it would be best to lay out a set of instructions, the purpose of which was to avoid alarming Mother Rainey at all costs. "You need to be quick about it. And don't go out the same way we came." He pointed toward the other end of the hallway. "Go down the other set of stairs back there and turn left. You'll see a door that leads to our backyard. Leave out that door. Turn either way and walk around our house. After that, I don't care what you do."

"Got it," she said, not sure that she actually did. "And thanks, Grant. I didn't mean to get pissed at you."

"Whatever," Grant replied, then he flicked his hand out as if to rid her from his life forever.

Dakota opened the door and slipped inside. The room was dark, and she felt for a light switch along the wall. After turning it on, it took a few seconds for her eyes to adjust to the light, but already she could make out the outline of a person lying on a floor mattress. Though it couldn't possibly be her mother. Her mother wasn't a big woman by any means, but this person, curled up in a fetal position, looked like a child. Great. It would be just her luck to spend all night looking and end up in this god-forsaken place, just to find her mother wasn't here. Still, she moved closer. "Mom," she said, just in case. "Mom." Again. She knelt down beside the mattress and nudged the person on the shoulder, which resulted in movement, a head turning, which was about when Dakota noticed that it wasn't a child, but in fact her mother, except more like the *Walking Dead* version of her mother. Her hair was matted with blood, with the remnants of a cut above one of her red eyes and a purple welt on her cheekbone.

Even though she'd been warned, the sight startled her. "It's me, Mom," she said, trying to remain calm. "Dakota."

"I know who you are," her mother said, her voice scratchy, almost inaudible. "What are you doing here?"

"You've been gone for two nights. I tried calling you, but it kept going to voicemail."

Her mother groaned as she lifted herself into a seating position, her breathing heavy and uneven. "How'd you find me?" she asked, as if that were the most pertinent question.

"I went to the Handlebar. I talked to Wilson and some guys at the bar. They thought you might be here, so I came. Then some kid downstairs told me you were up here and that you fell down the stairs."

"You shouldn't be here, peanut."

"Yeah, well, neither should you."

"Fine. But if you've come here to yell at me... to tell me I'm a shitty mom... then you might as well leave."

Dakota paused. Lately, it had become obvious that her "you're the worst mom in the world and you need to get your shit together" strategy wasn't working. That she had to come up with something new. Even the internet info she'd spent hours browsing through referred to addiction as a sickness, a disease that needed treatment like pneumonia or cancer. Not that she didn't already know that. Not that it was easy when you had to live with that person.

"I don't want to yell at you, Mom," she responded. "But right now we need to get out of here."

"Okay," her mother said. She attempted to stand up but stumbled forward.

Dakota moved like a cat to catch her, digging her shoulder into her mother's armpit and propping her up. "You must have hurt your leg."

"It's my ankle."

"You fell down the stairs. Do you even remember that?"

"Yeah. I kind of do."

"So you fell down that first night and you've been in this room since?"

"No. I passed out the first night and fell down the next."

Dakota's mouth dropped. Her mother's escapades never failed to shock her. "So you were here twenty-four hours before you fell?"

"What is this... a fucking inquisition?"

"No, Mom. It's not an inquisition."

She took her mother's arm then, draping it around her shoulder to take the weight off of her ankle and guiding her into the hallway, toward the stairs that Grant had told her about. In the distance, someone had turned the music up. They kept walking, down the creaky stairs, her mother having to stop three times to rest, until they ended up at the bottom, where she heard voices again. Footsteps. She held her mom back and peeked around the corner. Two people moving in a direction opposite from them, one of them as wide as a truck. She remained still, practically holding her breath, until they disappeared into some other room.

"We have to go out the backyard," Dakota said once they reached the back door.

Her mother bent over and put a hand over her stomach.

"I don't feel so good," she said. "I think I'm gonna puke."

"You're not gonna puke, Mom. It's been two days. You probably just need your medicine."

Even while exiting a crack house, Dakota couldn't bring herself to say the H word, medicine seeming like the perfect synonym.

"And I definitely can't walk much more. My ankle is killing me."

"I can try to call Gina for a ride. But she hasn't been answering her phone."

"She probably turned it off," her mother said, as if it were an everyday occurrence, even though it wasn't. "You're better off with Uber."

Dakota bit her tongue. She had questions about Gina and the events of the past forty-eight hours, but figured it was best left for another day. Instead, she took her coat off and put it on her mother. They made their way out the door and into the snow.

July 9–July 26, 2019

Chapter 30.
Exslydia Fields

Of the many *Dateline* episodes Dakota watched in Rosie's basement over the years, the cold-case episodes never failed to pique her interest. How one detective could read the same case files, interview the same witnesses, and come to completely different conclusions than the original detectives decades ago. Sure, there were times when technology played a role. DNA testing coming to the rescue, if crime techs had been savvy enough to collect decent crime scene samples at the time. But usually it was something that one person noticed that another didn't. Like the *I Spy* books she loved as a kid, when her mother scoured the page for ten minutes looking for the monkey she couldn't find, after which Dakota, in a matter of seconds, spotted it sitting in a tree.

Apparently no one had noticed Anika Powers. She'd been sitting in a tree at Muncy's Tavern the night of the brawl she likely instigated.

"You think they even questioned her?" Dakota said after their post–Katie Larsen debriefing, the two of them sitting in the Subaru outside of Starbucks, both of them nursing iced coffees.

"They probably had no reason to," Rosie replied.

"I'd say revenge is a decent motive."

"Especially when no one believes you."

By then, they'd concluded that, years ago, Greg Coleman raped a young Anika Powers, and that she had retaliated in some manner.

"Though I have a hard time seeing Anika as the actual killer," Dakota said. "I bet she got Albert to do it. Killer couples."

Rosie tilted her head. "Interesting. But I'm putting my money on Stanley. Dads can be protective of their daughters. And you gave your number to Stanley and Helen, not Anika. What if they kept it to themselves?"

"And Anika went to them after we mentioned the murder?"

"We both saw Katie's face when you asked her about him. That had to mean something."

Later that night, even Lucinda got in on the act as they hung out by the backyard patio, enjoying an unusually cool summer evening. "That's one helluva story," Lucinda observed after hearing about her granddaughter's recent adventures. "But you've done all you can do. You should get back to normal life. Enjoy the rest of the summer."

Normal. It sounded good in theory. And wouldn't her life be closer to it if she could put the whole murder thing to rest? Never speak to a Coleman, Bonardi, Boland, Renfors, Larsen, or Powers again. Instead, just wait for the DNA test to arrive in August, then revisit the father search at that time. Yet she needed some degree of closure. Something to wrap it all up in a neat bow. Which was why, the next morning, she sent out what she hoped to be her final text message to Alice Benning.

Hi Alice :)

I thought I'd share some observations based on my investigation. Tell Waller if you must.

The tar from the murder scene could be from either Albert Renfors or Stanley Powers, both of whom were employed at the Zionsville Public Works department at the time.

Anika Powers was likely raped by Greg Coleman but it was not reported to police and no one believed her at the time. Still, a decent motive for her to set things in motion.

I'm wondering if Stanley has the murder weapon. Just a hunch.

Blinking ellipsis for like five minutes.

Alice: *How do you know about the rape?*

After Katie's revelation, and based on another hunch, she'd revisited Marjorie Jenning's Insta page and clicked on a link to LinkedIn on one of her blogs. As it turned out, Marjorie had received a college degree in psychology from Ohio State and during the years of 2004 to 2007 worked at the Alliance Counseling Center in Zionsville, which specialized in crisis intervention. And rape.

Dakota: *Her daughter told me about it. And there could be other witnesses who knew. Jenna Beal and Marjorie Jennings are friends and Marjorie may have been her rape counselor back when this happened.*

Not to mention Albert and Stanley. Or her mother.

Alice: *Is this a dream you had? Is any of it true?*

Dakota: *Could be both. LOL*

Alice: *Astounded face emoji*

* * *

It was approaching the end of July, the sudden descent

of summer becoming apparent, that Dakota decided to take Lucinda's advice and at least try to enjoy the rest of the summer. Though for some reason she equated that enjoyment with Carlos. And while they'd certainly become friends, reveling in their day-to-day banter in the diner, there'd been no concrete signs that he thought of her in any other way. Dakota resigned herself to that fate, reasoning it was nice having a guy for a friend, until a low-risk opportunity presented itself. Rosie had recently received great news and would be showing her latest painting at the local art gallery's young artists exhibit. Which meant she could ask Carlos to attend the exhibit with her, under the guise that she would be going anyway. It would give her an out of sorts, if he thought she was asking him out on a date (which she was) and didn't want it to be a date.

"So, Carlos," she said, encountering him in the kitchen, her nerves revving up like an untuned engine. "I wanted to ask you something."

Carlos had been unloading the Hobart but didn't seem particularly stoked for continuing down that path. He glanced up at Dakota. "Can I help you, Ms. Lodi?"

Dakota gulped in a heap of the steamy kitchen air and moved closer. "So, I'm going to Rosie's art exhibit on Friday night and was wondering if you might want to come along."

"Rosie has an art exhibit?"

Either Carlos was completely oblivious to the outside world or was intentionally trying to make things difficult. She couldn't decide which was worse.

"Yeah. She's, like, a really great artist. Which is why she's showing a painting at the exhibit. I'm going no matter what. I just thought you might like to come. With me, that is."

"Should I invite anyone else?"

Was this guy serious? Had he not recognized the gravity of the moment? "I'm inviting only you, Carlos," she responded, laying out the ultimatum.

He scratched at his chin and paused as if to consider his options "I see," he said. "Like a date?"

"Yes," she replied, an invisible hammer pounding against her chest. "If you're good with that. If not... you know... that's cool too."

"Okay, then. I'll go with you. On a date, that is."

"Really?"

"Definitely. I'm in. One hundred percent."

"Yeah... well, I'm gonna need one hundred and ten percent," Dakota said, beaming. Embarrassing, actually. She would have preferred to maintain her composure at the moment and act as if going out on a summer date with the hot dishwasher was not out of her norm.

* * *

Going on the first date of your life was humiliating enough, considering you were sixteen years old and every other person with a functioning brain and hormones around that age had probably been on multiple dates before. To make things worse, her grandmother decided to insert herself into the process.

"I never would have thought you hadn't been on a date before," Lucinda observed in her usual monotone. "You must be excited."

"I am," Dakota replied. "But it's not like I don't know him already."

"That's right. The guy at work. Carlos."

Sure, she'd mentioned him once or twice. Maybe ten times.

"But here's the thing, Dakota," Lucinda continued. "I wouldn't be a good parent if I didn't talk about... complications. Us Lodi women have a bit of a history with that."

She knew all about complications. Was she not living proof of that? Both Lucinda and her mother had babies at seventeen.

"It's just a date, Grandma," Dakota said, trying her hand at reassurance. "I wasn't planning to have sex with him."

"Yeah... well, no one plans to have sex. That's why they have that stupid *16 and Pregnant* show on TV."

Hey. She liked that show. Still, how many times had she and Rosie watched it while mocking the intelligence of its participants, proclaiming out loud that it would never happen to them?

"I admit I'm the last person that should be taking care of a baby," Dakota said. "But I'm not sure Carlos even likes me that way."

Lucinda shook her head. "You're underestimating a teenage boy's libido. And you're underestimating yourself. You're a nice person. You're interesting and attractive. Believe me, he's going to like you in that way. And while I'm not advocating you have sex with him, you need to tell me if things are going in that direction. We can take a trip to the Community Health Center to get you some pills."

Great. A conversation with her grandmother about birth control. Never in her wildest imagination had she imagined such a thing.

"I could do that," Dakota said, but wondering if she could.

Lucinda opened her mouth. "Truth squad" was all she said.

On the evening of her date, Dakota spent far too much time blow-drying and brushing her hair. She put on the outfit she'd bought at the mall with Rosie, a short black knit dress with spaghetti straps over a black-and-tan-striped crew-neck tee. A pair of black slip-on sneakers. She added the black leather bracelet Rosie had gotten her for her sixteenth birthday and applied a thin layer of lip gloss. Her intentions were to be her best self for one night. Once that was over, Carlos would have to be satisfied with the floor model.

Which he seemed to indicate on the way out to the car, after meeting Lucinda and talking about the weather for far too long. "You look amazing, Dakota."

"Thanks, Carlos," she replied with a smile. "And you're not so bad yourself." He had on tan prAna hiker pants and a black polo, much sharper than the jeans and T-shirts he usually wore at the diner.

The gallery was located in a refurbished industrial complex along the north side of the river, and as they entered the building, you could detect a distinct buzz to the place, the art crowd ambling about with their wine glasses, cheese, and crackers. It had high ceilings, exposed ductwork, and electronic rave music pumping out of a decent sound system. Paintings were set up on a series of random walls with track lighting. Sculptures on platforms. A giant centipede with creepy red eyes, constructed out of broken tiles, lying across the floor. In the distance, Rosario Peña, chatting up a small group of art aficionados hanging on every word, as if they were discussing something serious. They were obviously captivated by her friend, who appeared radiant. An indoor supernova, wearing a red, yellow, and blue floral-print, front-buttoned sundress over a white tee. Her hair was tied back, a stray bang wandering across her eye, her dimples clearly visible even from a distance.

Dakota grabbed Carlos's hand and led him out into the gallery, and he squeezed her hand back, caressing one of her fingers, sending sparks up and down her elbow. Then, as if he'd choreographed it beforehand, he smoothly transitioned into a hand around her waist, pulling her closer. Wow. This was going far better than expected.

The place was crowded but spread out enough so that you could get good views of the artwork if you were patient. And in some ways, the paintings took her mind off the developing sexual tension between them. She tried, at least, taking in the artwork with an open heart and mind. An oil painting of a boat tied up to a dock with a fading sunset in the background. A watercolor portrait of an old man playing the piano. A few modern pieces with paint splotched onto canvas, and mixed-media creations made out of fabric and what looked to be cutouts from colored construction paper. The sculptures were cool as well, especially the giant dragon made out of rusted cans and scrap metal that looked like a prop for a *Game of Thrones* episode and a humongous colorful ceramic pig on a wooden stand.

"I'm not sure why," Carlos said, eyes fixed on the pig, "but this is making me hungry."

Dakota smiled. "Rosie once told me that art can elicit a physical response." Not letting Carlos know that her physical response at the moment was due to extreme horniness. "So, if hunger is what you're feeling, I say just roll with it."

It was then, as if Carlos had read her mind, that he turned and kissed her on the mouth. Nothing too crazy, but soft and slow. Definitely sexy. "I've been wanting to do that all night, Dakota."

"Well, I've waited a whole month," she admitted, kissing him back, sliding the tip of her tongue over his mouth, which he seemed to like.

It wasn't as if they could make out in the middle of an art gallery, so they decided to journey to their ultimate destination, turning a corner at the back end of the room, where they faced a wall with Rosie's painting on it. There'd been a decent-size crowd around it at first, so they had to wait their turn until things cleared out. But once it did, they were rewarded. Set up before them, the painting, entitled *Exslydia Fields,* rested on a large yellow wall with a spotlight positioned at its apex. She let go of Carlos and took a step back. Carlos joined her so that they were side by side but not touching. He scratched at a spot below his ear and gave a slight humming noise. "Do you have any idea what it means?"

"I think I do," Dakota replied. "But maybe that's not the point. I think you're supposed to ask yourself that question and then come up with your own meaning. It's kind of like music. Right? Sometimes you identify with the lyrics. Other times it's the hook or something more subliminal like a background instrument or a drumbeat." She was flooding Carlos with artsy intellectual bullshit, but in some ways, she believed it.

"So I should assume you've seen this before," he said.

Dakota said she had but left out the details. She'd of course seen the painting before but not in its final form, only in the beginning stages where her friend, working with pastels, laid down the background one layer at a time. After that, she'd been secretive about it, covering it with a tarp whenever Dakota came by to inspect it. But there was no doubt about it. Rosie's final creation was the highlight of the exhibit. A young girl sitting in a field of windblown wheat. You couldn't actually see the wind, of course, but the way the tips of the wheat were bent made it so that you could almost hear it. Meanwhile the girl, with dark wavy hair and black eyes, stared into a large mirror. Except that her reflection was not her own face, but her face broken up into little pieces, like a photograph layered onto a sheet of glass that had been shattered with a hammer and then reassembled in an order that did not resemble a face. Eyes up and down, an ear stained with lipstick next to a mouth, patches of hair in places they should not be.

"She's very talented," Carlos observed.

"No shit," Dakota replied, something bursting inside her, the culmination of which she couldn't quite identify. Her throat tightened and she clenched her teeth, holding back tears.

"Are you okay, Dakota?"

How could she explain it to him? All that had happened to them over the past year? Those times spent in Rosie's backyard shed, her best friend laboring over one of her creations as their music played in the background. Rosie, too much in the zone to engage in conversation, probably wouldn't have heard you if you tried starting one.

"I don't know," Dakota started. "Like… I've known for a long time she was talented. But the fact that she's being recognized for doing it? And it's something she's always wanted? I guess I'm just proud of her, if that makes any sense."

"It does, actually. And it's really cool that you have a friend you care about like that."

She raised an eyebrow. "You think so?"

"It's not so common, Dakota."

They made the decision to leave then. Carlos kissed her on the cheek before suggesting it, a sweet gesture that gave her no reason to contest the decision. But first there was other business to attend to: a men's room break for Carlos and Dakota saying goodbye to Rosie, after which they'd meet up by the centipede.

Dakota crossed the room, stopping on the way at a desk that had paper ballots strewn about where you could vote on your favorite piece. She grabbed a pen and one of the ballots, filled out her choice, then folded the paper and stuffed it in the opening of a small metallic box. She lifted her eyes, taking one last glance around the room at all the people milling about and the lights and the paintings. She moved slowly, as if she wanted the moment to linger, coming up behind her friend and tapping her on the shoulder.

Rosie turned and fixed her with a big smile.

"Just so you know," Dakota said, "I voted for the pig."

Rosie shrugged. "Personally, I preferred the dragon. But to each their own."

Dakota lurched at her friend, draping her arms around her shoulders and giving her the hug of all hugs. "It's so fucking beautiful, Rosie. I don't even know what to say."

Rosie released herself from her friend's death grip but kept two hands on her shoulders. "I really appreciate you being here, D. Even if you had to bring your hot new boyfriend and you might have sex before I do."

"I wouldn't go that far. But he did kiss me already."

"I'm not surprised. You look incredible. I almost didn't recognize you at first."

Dakota shrugged. "Yeah… well, okay. But I'm really happy for you, Rosie. I think this could be the start of something big. And, like, you definitely deserve it. And you look great too. That dress… it's like a piece of art."

"Don't know about that, but I did want to stand out."

"Well, you did. And now I'm kind of sorry I didn't get to talk to you more."

"Believe me, you wouldn't have had the chance. Once these fucking art people latch on to you, they don't shut up. And honestly, D, they're boring as shit. Except this woman from the Langston Gallery… she wants to show my painting at their big exhibit this fall. She said I can actually sell it there. And when I asked her how much and she went…" Rosie lowered her voice an octave. "Well… you're young and inexperienced… so around eight hundred. But… if you work hard. If you develop yourself as an artist… I see no reason you couldn't make a career out of this."

"Are you serious? Did you tell your mother that?"

"You bet."

"You think she's coming around?"

"Not sure. But it helps when she sees dollar signs."

"Wow, Rosie. This is so amazing. Though I have to say I'm not that surprised. I've always believed in you. And that I get to be your friend… to see it all happen…"

Rosie bit down on her lower lip. "Honestly, D, if you make me cry, I am going to have to smack you."

"Fine then… I'll shut up. But we have to split. I guess I'll see you at work tomorrow."

"That's not gonna fly," Rosie replied, shaking her head. "You need to call me tonight after you get home. I want to know how the rest of your night goes."

Dakota gave her a devious smile. "I could be late though."

"Don't care what time it is. Just do it. Oh… and I will require details."

Next thing Dakota knew, Carlos had dragged her over to a patch of grass on a hill overlooking the river, somewhere between the gallery entrance and wherever the hell their car was parked. They lay down, and instantly he pulled her close. He kissed her softly on the mouth, and then, in what seemed to be a perfectly logical progression, began kissing her on her cheek, her neck, the nape of her neck down to the shoulders, finishing up at the lobes of her ears, which he nestled softly between his teeth. Who knew there were so many nerve endings in the human body? Even the crook of her elbow buzzed. It was as if she had no choice then, some invisible magnetic force sucking her in, and she kissed him back, slowly at first, until the two of them were like stars crashing into each other, bodies grinding, teeth gnashing, tongues moving in and out of each other's mouths.

Dakota came up for air. It was quiet and dark where they were lying, only the sounds of the river and the light of a crescent moon outlining their bodies. "You should have asked me out earlier, Carlos," she said to him. "We would have had a way better summer."

"You're right," Carlos admitted, "I was a chicken. It's just that sometimes I find you intimidating, Dakota. That probably sounds strange to you."

She laughed. Strange didn't begin to explain it. "Carlos, I'm, like, the least intimidating person in the world."

"The fact that you think that makes you intimidating. I mean, you're smart and you're cool. You've got your shit together. I guess that's something I'm not used to."

Dakota then surmised that Carlos had dated only mentally challenged hot girls in his lifetime. It was the only conceivable explanation, since she was about six time zones away from being cool and having her shit together. And obviously Carlos had not seen her last report card. But she could play that game if she had to. She placed her index finger on his nose and pressed it. "Anything else you want to add, Carlos?"

He moved closer, and she became aware of his breathing. "Seriously, Dakota. You can't deny this is unexpected."

"It is," she said, flashing her best sex-kitten smile. "But you need to shut up." She grabbed Carlos by the collar of his shirt and drew him closer. She kissed him on the mouth and lingered as her hand slid up his thigh.

February–March, 2019

Chapter 31.
One-Girl Intervention

In the aftermath of their crack house adventure, her mother spent the next morning holed up in bed, complaining about her head, stomach, and ankle. Whereas Dakota called in sick for school, with the intention of watching her, taking care of her, or perhaps just making sure she didn't run away again. She even dished up a late breakfast of coffee, toast, and jam, serving her mother in bed as if she were a queen. A queen with a purple welt under one eye. At least she'd washed the dried blood out of her hair, making her appear almost human. Yet not for a second did Dakota believe that her mother hurtling down a flight of stairs in a crack house would be a wake-up call.

Her mother seemed to appreciate the service. She scoffed down a piece of toast, then followed that up with a gulp of coffee. "Thanks for breakfast," she said. "But I still don't get why you're not at school."

"To take care of you," Dakota replied.

"I don't need you to take care of me."

"Apparently you do."

"Whatever." Her mother smiled. "Will I be getting lunch in bed too?"

Dakota ignored the request. "So, Mom, I was wondering. You still haven't told me what's going on with Gina. She hasn't responded to any of my texts."

For some reason, she'd been obsessing over Gina's bad phone etiquette. At a minimum, it presented a mystery that should be solvable.

"She probably turned her phone off," her mother speculated. "She drove to Texas to visit her brother. There's a niece getting married."

Was this breaking news or a multiple-choice test? Gina had grown up in Texas, and it was feasible that she might have a brother to visit and a niece getting hitched. But how hard would it have been to stop at a gas station or rest stop and message her back? Her mother's friend could be spacey at times, but was never rude.

"Should I assume she's coming back, then? After the wedding?"

"Never said that."

Dakota felt a jolt, as if someone had implanted an electrode into her brain and turned up the juice. "So she's not coming back?"

Her mother sighed. "People tend to desert me, peanut. That's just the way my life's always been. But for now, I need to sleep. We can talk about this later."

Her mother's cavalier attitude about the whole thing made her wonder if she was the butt of some practical joke. Gina had been her mother's running partner ever since she rolled into town three years ago. It made no sense that she would just split without saying goodbye. Did it have something to do with the drugs? Had there been a fight over money? And what did her mother mean by people deserting her? If you equated dying with deserting, then her father's heart attack might qualify. As would Dakota's father passing in a motorcycle accident years ago. Could she be referring to living people as well? Could any of that have something to do with why she took drugs?

Searching for answers, Dakota took one last shot at messaging Gina.

Hi Gina. Hope it's not too hot in Texas. When are you coming back? Mom's not doing so well and I can sure use the help.

Surprisingly, a response came back within the hour.

Sorry Kota. You're one of my favorite people in the whole world but I won't be coming back anytime soon. Be a rock for your mom. Do what you can to help her. We'll meet again some day. Promise. Heart emoji

* * *

Dakota felt more like a pebble than a rock, but at some point, she came to the realization she'd have to find some way to save her mother. They'd survived her mother's post–crack house recovery, but as February bled into March and Dakota settled into her school life–home life routine, it became obvious to her that nothing had changed. Sure, Gina had left, taking her transportation, financial support, and perhaps her mother's heart. But someone else had stepped in to keep the heroin train running: Sketch, a large, burly guy whose entire wardrobe consisted of orange Harley sweatshirts and who smelled like you might imagine a guy named Sketch might smell. Whenever he stopped by, he retired into the folds of their house with her mother, leaving after a minute or two, after which her mother's mood magically improved.

Truth be told, Dakota wasn't certain how to go about

it. Other than proclaiming to herself that she would save her mother, had she developed an actual plan to save her? She already knew that flying off the handle, accusing her mother of lying and being a bad mother, didn't work. At the same time, there needed to be some kind of confrontation. Though she'd have to go about it alone. Gina was gone. Aunt Evelyn didn't like them, and Grandma Lucinda probably lived in some fancy condo in Florida and didn't give a shit. Nor would it be fair to involve Rosie or Wilson. It would have to be a solitary effort. A one-girl intervention.

It was on a Wednesday, then, the twenty-seventh of March, that Dakota sat next to her mother on their living room couch, watching an old *Dateline*, biting at one of her fingernails. She'd worked out her intervention plan, spending weeks doing the research, correlating notes into bullet points in her bio notebook and committing them to memory. And as the TV light flickered, she went over it all in her head, concentrating on what she hoped would be a good opening. Then she waited until the time was right, until the *Dateline* cold case had been solved, and she clicked off the television.

"Mom," she said, a vise grip tightening around her chest. "I'd like to talk to you about a few things."

Her mother turned, and fixed her with a serious expression. "What is it?"

Dakota took in a deep breath before speaking. "I don't want to argue or blame you for anything, but I need you to be honest with me if you can. I know you've been doing drugs for a while now, and it's kind of scaring me."

She had intentionally avoided any accusations. Her mother had super skills when it came to derailing conversations, and she wanted to remain on point.

"You don't need to be scared," her mother said.

"I get it," Dakota replied. "But there are things you can't control. Wilson told me fentanyl is going around and that it can kill you."

"You talked to Wilson about me?" Her mother pressed her lips together. There was an edge to her voice.

Dakota nodded. "He helped me get Narcan. I have it in my room in case you OD. Though I'm afraid I might panic if I had to use it. So I thought... to avoid that... maybe you could explain this to me... like, why you like the drugs. That way I might understand better and then I could help."

Perhaps this was the turning point, when her mother told her to fuck off and she would slink back to her bedroom, defeated. But something in her mother's face told her otherwise. A softening around her eyes, the corners of her mouth stretching out.

"It's not so easy to explain." Her mother pressed her lips together and paused. "I don't like that I'm doing it, but when I do, it kind of erases everything. It makes me feel good... less alone, I guess."

"But you're not alone, Mom. You have me."

"But you're getting older, peanut. And some day you'll leave me too."

Dakota rubbed at her eyes. Would it be unprofessional to cry in the middle of an intervention? Probably not. But something about her mother's receptiveness had choked her up. If only she could follow that up with something meaningful. Except her bio notebook, the one with all her meaningful intervention notes in it, was stored away in her bedroom. Though she did recall a particular line that she'd underlined and highlighted.

"That just means you need something for yourself," Dakota said. "Something to make you stronger. I have some ideas, if you don't mind listening."

Her mother smiled and moved closer then, their shoulders touching. "You are something else, Dakota Lodi. Where did you even come from?"

"I'm pretty sure some guy impregnated you, Mom."

"Yes." Her mother laughed. "That would have been your father. And yes, I will listen to whatever you tell me."

Dakota felt a sense of relief. She was pretty much killing the intervention. Perhaps this could be a future career path for her. Interventions "R" Us. Mobile interventions, where you drive around in a van all day, and instead of delivering pizzas, help people with their drug problems. And it wasn't as if the next part would be that difficult, just a barrage of facts and future plans, which she had confidence in delivering.

"First of all, Mom," she started, "you have to go to rehab. I found this place in town that has really good Yelp reviews and accepts Medicaid, and you can get in next week. Rosie has her license now, and we can drive you there. And Mrs. Peña said I can stay at their house until you get out, so you don't have to worry about that."

"Okay," her mother replied, though a bit short of an endorsement.

"Then… when you get out, you can get your GED, which I seem to remember you've always wanted."

"Well, yes… but how long would that take?"

"Funny you should ask… but I called the community center in town. They have a GED class that only takes two months. You have to take a test at the end, but I could help you study for that."

"You're gonna help me study?"

Dakota shrugged. "Why not?" She hoped that wouldn't be a sticking point, but perhaps her mother could do it on her own.

"Is that it?"

"No, Mom. It's not. And this is the best part. I spoke with admissions at Zionsville Community College. They have all these cool programs you can sign up for, and if you went full-time, you could get a degree in less than two years. You like science, right?"

"Well, yes. But…"

"So they have medical coding, or a medical assistant, which I thought you'd like, and they almost guarantee a job when you get out."

"Not sure we can afford college, peanut."

Dakota had anticipated her mother's skepticism when it came to affordability. "That's where you're wrong, Mom. Ohio has these programs for community colleges, and if you qualified, it would be practically free. And I think we should move. Not to Cleveland. Just somewhere else in Zionsville. Wilson knows this guy that owns apartments, and we can get a place for six hundred dollars a month. And Mrs. Peña said I can work full-time at the diner this summer, so I'll be saving lots of dough."

Her mother reacted suddenly, putting her arm around Dakota's shoulder and drawing her in. She let out a sniffle. A single tear dribbled down her cheek.

"Mom," Dakota said, "are you okay? Why are you crying?"

Her mother used her free hand to cover her eyes. "I can't believe you did all this for me. I just don't know if I can do it."

"I know. It sounds like a lot. But if you do one thing at a time, it won't be. And you're really smart, Mom. You'll do great at school."

No response. Just more tears.

"So, can I call the rehab place tomorrow," Dakota continued, "tell them you're coming next week?"

"Yes" was all she could get out, because by then she was flat-out bawling, her body shaking, tears streaming down her face and staining Dakota's shirt. And while it was a bit unnerving and unexpected to see her mother cry, it felt as if something real had occurred, and the tears were good tears. Perhaps this was the kind of thing that happened in interventions. Successful ones, at least. A precise moment when two people experienced the same dream. When it felt as if things had turned, as if they already were better.

August 6–9, 2019

Chapter 32.
DNA Conversations

In the kitchen, they huddled around Dakota's cell phone, examining the AncestryDNA report that had just come over.

"Obviously this can't be true," Mrs. Peña started, her eyes fixed upon the colorful ethnicity pie chart, the presumed centerpiece of the report.

"They must have mixed up the samples," Rosie said.

Mrs. Peña cited a recent *Dateline* she'd watched. "Police mix up evidence all the time."

"Remember that *20/20* show, Mom?" Rosie added. "That woman in Massachusetts. She faked all those DNA tests."

"I think they put her in jail," Dakota remarked, trying to hang on to a thread of common sense. "So I'm guessing she had nothing to do with this."

"But I'd say the basic idea applies."

"So you're saying there's this network of people faking DNA test results somehow associated with this woman from Massachusetts. And that has something to do with my test."

Mrs. Peña tilted her head. "But there has to be some

explanation." As if her daughter's theory should at least be investigated.

"I'm just saying… it takes only one person," Rosie explained.

"That's not what you said," Dakota replied.

"That's what I meant."

"So you don't really know what happened here."

"Never said I did."

"So basically you can fill up a giant storage locker with what you don't know."

"You don't have to get all snarky on me. I'm just trying to help."

"It would have to be a really big locker though."
Rosie growled.

Mrs. Peña laughed and told the girls to knock it off. "Why don't you call technical support?" she suggested, and Dakota nodded, acting as if this had been an original idea of staggering brilliance, even though her intention all along had been to call.

"Hello, I'm Cora," the woman from AncestryDNA stated in a pleasant singsong voice that made Dakota think she was in good hands. "What can I do for you?"

"Well, Cora," Dakota said. "I'm a bit perplexed by my pie chart."

"Okay. Let's walk through it."

"I can only account for some of this." This being 43 percent of the DNA profile, made up from Ireland (17 percent), England and NW Europe (6 percent), Germanic Europe (13 percent), and Northern Mexico (7 percent), all of it explained by what she'd always heard about her family. The Irish-English heritage had been derived from her grandfather, Jameson Lodi, whereas Dakota's great-great-grandfather, a German immigrant settler in Ohio, marrying a young girl from Mexico almost a hundred years ago accounted for the rest.

"Is there something in the chart you didn't expect?"

"Well, yes... the 57 percent. How's that even possible?"

"Great question, Dakota. You see, a parent contributes half the DNA of a child, but it's never distributed fifty-fifty. That, and there's always some degree of error in these tests."

"Are you saying that the 57 percent in this chart would be from a parent, then?"

"Most definitely."

"So that's the problem, I guess... or maybe I don't understand the designation." She was referring to the ethnicity designation on the pie chart, the one that twisted her mind into a pretzel, eliciting an internal what-the-hell response upon digesting it. The same one that bewildered Rosie and Mrs. Peña.

Indigenous Americas Region-North.

Either it took a while for Cora to explain, or Dakota refused to understand, that the 57 percent ancestry designation on her pie chart, the one labeled Indigenous Americas Region-North, referred to Native Americans or North American Indians, of which there were an estimated 574 active tribes in the US, making it impossible to determine specifically which one her DNA came from.

"But how's this possible?" Dakota said. "We're from Ohio." Which she immediately recognized as perhaps the dumbest set of words that had ever emerged from her mouth.

Cora, most likely trained to not disparage a client's intelligence, explained that she was no Native American expert, but that most likely there'd always been Indian tribes in Ohio, after which she paused, perhaps to perform a Google search, then came up with Shawnee, Seneca, and Cayuga, just to name a few, which pissed Dakota off because it went contrary to the idiotic point she'd been trying to make.

"What about a labeling error?" Dakota inquired.

Rosie looked at her mother, and a "yes, that would be it" look passed between them.

"But you did the labeling," Cora said, her voice becoming more gravelly. Dakota got sick of it just the same.

"Could there not be a testing error?"

"You could always send in another test."

"But I'd have to pay for that and wait another twelve weeks."

"Yes, you would."

"Couldn't you just check in with the lab? What if someone there had a bad day?"

She was reaching by then. Bad days. Shoddy labeling. Testing errors. But what if it were all true? What if she was the error?

Cora tried changing the subject, perhaps sensing their discussion had headed off the rails. "Maybe we should focus on the match."

There had been a single DNA match that no one had mentioned up until that point. A woman named Dawne Berringer from Sioux Falls, South Dakota. A second cousin, first removed. Whatever the hell that was.

"So are you saying I should contact this person?"

"I don't see why not, Dakota. If you look underneath Dawne's name, you'll see an email icon. It means she's given permission to be contacted. This is not unusual. Our clients are often amenable to what you might call DNA conversations."

DNA conversations. Sounded like a load of crap on top of a pile of steaming garbage. But were there any other options? And she could sense, from over the phone, that Cora's patience had begun to dwindle. She'd probably rolled her eyes already, waiting for their conversation to come to its merciful conclusion. Certainly there'd be other clients in the queue, with far more intelligent questions to ask.

"Just so I understand this, Cora," Dakota said, wrapping things up. "This person, Dawne from South Dakota. She could have some answers for me?"

"It's possible," Cora replied. "But if not, she might be able to direct you to someone who does."

Afterward, they sat around the table. An uncomfortable silence pervaded the room, interrupted only by background noises. The hum of a refrigerator, the ticking of a clock. Rosie and her mother stared as if they expected something from her. But by then Dakota had entered a zone. One where the outside world existed on some hazy perimeter as random thoughts rattled around her brain, searching for a home. And so she'd been barely aware when Mrs. Peña tossed out an awkward comment about Dakota's sliver of Mexican heritage being interesting and unexpected at the same time. Yet she'd heard it. Which could explain what happened next. A game of word association. A trio of seemingly discordant thoughts, whose connections, previously unbeknownst to her, came together to form the perfect triangle.

"South Dakota," she said out loud, this being her initial thought, not coincidentally the home state of Dawne Berringer.

"Are you okay, D?" Rosie asked her, clearly concerned.

"Remember that guy Justin in seventh grade?"

"Not really."

Dakota ignored her. "He got all pissed off once because Allie Walker asked him if he was Chinese."

"Why would that piss him off?"

"Because he was Filipino."

Mrs. Peña put a hand on Dakota's shoulder and squeezed it. "Maybe you should lie down, Dakota. I could get you something to drink."

"No thanks," Dakota proclaimed, a smile emerging from one corner of her mouth. "But I think I might be onto something."

"Oh yeah?" Rosie said, using the voice of a nonbeliever. "What is it?"

Dakota stood up. "We need to go to the Zionsville Record," she said, her adrenaline ratcheting up. "Like now."

By the time they parked the Subaru, it had started to pour outside, the rain coming down in sheets. The two of them exited the vehicle, streaking through the unfortunate two blocks, then bursting through the front door of the Zionsville Record. They stepped up to the front counter, both of them drenched, steady drips of water pooling onto the floor.

Across the room was Alice Benning, at a desk in front of a computer screen just like she was the last time Dakota had seen her.

"Hello, Alice," Dakota said, forcing a smile.

Alice turned. "Oh… hi, Dakota."

"This is my friend Rosie."

"What can I do for you girls on this beautiful day?" Alice said ironically, the rain outside having transitioned into a herd of thundering elephants.

"You don't have a towel by any chance?" Rosie asked.

"I don't. But I do have some news," Alice said, eyeing Rosie, as if it was not the best time to talk about it.

"It's fine," Dakota assured her. "Rosie knows everything."

Rosie smiled and nodded as if to confirm.

Alice appeared skeptical but continued. "Well, I spoke to Waller this morning, and he's definitely interested in the information you provided. I did, however, get the feeling he knows more than he previously let on."

"Do you think they'll get the search warrant to look for the gun?"

"Don't know about that. They're going to be conducting interviews, at least. And Waller wants me to reveal your identity and give him your contact information."

"Well, that's great, Alice. But actually, I've been thinking about that police report. You know… the one with the list of everyone arrested during the bar fight. I'd like to see that again, if it's possible."

Alice shrugged, then beckoned them to follow her into the office area. And you could tell her wheels were turning. Something about two waterlogged girls showing up unannounced at her workplace had gotten her attention, and she sat down at her desk and began to type away. In less than a minute, the list of those arrested at the bar fight was up on her screen:

Greg Coleman-Zionsville, Ohio

James Coleman-Zionsville, Ohio

Albert Renfors-Zionsville, Ohio

Orville James-Zionsville, Ohio

Shamus Westwood-Columbus, Ohio

Randall Cronin-Columbus, Ohio
Lenny Braverock-Manderson, South Dakota
Jake Weston-Rapid City, South Dakota

Dakota's eyes focused on the bottom of the list. She'd seen the names before, but this time they stuck out like a swollen thumb.

"Can I ask you a question?" Dakota said. "What was the name of the bar again?"

"Muncy's Tavern," Alice replied.

"Was it a nice place?"

"You could call it a shithole, if you wanted to be kind."

Dakota smiled. "So maybe you can explain something to me. You have these two guys from South Dakota working in Columbus, and they decide to go out for a drink since there's nothing better to do. So they get in a car and they start to drive. And somehow they end up an hour away in a dive bar in Zionsville. Are you telling me there are no dive bars in Columbus?"

Alice shifted her shoulders upward, and her lips disappeared into the folds of her mouth. "What does this have to do with anything?"

"Jimmy Ray Coleman told me the fight didn't start with Greg and one of the bikers, but with a Mexican guy that came to the bar with Anika."

Alice lifted her eyebrows. "I don't understand."

"What if the Mexican was not really a Mexican?"

It came out sounding like an offensive joke with no punchline, and she could tell neither of them knew what the hell she was talking about. She took her phone out anyway and laid it on the desk. She'd start with Jake Weston.

"Ever been to Rapid City, Alice?" Dakota asked, typing it into her Google Maps search.

"Can't say I have," Alice responded.

Dakota read out the blurb that came up at the top of the page. "Rapid City. East of the Black Hills National Forest. Gateway to Mt. Rushmore. Population 75,258."

"Is that supposed to mean something?" Alice said.

"Not sure," Dakota replied. "Let's try Manderson."

This time, it took a while to digest what they were seeing, since Manderson appeared to have an alias: Manderson-White Horse Creek, a census-designated place in East Oglala Lakota Unorganized Territory. Population 626. Dakota then enlarged the map on the upper right-hand corner of her screen and immediately noticed a significant portion of the map highlighted in green. This was a different color than the rest, with Manderson smack in the middle. This part of the map was designated the Pine Ridge Indian Reservation. Home of Lenny Braverock.

* * *

After her interlude at the Zionsville Record, Dakota was faced with a series of conundrums. Not only did she have to come up with some way to phrase an intelligent email to Dawne Berringer about their long-lost heritage, but she had to deal with her best friend's skepticism on the matter.

"I don't see how you get from some guy getting into a bar fight to him being your father," Rosie said. "You're making too many assumptions."

She had a point. The DNA results had not specifically identified Lenny Braverock as her father, nor had it mentioned the Lakotas, which meant that technically her father could be a completely different person from any of the 574 federally recognized tribes.

"There's just too many coincidences," Dakota reasoned. "It's the only rational explanation."

Rosie moved her hands around. "So some guy from South Dakota passes through town one day and makes a baby."

"You make it sound so romantic."

"Then two years later he comes back. For what? To see you and your mother."

"Apparently we were worth it."

"And then he goes to a bar with Anika, who you're saying he knows for some reason, and gets into a fight with the person you thought could be your father. And the other person that your mom said was your father is also there and says the guy you now think is your father is Mexican."

"I know. It's, like, totally fucked."

Which was pretty much her grandmother's reaction to the news later that night as they sat on the living room couch, trying to make sense of it all. Lucinda sipped at a neat bourbon as she examined the report. An episode of *CSI* was on the television, with the sound turned down. "You wanna tell me what this means?" she said, a look of pure befuddlement on her face, like she'd just opened a foreign language app to order something from a menu she could not read.

"It means my father was a Native American."

"Jesus" was all she said then, shaking her head back and forth.

"And I think he could be Lenny Braverock."

"Where do you see that? And who the hell is this Dawne person?"

"It's convoluted, Grandma. But believe me, I've done my research."

"This is crazy. It makes no sense. I told you we

shouldn't have done this."

"So you never heard of Lenny Braverock before?" Dakota asked, ignoring her grandmother's I-told-you-so moment. "Mom never mentioned him?"

"Not even once."

"Seems like something she might have brought up."

Lucinda fixed her with a hard stare. "Your mother was good at hiding things, Dakota. I think we both know that by now."

No doubt her mother was the master of all things hidden. But at some point, you had to use what little common sense you had. The fact that Cousin Dawne had shown up on her DNA report and resided in the same state as Lenny Braverock had to be more than pure happenstance. There were forty-nine other states Dawne could have been from. And so she resigned herself to her only option. The one Cora had put forward on their call that afternoon. She retired to her bedroom, where she shut the door behind her and made a crater out of her pillows before settling into her bed. Bringing up the AncestryDNA app, she selected the email icon underneath Dawne Berringer and began to punch in letters. The letters formed words, all of it pouring out of her, like water funneling through cracked glass.

Hi Dawne,

My name is Dakota Lodi. I am sixteen years old and live with my grandmother in Ohio. I sent out for an AncestryDNA test months ago because I was trying to find my father, and what do you know, the report came back today and said you are my second cousin, first removed. Imagine that! According to the cousin chart on Google, it means we share great-great-grandparents. I have no idea who those people are. Anyway, would you by any chance know anything about a person named Lenny Braverock, who I think might be my father, even though he didn't show up on the report? He is likely a Lakota Indian and lives in Manderson, South Dakota, on the Pine Ridge Reservation. Any information you have about this person I would greatly appreciate. And I'd love to hear your own story if you were willing to share that. Thank you so much.

Dakota Lodi

The reply came quickly. Next morning, in fact, with a time stamp of 12:09 a.m., which she'd missed since she'd been fast asleep. Astonishing, really. When she opened it, there was an email the size of the five books of Moses.

Dear Dakota,

How surprising to get your email. Would "welcome to the family" be appropriate? I think so.

So. You want to hear my story? Great. Grab some popcorn. Ha ha.

Here it goes. I, Dawne Berringer, am a 100% certifiable Lakota Indian. The thing is, for most of my life, I did not know that. I was adopted off the reservation by a white family (although I've heard my mom had some Cheyenne blood) and grew up in Sioux City, South Dakota. Presumably when I was nine months old. Not sure how much you know about Indian adoptions, but it's right beside the stealing of ancestral lands and the forced reeducation of Indian children at Christian boarding schools on the list of shitty things our country did to them. And in many ways it was on purpose, a blatant attempt to dilute their culture, done at the slightest hint of a family problem, even when extended family members were perfectly willing to raise those kids. Not sure if all that applied to me. Haven't been able to get the whole story. But it's crazy to think this happened in the ole US of A. Oh. And should I mention they tried to make up for it by passing the Indian Child Welfare Act of 1978? Except I was adopted in 1977. Lucky me. But I guess I had an decent childhood. No point in getting into that here, except that my mom died a few years ago, which was when my dad told me all about this and I sent in my DNA sample. To make a short story long, I eventually accessed Lakota adoption records and found my birth mother and a sister. I have relationships with both of them, but it's a work in progress.

As far as Lenny Braverock is concerned, I've never heard of him. And since our respective family tree lines are somewhat separate, it is unlikely that they socialize. That being said, there's a very good chance they know of each other. If you are willing to provide me with all your contact info, I can send that along to my sister. She's a good person and probably won't blow you off. Does that sound good? I hope so. And I do understand your predicament. How strange is it to wake up one day and find out you're not the person you thought you were? Though you can look at it as an opportunity. I've tried to do that.

I do wish you luck, Dakota. And feel free to contact me at any time.

Dawne Berringer

Dakota's stomach felt as if it had been coated with warm, buttery sugar after reading Dawne's email, and she immediately replied with a thank-you, a smiling face emoji, and her cell phone number. But a few days later, her warm feelings had faded, replaced by an undercurrent of nerves, which her grandmother appeared to detect.

"I can tell you don't like waiting," Lucinda observed.

They were in the kitchen eating breakfast, after which

her grandmother would drive her to work.

"I wish I could be more patient," Dakota replied. "But under the circumstances, it's just not easy."

Lucinda produced an all-knowing smile. "I have a feeling something's gonna give on this. If not, we'll figure it out. Right?"

Dakota agreed, but she hadn't reasoned it out in her head yet. What her next steps would be if her recent request to Dawne turned into a dead end.

At the diner, she attempted to navigate her post-date, post–DNA report universe. She had yet to clue Carlos in on her recent discoveries, thinking she'd wait until it was all resolved, but she felt guilty about it. Like not revealing every detail about her life made her unworthy of being a girlfriend. Still, Carlos had a way of making her feel better about herself, and as she carried the last set of dishware into the kitchen and dropped them into the sink, she smiled and nudged him gently on the hip before heading back to the dining room, where she wiped coffee circles from the table in the corner.

She felt it then. Her phone, buzzing away in her back pocket. She pulled it out. *Hi Dakota,* it said, the beginnings of a text message from a number she didn't recognize. It had to be a scam. Some guy wanting to sell her into sex slavery, or a dude sitting on a couch in Nigeria trying to steal all her money. Either way, she opened up the message, thinking it could be amusing. A good story to tell. Except when she read it, her eyes popped right out of their sockets.

This is your brother.
Mato Braverock

April 10, 2019

Chapter 33:
Big Ocean

It didn't take long for Dakota's doubt to creep in. It started when her mother implied she had important business to take care of, and could she possibly check into rehab a week later, on the twelfth instead of the fifth, because that would be helluva lot more convenient?

Dakota tried to keep her cool. While her mother acting as if they were canceling a cheap motel reservation was disconcerting, it wasn't as if she was totally blowing things off. In the end, what difference would it make if she checked into the facility a week later? Though the woman at the rehab facility Dakota spoke to saw things differently, since apparently there was a line of druggies in town clamoring to get into their facility. That being said, it was normal for people to get cold feet in these situations. Was she aware that there were custom transportation services available for these cases? She was. In fact, she'd read about them during her research, though it had all seemed unseemly, imagining a bunch of thugs in dark suits, wrapping her mother up in a straitjacket and forcing her into a car with dark-tinted windows. Her best friend driving her mother to rehab sounded like a better idea.

It was on the walk home from school that afternoon when Dakota's doubt began to sprout wings. And when she reached the crest of the hill on Bramble Street and spotted two cars parked in their driveway she'd never seen before, her skin began to crawl.

Inside, they congregated around the kitchen table. Her mother was seated beside Sketch and some skinny blond dude wearing a jean jacket, next to a large bald man in a black Under Armour sweatshirt. Behind them stood a smaller guy sporting a plaid shirt and a black wool cap. His face was covered with dark stubble, and he had a series of teardrop tattoos underneath one eye. Immediately, Dakota's antennae went up. Her first thought was that she'd stumbled onto one of her mother's poker games, except that there were no cards. The next option was that her mother was preparing for one last bender before she went to rehab. But did you need to buy drugs from four people?

Something else then occurred to her that made her fingers tingle with bad energy. Her mother could be dealing, perhaps partnering up with Sketch and selling to the other three. It could explain the *important business* she'd mentioned, as well as the mystery of their disappearing $1800 debt last year, if her mother had been involved in dealing all along. A thought almost too harrowing to consider, since it meant she'd been totally oblivious.

Dakota wiped sweat from her forehead. She sensed that things were falling apart. For some reason, she locked eyes with the teardrop tattoo guy, who had no problem returning her gaze, eyes unblinking, his face rigid and hard. Dakota felt a chill run through her. She had the sudden feeling that she could be in the wrong place at the wrong time.

In her room, she lay down on her bed, her mind too

frazzled to study for her history test. Her best option was to wait it out. All drug deals had expiration times. Did they not? Let it blow over. Then give her mother hell. Not that it would accomplish anything. What was that definition of insanity again? The one about doing the same shit over and over again, expecting different results. She could be a poster child for that one.

Suddenly, she heard a loud crashing noise, as if a meteor had dropped out of the sky and landed on their house. Then voices. Loud voices. The sound of breaking furniture. Had there been a disagreement? A drug deal gone bad? Oh shit. If only her bedroom door had a lock. If only her room had a window for her to crawl out of. Instead she got off the bed, her heart thumping away. The noises amplified, ringing in her ears. In the distance, a siren. Police? Ambulance? How could you tell? She cracked open her bedroom door and could see only a sliver of what was happening. A flash of blue. The back of someone's head. She stepped out into the hallway and the sliver spread out. Their living room had morphed into a fighting octagon. A cop wrestled with her mother on the ground. Her mother swung a leg out as if trying to kick him, but came up short. Behind them, the remnants of a broken chair. An upturned coffee table. The front door swung open. Sketch slugged teardrop guy in the stomach and rounded for another go when the bald guy tackled him from behind. A burst of cool air followed by more police streaming in. Dakota stepped forward. Her mother had been turned onto her stomach, one cop holding her down while another applied handcuffs. Dakota had the foolish notion that somehow she could help her mother. If she could only speak with someone in charge, clear up the misunderstanding. Explain that she was sick, that soon she'd be going into rehab and had nothing to do with this.

"Hands up," she then heard. Another officer. This one with a gun, or was it a taser, pointed right at her face.

Dakota obliged, her hands shaking as she lifted them into the air.

"Keep your hands where I can see them," the officer snapped. He was young, likely in his twenties. And nervous too, his hands unsteady. "Who are you?"

"Dakota Lodi," she replied, her voice starting to fray. "I live here."

The cop pointed with his free hand. "Get back into your room and close the door. Now."

Very explicit instructions. Still, she had questions. Like what the hell were all these people doing in her house? Was her handcuffed mother in big trouble? And how long would she have to wait in her room? Would someone be coming to get her, and if so, who might that someone be?

She made her way to the corner of her bedroom, thinking it could be the safest possible location, when a loud boom rang out. Then a second one, followed by a scream. She dropped down to her knees, lowered herself beside her mattress, digging her face into the carpet, with her hands over her ears. A gunshot. Someone had been shot. She began to hyperventilate, hoping it wasn't her mother. Her head was all dizzy, as if she might pass out. Then more sirens. Voices getting louder. A thud, like someone hitting a wall. She took out her phone and found her contacts. She selected Rosario Peña. Her fingers were trembling, but somehow she managed to bang out a text.

Help. Mom's being arrested. Gunshots. Come get me if you can. Very scared

Less than a minute later, Rosie responded:

Be there soon

Dakota couldn't say with any certainty how long she remained hidden away in her bedroom. Just that eventually the noises died down and she could hear people talking. She heard a bang against the door, and at first feared it to be another gunshot, but the sound was more spread out, muffled, and followed by two more bangs, and she realized someone was outside her door knocking. "Come in," she said, raising herself into a sitting position beside the mattress.

A tall Black man eased his way into the room. He wore a light tan jacket and black pants, not a uniform, but by his confident demeanor, she could tell he was an influential person, a man in charge. "Dakota," the man said.

"Yes," she replied, her knees all creaky as she stood, wiping carpet dust off her jeans.

"I'm Detective John Waller with the Zionsville Police."

"Is my mom okay?" Dakota asked with a sense of urgency. "Was she shot?"

Waller offered a grin, not a smile, but a projection of warmth, nevertheless. "No. Your mom is fine, but she's been taken into custody."

"What'd she do?"

Waller stepped further into the room, closed the door behind him. "I can't really get into that, Dakota. It's up to the DA as to what charges they file."

"Will she be coming back tonight?"

But she already knew the answer to that question, as did Waller, who moved his head side to side, almost in slow motion, as if that might soften his message. "Sorry, Dakota. Does anyone else live here with you? Do you have a place to stay tonight? Relatives nearby?"

She gave him the quick story of her life. Living alone with her mother. Father, dead at two. An aunt in Cleveland that wanted nothing to do with her and a grandmother in Florida that didn't give two fucks. Not exactly your happy ending.

"All right then," Waller responded, drawing the words out.

Dakota took in a ragged breath and waited. In a different universe, she would have liked Waller. You could tell he was a decent person. Especially for a cop.

"I texted my friend," Dakota blurted out, as if just remembering. "Rosario Peña. Her mother is Camilla Peña. She owns the Sunrise Diner."

Waller nodded. "Good. But I can only release you to an adult. Otherwise I have to contact emergency child services tonight. In the meantime, you should gather up some clothes. Enough for a few days."

"A few days?"

"At some point, you can come back here to pick up all your stuff. I can arrange that with you. But right now it's a crime scene."

Awesome. A crime scene. And what did Waller mean by "picking up all your stuff"? Had he intended to use the word *all*, or had it been a slip of the tongue? Would she be coming back to Bramble Street just for her stuff? Not to live there anymore?

Either way, she did as she was told, gathering up a few pairs of socks, some undies, and a few tees. and stuffing them in her backpack. In the hallway she sensed something was off. The world seemed muted, as if she were underwater and could only detect garbled sounds. And even once Rosie arrived, thankfully with both her parents in tow, she couldn't quite comprehend what was happening around her. Her best friend surged forward to hug her. Rosie's parents were deep in conversation with Waller, after which they came over for more hugs. Some words from Mrs. Peña she couldn't quite make out as they guided her through the hallway. Past the living room that didn't resemble a living room anymore, since a tornado had obviously ripped through it. Scattered pieces of furniture. A hole in the wall the size of someone's head. Blood stains on the carpet. It was then that she came to a sudden realization. That she had been a dumb-as-rocks fifteen-year-old, and that turning sixteen hadn't made her any smarter. That she had failed her mother by not getting her into rehab earlier. That the whole sordid fucking thing had been her fault.

Outside, they passed a cop unspooling a roll of crime scene tape. She slid into the backseat of a Subaru, Rosie coming in from the other side, nestling up to her. Mrs. Peña flipped the ignition, while Mr. Peña rode shotgun. Something cracked inside of her. A tiny fissure, at first. She rested her head on Rosie's shoulder. Then, as if a lifetime collection of tears had been waiting for their opportunity to be freed, she began to cry, tears trickling down her face, dripping onto her friend's shoulder, her body beginning to convulse. Rosie drew her closer as the fissure expanded. She closed her eyes and sensed a pool of tears carrying her down into the earth, flowing downhill through stones in a creek bed, turning into a creek before emptying into a river, stretching for miles and miles until it reached the ocean. In the ocean, the waves came over her. She could not swim. She could not breathe. It was no use. The ocean was big, and it swallowed her whole.

August 9–13, 2019

Chapter 34.
We Are All Related

They set up the Skype call for 8:00 p.m. Eastern Time. Their text exchanges had been businesslike, as if they were setting up a doctor's appointment. Dakota made the call suggestion. Her presumed-to-be brother had responded with a *sounds good.* When she provided Rosie's phone number for their get-together, explaining that her best friend had a killer monitor, Mato came back with an *OK See u then.* If nothing else, she could tell he wasn't the loquacious type.

By then, Dakota had no choice but to tell Rosie about her newfound relative and the fact that she'd be meeting him for the first time in her bedroom, on account of the monitor.

"I can't believe you have a brother," Rosie said, bouncing on her toes. "How freaking exciting is that?"

"It's starting to sink in," Dakota replied, but truth be told, she'd only scratched the surface of its meaning.

"Did he mention your father?"

"Nope."

"That's odd. It could be he's the gatekeeper. Like you have to get through him first before you meet the wizard."

Dakota had worn her dark gray ringer tee with black-trimmed cap sleeves over light gray jeans, along with a layered beaded necklace. If there was to be an initial test to get past the gatekeeper, then she would at least look good. Though her heart pounded in her chest when she thought about what she'd say to her brother. She had not prepared decision trees like she'd done before her visit with Jimmy Ray. Only questions. Such as why her father had been absent from her life for sixteen years. What was he doing with Anika at Muncy's Tavern fourteen years ago? Or if he knew anything about the murder of Greg Coleman.

It was like jumping into a bucket of ice water the first time she saw them. Goosebumps covered her arms, hands trembling, her adrenaline shifting into overdrive. And it wasn't as if either of them knew how to begin, which made things awkward, there being four of them not helping. Rosie sat on the bed in a cross-legged yoga pose directly behind her. The other two were on a couch, 1200 miles away. The one she presumed to be Mato, probably a year or two older than her, wore a black-and-blue sleeveless athletic jersey with the words *Mahpiya Luna* on it that showed off his slim build and muscular arms. He had slightly lighter skin than the younger girl sitting next to him, with some version of a fade cut, buzzed around his ears, a small patch of moderately curly dark hair atop his head. Definitely good-looking.

"Hello, Dakota," he said, producing a modest smile, the inertia of which caused the skin around his mouth to cave in. "I am Mato Braverock. And this here is my sister Zaylee."

Zaylee leaned forward on the couch but didn't acknowledge her. She had long black hair that framed her thin, angelic face. Her skin looked as if it had come through an Instagram filter.

Dakota tapped her toes against the carpet. "It's really nice to meet you, Mato. I'm Dakota Lodi, and behind me is my friend Rosie."

Rosie slid forward and waved. "Hey, Mato. Zaylee."

"Oh," Dakota added, "and we're from Zionsville, Ohio, in case you didn't know that."

Mato's smile widened, after which an uncomfortable silence ensued. And though in a scientific-measurement-of-time sense it likely lasted only a few seconds, it felt more like light-years. Mato glanced at Zaylee before lowering his chin. Dakota tried to unearth something that didn't make her sound like a raving ignoramus. When Mato lifted his head and moved closer to the screen, his expression turned into something more serious. "So," he said, "how should we start?"

Dakota shrugged. "You could tell me how you got my number."

Suddenly, Zaylee leaned over and whispered something into her brother's ear. Mato playfully pushed her aside, but Zaylee persisted and came back at him, and the two of them shared something in confidence. There was an ease between them that came across the screen, and for some reason she liked that.

Mato produced an exasperated look a parent might come up with before chastising a bratty child. "Zaylee would like to talk to you first. She says she has valuable information."

Dakota clasped her hands together to stop them from shaking. "How old are you, Zaylee?"

"I'm twelve," Zaylee replied.

"And you're in middle school?"

"Yes. I'll be in seventh grade this year. At Pahin Sinte Owayawa. We call it the Porcupine School, because it's in Porcupine."

Dakota had studied the reservation map last night. Porcupine was the town next to Manderson, slightly north of Wounded Knee and east of Pine Ridge. "So, what's this valuable information?"

Zaylee took a deep breath. You could tell she was nervous. "I have this friend, Lydia Dull Knife… or maybe she used to be my friend. She's been at my house before, and we rode horses one time. But yesterday, I see her at the park, and she gives me an envelope. Says it's from her mom, Lena. Says don't open it. Give it to Mato. Of course I open it later. It's a note with your name and phone number. It says call Lena Dull Knife if you have questions."

"And who's Lena Dull Knife?"

"Lydia's mom."

Could it be that Lena Dull Knife was Dawne Berringer's sister? Unless they were playing some psychotic game of telephone, where the message came through her sister's mother's brother's cousin or something crazy like that. Then it dawned on her. Not only had she discovered a brother, but a sister as well. How cool was that? Still, the entire purpose of her quest had been to find her father. She had to come up with some way to slip that into the conversation, casually, as if talking about the weather.

After the message revelation, Zaylee ended up leaving, and Dakota chased Rosie out of her hiding spot. It was just the two of them then, eyeing each other across the miles.

"She'll be quite the heartbreaker," Dakota said.

"Already is," Mato replied.

"And I'm assuming that's not the whole story."

"It never is."

Dakota smiled. Somehow it felt more comfortable with just the two of them. Mato's perpetual grin had something to do with it. "Perhaps you could start with Lena."

"I know Lena. Her son Justin plays basketball at Pine Ridge, and I play at Red Cloud, so we've run into each other. And I heard once we might be distant cousins. But I did call Lena when I got the note, and she said she got your number from her sister. But I don't think her sister lives on the Rez. Lena said she's an apple."

"What's that?"

Mato paused, as if he were measuring what to say next. "I don't mean to be disrespectful… but it means red on the outside, white on the inside. If I had to guess, I'd say the daughter was adopted off the Rez and grew up in a white family. That happened to us a lot back then."

"I'm pretty sure we're talking about Dawne Berringer," Dakota said. "She's like my second cousin, first removed. I gave her my number and the name of your father, and she said she'd pass it along. To Lena, who I'm guessing told you that I was your sister."

"Not exactly."

"What do you mean?"

"I did talk to Lena about it. She told me you were someone who thought you could be my sister. But I already knew you were my sister. When I saw the name. That's when I knew it."

"I don't understand."

Mato pursed his lips and blinked a few times. "It's not easy to understand. You see, when an Indian tells a story, it's never just one story. There's one that leads to another and another one after that. Sometimes it circles back to the beginning. Sometimes it doesn't."

More than one story. Circles. No circles. Suddenly, she got the feeling he could be duping her or trying to teach her a lesson. Yesterday, the day before she received his text message, Dakota had gone to the library and took out a book on Lakota history, where she'd come across a passage on Iktomi, the spider trickster, a Lakota mythological figure often found in children's fables. In one of the stories, Iktomi fooled a group of pheasants by telling them to close their eyes while he sang to them. Meanwhile, he killed some of the unsuspecting pheasants. While they roasted on a spit, Iktomi heard a disturbance in a nearby tree and climbed it to see what was going on, after which a wolf came by and stole his dinner. Could this have had something to do with the story Mato seemed reluctant to tell? And if so, what would her part in the story be? Iktomi? The wolf? Hopefully not one of the dead pheasants.

"Is this some kind of joke?" she asked him. It had to be. One of those gatekeeper tests Rosie had alluded to.

Mato shook his head. "No. It's no joke. But I can set up a call with my uncle Ed. He wants to meet you, and he knows more about this than I do."

"Can't we just ask your father about this?"

Immediately, it looked as if a sharp object had pierced Mato's midsection. He bent over and peered down for a second, before readjusting his position back up. Even through the monitor more than a thousand miles away, she could see that his eyes had turned watery. "I'm sorry," he said. "I should have told you this first. My father... he passed away... like six years ago."

The revelation ripped through her like a runaway freight train. Pancreatic cancer, he explained. It had moved through him quickly, with barely any time for convalescence. Mato had been eleven at the time. Dakota had been ten, worlds away in Ohio, not knowing what had happened to a father she never knew. She didn't know how to react to such news. And sitting in her best friend's bedroom didn't seem like the right place to process it.

"I'm so sorry, Mato," she said, the blood continuing to drain from her head. "I had no idea." She had the urge to keep saying the word *sorry*, put it on a repeating tape loop, since there were multiple reasons to apologize. For bringing the subject up in such a clumsy manner, for his devastating loss, for his family's devastating loss. And how, looking back on it, she could tell, the second Mato had uttered the words *passed away*, he'd undergone a physical transformation, his previously lighthearted demeanor vanishing into the South Dakota air. By then it had become apparent: Mato Braverock wanted to be anywhere else in the world but on a Skype call with his newfound sister.

"It's not exactly great news for you either," Mato responded, and she appreciated his attempt to wave it off like he didn't care. Even though it was not great news for her. There'd be no channel catfishing or four-wheeling or whatever the hell it was that dads did with their daughters. Not that she had any claims whatsoever on this man who donated his DNA to her and not much else. She thought about her mother then and still couldn't rationalize her lies, even though they were only half lies, an epiphany that hardly provided consolation.

They ended the Skype call prematurely but made plans to talk again over the weekend. They hadn't shared much of their lives with each other besides their both having a dead father, a younger sister, and an uncle named Ed.

She sat slumped over on Rosie's bed. A few tears trickled down her cheek, and she stubbornly wiped them away with her forearm. By then, Rosie had come back into her room.

"I need to be done with this," Dakota said, still choked up over the call, barely managing to get the words out.

Rosie draped her arm over her friend's shoulder. "He seemed nice," she observed in a tone meant to communicate she didn't really know what else to say.

Dakota straightened up and cleared her throat. "We live in completely different universes, connected by only a double helix." She thought back to Dawne Berringer's email and how it referred to her relationship with her new relatives as a work in progress. She had brushed that part of it aside at the time, not quite grasping the concept. That after the initial thrill of discovering new blood relatives, meeting them for the first time might not live up to the fantasy you'd constructed in your mind.

"You know," Rosie said. "This whole thing is probably surreal for them too. You might need to be patient. Take it slow."

Taking it slow could be an option, but for some reason she pictured her and Mato spending their whole lives peering through each other's looking glass, not actually seeing each other. "I get it," Dakota said. "It's just that sometimes I feel like I'm a lost child."

* * *

The next day after work, Dakota went right back at it, depositing herself in front of Rosie's monitor once more, dialing up the number for Ed Braverock that Mato had provided less than twenty-four hours ago. Having changed from her sweat-infused work clothes into a dark purple tank top over dark khaki-colored shorts, she tapped against the armrest on her chair, not able to dredge up the same level of anticipation she'd felt the night before. After finding out about her dead father and likely insulting her half brother in the process, the prospects of meeting her half-uncle didn't seem all that exciting.

Or so she thought, until the monitor came to life. Before her was a person she surmised to be Ed Braverock, a large bear of a man. Somewhere in the vicinity of three hundred pounds, except that he was tall, and the weight appeared evenly distributed across his large frame. He wore an extra-large Los Angeles Lakers jersey, and his arms stretched out like the wings of a condor. Behind him sat a brown sectional against a bare white wall with what must have been twenty people draped over and around it, nestled among its cushions, positioned on armrests, lying about the carpeted floor.

Just then, Ed let out a high-pitched whistle and the crowd began to settle. Two of the younger kids had been wrestling on the floor, and they ceased what they'd been doing and gathered themselves, while Zaylee flashed her a peace sign from the cozy corner. Even Mato looked up with a placid expression. The rest of them had come to attention by then, staring at the screen as if they were watching a mediocre Netflix movie with subtitles.

Dakota, a bit embarrassed by all the attention, forced a smile and waved, saying, "Hello, everyone," wishing she could have come up with something more poignant.

Ed faced the camera. "This is our new friend, Dakota Lodi," he proclaimed in a booming voice. "Not sure if your mother told you this, Dakota, but the Lakota meaning of your name is friend or ally."

Her mother hadn't told her shit, but no point in going down that road. "Honestly, I did not know that."

Ed smiled, as if he didn't care one way or the other. "I'd like to start us off with a prayer."

Okay. No one mentioned anything about religion. But she could roll with that. And she could tell Ed was at least trying, sharing that tidbit about her name to make her feel more comfortable.

"Aho Mitakuye Oyasin," Ed chanted. "We give thanks to everyone present, especially our guest, Dakota Lodi, who has joined us all the way from Ohio. As well as the animals and birds. Insects, trees, and plants. Rocks, rivers, mountains, and valleys. The Indian tacos we'll be eating today, and all of its ingredients. The meat. The beans and cheese. Salsa. Lettuce. Tomatoes. And let's not forget Sonia One Feather's secret fry bread recipe. I'd also like to give a special thanks to Mason Iron Cloud for agreeing to not add beans to his tacos today. We all remember the last time. The release of noxious gas. The forced evacuation."

The crowd erupted in laughter. Ed was quite the comic genius. The whole taco bit, pure gold. And Dakota laughed as well, going along with it until the noise died down, and she leaned forward, tucking a strand of wet hair behind her ear, suddenly wishing she'd paid more attention to her appearance. "I have to admit," she then interjected. "That may have been the best prayer ever."

"Glad you enjoyed it," Ed replied. "But you should move closer to the camera now. Everyone's going to come up and introduce themselves, and I want to make sure they can all see you."

And so the procession began, as if choreographed. First, the matriarch of the family, her new grandmother and keeper of the fry bread recipe, Sonia One Feather. An old woman with long gray hair, who stuck her face so close to the camera that the wrinkles on her face appeared like rivulets carved into small hills of clay. She bowed and said, "Tanyan yahipi!" after which Mato and Zaylee came up. Zaylee offered a small wave without saying anything, while Mato just said, "Hey there." Then the parade of new relatives. Ed's wife, Juliana Spotted Bear. Her other aunt and uncle, Daria Braverock, along with the aforementioned keeper of the noxious gas, Mason Iron Cloud. The Braverock cousins, Stacy, Wendell, and Wesley, followed by the Iron Cloud cousins, Clayton, Ella, and Ryan. Her granduncle, Justin Big Crow. His son, George Big Crow, and his wife, Linda Black. Her second cousins, the wrestlers Troy and Austin. The whole time, Dakota kept her smiling mask on while greeting all these people she did not know and who did not know her. She wondered if they would remember her the next day or give any thought to her existence in the future. She had the odd feeling she might never see them again.

After the intros, Ed mentioned something about one-on-one time, after which the monitor went dark. Dakota closed her eyes and took in a few meditative breaths, wondering what the hell had just happened, thinking Dawne Berringer had hit on something when she wrote how you wake up one day to discover that you've become a completely different person. Not that she'd alluded to the eighteen new relatives eating tacos and fry bread that you could not partake in since you were 1200 miles away. Perhaps Ed could provide some clarity on that new person.

Eventually, Ed Braverock reappeared in a small room that resembled a closet. There were stacks of boxes and a surrealistic painting on the wall of a canyon with a river running through it. The scene looked familiar, like she'd seen it before.

Ed eased himself into a half-sized chair and wriggled around, trying to get comfortable. "They don't make chairs for big Indians," he said with the hint of a grin. Seeing him at close range, there was something about him that Dakota liked, although she couldn't say what that something actually was. Perhaps it had to do with his boyish face, his short dark hair with the tiny cowlick in the back, or the way the corners of his mouth turned up slightly at both ends, making him seem as if he were constantly amused. Like a person who just played a cruel practical joke on you, but afterward you couldn't find it within yourself to be mad at.

"So, what do you think?" Ed said.

Now there was a loaded question.

"It's been great to meet you and your family, Mr. Braverock," Dakota replied, trying to be diplomatic about it.

"Call me Ed. Please."

"So, Ed. You started your prayer off with some Lakota words. I'm curious as to what they meant."

"Mitakuye Oyasin," he replied, leaning forward. "It means we are all related. Somewhat ironic in our situation since it's not intended for just the immediate family. More so for giving thanks to all of creation. How we are connected to all living things as well as inanimate objects."

"Like tacos," Dakota commented with a smile.

Ed laughed. "Especially tacos."

Dakota liked that he'd laughed at her lame attempt at humor. It made her more comfortable, almost as if she could trust him. "To answer your first question, Ed, as to what I think… I have to admit it's overwhelming. You have such a big family. I live alone with my grandmother."

Ed tilted his head slightly. "What about your mother?"

"Oh… well. Sad to say, she's in prison… here in Ohio."

Ed leaned forward in his chair and his eyes widened. "I'm sorry to hear that, Dakota. If you don't mind me asking, what is she in for?"

"Mostly to do with heroin. They sentenced her to four years, but she can get out earlier if she behaves herself."

"It must have been hard for you. But you're lucky she's alive. I assume Mato told you about your father."

"He did. It was really sad for me to hear about that."

"It was tough for them. But their mother, Janice, is a mountain of a woman. She holds them all together. And Mato is strong. I worry about the girls though. Especially the younger one."

"Oh, yes. I met Zaylee on the Skype call."

"That one's trouble. But in case you didn't know it, you have two older sisters, Santana and Javin. Good kids. Santana graduated from college and works in Seattle. Javin lives in Rapid City and is taking classes at the community college. We're all proud of them. Your father never graduated high school, but he made sure his kids valued an education."

"That's really impressive," Dakota observed, trying to take in the fact she had two new sisters, half expecting that more sisters could be bursting through the wall behind Ed at any second.

"Honestly, your father was one of the smartest Indians I've ever known. And that's saying a lot. Always had something going on. Fixed cars, had a horse farm… even raised buffalo for a while. Then he got that job with his buddy Jake, setting up the conventions. Too much travel, but the money was good. That's how he met your mother. In Columbus, if I remember correctly."

"My mother met him at a convention?"

"No. At a Kenny Chesney concert, after the convention. I think she was there with a friend."

She recalled Lucinda's account of her mother attending a concert with her friend Anika. The lost weekend.

"So you're telling me I was conceived at a Kenny Chesney concert."

Ed slapped his knees, letting out a howl. "More likely it was some time after, but I never got those details."

Dakota smiled. "That sure is interesting news."

"What... you don't like Kenny Chesney?"

"I wouldn't say he's my favorite. But I might have to reconsider."

"Just so you know, Dakota, Mato doesn't know all the details. I told him about you when he turned sixteen. That's how he recognized the name, which was why he brought me that note he got from Lena. We're actually related, so Lena had no problem talking to me. Said she got your number from some woman in Sioux Falls who said you thought Lenny Braverock was your father. But what I can't figure is how you found that out. Unless your mother broke her promise, that is."

Dakota heard the word *promise* and immediately felt a giant tourniquet tighten around her lungs. "What do you mean... promise?"

"Are you saying she didn't tell you?"

Dakota told him then. About her mother's lie, the DNA test. How she got caught up in the Greg Coleman murder investigation as she looked for who she thought to be her father. How she'd put everything together once she saw the ancestry pie chart, the match with a woman from Sioux Falls, and went back to see the arrest report from the bar fight in the *Zionsville Record* with Lenny's name on it. Lenny, being from South Dakota, just like the woman. And from Manderson, which happened to be on the Pine Ridge Reservation.

Ed had listened to her intently the whole time, his brow furrowed, eyes shooting laser beams through the monitor, which Dakota took as a sign of deep concentration. But once her story ended, he leaned back in his chair and let out a small gasp of air. "Mmmm," he said, moving his head side to side. "You are a smart one, Dakota Lodi."

"What about that promise?"

"I could tell you about that. But the first thing you should know is that you've met your father before."

She felt a surge of blood reaching her toes, the tips of her fingers.

"You were too young to remember," Ed continued. "He worked the convention in Columbus every year. So he visited you and your mother a year after you were born and then again when you were two."

"That's when the bar fight happened." She knew it. The reason he'd traveled the fifty-plus miles from Columbus to Zionsville had nothing to do with the shithole Murcy's Tavern.

"That's right, except soon after that, Janice found out about you. Let's just say she wasn't too happy about it. Lenny told me she threatened to cut off his dick with a hunting knife if he ever ended up anywhere near the state of Ohio. Janice was good at making you think she'd do something crazy like that, and Lenny wasn't about to take chances."

"So the promise my mom made was to not tell me about him?"

"Don't know if it makes you feel any better, but from what I heard, your mother fought him over it."

It didn't make her feel better. Still, there had to be a missing link to the story. Something connecting her birth parents and Anika to the rumble at Muncy's Tavern.

"Maybe you could help me understand something, Ed. Why did my father go to the bar with my mother's friend and get into a fight with a guy that was murdered two nights later?"

"Ohhh... that's a good one," Ed replied, smiling for some reason. "That was a long time ago... and a rough time for the family. The detectives flew out here to question your father about the murder, and he had to use Janice as his alibi. No way he could be in two places at once. And your father... well, he only gave out pieces of the story. The only thing I do remember was him saying he'd been a pawn in some kind of game. That the friend had an agenda to stir up trouble, and the guy who was murdered went off on Lenny, and that it had something to do with you."

"That's ridiculous. I was two at the time."

"Like I said, there was something happening beneath the surface. Jealousy, if I had to guess."

"And they were never going to tell me about this, were they?"

"That's not true, Dakota. They talked about telling you when you got older, but of course your father's dying took care of that. After that, it was up to your mother."

Afterward, Dakota could not deny the meeting with Ed Braverock and her new relatives had been a revelation. Yet there was almost too much to consider. Two older sisters she hadn't known about. The details of her mother's secret being relatively simple, and the fact that she'd met her father before, and that his reason for being at Muncy's Tavern might have had something to do with her. Naturally, she went back to her conversations with Ed, wondering about things she should or shouldn't have said. Yet there was something else that irked her. Something that had nothing to do with a bar fight or the murder. Something she couldn't quite put a name to. And it didn't help that two days after the Skype call with Ed and her new band of relatives, Dakota hadn't heard a peep from Mato. Not that they'd made any arrangements. Still, there was a sense of unfinished business, unidentifiable things that needed to be resolved.

She fired off a text message.

Hi Mato. Would you be willing to talk again.

To which Mato responded immediately.

OK

They set up a meeting for Tuesday around dusk.

This time, Dakota took the call on her cell phone in her grandmother's backyard, using FaceTime instead of Skype. Her plan consisted of a casual approach, wearing her red Sunrise Diner tee over frayed denim shorts. Time spent on her physical appearance consisted of a compulsory brush of her hair and nothing more.

"Hey, Mato," she said once they connected, waving at him with her free hand. The wind blew her hair around, and she talked herself into not caring about it. She turned the phone into landscape mode and moved it around slowly, giving him a panoramic view of the house and yard. "So, this is my grandmother's house," Dakota told him. "It's where I live now."

"You have lots of trees," Mato observed.

"I suppose it's nothing like where you live."

She knew her grandmother's backyard could not compare to the stunning vistas of the reservation she'd seen in photographs, with its serene grasslands, the rolling hills and buttes of the Badlands, but she wanted him to know something about her.

"By the way, Ed told me he thinks you're okay."

Dakota smiled. "Just okay?"

"If Ed Braverock says you're okay, it means something. Otherwise you're not okay, if you know what I mean."

"I'll take it as a compliment, then."

"He said he could see our father in you. That you had his eyes and his humorous nature. He seemed a little spooked by it, actually."

"I don't remember being funny."

"It's not like that. Our dad wasn't a jokester, but he had a way of looking at things."

She felt her skin tingle. That something had been passed down to her from a man she'd only met when she was too young to remember appealed to her for some reason. As if there were some kind of connection between them.

"Would you say he and Ed were similar?" she asked, trying to find a reference point, something to hold on to.

"Uncle Ed's a bit more boisterous than our dad was, but he's been like a father to me."

"I can't imagine having such a big family, Mato. It must help to have that support."

"Sometimes it does. But other times it's just more people getting into your business."

"I have a question then, if you don't mind. When I talked to Ed, he said he was the one who told you about me. I'm just curious what that was like for you."

Mato swatted at something in the air, perhaps stalling to come up with the right words. "Actually," he said, before pausing for a split second, "it was Ed and Daria who told me about you. They went to my mom to get approval first."

"It must have been a shock," Dakota replied, wondering how that conversation might have gone. Not once since the Skype call had she considered Mato's mother, although her skipping out on the get-together had been noted. Yet she'd obviously given her stamp of approval for Ed and Daria to reveal details about her existence when she probably could have kept the secret if she'd wanted to.

Mato said, "Definitely. My older sisters didn't take it so well. They were angry at first. And honestly, I didn't know what to feel at the time either."

"And then you got the note."

"That's when it all came back. I have to say, I hadn't thought much about you. I was probably in denial in some ways."

"I know, Mato. It's strange. Isn't it? I think it's strange for both of us."

Dakota took a bit of a break then. Letting the strangeness settle as she walked through the yard toward the house. By then she'd developed a crook in her shoulder on account of holding the phone up for so long, and so she melted into one of the patio chairs, resting her elbows on the table while still holding the phone out.

"So, what do you do in Ohio for fun?" Mato asked.

Fun and Ohio. Two words that she'd never used in a sentence before.

"Just being in Ohio alone is fun enough," Dakota

quipped. "But I've spent most of my summer working. Rosie's mom owns a diner in town, and we both work there six days a week." She pinched at her Sunrise Diner shirt, pulling the sun away from her skin to show him.

Mato offered a half grin. "Do you get free food with that shirt?"

"All you can eat." Dakota patted her stomach.

Mato's grin widened, and he let out a laugh that appeared to be genuine. "So, what will you do with all that money you earn?"

"I wouldn't mind buying a car someday. It's embarrassing that I don't have my license, since I turned sixteen last March. Although my grandmother did say she'd take me for a driving lesson one day."

"Driving lessons from your grandmother. Sounds weird."

She thought of Mato's grandmother, Sonia One Feather, and tried picturing her behind the wheel of an automobile, the image not sticking.

"I know. But you have to meet her. She has a job remodeling old cars. And she used to race when she was younger."

"Hot-rod granny."

Dakota lifted a finger. "Okay," she said, jumping out of her chair. "I can see that you don't believe me." She streaked across the grass, then down to the driveway, where she stopped ahead of the Thunderbird, holding the phone out again so that he could see it.

Mato's eyes bulged. "Are you kidding me?"

"Next time you make fun of my granny, you can remember this."

"Point taken," Mato replied, holding a finger up in

the air, as if to signal something. "But now I have to show you my main mode of transportation." And just like that he was off, his phone facing down into the dirt. Dakota expected an old car or motorcycle to come into focus, until it settled upon Mato's foot next to the bottom of a fence post, then swung upward to reveal a stable with horses.

"Holy shit" was all she could say.

"They're not as fast as a car but way more fun, and you can get places cars can't."

"This is blowing my mind, Mato. They're beautiful."

"In case you didn't know, horses are a huge part of Lakota culture, going back a few centuries. They're considered to be our equals. But I think they know they're superior."

Mato captured a panoramic view of the stables and introduced her to the horses, like they were drinking buddies from school. Starting with the two in the back end of the stable, a black one named Raven was standing beside Tokala, a brown horse with a white patch around its neck. A smaller gray pony with black speckles, Canotina, appeared in the middle of the stable, chomping at a bale of hay and stamping its feet between bites. It looked to be rambunctious with a sprinkle of attitude mixed in, and Dakota got the sneaking suspicion the pony belonged to Zaylee. Just then the other horse in the stable, a large muscular brown one with a black mane, trotted in their direction. Its head bobbed up and down, and Dakota could have sworn it was smiling. When it reached the fence, Mato must have adjusted the position of his phone, because the next thing she knew, it was as if he had posed for a selfie, the horse's face nuzzling into his shoulder as he ran his fingers through its mane.

Dakota felt a pang in her heart, at the same time thinking she could be interrupting an intimate moment. "That is so freaking adorable."

"This is Wakanda. It means Great Spirit in Omaha. Wakan Tanka is the Lakota word, but for some reason my dad picked Wakanda. It was his horse, and he gave it to me before he died."

"That's really cool, Mato. Did your dad teach you how to ride?"

Your dad, she had said, simultaneously wondering at what point she could refer to him as *her* dad. Certainly not at that moment. She at least had enough sense to not do that, as if intuitively she knew she hadn't earned the right.

Mato said, "Yeah. When I was four."

"This is a stupid question, probably. But can you ride Wakanda to school?"

"No. They have a no-horse-shit rule at school."

Mato winked at her then and Dakota laughed, wondering if he was messing with her, thinking he probably was, as she entertained the possibility of Red Cloud High having hitching posts instead of bike racks.

Mato continued. "I guess if there's one thing you should know about me, Dakota, it's that riding is my favorite thing to do in the world. That and basketball, which I guess makes two things."

"That explains why you were wearing a basketball jersey the first time we met."

Mato nodded. "I'm going into my senior year at Red Cloud High, and I'll be captain of the basketball team. We call it Rez ball here. It's way faster and more exciting. Anyway, my dream is to go to college and play. My grades are good enough, but I'll need a scholarship."

"Is that possible?"

"Hard to say. Recruiters don't make their way onto the reservation that often. Except I play on a summer AAU team. It's like a regional Indian all-star team. And this weekend, we're traveling to Minnesota to play in a tournament, and lots of recruiters are supposed to be there."

"Sounds exciting. I sure hope it works out for you."

"How about you? What year are you going into?"

"I'm going into my junior year. But I have to confess I'm not the best student. From a grades perspective. I guess I have attention problems."

She remembered Ed's comments about her father not graduating high school. Could it be that he'd had issues paying attention as well? Something else he might have passed down to her.

"I get that. School can be boring."

"You could be onto something, because I like to learn new stuff and I have a library card. Oh… and I should tell you… since we're talking about things we love, that I'm super into music. I'm not gonna lie, Mato. I can make playlists in my sleep."

When they were done, they stared at each other through their respective screens, the two of them looking exhausted, as if there was much more to say. And they'd left out giant portions of their lives. Dakota hadn't even mentioned her mother, or Carlos, or the quest to find her father. And Mato never shared much about his mother or sisters or what it was like to have a father die when you were eleven. Still, the feeling of something shared permeated the air, shortening the miles between them.

"That wasn't too bad," Mato then observed, as if their thoughts had been synchronized.

"It was really nice, Mato," Dakota replied. "I've been so nervous about calling you."

"I know what you mean. We should text now and then. Stay in touch."

"Definitely. And maybe I could come up to visit you someday."

"Don't know when you have winter break, but if you could time your visit with the Pine Ridge game, that would be good. It's a huge rivalry and the crowd is insane. I can almost guarantee you'll see parents fighting in the stands."

"Parents fighting," Dakota declared, her spirits soaring at the thought of it. "Well, now you've piqued my interest. I am definitely coming."

Mato laughed. "It's settled, then."

"But I warn you, I'll probably come up there and make a fool out of myself."

"It's not a big deal. Just be yourself."

"If I only knew who that was, Mato."

He chuckled and looked right at her through the screen. They were 1200 miles away from each other, but it seemed to Dakota that he could be in her grandmother's backyard, until he paused and an unsettling silence filled the air.

"Is everything good?" she asked.

"It's nothing," Mato said. "My father... our father... used to tell me there's meaning in silence. But what I wanted to say was, there's a good chance if you came here you'd feel uncomfortable at times. I'm sure I'd feel the same way if I went to Ohio. And I can almost guarantee some people here will give you shit."

"Does that mean I'm a wasicu or an iyeska?"

Mato produced a self-conscious smile. He would have known the two Lakota words, wasicu for white person and iyeska for half-breed. Terms Dakota had encountered during her reading, although she couldn't say with certainty if they were factual or derogatory, or maybe both, depending on who delivered it. "I can see that you've done your homework. But if I were to give you advice, I'd tell you to keep it real. If you do that, most people here will come to respect you. Don't try being two different people at the same time."

"Not sure I understand."

Mato furled his lips, and you could tell he was deep into one of those meaningful silences again. He angled his head slightly, and his eyes rolled up to the sky as if he were tracking a bird. "Let's put it this way," he finally said. "You're no Indian, Dakota Lodi. But you are my sister."

August 16–20, 2019

Chapter 35.
Friends with Benefits

You would have thought the last weeks of Dakota's summer would have been uneventful. Just the law of averages working its mojo, the undeniable insanity that had taken over her life having to end at some point. But then of course you'd be wrong. Perhaps there were those in the world not suited for normalcy. Dakota was beginning to suspect she might be one of those people.

It all started with the call from Alice. The Greg Coleman murder investigation had been wrapped up. Or so it seemed.

"They arrested Stanley Powers," Alice revealed, her excitement palpable through the phone. "And my sources tell me he confessed."

"How'd that happen?" Dakota asked, feigning interest. She honestly did not care anymore. Wouldn't it be best if they all moved on?

"The detectives used the information you provided about the rape, confirmed it through the witnesses you mentioned, then got a warrant to search Stanley's house."

"Should I assume they found something?"

"Yes. The gun. I guess there was a Facebook post from

a gun show at the Elks Club last year. It turns out Stanley Powers liked showing off his antique collection, including three World War II Lugers."

"Does a person need three Lugers?"

And if Stanley used one of them to commit the murder, why wouldn't he have disposed of it? Unless it was valuable and he figured no one would ever peg him as a killer.

"Don't know," Alice said. "But they did ballistics tests, and one of them matched the murder weapon. Apparently the fact that it was a Luger was important too. Presumably drug gangs use them sometimes because they're untraceable. Which could have been why they focused on the bikers years ago."

"Wow," Dakota replied. "Who'd have thought guns were so complicated?"

"And one other thing, Dakota. I hear Waller is going to contact you about an interview. And I'm pretty sure he's gonna take your phone to check out that text message. From what I hear, they're still looking at Albert and Anika as accessories. Though there's only circumstantial evidence against them, and they've already lawyered up."

"Not a problem. I could talk to him."

Though giving up her phone wasn't exactly great news. How long would it be for? And if Waller were to interview her, what would she even tell him? She certainly wouldn't lie, but perhaps she wouldn't volunteer any of her wacky theories. That just because the gun belonged to Stanley didn't mean he'd fired the fatal shot. That she still favored her family togetherness theory, all three of them playing some role in the murder. And what about that Luger? If the cops knew that drug gangs sometimes used Lugers, then perhaps Stanley knew that as well. Could the family have used the bar fight as a smoke screen to commit murder a day later, thinking they'd pin it on the bikers? It seemed far-fetched. No point in bringing that up. As well as Albert. The tar implied he could have been at the murder scene, but she knew nothing about him. And sure, she hadn't been particularly impressed with Anika, but the woman had once been her mother's friend, not to mention the daughter of her nemesis. A nemesis she kind of felt sorry for—she didn't feel the need to help the authorities take her mother. Either way, the new detectives seemed to be doing their jobs. They could likely figure it out without help from a half-baked sixteen-year-old girl and her dyslexic best friend.

"Are you okay, Dakota?" Alice then asked. "You don't sound too stoked about this."

Apparently it was not so easy to hide her apathy. "I've had a lot going on, Alice." Then she told her. About the dead father. Her new siblings. Even tossed in some minor details about their conversations. Her brother being a basketball player. A few choice words on tacos and horses.

A few days passed before the package arrived. A large manila folder sealed with scotch tape sent from Ed Braverock of Manderson, South Dakota. Dakota had some idea as to what was in it. At the tail end of the Skype conversation with her uncle, she'd phrased a question. Wouldn't a girl who recently discovered the identity of her father want to see a photograph of that father? To which Ed had tilted his head and remarked that they didn't take too many photographs, but he'd dig around to see what he could find. She should have known he was punking her. He'd had that same shit-eating grin on his face throughout their entire meeting. And so she stored that piece of information away as she took the envelope into her bedroom and pulled out a stack of three-by-five snapshots that knocked the wind out of her. They were different childhood versions of her, obviously taken by her mother and sent to Lenny (or more likely Ed, so that Janice wouldn't know). One for each year, with captions in black marker on their backs, signifying her age:

Three years old. In a red jumper with suspenders, about to attack an ice cream cone somewhere in the vicinity of Main Street.

Four years old. She couldn't recall ever going to the zoo, but there she was, smiling in front of the lion cage.

Five years old. Was that not the Band-Aid-brown couch in her grandmother's living room? No wonder she looked sad, unless it had something to do with her ratty jeans and that ghastly green T-shirt with the unidentifiable dark stain below her clavicle.

Six years old. Dressed for Halloween as her idol, Princess Leia.

Seven years old. Halloween and Princess Leia again.

Eight years old. Darth Vader this time, although she remembered wanting Chewbacca, but the Halloween store had run out of them. Taken at the parking lot of Willowbrook Gardens in North Zionsville.

Nine years old. First day of fourth grade at Beech Elementary. It would be her last year with the Star Wars backpack, but here it was, the final encore etched on film.

Ten years old. First day of fifth grade at McIntyre Elementary. She didn't know it yet, but later that day a girl named Rosie would introduce herself.

After studying the photographs for what seemed to be forever, she went back to the envelope and realized there were a few more tucked in its back end. She emptied the contents onto her bed, and immediately the hairs on the back of her neck stood up. The first shot was of a man she assumed to be Lenny Braverock, sitting in an oversized chair with a two-year-old Dakota Lodi on his lap. This would likely have been taken around the time Lenny went with Anika to Muncy's Tavern. Lenny's was mouth parted slightly to show his teeth. Little Dakota leaned forward as if she were about to attempt an escape, a giant candy-apple smile plastered across her mouth and her hair flying all over the place. But it was the second photo that confirmed the man's identity. A five-by-seven portrait of her father. On the back, a caption scratched out in pencil indicated it was him, taken about two years prior to his death. She turned it over, her eyes beginning to water as she examined it. In a field, he stood next to a horse that looked a helluva lot like Wakanda, both of them staring directly into the camera. Behind them, you could see blue sky and the tips of tall grasses arching in the breeze.

Her first observation: her father was not tall from a physical standpoint but appeared large in stature. He wore blue jeans and one of those heavy wool work shirts you sometimes saw construction workers wearing in the winter. He had a square-shaped face and long black hair that fell somewhere in the middle of his neckline. When Ed claimed she had some of his features, he wasn't kidding. When she saw the way his dark eyes tilted slightly toward his small nose that flared out gently on both sides, she knew some unseen genetic code had come into play. As far as his humorous nature was concerned, there appeared a hint of a smile even though his mouth was closed.

For some reason, and despite the scant details about

him revealed during the Skype calls, Dakota began to attribute traits to this man she'd never known. Her initial impression was that you wouldn't want to mess with Lenny Braverock. He looked wiry but strong. He wouldn't take kindly to liars or people with their own selfish agendas, but his first inclination would be to avoid conflict. He'd be willing to give those people a chance, but not more than one. Unless you were blood, in which case he might be more forgiving. He'd be a man of few words, but when he spoke, the words would count. With his children, he'd be stern but patient. He'd teach them about the world as he knew it. He'd be frustrated when they faltered but would be slow to anger. In no way was he perfect. Sixteen years ago, he'd slept with her mother out of wedlock. A mistake had been made, yet here Dakota was, sitting on her bed as a result of that mistake.

August 25, 2019

Chapter 36.
Notes from a Visit
to the Ohio Reformatory
for Women, Part II

Once again, Dakota found herself in the visiting room at the Ohio Reformatory for Women. Being a few days away from the start of her junior year at Zionsville High had made her nostalgic for the summer in some ways, and as Lucinda dropped her off at the prison's main entrance, she imagined the past unfurling itself onto the future.

She hadn't seen or spoken to her mother since the last time she'd been here, three months ago. And though she'd harbored doubts about how things might go on the drive up, she felt a sudden surge of confidence. Especially after being escorted to the visiting room, where she found the same exact table she'd sat at the last time, as if it had been assigned to her. As if it was her second day of first grade, as opposed to her first.

Minutes later, Victoria Lodi made her visiting room entrance, sporting the ubiquitous orange jumpsuit. She smiled when she saw her daughter and approached her slowly, as if she were strolling down a runway in a fashion show.

Dakota stood up to face her mother. She lunged forward and threw her arms out, wrapping them around her mother's shoulders and drawing her in, something unexplainable overcoming her at that moment. Could it be that her mother looked better than the last time she'd seen her? More alert and less edgy, her wavy blond hair looking as if it had been washed and trimmed. Did they have hair stylists in prison?

Once they sat, her mother began tapping her fingers on the table, examining her like a detective searching for clues. "You look different," she said.

"I had my hair cut," Dakota replied.

"You see yourself every day. You wouldn't notice."

"I put some weight on," Dakota countered, figuring that could be it.

Her mother scratched at her chin, not buying it. "Have you been out in the sun lately?"

"It's summer, Mom."

Her mother leaned back in her chair. She pressed her tongue against the inside of her mouth, forcing her cheek outward. Then, finally, "Oh, shit. You're having sex."

Dakota shrugged, trying to remain calm but sensing the blood rushing toward her face. "I'm not having sex. I went on a few dates with this guy Carlos that works at the diner."

"Well, if you do have sex, you better use protection."

Dakota gasped. Victoria Lodi had always been a drag racer, speeding through her daughter's emotional landscape. A to Z in one second. "I've got it covered, Mom," she said, her attempt at a pun falling flat, but not feeling the need to explain.

"Because if I find out you're pregnant, I'll escape from

this hellhole and I'll find you."

"Good to know."

"Is he hot, at least?"

"I really don't want to talk about this."

"Fine. But if he doesn't lock you up soon, he's gonna regret it. You're one of those girls that hasn't peaked in the looks department, if you know what I mean."

"So what you're saying is, Carlos would be smart to buy low."

"Exactly."

They chatted about normal things, which was nice for a change, even while Dakota dreamed up ways to shift the conversation to her recent discoveries. But she didn't want to push it like she'd done on their last visit. Instead, she bragged about saving money by working at the diner. About Lucinda having promised to teach her how to drive, and that a week from now she'd be starting her driver's ed class after school. The beginning of her junior year was less than a week away, and she'd been counting it down, like a death sentence.

Her mother then took her turn, telling her not to worry about Carlos. If he didn't want to be her boyfriend, there were plenty of fish in the sea, and once you caught a new fish, you'd forget about the first one. She'd been adjusting to prison life, but that didn't mean she liked it. The food sucked big-time, and the noises at night made it difficult to sleep. She promised to do her best to stay out of any conflicts, but the laws of reason in this place had their own twisted versions of logic. On the not-so-bad side, she'd completed her drug rehabilitation program, although the urge to use still hit her every once in a while. At least the prison offered some decent programs. She could get her

GED, and there were community service projects where you could work with dogs or other wildlife, and vocational programs like cosmetology or horticulture. Four years was a long time. She might as well do something constructive to make the time pass.

They had about fifteen minutes remaining when her mother casually said, "What else is new?" in a way that made her think she actually wanted to know.

Dakota sensed an opening. "I wanted to talk to you about something, Mom. But I don't want you to get angry with me. Because you are my mother... and you see... I've discovered something lately... about myself, and us in some ways... and I wanted to tell you about it... and..."

"Get to the point."

"Lenny Braverock." She practically shouted it out, then waited for the blowback, hoping she could survive the first few seconds at least. Except a bemused expression took shape on her mother's face as she crossed her legs. Under the circumstances, she appeared way too comfortable, as if she'd expected this.

"I'm impressed," her mother said. "How'd you find out?"

The response caught Dakota off guard. "Not sure we have time for that today, Mom. But I will say it was quite the harrowing journey."

"I'd sure be interested to hear about it someday. You know they have phones here."

Dakota nodded. "Did you like him?"

Her mother looked as if she was searching for the memory, and her mouth stretched out slightly. "I did. But... you know... it wasn't like we were a thing."

"Did you know he was married at the time?"

"Not when we made you."

The thought of them making her gave Dakota the hee-bie-jeebies. Like they'd installed a piece of furniture with less-than-accurate instructions. And where had her creation even occurred? Most likely it had been after the Kenny Chesney concert. Probably in some dingy motel room with peeling wallpaper and a creaky bed. Yuck.

"I saw the photos, you know."

"Really... I'm surprised they saved them."

"Uncle Ed sent them to me. I talked to him on Skype. He's a pretty cool guy, actually. And I met my brother, Mato. He's a year older than me, but I really liked him. And did you know I have three sisters?"

Her mother ignored the last question, but obviously she knew everything. "Well... weren't you a busy bee."

"Can I ask you about something else? Something that's been bugging me? Like how come you weren't at the bar the night of the fight at Muncy's Tavern?"

"I was home with you."

"And Lenny had been there too. Before he went to the tavern."

Her mother smiled. "My... you have learned a lot."

The dam in her brain broke then. Water, rushing everywhere, flooding the visiting room. "Then how did Lenny end up at the bar with Anika? And why would he get into a fight with Greg Coleman? Ed thought it had to do with Greg being jealous. Something to do with us, even. And because of the rape, Anika brought Lenny over, knowing that would stir up trouble. You wanna hear my theory? They used the fight as a pretext to kill Greg so that the cops would blame the bikers. Like they planned it afterward. Rosie thinks Stanley was the mastermind. I'm not sure about that, but it was his gun, and he's the only one they arrested. Anyway, what I still don't get is why you told me Jimmy Ray was my father."

Dakota could hardly breathe when she finished, and she fixed her eyes on her mother, trying to discern if her barrage of questions and statements had struck a chord. It didn't appear that way at first, because her mother mentioned something about their time being done and suddenly stood up, glancing at the ceiling while wiping sweat from her brow. "Come here," she then said, fixing her eyes on her daughter.

Dakota made her way over. Her mother grabbed her hand and squeezed it. It was cold and clammy. "Sometimes it's best if you just leave things alone," she said. "Otherwise, it will follow you around, and not just when you're awake."

"I get it. It's just that I have so many questions."

Her mother released her hand, a faint grin slowly forming across her face. "Well," she started. "I'm assuming Ed told you about the promise, which is why I never told you about Lenny. And once he died, I figured that I'd already picked someone to be your father and there was no point in you getting into this whole mess. Besides, you never seemed that interested in him, and so it never occurred to me that you'd go searching."

"I met him, you know. Jimmy Ray. We went for a ride in his boat. I liked him. I can see why you guys were friends. Anika... not so much. Though I did talk to Katie a few times, if you can believe that. I wouldn't say we're friends, but it's not like I hate her anymore. She's the one that told me her mother was raped... that you didn't believe her."

"It wasn't like I didn't believe her. It's just that Anika was a bit of a drama queen back then and didn't always tell the truth. And… you have to remember, Greg was my friend too."

For some reason, her mother's admission about Greg shocked her. All this time, she'd never once considered that Greg had been her mother's friend. She totaled up her mother's misfortunes, all of them happening within a brief moment in time. That fourteen years ago, Lenny Braverock cut off contact with her, two friendships had ended, and a third friend had been murdered. For a nineteen-year-old girl, it must have been a lot to deal with.

Dakota pursed her lips, then nodded as if she could accept her mother's analysis, that she'd pushed it far enough.

Her mother put her hand in the pocket of her orange jumpsuit and looked up, her eyes all watery. "I worry about you sometimes, peanut."

"You don't need to worry about me, Mom," Dakota contended. "I'm going to be okay."

"I can see that. But you still need to be careful out there."

"I will. But I wanted to say one more thing before I leave." In fact, she'd been thinking about that one more thing since her grandmother pulled into the prison parking lot, or perhaps going back to the night of her mother's arrest. Something that she'd kept hidden all summer. Though it had always been there, like a tick burrowed into her skin. "I'm sorry, Mom… that I messed things up for you, and I kind of feel like it's my fault that you're here. That I should have done better."

Her mother shook her head. "None of this was your fault. I'm the one who decided to sell drugs. I'm the one responsible for my actions. Only me. Understand?"

Dakota said she did, and her mother came closer,

placing a hand on each of her shoulders. She kissed her daughter on the forehead, said goodbye, then turned and headed back toward the exit.

Once outside the confines of the prison, Dakota sent Rosie a smiling face with an open mouth and cold sweat emoji. She texted Carlos, *I can't wait to kick your ass at bowling,* in reference to their date that night, then followed that up with a *Miss you* message to Gina. She searched for the Thunderbird and quickly spotted it in the last row of the parking lot, like a lime-green spaceship in an otherwise empty field. Her grandmother had promised a driving lesson that afternoon, and if they somehow survived that experience, there'd be a trip to Target to pick up picture frames and school supplies. Later, Dakota would frame the two photographs of her father and place them on her dresser. That night, she would send out a text to Mato, asking him to thank Uncle Ed for mailing the photos and saying she hoped his AAU tournament went well. She wouldn't expect an immediate reply, as Mato wasn't the kind of guy to hover about his phone. Yet he always texted back at some point. Not that anyone would accuse him of being chatty. But she'd already decided she liked that about him, mostly because he got right to the point instead of talking about useless bullshit like most people did. For instance, in one of their exchanges, he brought up the idea of her visiting him again, claiming that besides attending one of his basketball games, he could arrange it so that she could meet her older sisters. Perhaps even teach her to ride Wakanda if they had the time and she had the guts. Which she said she did, even though the thought of mounting the giant beast she'd seen on their last Skype call frightened her.

Dakota stepped onto the blacktop and moved slowly,

slicing through cars in the parking lot. She'd made the same trek three months ago, but the events of that day had occurred a lifetime ago, and there was only a mild sense of déjà vu. *I'm going to be okay,* she had told her mother back in the visiting room. At the time, it seemed like a lot to live up to. Being okay. And sure, they were just words. Words likely spoken to allay her mother's fears in a prison visiting room. But as she approached her grandmother's car, those same words bounced around her cranium, and she said them once more.

No one else heard them. They were just idle waves of sound, but she repeated them like a mantra and smiled as the words washed over her.

Because at that precise moment, she believed them to be true.

Acknowledgements

Apparently, it does take a village to make a book.

There would be no, Under the Family Tree, without my great editor and mentor, David Griffin Brown of The Darling Axe. After reviewing my first draft, he recommended that I "burn down the house," but he delivered it in a way that made me think writing a novel was something I could pull off. After multiple rounds of edits, a zoom call, and David answering far too many email questions from me, that's exactly what happened.

There would be no, Under the Family Tree, without my wife, Karen Feinstein, who's love and support kept me going when writer's doubt crept in. It's not so easy being the wife of a person whose head often resides in storyland, but Karen was there from the beginning, giving a thumbs up or thumbs down to passages, scenes or entire chapters, all while making me believe that I wasn't wasting my time. Seriously, there should be some kind of medal for this.

My daughter, Sarah Geller, a fabric designer in New york, not only gave me a thorough analysis of my first draft, but fashion advice for my characters as well. "Rosie wouldn't be caught dead wearing that," she declared, opining on a particular choice I had made. She then proceeded to make Pinterest boards for both Dakota and Rosie, and helped me select which outfits they wore in many of the scenes. In addition, she provided invaluable feedback on my book cover design options.

Other family members came to the rescue as well. My mother, Harriet Feinstein; son-in-law, Mitchell Geller; sister, Karen Clark; and sister-in-laws, Susan Lanphere and Kirsten Petrizzo, all gave me input on various versions of my manuscript. Whereas my niece and nephew, Jenny and Bobby Clark, offered astute observations on the cover design, which were eventually incorporated.

As to the industry experts. I had the best beta-readers ever. Janel Garcia, Kara Aisenbrey and Davy Kent. Kara and David also proved their versatility by doubling as proofreaders. Amaryah Orenstein and Nathan Bransford provided incisive feedback on my opening chapters, and Nathan added expert advice on the self-publishing industry.

It was a pleasure working with the professionals at Cover Kitchen. The collaborative effort with the creative director, Xavier Comas and designer Rafa Andres Pio, progressed seamlessly and I ended up with a book cover that exceeded my expectations.

Gary Feinstein had worked in science related fields for most of his life. But all of that changed during a cross-country Covid road trip out west. Perhaps it was the thin air of the Montana mountains that rewired his brain, making him believe he had an untapped creative side. Back home, he hunkered down with his family and learned that baking sourdough was a wonderful thing. He started writing and never looked back. The result is his debut YA novel, Under the Family Tree. Gary was born in New York and has lived all over the northeast. Currently, he resides in Haddam CT, with wife and fourteen-year-old dog, near the 400 mile Connecticut River.

Reach out to Gary on www.garyfeinstein.com, or follow him on X, @gfeinz.